David J Walkden has been a pirate, cosmonaut, trapeze artist and an adult film star. He has run with the bulls in Pamplona, conquered Kilimanjaro, been to Everest base camp and really likes red wine.

Nowadays he enjoys walking up mountains, almost exclusively in the rain and running a drug cartel from his rather nice three bed semi-detached house in The Lake District, England. He hates cats and happy people.

He is currently number two on Guatemala's most wanted list.

Dedication

For Teeny Tiny Brontosaur Hobbit

David J Walkden

The Book of Shenanigans

Austin Macauley Publishers™
London * Cambridge * New York * Sharjah

Illustrated By: Joseph Hartley

A CIP catalogue record for this title is available from the British Library.

ISBN 9781398400948 (Paperback)
ISBN 9781398400894 (Hardback)
ISBN 9781398400917 (ePub e-book)
ISBN 9781398418158 (Audiobook)

www.austinmacauley.com

First Published 2022
Austin Macauley Publishers Ltd®
1 Canada Square
Canary Wharf
London
E14 5AA

Acknowledgments

Debbie “Beady Eye” Frobes, for bringing her proof-reading expertise to the party.

Thanks also to Joseph “Tequila Shot” Hartley for bringing this book to life with his wonderful illustrations.

Chapter One

"Oh bugger. I did not expect that." – A watching entity

Trafford Business Park, Manchester

Geoffrey Pike, the person with the greatest potential for evil in the whole-wide world, was thirty-three years old, hungover, miserable and stuck in traffic. More specifically, he was the traffic that everyone else was now stuck in. He rested his forehead on the steering wheel, jerked the ignition key and prayed for his orange Mini to start. Once again, the slow engine grind petered into silence.

"You really need to get this seen to, dude," beamed Rob, who filled the passenger seat completely with his twenty-one stone frame, the top of his balding head perfectly tilted against the roof of the car.

Beep! Beep! Beep! Beep! The car horns behind them reached a crescendo of disapproval.

Geoff looked up. It was less than thirty feet to the car park. "You'll have to give me a push and I'll sort it out later."

"I'm afraid that's not going to happen, amigo. First, pushing this car would be way too humiliating for a man of my standing. I mean, what would my ladies think?" winked Rob.

Geoff shivered. "Don't be stupid, all women hate you. You haven't had sex for months, maybe even years. And anyway, let's remember I'm the one giving you a lift."

"Technically, you're not actually giving me a lift. You're holding me in a stationary orange box that's held together by rust. Let's be honest, this is more like a hostage situation."

"Come on! It's my car and I'm driving you to work like I always do. I can't push and drive."

"Secondly, it's raining and I'd get wet," added Rob.

"It's Manchester. Of course it's raining."

Rob's blue eyes narrowed, creasing them even deeper into the wasteland of his face. "Is this because you're worried that the wonderful Rachel will see you? She barely knows you exist. What you have with her is just, well, nothing. Boo hoo! She's with Scott, who's your boss and who'll bust your balls if you're late again."

Geoff closed his eyes and sighed.

"Tell you what. Seeing as you're my best friend in all the world," said Rob, making a fleshy heart shape with his two thick hands, "you can push and I'll drive."

"What?" exclaimed Geoff. "You can't drive. No one will even give you lessons. Your last instructor called you a menace to society before you put him in traction."

"That wasn't my fault."

Geoff raised his eyebrows sharply.

"Okay, maybe I did have something to do with the traction part, but this wouldn't be proper driving. Your car is broken down, so it's just going to be a bit of steering and a smidgen of braking. Come on, what's the worst that could happen?" The beeps of the car horns behind them began to build up again adding a bold exclamation mark to Rob's point.

There was a sudden sharp knock on the driver's window, which Geoff rolled down. "Sorry about this, we're having a few minor engine problems," he explained.

"Pike and Billington? What a surprise," barked a grey-suited figure tapping his watch. "Sort out your minor problems immediately, or at least bump it up on the curb so normal people can get into work."

"Sorry. It's just that the pavement is too narrow so we're going to have to push it to the car park." Geoff cleared his throat. "Don't suppose you could give us a hand?"

The figure snorted, turned and strode back towards the line of waiting cars.

"Speak of the Devil, I do believe that was Scott Noble." Rob gave a slow shake of his football-sized head and laughed. "I say this as your only true friend, you've finally hit rock bottom. Losing out to a bloke with a moustache like that? That's gotta hurt. On the plus side, now is the perfect time to reconsider your life choices."

"Please don't."

"I mean it's not even a goatee, or a hipster beard. They'd be sort of acceptable but no, we're talking about a thick greasy porn star 'tache. Scott and his fucking creepy facial hair has stolen the love of your life and made you his bitch."

"Just piss off," muttered Geoff.

"Of course, if that's how you feel I could just get out and walk, letting you keep all the glory of pushing and driving this rust bucket to yourself."

"Okay, I'll push. Just let me do this first," snarled Geoff, watching Scott disappear. "ARRRGGHH!" He double fisted the steering wheel, adding his own pathetic horn to the symphony of beeps behind him.

"Feel better?" asked Rob pulling out a pair of black leather driving gloves from his raincoat.

"Why have you got driving gloves?"

"These are not driving gloves," replied Rob, making jazz hands. "These are my steering gloves."

Geoff opened the door and walked to the back of the car. "God, I hate my life," he muttered.

The rain began to lash down even harder. Drenched, Geoff looked back at the line of cars filled with his smug dry colleagues, all of whom, with the exception of Rachel, he decided he now hated. He looked down at the scuffed rear bumper of his Mini with its faded Alton Towers sticker. He was beginning to hate his car. He looked up at the podgy roundness of Rob beaming encouragement from the driving seat. He definitely fucking hated Rob.

Hating everything that he could see, Geoff hurled himself against the cold wet metal of the car. The initial shock of man versus machine pushed the car a good two inches forward. It stopped and rolled back three.

"Come on, you've got this," shouted Rob. "HEAVE!"

Geoff looked down at the waves of rain bouncing up from the tarmac. So this was his life now, a grey blob of nondescript misery? The slam of a heavy car door brought him back to his senses. Peering through the Mini's wing mirror, he saw an unmistakable shape five cars back. Rachel. Umbrella in hand, she began to walk towards him. For once Rob was right. Rachel would never fall in love with him, especially if she saw him like this. He had to change. From nowhere a slow, deep voice echoed in his mind.

10 9 8 7 6 5 4 3 2 1

Ten. Nine. Eight. Seven.

All the items of his hatred began to coalesce.

Six. Five.

Geoff realised that his life need not be like this.

Four. Three.

That he was born for a great purpose.

Two.

He gritted his teeth and tensed his muscles.

One.

His time was now.

We.

"What are you waiting for, you little pussy?" whispered Rob in his right ear. "Arrgghhh! Get back in the car and steer."

Geoff hurled himself forward.

Have.

His angry face crumpled against the back window of the Mini, so only Rob saw the colour of his eyes change from pale blue to the most furious of red found only at the centre of suns, volcanoes and the deepest, darkest canyons of Hell.

"Wow." Rob's grin widened. "I did not expect that."

To his watching colleagues Geoff was just pushing a small car in the rain. However, Rob had pressed the brake pedal down to the floor and pulled the handbrake up as far as it could go. Despite his meddling the Mini creaked forward, inch by grindingly painful inch. "Put your back into it. Your lovely Rachel's going to watch you fail."

Without checking where Rachel was Geoff pulled back and flung himself at the car once more.

LIFT OFF!

"Whoop!" cried Rob, releasing the handbrake and removing his foot from the brake pedal. The car flew forward, resulting in two significant events.

The first was that without the balancing support of the Mini, Geoff found himself leaning at an angle of forty-two degrees to the road. He crashed face down in the middle of the puddled tarmac. Instinctively his palms took the greater part of the collision with the earth's surface, causing them to graze raw and bleed as a dozen or so small loose black stones pierced his skin. The rest of the impact was taken by the top of his forehead. He bounced.

"Oww."

Geoff's cry didn't reduce the sting, or the suffocating embarrassment that consumed him as he lay there, spreadeagled and bleeding in the middle of the road. He did not move. He simply did not have the necessary will and remained motionless in the mixture of dirt, rain and humiliation. He closed his eyes. At least he'd moved the car forwards though he couldn't tell how far. The number of people gathering around him was increasing and he made the connection between the smart clicking of heels and the arrival of Rachel. The clicking stopped inches away from his head.

"Are you okay?"

Rachel's soft velvety voice sliced into Geoff's consciousness. He opened his eyes and tried to focus on the tarmac. It was shiny and black, very close and very blurry. Without looking up, he knew exactly what Rachel would look like. She'd be clothed in a white cotton blouse and a black pencil skirt and jacket. Her large green eyes would be smiling at him warmly with more than a hint of pity. That did spoil it a bit.

"I'm fine," said Geoff, eyeballing the tarmac. "It's just minor car trouble. You know what it's like with these classic cars."

Rachel paused for a couple of seconds trying to find something to say before the developing situation saved her. "Is that Rob driving your car?" she asked.

"Yes, it is Rob, but he's not really driving," Geoff corrected, his voice muffled by the tarmac. "The car's broken down so it's more like glorified steering. He's moving at two to three miles an hour tops, so he'll need another push from me just to keep going."

"It looks a bit faster than that," said Rachel.

"It may look like it's going faster but I can assure you it isn't. It's just basic physics at work."

"Are you certain you don't need any help?"

"No thank you," replied Geoff. "This is all under control[1]."

"Okay. I'll see you later," said Rachel as she started to walk off.

Well, that could have turned out far worse, thought Geoff, when the second event occurred. Rob's sausage-like fingers twisted the key and the Mini's engine roared back to life.

Geoff's head jerked up. "No! Please, not this."

Φ

Stepping out of his black Volvo, Scott, who had driven into the car park through the exit lane, realised that things were different. Straight off he didn't like that. There was a noisy commotion taking place one aisle down. A handful of people were cowering between cars and there were a couple of high-pitched screams, one of which sounded a bit like Pike.

"This is great!" someone else shouted.

It was when the "–eat" hit Scott's eardrums that a battered orange Mini skidded around the corner.

Bang! was quickly followed by metallic grinding as the Mini scraped against the front grill of a VW Polo. The headlights popped out and the front bumper sheared off the stationary car.

---

[1] Spoiler alert. For those of you who are of a fragile nature, do not like living on the edge and certainly do not like sudden surprises, this statement by Geoff is factually incorrect. Things were not under anyone's control, least of all his.

Two things struck Scott. The first was that this car was Pike's broken-down shed. The second was that Billington was driving. For the briefest of seconds their gazes locked. Scott flinched away. He did not like what he'd seen through the windows of Rob's soul. He wasn't even certain that Rob actually had a soul and if he did, it was inky black, malicious and very pointy. In a rushed heartbeat Scott turned on his heels and ran[2].

𝕽

Rob was in a very happy place. His grin was all teeth and sharpness, a look usually reserved for homicidal cats finding cornered rats. His past driving failures had been rooted in being told what to do by ugly descendants of apes. Now fate had given him a far more effective method of learning how to drive. He just needed a victim. He just needed a Scott. Leaning over he completed a perfect Scandinavian drift around a tight corner and smiled.

Scott was on his hands and knees cowering between cars, his fingers fumbling the infrared remote.

The Volvo lights flashed on.

"Shave your…"

"Arrgghhh," Scott screamed.

"…creepy moustache off!"

"CRASH!"

β

Two hours later, Geoff sat on the top step, hands in pockets, watching what was left of his Mini being hoisted up onto the recovery wagon. "I can't believe you got us fired."

"Screw that. I can't believe I can drive," said Rob, fishing a pack of battered red Marlboro's out of his stained raincoat.

---

[2] This can be equated to being an unbearably cute Norwegian Blue button-nosed, lop-eared rabbit, resplendent with a pure white fluff of a tail, standing in the middle of the M25. Your right foreleg reaches out and your paw beckons over a thundering eighteen-wheeled juggernaut. You smile. Your name is Gus and you have three options available to you: freeze, flight or fight. Unfortunately with so much pride at stake, you decide to fight the oncoming metal monster with your near perfect use of the ferocious 'death bite'. Though perfectly executed, this doesn't slow the beast down. Everything goes black, which even rabbits know cannot be a good thing.

The low loader crept away as the last of the broken glass and twisted metal was swept up. Geoff sighed and ran his fingers over the deep scrape marks on the sides of his shoes. "Were you really going to run Scott over?" he asked.

"What do you mean?" smiled Rob. "I did run him over."

"That's not really true. Scott was hiding behind his car which you hit so hard that part of it collapsed on him."

"But he left in an ambulance so that's gotta count?"

Geoff shook his head. "What I don't understand is how you got it started?"

"Beats me," replied Rob.

"And why aren't the police pressing charges?"

"Private property? Your insurance will cover it anyway. Just stick to the story. I was placed in charge of a car without adequate risk assessment. The engine fired up, I panicked and understandably bad things happened."

Geoff watched Rob's immense mass skip down the remaining steps and turn back towards him, grinning wolfishly.

"Where are you going?" asked Geoff.

"Where else? The pub, stupid."

Neither Rob, nor Geoff noticed the curious murder of crows circling high above them, or the two figures that had been standing on a pedestrian bridge watching them for the last three hours. The taller figure, a slim woman with chalk-white hair, handed the other, a very short man in a red smoking jacket, a thick envelope. The man scowled and threw his half-smoked cigar onto the floor. Grinding the Cuban heel of his boot on the embers he stalked away and clicked his fingers. The rain immediately stopped.

"Is that the sun?" asked Geoff. "I hope we get a rainbow?"

"So do I," said Rob as he barged open the door, allowing Geoff to enter the snug of the Rose and Crown.

∞

This action triggered something 14,500,000,042.4242 light years away from Manchester at the very centre of the universe. An incomprehensibly large cog of gleaming adamantium churned ever so slightly against a set of other unbelievably large, but ever so slightly smaller cogs. In turn, each one of these churned against sets of impossibly large, though ever so slightly smaller cogs.

And so on, and so on, and so on, and so on. Eventually, the final smallest cog, the size of Manhattan, clicked into place.

A watching entity, who had been silent for over eleven billion years, bit his lip and mumbled seven words. “Oh bugger. I did not expect that.”

Chapter Two

"I guess that's what you get for being a virgin in the company of sinful monks."
– Sam Spade

Freemasons Hall, Bridge Street, Manchester

The Derby Room of the Freemasons Hall is not blessed with an abundance of natural light. The Freemasons and others who use it prefer it that way. Cavernous with vaulted ceilings and Corinthian columns, it was now host to only four figures. One, clean shaven and wearing a tired black blazer, was eating at a large dining table with three musty books spread around him. Two, almost identical in their immense, black-suited bulk, stood either side of him like a couple of stone statues guarding an ancient temple. The remaining figure, noticeably trimmer, was busy serving food and wine. Four thick candles illuminated the table but failed to penetrate the corners of the room and cast weak shadows into the darkness. With a flourish, the seated figure splashed a pink highlighter pen over the closest book and appeared to smile.

From the furthest recess a deep voice spoke. "You do know that book is literally priceless, Brian."

Brian put down the pen and the voice continued, "*The Pnakotic Manuscript of the Dead* has been out of print for over a thousand years. You'll get into serious trouble if they find out that you're highlighting parts of it."

The two hulks grunted and started towards the voice but stopped when Brian shook his head.

"Well, if it isn't my old friend Samuel Spade. I thought we'd agreed that you no longer had any Northern privileges? In fact, I recall that you have no privileges left at all," Brian said.

"I think you made that decision in my absence," replied the figure, stepping out from behind a pillar.

"Indeed I did. But who could blame me considering how things ended? And thank you for your concern, but I own all of these manuscripts so I can annotate them as I see fit."

"I see you're as trusting as ever?" said Sam, looking down at the pentagram on the floor and the faint purple tinge hovering above it. "Are you going to invite me in? Or shall we continue like this?"

"By all means enter but strictly no funny business. *Desino*," Brian smiled, twisting his right hand as if he were loosening a petrol cap. The purple glow dissipated and Sam continued his slow walk to the centre of the room. This time the two figures sprang around the table, placing their considerable bodies between the visitor and their master. As the three met, Sam stopped and raised his arms. The larger of the two patted him down and pulled out two pristine Luger pistols from brown leather shoulder holsters.

"*Reddo*," said Brian, his fingers twisting the imaginary petrol cap shut. Wisps of purple reappeared at the edges of the pentagram.

"Be careful with those, they're priceless," said Sam. The lower half of his face was now free from shadow and showed a firm jaw and pinkish lips.

The guard turned, placing the pistols on the table.

"Have you ever thought of joining us in the twenty-first century? We have some excellent new ways of killing people," said Brian. Releasing the magazine, he popped out the first of the eight bullets and tapped its tip on the edge of the table. "That said, these dumdum bullets look like they could still do a decent job. World War II[3]?"

---

[3] Dum-dum bullets are great fun and a wonderfully effective way of stopping people literally dead in their tracks. However, those well-known party-poopers the Germans helped get them banned in 1898, calling the wounds they inflicted 'excessive and inhumane'. Consequently, the Hague Convention Declaration IV 3 prohibited the use of expanding bullets in international warfare. The British delegate to this convention, Sir John Ardagh, had the right idea of warfare being a bloody big game of tag when he stated that, "The civilized soldier when shot recognizes that he is wounded and knows that the sooner he is attended to the sooner he will recover. He lies down on his stretcher and is

"Spanish Civil War, and the last time I fired those a lot of people died," replied Sam.

Brian raised the gun and aimed through the iron sights. "So would you prefer to be shot by this one?"

Sam shrugged and handed his raincoat to the lean figure by his side. "Thank you Hunter. You're looking well."

Hunter gave a cordial smile. He had a stiff military posture and sharp white hair. His piercing brown eyes, cruel smile and tips of numerous occult tattoos peeking over his white collar and cuffs confirmed that he was far more than a butler.

"Would you like a drink?" asked Brian.

"Whisky. Jura Superstition, if you've got it."

Hunter nodded.

"So what's with the Minotaurs?" said Sam, cradling his glass.

"They're a recent acquisition. You cannot be too careful especially in our game."

"You still hold a Chair at the University? Rumour has it you were using students to help summon daemons?"

"Nothing was proven but the Board of Governors did get a bit shirty with the media coverage. They cloaked it under a charge of improper conduct and stripped me of my professorship," smiled Brian.

"What about the TV work?"

"What do you think happened?" Brian's smile all but gone.

"Shame. Didn't the papers call you the thinking housewives' crumpet? Just so you know that had nothing to do with me." Sam took off his hat and placed it on the table. In the candlelight there was something playful in his blue eyes.

---

taken off the field to his ambulance, where he is dressed or bandaged. Your fanatical barbarian, similarly wounded, continues to rush on, spear or sword in hand; and before you have the time to represent to him that his conduct is in flagrant violation of the understanding relative to the proper course for the wounded man to follow—he may have cut off your head." Mind you, the Germans did get with the whole excessive and inhumane slaughter programme with pretty much everything they did after that.

"I know that, but you did do something far worse," said Brian, his mouth tight. "You stole from me."

"You want to be careful with those carbohydrates," said Sam, pointing at the remaining potatoes. "They'll kill you."

Brian chuckled. "So why have you come to see me now?"

"I thought you might kill me first and ask questions later so I went away."

"Justice is revenge. Revenge is justice. Didn't Tarantino say that in one of his films?" asked Brian.

Sam shook his head.

"No matter, he should have done. I want justice. I want my justice now, Samuel."

"See what I mean? You're not really happy to see me at all."

"Of course I am, just a bit surprised that's all."

"Speaking of surprises, don't you want to know about Emily?" asked Sam.

"Why? She is literally dead to me. If you cast your mind back, you'll remember that she was the root of our problems, but we digress. Why are you here?"

"I will get to that," said Sam, pointing at the furthest book. "May I?"

Brian nodded.

Sam reached over. "*The Pnakotic Manuscript of the Dead,* good choice for a bit of light reading. Do you know that only three original copies exist? The Vatican Apostolic Library, the CIA vaults at Langley, and yours. The Catholics got seriously pissed when they found that one of their orders was worshipping Pnakotic twenty-four seven. Fun fact – all the copies are written in blood on the skin of virgins sacrificed to Pnakotic by those monks. I guess that's what you get for being a virgin in the company of sinful monks. You met Pnakotic? She's a decent stand-up type of daemon but don't piss her off. She's got a temper."

Brian shook his head. "I often wonder what your true daemonic name is. I doubt that it's Samuel Spade. My sources say you've been around for two thousand years though I personally think you're far older than that."

"That would be telling. If I gave you my true name and you had some of my blood, you could summon me and bind me to your will if you were powerful enough," said Sam, his unblinking eyes locked on Brian's. "But I don't think you are. Powerful enough, that is."

"Well, there may be a time when we have to find that one out. Until then why don't you cut to the chase?"

“I have information that should repay my debt,” said Sam, his eyes no longer playful.

“Really? That would have to be extremely valuable information.”

“It relates to an item that you have spent the last decade trying to acquire.”

“There are many items I’ve been trying to acquire.”

“True, but there is only one that could change absolutely everything for you.” Sam took another small sip of his whisky. His glass was empty. “And it’s coming back into circulation,” he added.

“You better not be teasing me,” said Brian, picking up his steak knife like a serial killer arriving at work, his eyes all shiny and wet. “That item has not been seen or heard of for over seventy years. There hasn’t even been a credible whisper of its whereabouts for decades and you bring me petty rumours of its reappearance. You have no idea how disappointed I am, Samuel. Disappointed and angry.” He plunged the tip of the knife into the *Pnakotic Manuscripts of the Dead* manuscript. Breathing heavily, he looked into Sam’s eyes. “Kill Bernie.”

“Hey, Brian, calm down,” cried Sam, pushing his chair back and jumping to his feet while Bernie grabbed him from behind by his lapels.

Sam hovered a good six inches above the floor, feet flapping like a man dancing the quickstep. The other Minotaur, grunting with well-practised menace, clutched a black military dagger. It looked like a toothpick in his hand.

“I am calm, Samuel. Hunter, what do you think would go well with Mr Spade’s hearts?”

Hunter thought for a moment before replying, “Sir, I would suggest I fry Mr Spade’s hearts with shallots and a red wine reduction. Add some of those spicy wedges you like and pair it with a bottle of the Artadi Vina El Pison 2012. The notes of liquorice and wild herbs will get the most out of the big flavours the meat has to offer.”

“That sounds absolutely delicious. Right, now that’s decided would you like to do the honours, Saunders?” asked Brian.

“Stop! I’ve got more!” shouted Sam, his cry echoing in the vaulted shadows of the ceiling.

“Desist. But before you utter another word Samuel, please understand that this really needs to be concrete information. The alternative is.”

Bernie dropped Sam to the floor.

“The Devil is making a personal trip to Manchester to find the item,” said Sam.

"So? That does not get me any closer to owning it," pressed Brian. "Let me guess. You can tell me where it is, I thank you and cancel your debt?"

"No, but I can help you find the Devil and possibly the item."

"Let's follow this to its logical conclusion. I confront the Devil but there is no actual item. You have made a deal with him and I meet with a grisly end, effectively clearing your debt to me. I go to Hell and mankind remains under the ridiculous yoke of Christianity. Surely you can see my reservations?"

"My coat Hunter?" requested Sam.

Brian raised his eyebrows and Hunter passed over the mackintosh.

Sam ripped open the weakened lining and pulled out a large brown envelope and placed it in front of Brian.

"You know how much I like presents. Surprisingly weighty, what could it be?" Brian tore into the envelope, releasing three translucent pages that fluttered to the table. Drawn by instinct every pair of eyes followed them as they cast curious and everchanging golden shadows in the flickering candlelight. Once the pages stopped, eyes widened, heartbeats quickened and pupils grew larger.

The cover page was dominated by an ornate silver spear with a collection of people trying to climb it. Above this in shimmering golden lettering was *Book of Shenanigans.*

Brian looked up. "Oh my, I think you may have outdone yourself, Samuel."

St John's Court, Manchester

Sam recognised the clicking of expensive heels on the wet cobbles of St John's Court. A dozen seconds passed before a tall woman in her late twenties turned the corner.

"You're late Em." Judging by his tone, this was a factual observation that Sam had made many times before, in many different places.

"Well, that is hardly the sort of welcome I was expecting Mr Spade," said Emily. Her curly red hair cascaded down either side of her face from under a blue hat. "When are you going to kiss me?"

Sam pulled her lips to his. "Weren't you slightly concerned?"

"Why? Don't you have this famous knack of avoiding trouble[4]?"

---

[4] The hype surrounding the daemon known as Samuel Spade and his ability to avoid trouble is, in fact, well deserved. A little known statistic is that during his existence he has successfully avoided taking the blame for 87.4% of his actions. However, there was a well-documented incident that took place in Turin, Italy, on 1st April in 1098 that

"You shouldn't always believe the hype."

Emily smiled. "Was it like your comic?"

"Every damn part of it," Sam replied.

There was a short pause as they each grappled with what that meant.

"Did he seem well?" asked Emily.

"He's put on a few pounds but he's in good spirits."

"Did he ask about me?" Emily's dark green eyes widened.

"Some."

"That doesn't sound overly promising. Using your undoubted talents as a private investigator, what do you deduce from that, Mr Spade?"

Sam kept his thin smile but remained silent.

"Does he even know where I've been?" asked Emily, her voice quivering.

"I'm not sure he does and we had other matters to deal with."

"Really? Did Daddy like his present?"

"Daddy?" snorted Sam. "Daddy threatened to eat my hearts with spicy wedges and a nice bottle of wine."

"That only shows how much you mean to him," whispered Emily. "You hurt him just like I did."

Sam kissed her forehead. "I'm not going to go over that again but he seemed impressed with the pages. We may be able to put all of this behind us."

"See? You'll regain his trust in no time."

"That is the last thing I want for me or for you. Your father is an extremely dangerous man, dabbling in matters that he cannot understand, or cont." Sam's mobile burst into life. "Spade."

"Good news," replied Brian.

"It's real?"

A loud burst of thunder announced another heavy deluge of rainfall[5] as Emily took shelter under a nearby doorway and pulled out a black tablet.

---

involved a bearded Sam Spade, copious amounts of wine and a funeral shroud. For this, he did get into serious trouble.

[5] The Mancunian rainfall is not, as some would have you believe, the result of geographical and climatic factors. It is actually a soggy side effect of Manchester being the European Headquarters of the Elemental Air and Water Lords or EAWL for short. For a period this general dampness proved to be exceptionally good for the cotton industry and therefore England. Now, it just makes southerners stranded in the North feel completely miserable. The practical exams, which are the cause of most of the rain, are spread over the year and take place in the following months: January, March, June, August, October, November, and December. For those who wish to study at the EAWL

"Correct."

"So my debt is paid?" asked Sam.

"I only wish it was as simple as that but I have a number of questions. The first being, how did you happen upon this first edition bone fide Word of God? It's not even your side."

"You know I no longer have a side and a daemon never reveals his sources. It's bad for business."

"Fair point," accepted Brian, "but the provenance of this item is still important to me."

"The fact that you have it and now know it's real is far more important than its past," said Sam, looking at Emily tapping away. The ridge between her eyes furrowed, her red lips pursed to the right.

"What about God? What does the all-seeing, all-knowing old chestnut want from this?"

"I can't help you with that. Divine wisdom and planning of God is way above my pay grade," replied Sam, "and like you said, it's not from my side."

"I find it perplexing that it has taken over two thousand years for him to write a sequel. I always thought of God as a one hit wonder but I could be wrong. All these years his publishers must have been going frantic for new stuff. Millennia pass, people stop going to church, stop praying, stop believing, and then, miraculously this pops up," said Brian. "And then there's the fact that we both appear in it. Did you notice how I'm always smiling? I look like an absolute idiot."

"I didn't see that," smiled Sam.

"Have you got the rest? The cover says it's a bumper sixty-four page issue."

"No. That's all I've got," said Sam, watching Emily raise her arms and slide the tablet back into its case. "All I want is a clean slate for us."

"Would that I could, but you are in this comic, so logically you're going to be part of what happens next whether you like it or not."

"Me on page two doesn't mean that I'll still be around by page sixty-four," reasoned Sam.

---

applications should be sent with a hand written covering letter to Professor Erwin McSweeny, Elemental Air and Water Lords European Headquarters, Applications Department, 124b Oxford Road, Manchester, M3 9RD.

"True. You may not make it to the very end but I'll wager your role in this story is far from over. So why don't we get back to you clearing your debt to me?"

"And Emily's," added Sam.

Brian sighed. "Unfortunately, I require significantly more from you for that," he said.

Sam did not reply.

Brian went on. "Let's say I can foretell your future and I predict that you will agree to work for me until this matter is settled."

"I'd say that you're insane. Why would I put myself between you and two Gods? Look at my business card. I'm a private investigator specialising in the return of missing cats, dogs and errant husbands," said Sam in an even tone. "I'll help you find the Devil, but that's all."

"We'll see about that, Samuel. Emily was in Hell and now she isn't. Do you follow me so far?"

"Yes."

"So as a previous inhabitant of Hell she's an honorary daemon. Therefore, if I know her true name and have some of her blood, I will be able to summon her whenever I like. Are you still following?"

Sam could feel the blood pumping into his balled fist.

"If you think that your past employer was nasty to her just think what I can do," said Brian. "Imagination is such a human trait."

"But she's your daughter." Bright anger sparked as Sam's eyes turned red.

"And you are her lover. Do you want me to make Emily's life a living hell?"

Sam felt his stomach tighten.

"These pages may have cleared your debt with me but not Emily's. That falls down to you."

"I could kill you," said Sam.

"And my Minotaurs or Hunter will either prevent that, or if you are successful, rip you and then Emily limb from bloody limb. I'm not a monster Samuel, and that isn't the result I want. So, if you give me your word that you will see this to the end, I will give you my word that both yours and Emily's debt will be wiped clean."

"But the chances are –"

Brian interrupted, "Yes, the chances are that this will be very interesting for everyone involved. Why don't we just see how the chips fall?"

Sam clenched his jaw. "You have my word. If you get your item or the Devil returns to Hell and there are no further leads, our debt is cleared."

"Excellent. I'll send over the paperwork. Always a pleasure, Samuel." There was a pause. "I said, always a pleasure Samuel."

"Never a chore Brian."

"Well? Are you going to tell me what that was all about?" asked Emily.

"It's genuine so that should be true for the other pages but we need to talk about your father."

"Oh," was all Emily could muster.

Sam pulled her towards him.

"Didn't you say that the heart wants what the heart wants?" whispered Emily, feeling the heavy beat of Sam's two hearts.

"I want you too, always and one hundred percent," said Sam.

Emily smiled.

"I'm going to do some work for him," he said.

For some time, Emily and Sam said nothing. Finally, she looked up, her green eyes fierce. "You do realise, Mr Spade, that when I said that you'd get along I didn't mean putting the fucking band back together. I don't suppose that you would consider relocating to somewhere less dangerous? I've heard Mogadishu is great this time of year."

Sam shook his head. "I'm tired of running Em."

"This is about that stupid comic?"

Sam rolled his eyes and considered whether now was the right time to point out that it was a graphic novel and not a comic, but instead he just nodded.

"Okay, talk to me," said Emily.

"I'm going to check in on some of my past associates."

"You're going back to Hell, aren't you?"

"I am a daemon and that's where I've got friends."

"And enemies," added Emily.

"Don't worry, remember I have this famous knack of avoiding trouble."

"Didn't you tell me not to believe the hype less than ten minutes ago?"

"I was being modest," replied Sam.

"Modest and handsome," Emily repositioned the knot of his tie, "and really fucking stupid. What if you don't come back?"

"I will," Sam paused, "but if I don't, promise me that you will get yourself as far away from Manchester as you can. A Biblical shit storm is coming and everybody is about to get very wet."

Chapter Three

"I've also got some nice commemorative tea towels of me in full formal regalia if you would prefer?" – Archangel Gabriel

Lift 124, Central Complex, Heaven

Simon Broomhead was sweating. He was also dead, a fact he was trying his best to ignore as he had far more pressing matters to deal with. Pushing up his black spectacles, he stepped inside the large lift. Gradually the number of people thinned out and by the two hundred and thirty-seventh floor he was left smiling at a fresh-faced woman in her late twenties with shoulder length black hair. Her body was slender and her face was somewhat angular with high distinctive cheekbones. Her royal blue dress clung to the curves of her hips and ended just above her knees. The colour had obviously been chosen for the way it matched her eyes, which sparkled like sunshine on water.

"Hi, going to the top?" asked Simon in a crackly voice.

"No, I'm off at three hundred and one," replied the woman, holding a clutch of beige files.

"Sounds important," he said.

"Not really. I work for one of the older saints, Basil the Great. Have you heard of him?"

Simon shook his head. There were an astonishingly large number of saints and angels in Heaven, and Basil the Great was definitely a new one to him.

The woman frowned, a look that didn't suit her. "Not many people have but he was very big in Greece and Russia with the whole Orthodox Christian thing. You know the Cathedral with the multicoloured domes in Moscow?"

"I think so," replied Simon.

"Well, they're his."

"He's got property in Moscow?"

"No, silly, I mean they're named after him," she said. "He's like Father Christmas without the white beard, red costume, flying reindeer and Coke advert, though he still gives children presents and that's the part he likes the most. He's very sweet but someone has to balance the books and that's where I come in."

Simon looked confused.

"I'm his accountant," she said with a smile.

"What! You're an accountant?"

"Yes I am," she replied.

This woman was the first accountant Simon had met in Heaven. Everyone else seemed to have a life-affirming story of helping the weak and needy. In this, children and cute animals were firm favourites. Accountants, lawyers and especially bankers were noticeable by their absence.

"And what about you?" the woman asked.

"A business meeting," replied Simon, sucking in his stomach. The red knitted tie and the blue linen blazer were his personal nod to his strong afterlife work ethic. "Do you enjoy it?"

"Being in Heaven? Of course, don't you?" she asked.

Simon nodded and gave a weak smile for the remaining few seconds it took to reach floor three hundred and one.

The woman stepped out of the lift and turned. "I'm Isabel but my friends call me Izzie. Have a great day. Hope to see you soon."

"I'm Simon. Pleased to meet you, Isabe..." The doors closed, guillotining the conversation and leaving Simon as the sole occupant of the lift. He smiled. Isabel was the most beautiful accountant he had ever met, living or dead. Where was she from? What qualifications did she have? What did she like? What made her laugh? How did she die? And why was she here?

At the six hundred and sixty-seventh floor Simon stepped out and followed the signs. Eventually he came to an imposing set of double doors. To one side there was a shiny brass plaque: "Archangel Gabriel, Acting CEO of Heaven."

Five minutes later Simon was explaining, "Sir, please refer to the interim report, page one hundred and six, section five point three, subsection seven," while offering his own copy. "I've highlighted a number of inadequacies with the current system. Budget cuts together with the inherent difficulties of."

"Be quiet," said Gabriel with the measured authority of someone who expected to be instantly obeyed. He had a deep tan, a full head of greying hair and a meticulous beard. His most striking feature, however, was his unearthly cobalt eyes. Scrupulously suited, rumour had it that he shared a Venetian cobbler with the Devil on a shoe-for-shoe basis.

Simon fell silent, his brow knitting up and giving droplets of sweat new channels to navigate down. Being dead was significantly more trouble than he ever could have imagined when he was alive.

Gabriel took a minute of thoughtful silence before speaking. "Let me clarify. For the very first time since the day of Creation we do not have the precise location of the Devil?"

Simon's Adam's apple bobbed furiously.

"The Devil is lost." Gabriel's voice was reassuringly rich like an antique mahogany table. "And we are sure this is an accurate appraisal of the situation?"

Being a middle management accountant in his previous life Simon knew a dangerous rhetorical question when he was asked one. He ventured a cautious nod and pushed up his glasses. Blood thumped through his brain like the beating of a thousand drums.

"Splendid." Gabriel strode around the desk. "Though perhaps my optimism may have been misplaced. It is not splendid. It's not good, fine, or even mediocre. This is a complete disaster. During the past five thousand years, we have never lost the Devil[6]."

Simon's legs no longer worked as legs should. They seemed to be filled with damp sand and despite a desperate urge to run he remained bolted to the chair. He stared at the shiny black shoes to his right. They were truly exceptional. A powerful hand gripped his shoulder.

"Mr Broomhead, we can dispense with formalities."

"Thank you sir."

"Gabriel. You can call me Gabriel."

"Thank you sir. Sorry, I mean, Gabriel," said Simon as he looked up. The dimensions of the room were immense with wooden panelling surrounding him on three sides. To his right a floor-to-ceiling bookcase was crammed full, with a

---

[6] The 2.4% of you who need to dot the i's and cross the t's and submit your tax returns before Christmas – this statement is incorrect. The Satanic Tracking System (STS) was first piloted in 2054 to 2050 BC as a covert operation in response to rumours that the Devil was spending way too much time in the Rose and Crown pub during Heavenly working hours propping up the bar and mercilessly monopolising the karaoke. After 2050 BC the STS received a generous black budget from the Ways and Means Committee following the Devil's fall from Heaven after a particularly heavy session at the aforementioned Rose and Crown. Sadly, karaoke nights were never the same after that. Which just goes to show what you can miss when it's gone.

prominent shelf devoted solely to modern self-help books. Opposite, a dozen famous paintings were surrounded by hundreds of black and white photographs of Gabriel welcoming famous people to Heaven. Everyone was smiling and having a great time.

Gabriel's grip strengthened and Simon found himself standing and walking to the full-length window behind the desk like a clockwork automaton.

"Do you think that the Devil is currently located on the Mortal Plane?"

Simon nodded.

"And how do you suggest we rectify this?"

"Well, err. Couldn't we just find him?"

"Exceptional!" Gabriel exploded. "Thinking like that will ensure the safety of every soul you see before you."

At this height the full expanse of Heaven spread out before Simon. It was a mass of glistening spires; ornate shimmering domes; sweeping boulevards; grand piazzas; and pockets of lush, manicured greenery. He could barely make out the thousands of tiny figures crawling over this paradise.

Gabriel brought him back with another question. "And how exactly do you intend to do this?"

"Err…couldn't we…use Heavenly Operatives?"

"Using HOs to find the Devil? Mark my words you are going to go far with such outside-the-box thinking." A long tense pause followed. "But sadly no. Not unless you wish to break the Divine Word of God?"

Simon's face flushed.

Gabriel continued, "Let me explain. In the 1970s, negotiations took place to reduce the number of operatives on the Mortal Plane. For both sides the expense was far too much. A cost benefit analysis had already proved this, so a treaty was signed on 4th May 1979."

Simon nodded slowly to indicate that he was taking in every word. One thing he had learned was that saying absolutely nothing to those in positions of power worked fine, nine times out of ten.

"Low level operatives were allowed to remain if they wished, though they were banned from acting on official business. To my knowledge all of ours came back. Consequently, we no longer have resources on the Mortal Plane and we cannot deploy any additional assets from Heaven."

Having sat down, Gabriel asked, "So the question remains, how are we going to find the Devil?" He clapped his hands and a huge transparent 3D image of

Earth appeared in front of the desk. Rolling mountains, rivers, lakes, cities, forests and dark green jungles began to spin on its axis. "Trixie, miracles in the last six hours?"

Forty lights flashed into existence as Simon unmerged himself from the Amazon Basin. "What do the colours mean?" he asked.

"A red light signifies an evil miracle while the blue ones are ours."

"Oh, I see."

"Trixie too large." The globe shrunk to two metres wide. "The number of miracles is interesting. We would expect to find two or three for this period. Which means what, Mr Broomhead?"

"This was a planned operation?"

"Go on."

"To camouflage the Devil's entry point?"

"A logical assumption and one that I concur with."

Looking through the globe Simon asked, "Sir, does it tell us where the Devil went?"

"Not as such. These are all minor miracles and anything to do with the Devil would be automatically flagged up as a major miracle. We even have a number of friends on the other side who have told us that all hell has broken loose." Gabriel coughed and smiled. "No pun intended."

"You have spies in Hell?" asked Simon.

"Of course we have. This is the eternal fight, Mr Broomhead, and the forces of evil are, by their very nature, extremely sneaky individuals. But alas, our sources cannot actually tell us where he is or what he's intending to do." Gabriel's eyes turned purple.

Simon froze. He felt sure that something bad was about to happen.

There were two sharp knocks on the office door.

"Come in," ordered Gabriel.

Simon heard the heavy wooden door swish open and close with a jolt. He felt a strange urge to turn around to see if polythene sheets for his soon to be lifeless body were being laid out on the floor behind him but all he could do was weakly return the archangel's smile.

Gabriel pointed behind Simon. "I believe that we have found a solution to our problem. Please meet Mr Smith, one of our most talented Heavenly Operatives."

Six heavy footsteps brought Mr Smith to Simon's right where he towered over him.

"Pleased to meet you," crackled Simon.

Mr Smith looked at Simon with the cold silence of a shark and pulled a six-inch metal baton from the inside pocket of his suit. Wrapping his thick fingers around the tube he twisted it sharply through one hundred and eighty degrees. Simon's eyes widened as the baton quadrupled in size. Mr Smith now smiled.

Simon felt the blood rush from his face. He turned to Gabriel. "Sir, I don't think this is necessary." Before there was time for a reply the air whooshed beside him. Simon closed his eyes and waited for the impact. A couple of seconds passed before he became aware that Gabriel was saying something.

"Please pay attention Mr Broomhead. This is not the time for daydreaming."

Simon opened his eyes. Mr Smith was using a pointer to identify somewhere in the north of England.

"Once we correlate this information and merge it with the locations of the miracles, we can conclude with ninety-eight percent certainty that the Devil entered the Mortal Plane on the outskirts of Manchester, England," said Gabriel, adding a jolly, "Pretty nifty eh?"

Simon swallowed hard.

"And Mr Smith will seek out and smite whatever mortal vessel the Devil is using and send him straight back to Hell."

"Sir, I thought we couldn't despatch any HOs?" asked Simon.

"That is correct. However, Mr Smith is currently suspended, which means that technically he is no longer an operative."

"That's pretty sneaky," blurted out Simon.

"I know. It's genius. I've personally reclassified his status to that of a Technical Administrative Support Officer," explained Gabriel.

"So he's not a Heavenly Operative?"

"No. Which means he can go and sort this mess out."

Simon estimated the damage that Mr Smith could inflict armed with the standard supplies of a Technical Administrative Support Officer: a stack of orange Post-It notes; a ballpoint pen; a mid-sized Pritt Stick; and a twelve-inch Perspex ruler. It hovered somewhere between a great deal and truly horrific. "That's great," he finally said.

"Indeed it is. However, Mr Smith does need a guide who can show him the ropes, local customs and the like. He will take care of everything else."

Simon glanced back at Mr Smith and decided that everything else would involve pliers, imaginative uses of the standard office supplies and gallons of other people's blood. He shivered.

"That someone will have the opportunity to make a real difference in the war against evil," declared Gabriel, his cobalt eyes burning into Simon.

Despite Gabriel's concentrated gaze, a wave of relief swept over Simon. Accountants, especially in the afterlife, were definitely not the right people to make any real difference in the war against evil. He began to motion towards the door. "Sir, I realise that protocol probably prevents you from saying, but can you tell me who is the other officer?"

"No problem at all," replied Gabriel, walking around the desk. "Though I think it's pretty obvious."

Simon frowned and looked around the office.

"It's you Mr Broomhead," smiled Gabriel, slapping Simon hard on the back.

For a couple of seconds Simon stood there. "But I'm no operative sir," he eventually whispered.

"Precisely my boy, which makes you perfect. We can't pull the same trick with another existing operative now, can we? No, that would simply not be fair."

"But I thought that you said it was genius?"

"It is," confirmed Gabriel, "but it wouldn't really be cricket. Not with two of them."

"Surely you need training? Years and years of training?" said Simon.

"Like I explained, Mr Smith will deal with all the smiting. So no training required on your part. Just aim him at the Devil, stand back and wait for the fireworks." Gabriel beamed as he walked behind his desk.

Simon grimaced and gripped the back of the chair.

"This is one of those tricky need-to-know situations and you already know and we certainly don't want anyone else to know now, do we?" asked Gabriel.

Simon tried to reply but found that he could only take in a couple of extra-large mouthfuls of air.

"That's the spirit. Think of this as a real opportunity for you. If only I was a thousand years younger and not bogged down by all this bureaucratic nonsense I'd be joining you like a shot."

"But it's…it's…" Panic rose in Simon's voice. "Couldn't someone..."

"Else, Mr Broomhead?" Gabriel pounced. "Regrettably not. You were right to come directly to me but it makes you part of this now."

“Why does Mr Smith even need me?” asked Simon, realising that Mr Smith hadn’t uttered a single word since he arrived. “Isn’t he English?”

“Yes, of course he is. He can trace his ancestors right back to Boudica but as I said before he is currently suspended.”

“Why was he suspended?”

“Minor disciplinary issues,” replied Gabriel, staring disinterestedly out of the window.

“What issues? I think I have a right to know if I’m going to have to work with him.”

Gabriel paused before replying. “As a rule I would never discuss such matters. I’m certain it breaks a whole raft of HR policies and I for one do not want them coming after me again. However, given the covert nature of this operation and the fact that it was sprung upon you I suppose I should explain. Mr Smith was suspended for a single minor transgression.”

“And when was this?”

Gabriel picked up a thick blue file from the desk and leafed halfway through it. “Here it is. September.”

Simon nodded. He had no idea what standards of behaviour were expected of Heavenly Operatives though a six month suspension didn’t sound that bad.

“3rd September AD 1098.” Gabriel closed the file and placed it back on the desk.

“What?”

“Mr Smith was involved with the mass beheadings of Muslims at Antioch during the First Crusade. Things got a bit out of hand, all that sun and sand.”

“But why didn’t he go to Hell?” asked Simon.

“It was all done in God’s name, so the original charge of genocide was reduced to unnecessary roughness, on the understanding that Mr Smith would plead guilty and promise never, ever to do it again. The person who stands beside you has served his time and is itching to get right back into the action.” Gabriel smiled at Mr Smith.

“I bet he is,” said Simon under his breath.

“So why don’t we get back to the matter in hand?” said Gabriel.

Simon fell silent. He could think of nothing more to say. His breathing grew ragged and the room began to pixelate and spin.

“Welcome to my A-team Mr Broomhead,” said Gabriel. “I do love it when a plan comes together.”

Thud!

Simon collapsed backwards. A minute later he woozily came to. His head was between his knees and he was sitting on the same chair as before. There were no polythene sheets behind him.

"Excellent, you're back with us," said Gabriel.

Simon swallowed and pulled his head up slowly.

"Oh, I almost forgot, a little memento for you," said Gabriel, handing Simon a cheap silver plastic ballpoint pen.

"Thank you sir."

The black writing on the side of the pen stated, "Archangel Gabriel – always here for your spiritual needs! Freephone 0800 04051979."

"I was persuaded into buying a job lot years ago and I've been trying to get rid of them ever since. The freephone number is disconnected but they still work as pens. I've also got some nice tea towels of me in full regalia if you would prefer? They were for the new millennium, one hundred percent Egyptian cotton."

"No, I'll stick with the pen," mumbled Simon.

"Wonderful. Now time for the photograph." Gabriel clapped his hands and with a creak a tiny camera sprang up to meet them at eye level.

"Bunch up. We'll have to get closer together. It's normally just me and one other person," said Gabriel as he and Mr Smith pressed up against Simon, who felt like he was caught between a rock and a very hard place.

"Say cheese," said Gabriel.

"Cheese."

The shutter clicked three times and three black and white photographs instantly appeared on the desk. They were so close that their faces seemed glued together. Gabriel and Mr Smith had broad smiles. Simon had the contorted grimace of someone who hadn't enjoyed the rollercoaster ride and would not be paying for the overpriced photograph once he got off.

"I think this one is the best," said Gabriel, pointing at the middle photograph. "Don't you agree Mr Broomhead?"

Sinaloa Cartel Compound, Tijuana, Mexico

At that exact same moment, Raul Gonzalez Garcia, a defrocked Catholic priest was also about to faint. As the High Priest of La Santa Muerte for the Sinaloa Cartel he was giving his flock an early morning blessing at their heavily fortified compound. The statue of Santa Muerte stood behind him. Thirteen feet tall, clad in a velvet crimson robe, topped by a human skull under a white silk veil, its bony hands gripped a large white orb and a bloodstained scythe.

Father Garcia's guttural beseeching filled the room.

"Santa Muerteee...

I ask you...

that you make your force felt...

against those who try to destroy me."

Coloured candles flickered on top of the two dozen human skulls scattered over the floor and altar. Each skull had belonged to one of Sinaloa's competitors.

Father Garcia's rich coppery face contorted as he gave the final liturgy in praise of Holy Death. The sicarios clenched their fists and bowed their heads in silence.

"White lady...

Black lady...

At your feet I bow."

The priest breathed out and his sharp features relaxed. Wiping beads of sweat from under his black scarf adorned with white skulls he spoke, "Leave with thunder in your hearts, brothers!" Raising his right hand his assistant pressed the play button and the opening chords of 'Santa Muerte' by 'El Cartel de Santa' rang out.

"Especial dedicación a mi Santa Muerte, Por protegerme y proteger a toda mi gente[7]."

---

[7] Translated as, "Special dedication to my saintly death, to protect myself and all my people."

Father Garcia went behind the statue, picked up a bright red chainsaw and ripped the starter rope. It snarled into life.

He held the pulsating blade high above his head, his muscles straining. Then as some of the congregation began to leave, he fell backwards. The whirring blade cleaved into the bottom half of the statue, spitting red cloth and dry bone skywards. Fainting, he convulsed and then without anyone noticing died.

Father Garcia breathed in the suffocating stench of sulphur and fresh paint. He looked around the deep pit and realised that he was no longer in Tijuana. Three torches were bolted to the sides too high to reach, their flames casting flickering shadows below.

"Padre Garcia?" a voice little more than a whisper startled him from behind. "Is that you?" it asked.

Father Garcia turned and saw a recently dead member of the cartel. "Alexis? Where are we?" he asked.

"You do not know?" asked Alexis.

Father Garcia frowned and asked, "Is this a dream?"

A silent Alexis stepped out of the shadows. He was naked apart from a plastic Casio watch. A machete thick with fresh blood swung by his side. He checked the time. "Oh no," he whispered, his voice like broken glass.

The watch started beeping. Soon the air was filled with beeps and screams, distant and close. Swallowing hard, Alexis looked away. Breathing in sharply he raised the machete and sliced an appendage off. Blood spurted between his legs.

"I want my mom. Aaaarrgghhh!"

"What!" exclaimed Father Garcia.

Falling to his knees, Alexis looked up. "Padre, please bless me," before jabbing the machete into his guts and wrenching it to one side. Blood and intestines spilled out.

"No!" cried Father Garcia.

Alexis swiftly brought the blade up to his right eye. "It's better than letting the orangutans do it. Aaaarrgghhh!" he screamed.

A large shadow appeared on the floor in front of Father Garcia. Turning he found himself standing in front of La Santa Muerte.

"He was not a true believer," she said. "Are you a true believer, Raul Gonzalez Garcia?"

He nodded.

She leant over, whispered something into his ear and sent the surprised priest gasping back into the world of the living.

A pale Father Garcia struggled to his feet, picked up the microphone and cried out, “La Santa Muerte wants Geoffrey Pike’s balls!”

No one knew who Geoffrey Pike was. No one cared, but everyone cheered. As they filed out, they all agreed that this had been a truly exceptional blessing.

Chapter Four

"You have the mark of greatness. Men have feared and respected you. You have wielded great power." – Ruby

O'Sheas Irish Bar, Princess Street, Manchester

Geoff stared at the closest stuffed leprechaun. Its single wonky eye seemed to be following him around the pub. Moving seats he looked up at Rob. "I didn't even know it was St Paddy's," he said.

"No shit shamrock," replied Rob, wearing a commemorative Guinness hat and a massive green 'Kiss me, I'm Irish!' badge.

"Don't know about you but I'm officially out of cash," said Geoff.

"No need to worry. My famous good luck will take care of us tonight," replied Rob, pulling out a money clip thick with notes and passing it over.

"Wow. Is that gold?" asked Geoff. "There must be five hundred quid here?"

"Nearer a thousand."

"How the hell did you get this? Please tell me you've still got all your organs?"

"Don't be stupid."

"Have I still got all my organs?" asked Geoff feeling his stomach.

"Don't worry I'm all about gambling responsibly," grinned Rob. "I got lucky with the football, that's all."

"How lucky?"

"Enough for us to stop worrying about tonight," answered Rob. "Remember things always happen for a reason."

Geoff turned the clip over, "What does DOH mean? And what's this inscription? Fortuna. Azothoth. Solus in mundo. Amare. Mephistopheles x."

"No idea," Rob shrugged. "Got it in a pawn shop just off St Anne's Square. They said it was German World War Two gold[8]. Pretty cool, hey? Why don't you go get us a beer?"

At the long wooden bar, a short weasel-featured man was busy serving endless pints of Guinness.

"Two pints Sean," said Geoff. "Bloody hell, you look happy."

Sean grimaced. "You know how much I hate the Irish, but I hate them even more tonight."

"I don't want to upset you," said Geoff, "but you do realise that someone has turned you into a leprechaun?"

Sean turned and looked at the large mirror that spanned the length of the bar. A deeply unhappy giant leprechaun stared back at him complete with a green hat and tunic, fake red beard and the same 'Kiss me, I'm Irish!' badge as Rob.

"You're badge buddies," grinned Geoff.

"Why does everyone in the world think they're Irish? I mean, look at Rob. He looks like a well-fed grizzly bear, not a pasty pinch-faced Celt."

"Come on, everyone is Irish tonight, even you," said Geoff picking up a flyer from a stack on the bar. "Who are The Wild Geese?" he asked.

"Tonight's live music. I had another band booked but they cancelled this morning. Two minutes later, this huge guy walks in and tells me that The Wild Geese will be playing here tonight. He didn't even give me a choice. There's your Guinness."

Geoff inspected their creamy white heads. He made out the words 'FUCK' on one and 'OFF' on the other. "Heh, you're getting really good at this."

"Too much damn practice," replied Sean.

---

[8] The clip was a bespoke item made of pure twenty-one carat gold gathered at Auschwitz. It was a very special present, for a very special Major of the Waffen-SS.

Drinks in hand Geoff turned to face a pretty young woman with white hair standing right behind him. "Sorry," he said as the creamy heads sloshed over the rims. The woman smiled and he smiled back. After a couple more steps he turned but she was gone.

At six o'clock a procession of six musicians filed past on their way to the wooden stage at the back of the pub. Like their battered instrument cases they came in widely different shapes and sizes. A minute later they were joined by another man. Standing well over six and a half feet tall he brushed the rain off his waxed coat, took off his black sunglasses and scanned the pub.

Two of the younger men, all smiles and laughter, took over the booth next to Rob and Geoff and were swiftly joined by the rest of the band. Seconds later one of the girls leaned around the corner and smiled. "Come and join us? St Patrick's the most sociable night of the year and you two look like you could do with some craic." Her playful voice matched the glint in her large brown eyes.

"So what brings you here?" asked the tall man who had a grey ponytail and a thin white scar that ran from his left eye to the centre of his upper lip.

"Hmm, it's a long story but the short version is him," said Geoff pointing at Rob balancing on a stool at the head of the booth.

"Well, I think that fate has brought us all here. I'm Seamus and we're The Wild Geese – your entertainment for tonight," he smiled, creasing his face. "This will be an honour for us all, Geoff."

Geoff stopped and frowned. He tried but couldn't remember introducing himself.

The three young men were cousins, Seamus Junior, Patrick and Michael. They had easy smiles and confidence that comes from knowing that women found them attractive. A smaller, wrinkled old man with wild eyes was introduced as Donald. The two women, Ruby and Sofia, were identical twins who wore black satin blouses and green and black tartan skirts.

"Have you just escaped from that wanker who does Riverdance?" grinned Rob. "Blink twice for yes and we'll save you."

"Please ignore my drunk and stupid friend," apologised Geoff.

"No worries, we get it all the time," said Sofia looking at Rob. "But I hope you know that Riverdance wanker is from Chicago and we're from Ireland? That's a big difference isn't it Donald?"

"Yes it is," snapped the old man who'd been silent. His voice sounded like dry branches being broken underfoot. "He's too disrespectful about traditional

Celtic music. It's all about the money for him, not the passion. He's not as bad as Franco though."

"Behave Sofia, and Don, let it go," laughed Seamus. "Please don't tell these new friends of ours how you fought against Franco in the Spanish Civil War with the International Brigade."

Geoff thought about this and did a rough calculation. "That would make you well over a hundred years old?"

Donald broke into a craggy smile and was about to speak when Seamus beat him to the punch. "Which is why I don't think he should tell you about it. You'll end up thinking he's mad, or worse still, you'll start believing in leprechauns and fairies."

As drinks flowed, it turned out that they were blood relatives from Munster, a county in Ireland and were touring around Europe.

In a pause in the conversation Ruby excitedly cried, "I should read your palms."

"She's got the Gift," drawled Seamus, cradling his whisky. "I wager that you'll both learn something about yourself and your destiny if you let her work her magic."

"Me first," said Rob, thrusting his hand towards her.

"Now let me see what we've got here," Ruby said, frowning as she traced the lines crisscrossing his fleshy palm. After a minute she looked up. "You have the mark of greatness. Men have feared you and respected you. You have wielded great power. Though this has taken place in another life, you will regain your position of power very soon."

"And that," said Rob taking in the booth, "is the way I roll."

Geoff shook his head. "Come on, you wouldn't know great power if it came up and stole your pint."

Ruby continued, her voice tinged with sadness, "You will also find a love that will bear you seven sons and seven daughters in this life, or more likely the next."

Rob raised his eyebrows and caught Sofia's gaze.

"It's your turn," said Ruby, reaching for Geoff's palm. "This is such an honour."

Geoff's brow creased tightly. He felt like he'd been hurled through the looking glass and on this side, Rob could drive and pretty women found them both attractive.

Ruby's right index finger slowly hovered over each line as she gazed down.

To his surprise Geoff realised that all conversations in the booth had ceased and complete strangers were gathering around them, their eyes fixed upon Ruby and his palm. *People on this side took palm reading far too seriously*, he thought.

Ruby muttered a series of 'mmmhhs' and 'aaahhhs' but that was all.

A glistening silver pendant fell out of Ruby's blouse and caught Geoff's eye. It was a misshapen pentagram with a dark red stone in its centre. Uncomfortable with the silence he blurted out, "That's an interesting piece of jewellery."

Ruby glanced down. "A family heirloom, same as the Gift. Sofia's got one as well."

"Is that a ruby?" asked Geoff.

She shook her head. "No, it's a special soulstone."

"Oh," said Geoff. He had never heard of a soulstone. "What do you see?"

"I can see many things but I'm afraid that some of them I cannot tell you."

"Why not? I thought the whole purpose of this palm reading thing is for you to tell me stuff that's going to happen so I can get ready for it? You know, a bit like an early warning system for life?"

"But there are a few things I can tell you," smiled Ruby.

"Job? Money? Fame? Do you see a woman called Rachel?" asked Geoff.

Ruby's features pinched up. "I definitely can't see anyone called Rachel," she said quickly, "but this is your lifeline. Can you see here? There is a fork and it becomes deeper and continues on this side but completely stops at the other?"

Geoff peered at his palm. It looked red and sweaty. "Sort of… what does that mean?"

"Within you are two lives," Ruby replied. "The first is from birth and the other will only occur after the change. Follow this line, and you will find true greatness and fearsome power."

"You mean like Rob?"

"No. Rob has already wielded great power while you have not," said Ruby.

"And what about this one?" asked Geoff pointing at the stunted line.

"I'm unable to tell you what you already know," she replied.

"You almost had me there," snorted Geoff, looking at a grinning Rob.

"I am not joking, Geoffrey. Heed my words, your power can be far greater than anyone who has ever walked the Earth." Ruby's eyes were dark and wide. "Here," she pointed at the fork, "is where every part of your life can change forever. Whether it does, is all down to you."

Geoff shivered. "You're kidding, right? Did Rob put you up to this?"

Ruby shook her head.

"Are you certain, because I think that working out that Rob is the cause of all my problems could be my big life changer? He wrote off my car and got us both fired and that's just for today."

Ruby looked up at Rob and they both shook their heads.

"I'm not going to find God, am I?" said a puzzled Geoff. There was a sharp intake of breath across the booth. "Because I'm an atheist, just like Rob."

Everyone burst into laughter, even the curious strangers.

"What's so funny?" asked Geoff.

"Don't worry, you finding God at this time would be a very bad thing," smiled Ruby.

"Why would finding God ever be bad?" asked Geoff.

"It's a bit tricky. Let's just say your life is on the cusp of a great change. If you fulfil your destiny, you will follow this line and become more powerful than you can ever imagine."

"So all I need to do is avoid God and fulfil my destiny? Tick. That sounds easy," grinned Geoff. "So when is this great change going to happen?"

"Soon, very soon," replied Ruby.

Before Geoff could ask anymore Seamus pulled a gold pocket watch from his waistcoat and flipped open its hunter case. "Time for us to go and leave these good fellows in peace."

"Hang on, what about children?" asked Geoff.

"I'm afraid that you'll have no sons but possibly a daughter." Ruby lent over and gave him a kiss on the cheek. "I'm sorry, I have to go."

"We'll expect to see you boys dancing tonight," said Seamus. "We've been told that our music is very powerful."

When Geoff was certain that none of the band were within earshot, he turned to Rob and whispered, "That was massively weird, don't you think? What a load of bollocks."

"What do you mean? Ruby really knows her stuff. Like I've always said, you have greatness written all over you," said Rob.

Geoff shook his head and rolled his eyes. "You have never, ever said that to me."

"Really? Well, I've always intended to tell you that. Any case, I think I'm going to do some serious wielding of my old power with Sofia later on. As for the children thing, it's all about the size of your balls. I'm going to freshen up." Rob rose and disappeared into the throng.

Left alone, Geoff stumbled upon a simple theory that explained everything. The world had simply gone mad. Not in an obvious way, for it was far subtler than that. Everything felt slightly off kilter. He wondered whether the captain of the Titanic would have had the same thought just before they hit the iceberg[9]? While looking at his pint a sudden low-pitched creak startled him. He looked around but nobody else appeared to have heard it, as they were all still chatting and laughing. The exception to this was the white-haired woman he'd seen before. She was back standing at the bar, staring directly at him. She smiled at him and then she was gone. He looked behind him. The leprechaun with the wonky eye was definitely grinning at him.

A second later, Geoff heard the creak again. This time it was louder and more distinct. It sounded like steel crushing against ice. Lots and lots of ice.

[9] It was after a delightful meal in the first-class restaurant at 10.14 pm on the 14th April 1912 that Captain Edward Smith, of the Titanic, felt that something distinctly odd was happening. At the time he put it all down to questionable scallops he'd had for starters and decided to go straight to bed to sleep it off. It was only later at 11.40 pm that he wished he'd investigated exactly why he was really feeling that way but by then, of course, it was way too late.

Chapter Five

"What bucket of shit is she making you go apple bobbing in now?" – Jay 'Judas' Iscariot

Loading Bay 6, Bowels of Hell, Hell

With an explosive jolt, Sam Spade's hearts stopped midbeat. The air raced out of his lungs crumpling him to his knees. For the next lung-bursting minute he lay motionless on the concrete floor.

"Hello Sam. How have you been?" A thick East Germanic voice came from above two large polished black army boots that appeared by his side.

Sam raised his head just in time to get an extreme closeup view of an extremely large clenched fist. The impact sprawled him across the floor and left him looking up at the red granite ceiling. He carefully moved his lower jaw and clenched his teeth before asking, "Pretty good Lou. Yourself?"

The owner of the fist moved swiftly to Sam's right, unleashing a single rib-cracking kick. "Can't grumble. Do you want to take your coat off? This could get messy."

"No, I'm fine," breathed Sam spitting a mouthful of sour tasting blood over the floor. "How's the missus?"

"Thanks for asking, we're seeing a couples' therapist now," Lou paused before delivering another kick.

"Arrgghh!" grunted Sam.

"Happy wife means happy life," said Lou, a stubby, barrel-chested man who stood at just over five feet. Years of putting the fear of the Devil into new souls had resulted in him developing astonishingly large hands and oversized feet. "At least that's what I've been told," he added.

"I guess I had that coming," smiled Sam.

"You back working for the boss?"

Sam looked up. Lou was wearing military grey-black camouflage trousers, black braces, a pristine white T-shirt and a toothy smile. A small black 'AB' tattoo poked out of his sleeve[10]. "No, I'm here for information," he said, carefully massaging his side. It felt like at least one, or possibly two of his ribs were cracked.

Lou grunted and wandered off to a small collapsible table in the corner. Opening his lunchbox, he fished out a thick corned beef sandwich and offered it to Sam who shook his head.

"I like what you've done with the meat factory. Is that a new type of red?" asked Sam.

"Dutchlac brilliant tulip red," replied Lou between mouthfuls.

A dozen torches were strategically bolted onto the walls to ensure the most atmospheric shadows swayed and crept along every surface.

"Nice. The deeper red gives it a more intimidating feel," said Sam. "I like the new signs as well."

Lou looked at the large white sign above Sam. Thick black letters informed new souls:

<u>WELCOME TO HELL</u>

1. THOU SHALT NOT QUEUE JUMP
2. THOU SHALT NOT EVER THINK YOU CAN EVER LEAVE
3. THOU SHALT NOT LITTER
4. THOU SHALT NOT CRY FOR YOUR MUM
5. THOU SHALT NOT PRAY TO GOD
6. THOU SHALT NOT GRAFFITI
7. THOU SHALT NOT ASK FOR MERCY
8. THOU SHALT NOT ANSWER BACK

"We were going for ten, like the Commandments, but as you can see, we ran out of ideas at eight," said Lou thoughtfully.

---

[10] It may come as a bit of a shock to some people, but membership of the Waffen-SS was and still is, a pretty much "Go Directly to Hell. Do not pass Go. Do not collect $200." While this is not always true for members of the Hitler Youth, certain Catholic clergy should really take notice of this precedence.

"Top of the head you could try, 'Thou Shalt Not Disobey' and, 'Thou Shalt Not Be Late'?" suggested Sam.

"Wow. They're really good. Just let me write them down," said Lou, pulling a pencil and pad from out of his boot.

"It seems a bit dead," said Sam, getting to his feet. "I was hoping I'd be able to sneak in unnoticed."

"This bay's been taken off the rota while it's being refurbished. Management said you can't have people working on the décor when the meat train brings in the new souls. It makes us look unprofessional," said Lou, peeling a banana. "You okay so far? You can always go back down and curl into a ball."

"Would you still kick me?" asked Sam.

Lou nodded.

"Well, I think I'll stand." Sam stooped down to retrieve his hat. "Ready when you are," he said.

Lou walked to the centre of the room and gave Sam a solitary punch to his stomach.

"Uugghh!" Sam doubled over.

Lou took a bite of his banana and launched a vicious upper cut that took Sam off the ground, spilling his hat.

"I don't suppose that we are good now?" asked Sam.

"Well." Lou unleashed an almighty headbutt.

Sam collapsed in a well-dressed heap of pain.

"Now I think that we are good. Just so you know, that was nothing personal."

It took another twenty seconds before Sam got up and brushed himself down. "We both know that I'd be hurting way more than this if it was personal." He plucked a handkerchief from his trouser pocket and began to wipe away blood from his mouth.

"That's great, Sam," Lou laughed, showing his collection of gold teeth. "There are people here still seriously pissed off with you. It wouldn't look right if you turned up untouched. I've got my reputation to think about." Most of his hair had long since gone, leaving small patches of shaved grey stubble at his temples. His tight brown eyes had a perpetual sharpness to them.

"You know that if anyone was going to give me a kicking, I would want it to be you," said Sam.

"That means a heaven of a lot to me but like I said, there's still the people here you pissed off."

Sam put the handkerchief back in his pocket and smiled.

"I'm sorry about this," said Lou, pulling out a thick metal rod from his boot. "Now just so you know, this is going to really hurt." A minute later, he breathlessly said, "You can open your eyes now, Sam. I figured you'd want me to leave the face."

With a great deal more effort than before Sam struggled to his feet and picked up his hat. He shook Lou's outstretched hand.

"Safe trip and watch yourself. I'm guessing you'll be seeing Jay?" asked Lou. "He's a tricky bastard if you ask me."

"Ain't that the truth?" replied Sam. "There's a certain JC up there who agrees with you."

Lou's throaty laughter echoed around the bay and followed Sam as he walked into Hell. Snaking a path through the cramped streets and jumbled alleyways it struck him that everywhere was much cleaner than he could ever remember and that almost all of Hell was turning bright red. As the Devil's favourite colour Hell had seen more than its fair share of red but this was different. Every wall, cobblestone, door and sign had been repainted in the Dutchlac red of the meat factory. After cutting through another side street he entered, *The Thirty Pieces of Silver Sports Bar and Grill*, to the opening cords of The Doors, 'Break on Through to the Other Side'.

An island bar of polished marble and mirrors reflected the beautiful people who worked there. Hundreds of framed memorabilia items hung on the walls. Walking to the centre Sam passed the fez of Talaat Pasha[11]; Idi Amin's Victoria

[11] Talaat Pasha was the Grand Vizier of the Ottoman Empire and the driving force behind the Armenian genocide of 1915 to 1923 which claimed the lives of over a million Armenians. He was a charming man who sported a thick bushy moustache that really complemented his fez.

Cross medal[12]; Margaret Thatcher's handwritten Christmas card to her close friend General Augusto Pinochet[13]; and Ted Bundy's signed pair of crutches[14].

Sam had been standing at the bar for a dozen seconds or so looking at Peter Sutcliffe's black V-necked sweater[15] before something warm and wet grabbed his legs. He looked down and found a pair of jet-black eyes staring back at him. A pure white-coated seal pup's flippers were holding tightly onto him.

"Owhh. Owhh," the pup gave a soft howl.

"Heh buddy, you okay?" asked Sam as he bent down to stroke him.

The seal violently shook his head as a fat man wearing a faded Britney Spears Tour T-Shirt appeared. He had sweat patches under his arms and was out of breath.

"Sorry dude. These fuckers keep trying to escape," said the man, grabbing the seal from behind. "Arrgghh… he bit me!"

"Owhh. Owhh."

"Really?" asked the man walking off seal in hand. "We'll see who's laughing at nine o'clock."

Sam's eyes followed the man to the stage where he flung the seal into a cylindrical Perspex cage full of other pups. The seal righted itself and pushed its nose to the side, staring all the time at Sam.

"I'm not even going to ask," Sam mumbled.

A tall, lean, tattooed figure shouted from a side booth, "Fucking heaven Sammy! Get over here." He was wearing tight black leather trousers and a loose-

---

[12] Idi Amin (aka 'Lord of All the Beasts of the Earth and Fishes of the Sea') awarded himself a fake Victoria Cross. However, he is not the only person to have an incredible amount of medals that he didn't earn. Prince Philip had over twenty-five military medals and well over eighty medals when you count civilian honours and orders of chivalry. That's where similarities between these two world leaders end, with the polygamist Amin marrying at least six women including 'Suicide Sarah', a go-go dancer with the Revolutionary Suicide Mechanised Regiment Band and Prince Philip wisely marrying into the British Monarchy and their estimated net worth of £72.5 billion (2020).

[13] General Pinochet's 1982 Christmas card is signed 'To my BFF', from your sexy 'La Senora' Margaret Hilda Thatcher.

[14] It could be argued that Ted Bundy was America's most successful multi-talented performer ever, a true GOAT. Noted as a top-quality serial killer, rapist, and necrophile, he often feigned disability before assaulting his victims. However, this pair of crutches was never used in the field and is therefore purely symbolic. However, they are signed, "To my good friend Jay, hugs Ted Bundy xx."

[15] Peter Sutcliffe, 'The Yorkshire Ripper', wore this sweater under his trousers, exposing the genital area and protecting his knees that otherwise would have chafed terribly when assaulting women. Even in Hell this was considered by many to be too weird and way too wrong.

fitting vest with a faded ornate upside down cross printed in the centre. "How you doing brother?"

"Good to see you too, Jay. How's business?" asked Sam.

"Same shit, different day in this sunny part of fucking Hell. But I can't complain – it's all still sweet for the Jaymeister." Looking back at the girls seated in the booth in various states of undress he clicked his fingers and barked, "Scram! The adults are talking. Wanna whisky, Sam?"

"That would be good."

"Bottle of Jura in my office," shouted Jay at the bar as he marched to a side door. Once the whisky arrived Jay sat back on one of the tired leather sofas. "Heard you were back."

Sam raised his eyebrows and checked his watch. It had been less than thirty minutes since he'd left Lou.

Jay brushed his hand over his unshaven jaw and gave a short whistle. "You look like shit brother. Lou is a true professional. Want my bitches to get that blood out of your coat?"

"No, I think it helps. What's the fun in beating up on someone who's already been seen to?" replied Sam.

"Interesting logic but I'm not sure I agree. A lot of people here have struck you off their Christmas card list if you know what I mean? Not me, brother. You back working for the man?"

"No, I'm retired and just a tourist now."

"And yet here you are. Makes a man wonder why a disgraced daemon such as yourself would come back to Hell for a one hundred and one percent nailed-on ass kicking? You feel my confusion?"

Sam drained his glass and refilled it.

"Ah, you don't want to say," said Jay. "That's cool but I'm guessing that you're not here to reminisce about what we got up to back in the day?"

"I'm here for information," said Sam.

"My specialty. Information is valuable here, there and everywhere. But I'm reckoning that it must be super valuable if you had to visit me to get it."

"Just so we're clear. If you help me with this we're even."

"That's mighty white of you brother. So shoot. What do you want to know?" asked Jay.

"I know the Devil has made an unexpected trip to the Mortal Plane. Any idea why?"

Jay gave a long whistle. "So it's true? I've heard rumours but nothing concrete. No one has seen him but if he really is off the reservation, it's fucking hush-hush. None of his top boys have said a word to my bitches. My question to you is why the sudden interest in the man? You stepping up to major leagues? It can get pretty brutal out there."

"No, like I told you I'm just a tourist but I think whatever is happening has got something to do with this," replied Sam, pulling out three pages of the *Book of Shenanigans.* Even in the subdued lighting they sparkled as he lay them down.

"Sweet. You brought me a comic. Thank you ever so much." Jay spread the pages on the coffee table. "Just what I need: an incomplete comic which you and that bitch of yours are in. So?"

"Never call her a bitch, Jay," said Sam, his jaw tight. "Her name is Emily and if you don't want any trouble with me, you need to show her respect."

"Okay, chill. Her name is Emily," said Jay holding up his hands. "People get so fucking weird when they get messed up in love. It's not fucking natural brother. Give me another shot at this?"

Sam looked at him with fading red eyes.

Jay, taking this as approval, spoke in a slow even tone. "Is this something to do with that broad of yours? You know the one, that delightful, sweet psychopath. Emily?"

Sam frowned and started to speak but Jay continued, "Heh, chill, Sammy. I'm your friend so I've got the right to have a viewpoint. Calling someone a psychopath isn't disrespectful, at least not around here."

"All I know is that she's in danger," said Sam.

"Why does that not surprise me? What bucket of shit is she making you go apple bobbing in now?" said Jay as he poured himself another whisky. The ice crackled.

"Emily's being threatened by her father, Brian, who's also somehow messed up in this."

"So the bat-shit crazy madness doesn't stray far from the asylum. You know she's bad. Not like you and me, but seriously fucked-up badness. Once she got used to this place she started kicking-ass."

"You're wrong," said Sam.

"Am I? Did she, or did she not, know exactly what would happen to her soul if she sliced open her wrists?" Jay breathed in. "And yet she cut herself all the way up to her fucking elbows."

"She knew I'd been summoned back to Hell and it wasn't looking good. She wasn't thinking straight when she did it, that's all."

"Okay, I ask you who intentionally comes here? No fucking one. Why did she really do it? I'll tell you why, she knew that you'd get on your fluffy white charger and come and save her whatever the cost. Was it her idea for you to double-cross her father and give the man the only original copy of the *Necronomicon* left in the world in exchange for her freedom? I wonder if she knew it would make every major Daemon Lord who'd already said it didn't exist look like an absolute fucking idiot."

"I did what I did." Sam raised his eyebrows. "I know someone else who ended up here after taking a not so dissimilar path, apostate."

Jay's eyes narrowed and his features hardened. "That is just so mean. You know that I had no choice in that. It was all part of God's fucking plan and I was his fall guy. My fate was literally carved in stone. Listen, as your friend I'm begging you, do not let her fuck you up again."

"It wasn't like that."

"It never is brother," said Jay shaking his head, "It never is."

"Let's just agree to disagree on this. So, you've never seen this before?" asked Sam, pointing at the pages on the table.

"On my mother's life I haven't seen this before. Why would I?" replied Jay. "I deal in hard information not comics."

"Look at the seal and the craftmanship. This is the Word of God," said Sam, "and it's a graphic novel not a comic."

"I saw that, but do you seriously think it's real? It's just a fucking comic," dismissed Jay with a flourish of his right hand.

"It's real and someone is sending me pages anonymously."

"Even if it is real, speaking as one of the stars of his last big work, I think this new shit lacks a certain gravitas," said Jay. "It needs a seriously cool bad guy like the past one."

Sam sighed. "Putting your ego to one side, can you help me find out who's been sending me this? Being manipulated is one thing – the trick is to know by who and why. I can't see it being God, so it's got to be someone from our side."

"Right," said Jay, putting his forefinger on the middle crease of his upper lip.

"Have you heard of anything out of the ordinary that could be linked to it?"

"I don't want to get involved, but there are some rumblings that we don't do anything hardcore evil anymore. This new clean-up campaign is rubbing people up the wrong way. Hell, you know, should be exactly that: Hell. Certain people are talking about a possible change in the hierarchy," said Jay. "Starting at the very top."

"Go on."

"That's all I really know. There are whispers about taking it to the next level. As for me, I've got a good thing going on here so why fuck things up, when they're already so superbly fucked up?" said Jay, his green eyes sparkling.

"Where are these whispers coming from?" asked Sam.

"Some of the lower Dukes and Sister Muerte may be involved but I really don't care," answered Jay.

"Sister Muerte? She's always been ambitious but a move on the Devil is crazy. He'll annihilate her if he ever finds out."

"They're just rumours."

"What about this *Book of Shenanigans*?"

"I dunno, Sammy. Shit like this, if it is real, is one motherfucking clusterfuck just waiting to explode," said Jay looking at the cover. "Word of God. End of the universe? At least there's no zombies. Those things give me the creeps. Are you certain you really want to know?"

"Just spill. I need to make sure that Emily is going to be okay."

Jay blew out his cheeks theatrically, stood up and opened the top drawer of the filing cabinet. "I may have something. There's a man who deals with the seedier side of the manuscript market who may be able to help you. His name is Darius Bigelow, though he likes to go by the handle of DMan. Dresses a bit like you but he's short, fat and wears glasses. Last time I heard he was keeping a very low profile holing up at this address."

Jay wrote on the back of his business card and held it out, looking into Sam's blue eyes. "One thing, do not tell him I sent you. This is not me giving you an introduction. This is me giving you a name and address in confidence. Darius is the sort of man who likes to protect his privacy, if you know what I mean? He may, and I need to stress this, Sammy, be able to help you. Also, whatever you do, keep what I said about Muerte to yourself. She is one crazy bitch and I do not want her causing me any trouble. You dig that whatever happens now, me and you are square. Deal brother?"

Sam nodded and Jay released the card.

"And I implore you, Sammy, ditch that crazy broad of yours before you get seriously hurt. I know all about your hearts want what the hearts want, but sometimes the brain has got to pull rank and smell the fucking coffee." Jay pushed his right forefinger into his temple. "Or in your case the whisky and cocaine. You know I can remember when you used to be happy and that was when you weren't in love."

Sam stood up to leave and as he opened the door Jay walked up to him.

"We've got karaoke later on if you fancy it? Bit of 'Cigarettes and Alcohol' coming your way courtesy of the Jaymeister?" said Jay, meeting Sam's frown by raising both his palms. "Don't give me that look. Before you decide, it's not just karaoke, it's karaoke while clubbing baby seals. Cute as a button seals having their heads smashed in time to music. Fucking genius, eh?"

"I think I'll give it a miss this time. Real things to do," replied Sam.

"Fair enough but it's pretty insane when someone hits the sweet spot with the baseball bat and splatters brains all over the front tables and keeps on singing Dolly Parton's, 'Nine to Five'. The crowd goes fucking mental. Speaking of mental, you know who would be a natural? Emily. Heh, I'm just messing with you. Can't get enough seal cubs anyway."

Jay paused and looked seriously at Sam. "Let's hug it out. Be careful out there brother, and keep your head on a swivel."

Jay spent the next ten minutes pacing up and down his small office. Finally, he stopped, picked up the phone and dialled a number.

"Yo, Muerte. We've got trouble."

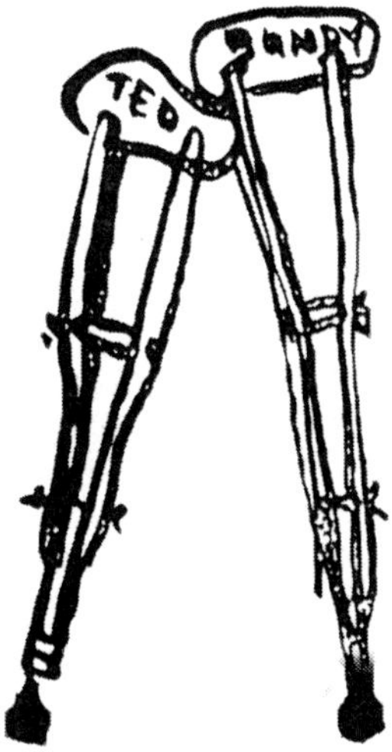

Chapter Six

"Screw being cute. I think that eating creatures with faces is all part of God's plan, don't you think?" – Mrs Thornthwistle

Thrifty Flowers, 121 High Street, Prestwich, Manchester

"A little pinch of this in his bedtime cocoa and you won't be disappointed, dear," said Mrs Thornthwistle with a soft sparkle in her eyes the colour of rain clouds. She pressed a small polythene bag containing a mixture of herbs and roots into the gnarled hand of her customer.

"Thank you ever so much," said Mrs Eccles, placing the bag in the side pocket of her tartan shopping trolley.

When Mrs Thornthwistle could no longer hear the rhythmic squeak of the loose back wheel of the trolley, she locked the door and flipped over the plastic, 'Sorry, We Are Closed' sign. "I thought we'd never get rid of her," she said to Mogwai, her shabby overweight cat curled up in the window display. "A dead cat bounce if you ask me."

Mogwai's eyes narrowed and he gave her a soft hiss before going back to licking his right paw.

"I was just checking that you're paying attention dear. Now let's get ready for our guests."

Walking over to the spotless reception table Mrs Thornthwistle chose the largest card in her collection; brilliant white with a striking pink rose and two purple crocuses surrounded by lush green leaves in the top left-hand corner. Picking up her fountain pen she wrote in purple ink:

Dear Customers,

Thrifty Flowers will be closed for the rest of the day due to the arrival of unexpected guests of supernatural persuasion. We hope to reopen on Monday 21st March. Sorry for any inconvenience this may cause.

Yours, Mrs Thornthwistle, Proprietor of Thrifty Flowers

"That should give the local gossips plenty to talk about," she said, smiling at her handiwork. Her smile quickly changed to a frown as she realised that it was utterly wrong to call the guests 'unexpected' given that she had closed at lunch to buy sandwiches and cakes for them. With a nasally sigh she ripped the card in two and wrote the same explanation without the word 'unexpected'. Satisfied she walked to the front door and wedged the card in one corner.

One hour and four minutes later, Mrs Thornthwistle stood staring at the large clock, her hands pressed firmly on her hips. "This will not do," she said, curling her thin lip and giving a loud tut. Turning on her heels she looked at the selection of sandwiches and cakes she had placed on stands ready for her guests. A couple more seconds tumbled by until the clock's hands made a single click as they moved into a perfect line. "This is all wrong." With a deep scowl she spoke directly to Mogwai, "I may have been mistaken but for the life of me I don't know how? My vision was very clear, the shop today at precisely five forty-five post meridiem by that clock. You were even lying in the window display. The only thing that is missing are my guests. It's too late to cancel the Set but I will be making a formal complaint after the meeting."

This time Mogwai looked intently at her and purred his agreement. She picked up the teapot and opened the lid. "My tea is never stewed and never served cold," and started towards the small kitchen at the back of the shop. She had travelled a dozen busy paces when there was a heavy cushioned *Thud!* behind her, followed by a gasping, "Owhhhh!"

Mogwai stopped purring. This new development required his full attention and he raised his head and looked out with newly critical eyes. Disappointingly it was obvious that the newcomer did not have anything of interest on his scrawny pink person so Mogwai yawned and stretched back out. While happy to keep an eye on proceedings this would not be spoiling his perfect day of doing absolutely nothing.

Mrs Thornthwistle stopped but did not look back. After a second, she continued to march away and had made another five paces when there was a louder, *Thud!*

She waited but this time there was no following, "Owhhh."

In the cramped back room Mrs Thornthwistle poured the tea away and waited for the old kettle to boil fresh water[16]. Closing her eyes, she concentrated but still could only make out certain words.

"That really blah blah blah!"

"Who the blah blah blah she?"

"Shouldn't we blah more blah with us?"

Four minutes later, Mrs Thornthwistle returned, tray and contents in hand. Annoyingly the shop still appeared empty. She cleared her throat and addressed her guests in her steely Scottish voice, "In my book tardiness should be included as an additional Commandment."

Over the years Mrs Thornthwistle had added fourteen Commandments[17]. She had always been perturbed that God, the universes' omnipotent being and the creator of all things hadn't given his children a far more detailed set of rules for

---

[16] While Mrs Thornthwistle's kettle did look old, it was actually ancient. You never would have guessed that it was over three thousand years old. It was the property of AuLoutine Reginald Constantinople, a rather beautiful and dashing member of the aristocracy of the Chthonians, a super-intelligent race of tentacled polymorphs, who had secretly frequented her shop via a wormhole. AuLoutine really liked to drink Yorkshire Gold tea whenever the stresses and strains of normal life proved too much for her. At this precise second AuLoutine, in a parallel universe, surveyed the utter destruction surrounding her and gave a really big sigh. The pointless three century war with the Phalagians, a super-intelligent race of twelve-legged spider-like beings, was drawing to an end. Their respective empires were now smoking ruins. She decided she could really use a nice cup of tea in her special mug sat with her tentacles wrapped up in her favourite towel.

[17] Mrs Thornthwistle's full list of additional Commandments are as follows:

11. Thou shalt be not be tardy.
12. Thou shalt have manners.
13. Thou shalt not be stupid.
14. Thou shalt be grateful.
15. Thou shalt pay taxes.
16. Thou shalt not be disrespectful to the British Royal Family (unless the person in question was originally Greek).
17. Thou shalt respect your elders and therefore your betters.
18. Thou shalt follow all grammatical rules in all forms of communication.
19. Though shalt not speak with your mouth full.
20. Thou shalt not get fat.
21. Thou shalt maintain the correct posture.
22. Thou shalt never answer back.
23. Thou shalt eat meat.
24. Thou shalt not be cowardly.

All told that would bring the number of Commandments up to twenty-four which Mrs Thornthwistle considered to be a far more suitable number. She would also like these carved onto a large tablet of Scottish granite by God.

proceeding through life. After all most people were complete idiots. Placing the tray down on the table she asked, "Do you not agree?"

Simon popped up from behind a large apple blossom tree. He smiled but this quickly turned into a painful grimace as he ran his tongue over his cracked lips. Planar travel has unfortunate side effects[18]. Atoms are broken into protons, electrons and neutrons, which are vigorously shaken in a large metal cocktail mixer. At the other side the resulting gloop is poured out and put back together. Invariably a small film of moisture ends up coating the bottom of the mixer which contains water, proteins, salts, fats and almost all of the body's dopamine. Consequently, planar travel is just not designed to make you happy.

Simon stared at Mrs Thornthwistle. With her grey hair scraped back into a severe bun he decided she was the human equivalent of a Scottish pocket battleship. "Really sorry," he said. "Something about major repair works at our end that messed around with the whole timetable. I'm Simon and my companion is, err…"

Mr Smith's head and incredibly hairy chest lurched into view. He looked like a strawberry blond, grizzly bear.

"…is Mr Smith and we've been sent by..."

Mrs Thornthwistle interrupted, "Yes I am fully aware of who sent you but I was wondering why you are naked in my shop?"

"Budget cuts," said Simon.

"Well, that's as may be, but even so. My name is Alice Elizabeth Thornthwistle, but you can call me Mrs Thornthwistle." She looked Mr Smith up and down, frowned and gave a brief shake of her head.

"It's a very nice shop you have, Mrs Thornthwistle," said Simon.

"Thank you, dear. Now would you like some freshly brewed tea? Do you take milk? Sugar?"

---

[18] This general loss of moisture also helps to explain why beings subjected to this type of travel can get an irresistible urge to drink a nice cup of sweet tea and eat as much chocolate as they can lay their hands, legs, or tentacles on, as this helps replace almost all of the precise elements that planar travel takes away and subsequently helps make them feel a great deal happier. Planar travel also has a tendency to make you lisp every other one of your words, making perfectly innocent words sound like *blah*. There is no adequate or understandable reason for this, though the leading theory on this topic simply states that it seems like a fun idea at the time. Fortunately, this generally passes very quickly.

"Milk and one sugar please. Actually, could you make it four sugars?" Simon paused. "Can I please change that to six?"

Mrs Thornthwistle passed over the cup and saucer and coughed weakly. "Are either of you of the vegetarian persuasion?"

Simon shook his head and looked at Mr Smith's hawk-like eyes and large teeth. It was like asking a Great White Shark if it wanted seaweed instead of sea lion. "No, we're definitely not vegetarian," he replied.

"Excellent. Did you know that Hitler was one of them and look where that got him? Screw being cute. I think that eating creatures with faces is all part of God's plan, don't you think? The whole, "be fruitful and multiply, and replenish the earth, and subdue it: and have dominion over the fish of the sea, and over the fowl of the air, and over every living thing that moveth upon the earth." Genesis 1:28 nicely sums it all up," said Mrs Thornthwistle. "But enough of that, why are you here?"

"The Devil is in Manchester and we are supposed to smite him back to Hell. Gabriel said that you may be able to help us?" explained Simon.

"Interesting. Would you like a sandwich?" Mrs Thornthwistle offered the generous selection of sandwiches spread out over a silver three-tiered cake stand.

"Thank you very much," replied Simon, still standing behind the bush.

"Right, how naked are you and your companion?"

"Completely, I'm afraid."

"Well, we can't have this conversation with you both naked," said Mrs Thornthwistle, heading back to the kitchen. A short time later, she reappeared clutching two towels. "I'm afraid this is all I've got for the moment."

Simon unfurled his tea towel. 'The Legends of Scotland[19]' gave a graphic account of individual Scots who did not like the English. He wrapped the tea towel around him inside out.

Mr Smith emerged with a large beach towel wrapped around his waist. The red lettering said, "My mate went to Alpha Centauri and all he brought back was this stupidly huge beach towel!"

---

[19] Working around a Saltire was: Robert the Bruce who killed English people; Rob Roy MacGregor who killed English people; Ian Brady who killed English people; Robert Burns who sent English people insane; William Wallace who killed English people; Irvine Welsh who sent English insane; Black Agnes who killed English people; Dennis Nilsen who killed English people; and finally, Nicola Sturgeon who just scared English people to death with her haircut.

“Please take a seat,” said Mrs Thornthwistle. “What can you actually tell me? To start with, do you know where the Devil is right now?”

“No, I’m afraid not but we’ve got ID cards,” answered Simon.

“ID cards?” she asked.

“Plastic cards with our names and photos on them.”

“Well, I suppose I should inspect them. May I?” Mrs Thornthwistle held out her hand. “Dear, you look a wee bit scared. Please help yourselves to more tea and sandwiches. I’m going to make some phone calls and when I come back we are going to have a nice chat about how I can help you find the Devil, and how we’re going to smite him all the way back to Hell.”

Chapter Seven

"He can have as much Guinness as he wants, but no more whisky!" – Rob

O'Sheas Irish Bar, Princess Street, Manchester

An audible buzz went through the bar as The Wild Geese took to the stage. Towering over the audience Seamus growled, "Happy St Patrick's Day. We are The Wild Geese from the Devil's own country. They say that he has all the best music, why don't we find out!"

The crowd became a heaving mass of expectations, whooping, whistling and cheering until The Wild Geese shattered them apart like a bullet slicing through fresh pumpkin. Fiddles, flutes and ferocious beats grew faster and faster, all fashioned around Seamus' hypnotic voice. As the band launched into another song, the traditional jigs of the ceilidh were replaced by something more primitive and savage.

Intrigued, Geoff stood up on the wooden bench of his booth to get a better look. "Bloody hell. It's like being at the zoo[20]," he said.

---

[20] The Definitive Party Scale (DPS) was introduced by Emperor Nero during a rather dull day in Rome on 11th November AD 63. It was drizzling and cold. The scale was devised by Nero himself who really, really liked parties as well as zoos. If Geoff had been aware of Emperor Nero's DPS, which gives no less than thirteen different categories, he would have ranked tonight as a solid Category 4. This would mean that it was classed as a 'A bit of a Raucous Party', which should include acts such as unnecessary fighting, simulated public fornication and vomiting. Even so it was still, in its fast-beating heart, just a party. At the moment it stopped short of being a Category 5 which is a 'Bloody Great Party', which should include Grievous Bodily Harm, actual public fornication, vomit drinking and synchronised dancing to exceptionally poor music e.g. The Birdie Song, or anything by Robbie Williams, the fat dancer from Take That. All of this was a million miles away from a Category 13 Party, 'Apocalyptic Fun', which could include the end to the world as we know it. It would all really depend on how far people wanted to take it but key aspects are likely to include: the election of a madman as the President of the United States of America; the election of a madman as the

Two women fell horizontally into the seats where the band had previously sat. The woman on top gripped the other's wrists and kissed her violently. They moaned and giggled.

Geoff looked down at the writhing mass of female flesh, bent over and carefully retrieved his pint. "Rob!" he shouted as the two women launched into another kiss, though this time with teeth. "Let's get another beer."

One pint of Guinness followed by a couple of double Jamesons later Rob said, "You should join in," and body slammed Geoff into the centre of the frenzied fray of dancers.

Geoff instinctively jerked and jolted to the primal Irish beats. Closing his eyes, he began to feel part of something much larger than himself.

Pop!

Geoff opened his eyes. All he could see was the tops of heads in constant motion to the music.

CREAK.

Everything and everyone was frozen. Geoff hovered above his own petrified body. *Am I dead?* he thought.

Before he could think anymore, grotesque alien features flooded the dance floor. People changed. Tentacles slithered around bodies, wings jostled, tails squirmed across the beer-soaked floor and everyone now had horns. Everyone that is apart from Geoff who still looked human.

Geoff spied a bloated body with over a dozen eyes dripping over his neck and shoulders, two red horns and a dark green tentacle sprouting thick from the centre of his chest. He could barely recognise his friend, but Rob was still wearing his Guinness hat and the oversized "Kiss me, I'm Irish!" badge.

Geoff dropped down and hurtled towards the Mancunian night. He rebounded a good six feet from the main door.

"Bloody hell!"

He tried to force himself through the floor, the ceiling and the windows before gazing at The Wild Geese. They still looked vaguely human but had jutting sharpened features and were totally naked. An aura of crimson energy quivered around their bodies and their instruments. Hovering behind them was a misshaped silver pentagram. It was at least six feet in diameter and was an exact

---

President of Russia; the resurrection of the dead; the Rapture; a drum and bass set by the Four Horsemen of the Apocalypse; and a charade drinking game that involves the correct guessing of nuclear launch codes.

copy of the pendant that Ruby had been wearing. Unlike everything else, the soulstone at its centre was pulsating rhythmically like a slow beating heart.

CREAK.

The music restarted. Everything went pitch black and then a red strobe light burst out of the soulstone. Geoff started towards the stage, his eyes locked on the peculiar stone. He inched forward. Blackness; red strobe.

He inched forward some more. Blackness; red strobe.

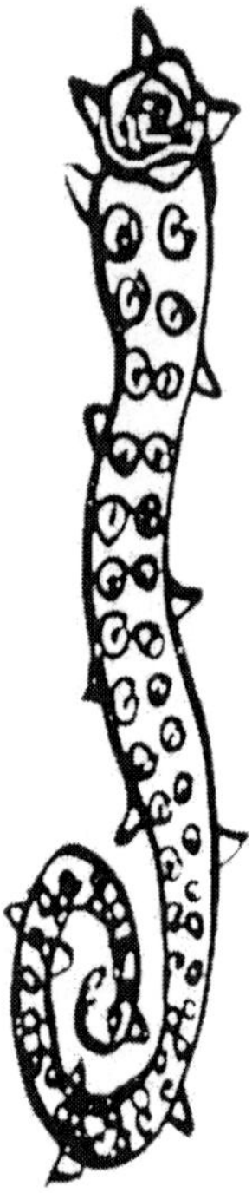

Something cold and wet touched him. Blackness; Geoff froze; red strobe. He looked down to see Rob's contorted face leering directly under him. Arms outstretched, the thick green tentacle wrapped around his legs pulling him downwards.

Blackness; Geoff thrashed out and kicked Rob full in the face causing the tentacle to uncoil. A bitter alien howl rang around the bar. Red strobe. Free, Geoff rose to the ceiling and looked down. Every single eye was staring directly at him.

Blackness; screams, shrieks, howls and wails.

Red strobe; grasping claws, tentacles, talons and maws strained towards him.

Blackness; Geoff flew to the nearest corner.

Red strobe; the mass of monsters jostled below Geoff who found he had nowhere else to go.

Blackness.

CREAK.

Instant silence. When the strobe returned everyone was frozen once more. Geoff, seeing his chance, whirled down through the mass of flesh and bone to the other corner of the pub.

Blackness.

Something else moved.

Red strobe.

The something else that moved was not grotesquely alien. It was the pretty woman with the white hair. She was walking slowly towards Geoff's physical body with a confident smile. She looked beautiful with pale blue eyes. He could smell the soft, light scent of her flesh; blossom and citrus. He tried to get closer but found he couldn't move. Helplessly he looked on as the woman eased through the crowd until she stood facing his inanimate body.

Who are you? he thought.

The woman looked up at him and placed her index finger on the centre of her lips. "Shush," she whispered. Moving his mousey brown hair to one side she leaned over and fully extended her thin tongue, licking from the base of his neck to his right ear. Once there she whispered in a syrupy Welsh accent, *"Tu es meus creatura,"* wrapping her tongue around each word.

"Ego Dominus Deus vester." Her blue eyes shimmered, her lips curling up into a smile. *"Ego vere tui similis chorum."*

Pop!

With a flash of burning whiteness Geoff's mind was catapulted back inside his body. The hideous creatures that writhed below him began to melt back into their human forms. Like an assortment of ghost train wax figures standing too close to a bonfire they gently oozed away. The Wild Geese were also back to their normal selves with their auras and the pulsating soulstone vanishing, their clothes reappearing.

Geoff was back in motion. Though desperately slow he could feel his body becoming more used to the movements that went with it. Before long, he was speeding up as the rules governing time lurched back into existence. Whirling away he saw the white-haired woman back at the bar. She smiled and aimed her left hand at him like a gun.

"Bang," she mouthed as she pulled the trigger.

Geoff spun away in real time and when he returned, she was gone.

As the fiddles fell silent Seamus growled, "We're going to take a break now. Hope you enjoyed that, Geoff. There's much, much more to come."

Everyone was now human. Given this, Geoff dismissed the idea of running away and decided the strange woman was the key to what had just happened. He traced a line from his neck all the way up to his ear. It felt sticky and tasted sweet. He knew exactly where she had been standing and began to ease his way through the bar. As he got closer, his heart banged harder against his ribcage. The woman wasn't there.

"You look like fucking shit mate," said Sean.

Geoff's eyes darted around.

"Same again?"

"There was a woman, she was standing right here. Did you see her?" asked Geoff.

"Can you be a bit more specific? I mean, look around you."

"She was special."

"Aren't they all?" said Sean with a wink.

"You don't understand! I need to find her."

"Find who?"

"That fucking woman," exclaimed Geoff. "She was pretty and had white hair."

"Same again?"

Geoff sighed, "Yes, I guess. Sean, don't take this the wrong way, but you seem different. Are you," he paused and frowned, "happy?"

"You know, I guess I am," smiled Sean.

"Why?" asked Geoff. "You were your miserable git self an hour ago."

Sean licked his lips before replying, "Life is pretty good and there are far worse things to do."

Geoff's eyes narrowed, "Are you ill? Do you want me to get a doctor?"

Before Sean could reply a large fleshy hand spun Geoff round. It was Rob, his blue eyes shining out of his red face. "Wow. What a great night," he said.

"You're normal," mumbled Geoff.

"We've spoken about this before, so you know I prefer to think of myself as well above average," replied Rob.

"That's not what I mean," said Geoff. "I thought you were some sort of monster. You had horns and really big fangs. Your head was that dirty red and black like Darth Maul and you had lots of these evil, glowing eyes and a big green tentacle coming out of your stomach. Everyone else was scaly, slimy tentacles, claws, horns, seeping wounds, bug eyes."

"Really?" Rob raised his eyebrows.

"Everyone was chasing me, but it wasn't me because I'd come out of my body. And now everyone is normal. It was so scary and you were part of it."

Rob placed his arm around Geoff's shoulders and yelled at Sean. "No more whisky for this young man. He can have as much Guinness as he wants but no more whisky!"

"Do you think someone spiked my drink?" asked Geoff.

"What? With lots of alcohol?"

"There was a woman who was part of it. I've got to speak to her."

Rob rolled his other hand down his bristles. "Let me get this right in your alcoholically fuelled hallucinations where I was this really scary monster there was a woman?" he said. "I can see exactly where this is going."

"No, it's not like that," said Geoff. "I just need to find her. She was pretty, white hair and had a black leather jacket."

"Are you certain she even exists? It looks like drinking and dancing doesn't agree with you, dude."

"Yes, she bloody exists," Geoff's gaze covered the pub. "She could still be here."

"But you've checked the bar and you can't find her?"

Geoff nodded.

"Manchester's a big place. You'll probably never see her again," said Rob.

After another minute scanning the pub Geoff spoke. "You're right. We should go home."

"Wouldn't you like to see Ruby after the show? I'd like to see Sofia if you know what I mean. Your mystery woman may even reappear. Did you see that Seamus dedicated the first part to you?"

"You can stay out if you want but I'm going home," said Geoff.

"No. We never leave a man down. Back to the bat cave," replied Rob.

Outside the heavens had opened and Manchester was getting wet once again.

"No taxis?" asked Geoff, looking up and down Whitworth Street.

"Not here. We're going to have to walk to the taxi rank at Piccadilly."

"But it's throwing it down."

Rob buttoned up his coat. "Come on, you're not made out of sugar and it'll sober us up and make the pizza taste better," he said.

"I guess," mumbled Geoff.

Between the clouds the inky-black sky was peppered with a sprinkling of stars. At ground level gaggles of drunk students meandered home as the sheeting rain bounced a couple of inches up from the pavement. As they walked on, Geoff thought that somewhere within all of this was the woman who had whispered something in his ear, something that felt important. As much as he tried, he couldn't remember a single word of what she'd said.

As they stepped into the back of a black cab, the woman crowding Geoff's thoughts was making a cup of tea and searching for biscuits in the kitchen of Flat 124 Barry Court, Withington. She placed her hands on her hips, frowned and cursed loudly.

The taxi driver flipped on his meter and turned around. "Good night lads? Like the hat. Where can I take you?"

"Cheers mate. Barry Court, Withington," replied Geoff. "Just off Palatine Road."

Chapter Eight

"I am truly sorry for ruining your plans, Mr Spade." – Emily

Hell Mouth Orchard, Hellside, Hell

It is notoriously difficult to measure time in Hell. Even souls who have been there for centuries often find that they lose track of minutes, hours, days and even years. The sky is forever fixed in a muggy burnt orange dusk of a summer's day hanging somewhere between daylight and darkness. Sam checked his watch. Seven-fifteen, which meant he'd been Hellside for just over two and a half hours. He winced and slowly rubbed his chest. His bones were already reknitting but that didn't stop them hurting. He was keen not to outstay his welcome, since it would undoubtedly lead to more cracked ribs, or something much worse.

After forty minutes of snaking through claustrophobic alleyways, Sam finally got to 1785a Hell Mouth Orchard, the address Jay had written on the back the business card. The area was utterly broken. Tumbledown ghettos populated by damned souls weren't anything new in Hell, but this place had a terribly lifeless feel to it. There was no red paint here, just a collection of pitiful dumps clinging to the barren hillside.

Under normal circumstances Sam would have staked out the property for a couple of days. That would help ensure that he didn't get any nasty surprises, but all of that would take time and that was a luxury in short supply for Mr Spade.

Checking the street, he went around the back of the house and kicked the half-rotten door in. Inside, what sunlight struggled to get in was met by a rancid stench of cats, cigarettes and cheap whisky. Hordes of flies buzzed around piles of rotting cat food. As he crept through what was once somebody's kitchen, there was a sudden hissing sound behind him. He spun around, Luger in hand, to face a pure white Persian cat arching its back.

"Hiss!"

"Shoo, you mangy fleabag," growled Sam, poking the pistol barrel in its round face.

With a further hiss the cat leapt off the table.

"I hate cats."

The walls of the adjoining lounge had a dirty yellow tinge to them. An ancient TV stood in one corner where more feline eyes tracked Sam's movements. He loosened his tie and collar in a vain attempt to get more fresh air into his lungs. A quick search of the rest of the house found a dozen or so cat carriers piled in the main bedroom, more cats and hundreds of unopened tins of cat food. There were no clothes or even a toothbrush. The bunched-up sheets on the bed suggested that it had been slept in, but he couldn't tell when.

"Jay must be wrong about this," muttered Sam as he reholstered his gun and passed back through the kitchen. Once outside he closed his eyes and took a couple of lungfuls of freshish Hell air. It was time to go back. He had no leads and a couple of broken ribs.

Sam's assessment of the situation then took a dramatic change. He felt a cold large calibre metal cylinder pressed hard into the middle of his forehead. He opened his eyes.

The owner of the gun spoke quickly, "Who the fuck are you?" Without waiting for an answer, he added, "Open your mouth. Wider!" The gun barrel was shoved into Sam's mouth.

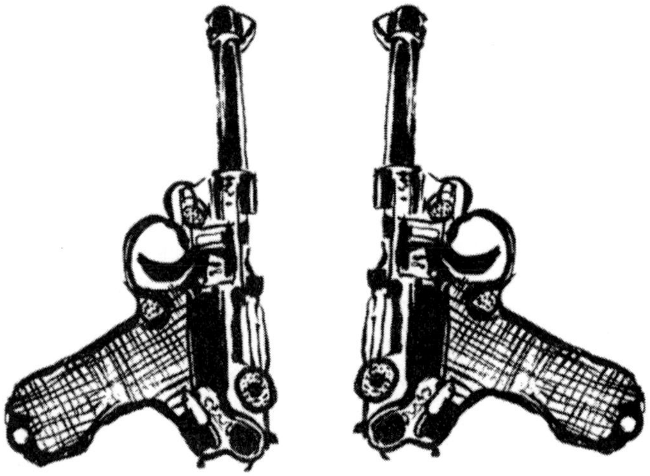

"Waahhh."

"Move and I will kill you."

Sam felt a trembling hand inside his overcoat pat its way to his pistols. Looking down he could see that it was a hand cannon, one capable of splattering every last ounce of his brains over the wall behind him.

"Waaahhh?"

The person slowly pulled the gun out of Sam's mouth and took three steps back. He was as Jay had described: a short fat man with a receding hairline, patchy beard and black glasses. What Jay had failed to mention was the hand cannon or his nervous disposition. A shudder ran down the righthand side of his body.

"You okay?" asked Sam, lifting his palms up.

"Do you want me to be okay?" accused Bigelow. He was wearing loose fitting grey jogging bottoms and a stained sweatshirt.

"Well, yes, I would like you to be okay, but at the moment I'd settle for that hand cannon of yours not having a hair trigger. I'm Sam Spade, a private investigator, and I'm looking for a Darius Bigelow. That wouldn't happen to be you, would it?"

"Introductions over, who sent you?"

"Nobody sent me. I don't suppose you want to put that cannon away?" suggested Sam.

"Why did you break into my house?" Bigelow scowled.

"I'm working against the clock and was hoping to discuss an urgent matter with you. Mind if I ask who is after you? I may be able to help."

"I seriously doubt that. Assuming that you get through the next five minutes with your life intact, all you would need to do is go and tell them where I am, or you could try to claim the bounty yourself."

"I don't know anything about a bounty but even if I did, I wouldn't do that. I have issues with authority, especially with those who are in power."

"We're not safe here. Go back inside," ordered Bigelow.

Sam walked back into the kitchen and sat down.

"You didn't need to break down the door, it was open, you idiot," said Bigelow taking the seat opposite Sam. Placing the Lugers on the table he levelled the hand cannon at Sam's midsection. A dozen cats appeared, tails up. "Did you hurt any of my cats?"

"No, of course not, I love cats."

"I know you despise them, so I'd appreciate if you do not lie to me."

"Look, a few hissed at me before, that's all."

"How few?"

"I don't know…a dozen? You've got quite a few cats here," said Sam looking at the Persian being stroked by Mr Bigelow. The cat gave him a look of pure hatred. "That one in particular didn't seem overly friendly."

"Did you touch any of them?"

"No," replied Sam. "I don't love cats per se, but I think despise is a bit extreme. Truth is they just don't like me."

"You're a daemon and cats don't like daemons, which is the reason why I like cats," said Mr Bigelow.

"Then you really should have made better choices in life, Darius. Eating cat food in a shit hole in Hell surrounded by daemons doesn't seem the best outcome for anyone," said Sam shaking his head. He looked down at the hand cannon. "You know if you miss me you won't have time to reload?"

"I'm not going to miss."

"Maybe," said Sam. "There really are a few questions I need to ask you." He handed over his business card.

"You find cats?"

"Yes, though they're pretty unhappy when I do find them."

Bigelow laughed. He had dark circles under his eyes and looked like he hadn't slept properly for weeks.

"Is it okay if I show you something? It's a manuscript of sorts and I'd appreciate your expert view on it."

Bigelow nodded. "Just so you know this cannon does have a hair trigger."

Sam eased five pages of the *Book of Shenanigans* out of his coat and placed them on the table. Darius stopped stroking the cat and spun the pages round. "What's this?"

"I was hoping you could tell me," said Sam.

Picking up the cover page Bigelow spoke slowly, "This is exquisite. The craftmanship of each page is quite remarkable. See here, the hologram appears to be genuine." He looked up. "What is a daemon doing with an unknown Word of God?"

"So you've never seen this before?"

Bigelow shook his head. "I have never even heard of its existence. Where in Hell did you get this?"

"Not here. Someone has been sending me pages on the Mortal Plane," said Sam.

"Could it be a forgery?" Bigelow pulled an eyepiece out of his pocket and examined the hologram. A minute passed before he looked up. "If this is a forgery, it is a truly excellent one. I could get this properly authenticated but I would need time and, of course, cash."

"No need. It's real," said Sam.

"Well, assuming your sources are correct this is literally priceless. I could easily find you a buyer."

"I'm afraid it's not for sale, but please read the other pages. It gets better."

Five minutes later, Bigelow frowned and cocked a solitary eyebrow.

"Thoughts?" asked Sam.

"It seems they are right. God does work in mysterious ways."

"I'm aware of that, Darius. Anything else?"

Bigelow shrugged.

"Why are you hiding here?" asked Sam.

"I'm afraid that certain people wish to kill me."

"Even in Hell that's extreme," said Sam. "Eternal torture is more our style."

"As we're trading questions mine is: why should I trust you? You did break into my house."

"Firstly, you're the one with the guns and secondly, I've shown you something that while not connected to your problems, is pretty damn interesting. The sort of interesting that could easily get me killed," said Sam with a shallow laugh.

"I suppose you have a point. Why do people want me dead? I honestly have no idea."

"Let's start with who wants you dead?" pressed Sam.

"Powerful people, that's all I know."

"Who have you been working for?"

"You know the rules. I would venture that we share a code of strict client confidentiality," said Mr Bigelow, placing the hand cannon down on the table.

Sam looked around before levelling his gaze at Darius. "But you are facing exceptional circumstances and my guess is that you are in dire need of help. What if I make it worth your while to relax and maybe bend those rules?"

"I thought I made myself clear, Mr Spade, my adherence to the code is not up for negotiation with you or anyone else."

Reaching inside his jacket Sam pulled out a very large roll of green Hell dollars and placed it between them.

Bigelow's dark eyes widened as he latched onto the roll and made a quick assessment of its value. He rubbed the thumb of his right hand slowly over the tips of his fingers. "That is a pitiful amount. I am deeply offended by your belief that I can be bought so easily."

Sam pulled another identically sized roll and placed it next to the other. He gave a thin smile.

"Of course, you may be right that I should be more open to new ideas. You are correct that my current predicament is somewhat unique." Bigelow looked deep into Sam's eyes and realised that there was not going to be any further rolls. He grasped at the two wads of notes but as he touched them Sam's right hand shot out and gripped him by the wrist.

"What were you working on?" asked Sam.

"I fail to see any connection but I'll answer any questions you have as honestly as I can," replied Bigelow. "You can trust me on that."

Sam did not trust him. Bigelow was desperate and he had lots of cats. He slowly released his grip. "What can you tell me?"

"I was collecting scientific pieces working on a blueprint for time travel. The most recent theorised that if you can make a large tear in space and have access to untold power you can actually travel through time."

"Is that possible?"

"No, of course not," snorted Bigelow. "It was just a theory."

"How come I've never heard of this?" asked Sam holding his jaw.

"All of the pieces were completed in utmost secrecy. My guess is that they didn't want the great Sam Spade to know about it."

"Who was working on this? A daemon?"

"No. All of the work was done by humans starting with Archimedes. He posed the original question of how time travel could be achieved, which the world's greatest scientists then tried to answer. Galileo; Michelangelo; Newton;

Einstein; Steenbeck; Hawking and many others have added to this body of work."

"But how could they work on the same theory if it was written in secret with hundreds of years separating them?" asked Sam.

"Simple. Each document was written in a complex code that appears to be known only to these scientists. They somehow found the previous work, added to it and passed it on to the next generation. I believe that they could have been part of a secret society that predates the Illuminati."

"How do you know that?" asked Sam.

"In a fit of puerile curiosity, I procured the services of a code breaker to make sense of what I was collecting. Eventually he used a variation of the Codex Sinaiticus to break it. And that's when all my problems started," said Mr Bigelow.

"What happened?"

"My code breaker was found dead and I narrowly missed the same fate."

"How?"

Mr Bigelow looked down at the hand cannon. "A squad of Minotaurs paid us both a visit."

"I hate Minotaurs," said Sam shaking his head, his jaw tight. "Who were the last scientists working on this?"

"To my knowledge Brout, a theoretical physicist who was key to the Higgs boson work, passed it onto Hawkins."

"You mean the God Particle guy?"

Bigelow nodded.

"Do you know if there are any living scientists still working on this?"

"With Hawkins dead I'm afraid I don't and interestingly all of them have gone to Heaven."

"Who were you collecting these for?" asked Sam, eyeing the Persian cat who stared at him with unblinking almond eyes.

Bigelow picked up the hand cannon. "If you want me to discuss this any further, I'll do a deal with you."

"I don't suppose it's worth mentioning your promise to answer my questions truthfully?" asked Sam.

"Probably not as this information goes over and above that and as you can see, I still have all the firearms."

"What do you want?"

"Your hat, coat and shoes." Bigelow paused and looked at the Lugers on the table. "I'll keep one of your pistols too."

"I'm surprised you don't want any of pages of *Shenanigans*?"

"On second thoughts I think I'll pass on that. I have a strong feeling that ownership of these pages will get you into far more trouble than even I'm in," said Mr Bigelow, forcing a thin smile.

"So there is a connection?" asked Sam.

Bigelow nodded. "I hadn't thought of it before but my work and your God written graphic novel are interlinked. Now if you would be so kind as to pass me your hat and coat? Trust me, this will be worth it."

Sam was right not to trust Bigelow. Not only did he have cats, he also had his money, one of his priceless Luger pistols and would soon have his coat, hat and shoes.

"The benefactor that I was collecting these works for was Pnakotic," said Bigelow.

"The Daemon Lord?"

"No, I mean Pnakotic that nice Chinese woman who lives down the road," Bigelow sighed. "Of course the Daemon Lord, you fool."

A shadow passed over the kitchen window. Every cat arched their back, fluffed up their fur and hissed at what remained of the back door.

"Run!" shouted Sam, diving off his chair. Bigelow tried to swivel to face the door whilst grasping the hand cannon. He was successful with the former but not the latter.

The back door burst open and a Minotaur covered in black body armour with infrared goggles appeared.

Rattattattat!

Bullets riddled Bigelow's face and upper body, clattering him backwards, sending everything on the table crashing down to the floor. As the final slug ripped into his lifeless body cat chaos erupted around the Minotaur.

Sam rolled behind the upturned table and grabbed the hand cannon. Against military grade body armour his Lugers would be as useful as peashooters on a tank. However, the hand cannon was an entirely different proposition.

Shaking the cats off him the Minotaur grunted, pulled his goggles up and began to clear the room. He kicked the chairs and the table to one side, though confusingly the table did not move. For a second the Minotaur cocked his head, looked at the table and raised his pistols. Sam dived to his right, levelling the hand cannon at the surprised daemon who was standing less than three feet away. "You looking for me stupid?" he asked.

"Yes," the Minotaur replied.

"Good." Sam pulled the trigger.

Boom!

The hand cannon roared through the chest armour, instantly exploding the Minotaur's two hearts. Falling to his knees he collapsed backwards as a look of confusion slowly spread over his face.

Clink.

Something dull and metallic rolled across the line towards Sam. In a heartbeat he started to sprint to the lounge.

Boom! The stick grenade exploded, hurtling him over the sofa where he landed in a painful heap.

Rattattattat!

Bullets sprayed the lounge. Sam considered whether he should try for the stairs or the front door. Neither looked promising. Going upstairs would leave him trapped, while going outside would almost certainly mean running into more daemons. As it was, he didn't have time to choose either of them. Another Minotaur stomped clumsily and quickly into the lounge and levelled the guns at his head. Sam closed his eyes. He wanted his hat and his final thought was that he was right when he told Brian he wasn't going to make it to page sixty-four.

Thud.

By the time Sam opened his eyes fifty plus stone of dead Minotaur had fallen to his knees. Two thick streams of blood poured down from under his jaw line as his pistols clattered to the floor. The massive head rocked backwards and forwards and then fell towards him.

"Aarrgghhh!" cried Sam as he half caught the horns of the dead daemon and wriggled free.

Emily smiled. She was holding two bloody stiletto daggers and his hat, which she threw to him. "It's got a few bullet holes in it," she said. "You may need a new one."

"Just so you know I had that under control. I was just about to disarm him and find out who sent him. Now thanks to you we'll never know." Sam put his index finger through one of the holes in his hat.

"I am truly sorry for ruining your plans, Mr Spade. I killed another one outside but I expect there'll be more coming. You can always disarm and interrogate them when they get here?"

"No, we should go, you might get hurt. Just let me check something."

Searching Bigelow's body was quick. He had Sam's two rolls of dollars and a black business card. "Pnakotic – Ravishing Souls since 450 BC Freephone 0666 16030659."

Sam flicked over the card. In black scrawl he could barely make out, "Sister M has a job." It was Jay's writing.

"I do believe that you owe me Mr Spade," said Emily.

"In my line of work I always owe someone and this time it just happens to be you," Sam replied. "But you really shouldn't have come here, it's too dangerous."

"For who?" replied Emily. "Any case I wasn't going to let you have all the fun now, was I?"

Sam looked around. The white Persian cat was staring at him, though its hatred had ebbed away. He gave it a brief nod and turned to Emily. "Did I ever tell you I hate cats?"

"Yes."

"And Minotaurs?"

Emily smiled. "Yes. On many occasions."

"But I love you one hundred percent," said Sam as he kissed her. "Now let's get the heaven out of Hell."

Chapter Nine

"Any of you sinners need a flogging before we go?" – Mr Smith

Thrifty Flowers, 121 High Street, Prestwich, Manchester

"So, you're the members of this Set thing? It all sounds a bit secret agentish to me," said Simon to the small group standing in a semicircle around him in the main shop at Thrifty Flowers. "How did you all meet?"

Rachel, still wearing her work clothes, was the first to answer. "Mrs Thornthwistle put a card in the local post office. I think I've still got it." She opened her bag and began to search. "Found it," she said, offering a small laminated card to Simon.

Dear People of Manchester,

"Hell is empty and all the devils are here" (The Tempest Act 1 Scene 2)
Do you feel that the world is full of evil?
Do you think that the apocalypse is just around the corner?
Do you want to do something about it?
If you feel strongly about the mess the world is in, please call:
Mrs Elizabeth Alice Thornthwistle on 0161 444 42424.
We will sort it out over tea and cakes.
No time wasters, vegetarians, vegans, Greeks, or those of a daemonic persuasion need apply.

Yours faithfully,

Mrs Alice Elizabeth Thornthwistle

Simon read the card twice before handing it back. "Do you really think the end of the world is nigh?"

"I don't know," Rachel replied. "It just sounded a bit more interesting than Zumba."

"And I take it all of you called her?" asked Simon, looking around. Everyone nodded and smiled, reminding him of something that he couldn't put his finger on.

Jacob Tucker peered out from behind a large potted apple blossom tree, which was coincidentally the same tree that Simon had hidden behind on his arrival. Strangely this coincidence had no deeper meaning, which on this particular day was coincidentally extremely rare[21]. "So who are they?" he whispered in a way that smacked of curiosity laced with heavy paranoia, exposing the hard wiring of his DNA. He bit into his BLT sandwich.

"Mrs Thornthwistle said they're emissaries of God," replied Sister Ruth standing discreetly next to him eating a chocolate éclair and sipping a cup of tea.

"Your God or my God?" asked Jacob.

"They're both from the same God – you know, the one who wrote the Old and the New Testament." Sister Ruth's pale features showed the merest hint of annoyance.

"Not at all," Jacob snorted. "Ours has a proper name and he's called Yehovah. He knows how to be a true omnipotent being. We've got creation, plagues, commandments, covenants, human sacrifices, stone tablets, pillars of salt, and the instant destruction of cities. Yours is just called God and he's all about love, turning the other cheek, doing the right thing, being charitable and compassionate. I say if you've got it, flaunt it."

"I don't think that's very fair. What about the *Book of Revelations*? It's got the destruction of mankind; the Four Horsemen of the apocalypse; scorpion-tailed locusts; Seven Seals; and the Beast. Isn't that enough violence and misery for you?" Sister Ruth was enjoying herself. Bible study classes with the nuns of the Order of Saint Gertrude of Nivelles and her Crazy Cats were never this much fun.

---

[21] On this day in the whole of the universe, there was precisely a 0.0000004% chance of any coincidence being simply a coincidence. Or, put more simply, there was a one in 259 million chance that a coincidence on this day was exactly that, a coincidence. However, Jacob and Simon using the same apple tree as cover was one of those extremely rare *actual* coincidences.

"Precisely!" Jacob smiled triumphantly. "And who is doing all of this? Not your God, it's the Devil, who, for the record, I don't believe in. These two must be from your God."

"Why on earth do you think that?" she asked.

"If they were from Yehovah they would have wings, golden armour, flaming swords and do all that old-style smiting talk. They wouldn't be drinking tea dressed like that."

Simon was wearing flared jeans and a black and white striped sweatshirt. Mr Smith had fared no better and was wearing extremely tight grey jogging bottoms and a grey sweatshirt that professed that his heart belonged to someone whose initials were 'PB'.

Sister Ruth sighed. "Is there a reason that you're hiding behind that tree? The whole purpose of this gathering was to meet our new guests."

"Well, we often get blamed for the crucifixion thing and as they're your God's angels they may feel the need to do something about it, something that could involve me getting hurt," replied Jacob.

"I'm certain they won't do anything to you. I don't even think they're actually angels."

"What do you mean?"

"If you'd got here on time you would have heard Simon say that they are Technical Administrative Support Officers." Sister Ruth frowned, it still didn't sound right.

"That makes them sound like they're from IT. But they have been sent by God?"

"Mmmhh…sort of." Sister Ruth bit her bottom lip. "Archangel Gabriel sent them under the auspices of Heaven and therefore, I suppose, God. They've even got ID cards."

Jacob placed his empty cup on the edge of a large terracotta pot, rubbing imaginary crumbs from his beard. "Why would angels need ID cards?"

"To help prove who they are to people who doubt them." Sister Ruth flashed a withering look at Jacob who gave her a warm comforting smile.

"Really? Wouldn't some amazing miracle prove their credentials?" he asked.

"Possibly but they aren't allowed to perform miracles anymore. Simon said they got banned in the 1970s. I don't think he was supposed to tell us about that so try not to mention it if you speak to him. He seems a bit nervous. Miracles or not, it doesn't matter to me because I have faith."

"Yehovah would never ban miracles," said Jacob flatly. "So they're not angels, have not been sent here by God and they can't even perform cool card tricks. Why are they even here?"

"Oh, that's the fun part," said Sister Ruth her eyes dancing. "They are here to destroy the Devil and they have asked us to help them."

"What?" spluttered Jacob. "The Devil?"

"Yes," she replied.

"The Devil is in Manchester?"

Sister Ruth gave a wide smile.

"I don't want to be difficult but is there any reason why you didn't think to lead with this?" asked Jacob.

"Sorry, I thought you knew. I didn't think you believed in the Devil anyway?"

"That's beside the point. Are you completely sure that getting rid of him is going to be fun?" said Jacob, happy with the sarcasm in his voice.

"Oh yes. They are going to find him and smite him all the way back to Hell." Sister Ruth gave the air a punchy right hook.

Jacob frowned. His perfectly good sarcasm was clearly wasted on this ridiculously deluded Gentile. "If I did believe in the Devil, which I don't, I'd back him against us and a couple of Technical Administrative Support Officers any day of the week."

"Simon also said the Devil will be limited in what he can do, just like they are."

"But won't the Devil, being the Devil, cheat and hurl fireballs the size of houses at us?" asked Jacob.

"I don't think the Bible mentions fireballs the size of houses, I'm sure I'd remember if it did."

"Well, it should," stated Jacob. "If I were the Devil, I'd be hurling fireballs every chance I got."

Sister Ruth looked down at Jacob and said, "Simon's giving me and your tree some very peculiar looks. I think we should go and meet him before he decides we're completely mad."

"I suppose you're right." Jacob emerged from his bush wearing a black hat, full black beard, black ringlets, black coat, shoes, trousers and spectacles. He belonged to a tribe that understood the fashion statement that dressing in black makes. "But for the record I've got a very bad feeling about this."

"That's because the Devil is here," said Sister Ruth, happy that such an obvious reason simply had to be the correct one.

"No, it's because if the Devil is real he will burn us all to crispy bits with his massive fireballs." After taking three paces forward Jacob was cut short by a harsh female Eastern European voice.

"We should befuddle the Devil to prevent him from using his fireballs."

"Arrgghh!" spluttered Jacob.

A diminutive nun wearing a green camouflage habit covered in apple tree branches whispered in his ear. "It is like that with the wild boars in the foothills of the Caucasus. If you can befuddle the alpha male, his herd will be yours forever."

"Sister Agatha," said Jacob, clearing his throat. "Sorry I didn't see you there."

"Where is Sister Agatha?" replied Sister Agatha raising her bushy eyebrows, allowing her eyes to dart around the shop. "Sister Agatha is part of the trees. Sister Agatha is part of the forest."

"Where did you get that knife from?" asked Jacob.

Sister Agatha brought the razor-sharp blade to an inch from his nose. "This is not a knife. This is a kilij from my days in Constantinople."

"Righty-ho. I think we're going to mingle," said Jacob as he backed away. He stopped and turned but Sister Agatha was gone. "Remind me, why did we let her join us? She terrifies me."

"We didn't know what she was capable of," answered Sister Ruth. "Still don't. Bulgarian nuns seem to have their own set of rules. All that time with the Russians has left them a bit…well…different. You know, now you mention it, I think she'll be quite handy when we face the Devil."

"At least she knew about the fireballs."

"You're right, she did," frowned Sister Ruth.

As they approached Simon's group, Jacob offered his hand. "Pleased to meet you I'm Jacob and you're one of our newly resident angels? Sorry I missed your speech, I was running late."

"I don't know about the angel part but I'm Simon. Pleased to meet you."

Jacob lent over and whispered, “Can I just check that you’re not still angry about the whole nailing to the cross thing? Our bad. I thought I’d sort out the elephant in the room, that’s all. Bash it on the head, so to speak.”

“Not a problem, that’s water under the bridge now.” Simon smiled. “Rachel was just saying that her partner Scott was run over by a Satanist this morning and we’re looking into him as a starting point to finding the Devil.”

“It was that fat pig Rob in his mate’s crappy car,” snapped Rachel, her pretty features pinching up.

“Aren’t they the ones you’ve been keeping an eye on from your work?” asked Sister Ruth, placing her hand on Rachel’s arm. “Is Scott okay?”

“Yes, but they’re keeping him in overnight. I was going to bring him here tonight. I thought it would be good to show him what we do. He’ll be really upset at missing out on all of this,” said Rachel, repositioning her straight hair.

“I can see how missing out on confronting the Devil with all his fireballs would upset anyone,” chipped in Jacob. “Personally, I can’t wait for it all of this to start.”

Simon gave Jacob a smile. “We’ve got ID cards,” he said, passing his over to Jacob.

“Looks new,” Jacob said. The back was completely blank apart from a thinnish black magnetic strip and a scrawled black signature.

“It is,” explained Simon. “This is all a bit of a rush job, and very hush hush. To be honest I don’t know if I’m even allowed to say that. I don’t know the correct etiquette of being a...”

“A Technical Administrative Support Officer,” helped Jacob. “Don’t take this the wrong way but you look a bit upset.”

“I had just been given some interesting news,” replied Simon.

“Don’t worry, I’m sure you’ll do absolutely fine,” smiled Sister Ruth.

“I hope so. I wouldn’t want to let anyone down,” said Simon.

“Do you know why the Devil has come to Manchester?” asked Jacob.

“To be honest, we have no idea why he’s here.”

“But if you had to answer it you’d say?” pressed Jacob.

“I’d say he’s definitely planning something big,” said Simon.

“Like the apocalypse?” asked Rachel.

“I don’t know,” replied Simon.

“What’s the plan when we find the Devil?” asked Jacob. “Are we going to have a bit of a chat? Possibly catch a movie?”

Simon looked at the bulk of muscle that was Mr Smith talking to Mrs Thornthwistle. "Mmm, I don't think so. Our orders are very clear, we are to smite him straight back to Hell."

"That does sound like a plan," nodded Jacob approvingly. "Smite is an excellent word. You know where you are with a bloody good smiting."

"I can't wait to see the Devil get what he deserves," said Sister Ruth, her hazel eyes sharp and shiny. "It's very exciting. I never realised that being a nun would be so much fun."

"Rachel, do you really think these two from work are going to lead us to the Devil?" asked Jacob, rubbing his right hand down his beard.

"I'm certain that Rob has something to do with this. He's an absolute shit and obviously very evil. I don't know about his mate Geoff but they got themselves fired today and the Devil is here so that can't be a coincidence. I've spoken to Mrs Thornthwistle and she has arranged for us to ambush them later tonight."

"Sorry. Did you just say that we're going to ambush people?" asked Jacob. "Real people? Real people you work with?"

"Used to work with," corrected Rachel. "They got fired."

"We are talking about the Devil being in Manchester after all," said Sister Ruth.

"And you're the force who is going to smite the Devil when we find him?" asked Jacob, looking at Simon.

"Well, yes, I suppose I am. With Mr Smith's assistance obviously," answered Simon, blushing slightly. "You know, I don't actually think that anyone has ever called me a force before." He gave his glasses a good clean.

"Please don't be offended, but I was actually referring to your companion Mr Smith," added Jacob.

"Oh right. Yes, that makes more sense. Of course, you're referring to Mr Smith. He does look like a natural born smiter." Simon's Adam's apple bobbed furiously.

"Don't worry, I'm certain you'll also be an awesome force to be reckoned with when the time comes," smiled Sister Ruth.

Simon pushed his glasses back up his nose and steadied his breathing.

"Aren't you concerned that we could tell the world about all of this?" asked Jacob.

"Not really. Gabriel said that even if people heard about it, they wouldn't believe it. The Devil being in Manchester definitely sounds like fake news."

"You may have a point," said Jacob. "I don't even believe it."

Sister Ruth flashed Jacob a disapproving look before turning back to Simon. "I don't know if you're allowed to say anything but what is Heaven actually like?"

Simon thought very hard before answering. He had already said too much about the mission. However, some positive information given to a true believer could hardly be a bad thing. "Heaven is really beautiful. It's very white and it's always sunny. There is hardly any litter and people are always smiling. It's a very happy smiley place."

"That sounds exactly as I imagined it," beamed Sister Ruth. "Just like Alton Towers but with a few more rides, no queues and everything being free."

Simon thought about the view from Gabriel's window and felt that he may have failed to capture the majesty of it all. Also, he couldn't remember seeing any rides.

"What is Archangel Gabriel like?" asked Sister Ruth.

In answering, Simon could only think of two things, the perfect shine of his shoes and his comprehensive book collection. "He seems efficient. Yes, Archangel Gabriel is very efficient."

Mrs Thornthwistle and Mr Smith approached the group with Mogwai sauntering by her side. The tabby cat was enjoying all the attention and free food.

"Right, dears, I think we should get this show on the road so to speak," said Mrs Thornthwistle. "After all, the Devil could be right around the corner."

"Sounds like a plan, Mrs T," replied Jacob.

"Let's go and do some bloody smiting," said Mr Smith. "Any of you sinners need a flogging before we go?"

It was not the deepness of Mr Smith's voice or what he was saying that terrified Simon. It was the happiness that shone out of his blue eyes as he said it that made him shiver. No one replied.

"Right," Mr Smith turned. "Just me then."

Chapter Ten

"Geoffrey Pike? Come with me if you want to live." – Gus

Barry Court, Withington, Manchester

At least two dozen people crowded the illuminated entrance porch to Barry Court. The rain, though slowed, still tip tapped on the cheap Perspex roof that sheltered the bulk of them. Roughly half were horizontal, crashed out in sleeping bags and threadbare blankets. They had the unwashed ragged look of the homeless with dirty clothes, pinched features and carrier bags of tumbledown possessions. They looked plump, wearing every piece of clothing they had, layer upon layer to keep out the night chill. Standing beside them, smartly dressed men and women in suits, scarves, gloves and thick coats stamped their feet for warmth, their eyes flashing about their unfamiliar surroundings. One of the things that united them all was that they were completely silent.

This fact didn't escape Geoff as he left the warmth of the taxi. Without pulling his gaze away he pointed and whispered, "Who the hell are they?"

"Dunno? Jehovah's Witnesses?" replied Rob.

"What should we do?"

"Well, Ruby told you not to find God so I guess we shouldn't invite them in."

"That doesn't make sense. Some of them look like they're homeless and why are they all staring at us?" hissed Geoff. "Do you think we are safe?"

"Don't be stupid, of course we're safe. Look, that's Miss Perkins from number 13 near the bins," said Rob, waving at their neighbour.

“What are you doing?” snapped Geoff.

“Being friendly.”

Even from this distance, they could see Miss Perkins glaring at them, her lips curled into a silent snarl.

“You’ve got to admit it’s a bit weird. All these people stood outside and no one talking,” Geoff looked at Rob. “Do you think they could be zombies? What if a weaponised virus has just been leaked by mistake and is about to wipe out the world’s population starting with Manchester?”

“What? Miss Perkin’s a zombie? I guess I’m back to being some monster?” Rob opened his pizza box with one hand and expertly flipped out the largest steaming slice, catching it in his mouth.

“I think we should run,” said Geoff.

“Where? You know I don’t like running and our flat’s just there.”

“I don’t know, Scotland? This could be the centre of it all. We could be looking at ground zero,” Geoff’s breath plumed in the cold air.

“What, Barry Court? Our Barry Court? You saying this is where life as we know it comes crashing down?”

“Yes. We didn’t see anything like this in town. Maybe my hallucinations in the pub were a warning? And what about that awful smell that comes from the basement in summer when it’s hot?”

“Our Victorian drains smelling bad is your basis for the total breakdown of civilisation? You’re beginning to sound crazy again.” Rob shook his head and started walking across the grassy verge towards the pathway that linked the main road to the flats. “Come on, they won’t bite,” he grinned. “It’s a no brainer.”

After a couple of seconds Geoff began to follow him. Standing alone under the streetlight seemed marginally worse than walking behind his large friend. Once they met the path the only sounds he could hear were the beat of his heart and the clicking of their footsteps. “They still look like fucking zombies,” he said.

Rob turned. “If they were actual zombies they’d be chasing us by now. Let’s just get in.”

“I suppose so,” whispered Geoff, beginning to match Rob’s stride to help reduce the noise of their footsteps. He began to silently count each step. One step; two steps; three steps; four steps; fi…

Scccrreeeettcccchhh! An old zipper pulled along its rusted track was quickly followed by half a dozen more.

"Are you happy now?" chided Rob. "All your talking has woken them up. Man up, these aren't zombies and I'm not a monster."

Geoff looked at the unbroken stares. Maybe Rob was right, they all did look human. He cleared his throat and walked towards them. "Hi. We live in Flat 124 so if we could get past you that would be great. We don't want any trouble[22]."

Every set of eyes were now completely focused on Geoff, who was less than ten feet away from the closest person. He turned. Rob gave him a fleshy thumbs up.

"Hi Miss Perkins. Have you had a good day?" asked Geoff.

"Uuurrrrggghhh," groaned Miss Perkins, lurching towards him.

"Run away!" shouted Geoff. Haring back down the path, he could hear the clatter of eager footsteps right behind him. Speeding past Rob, he imagined his friend's horrific amazement as the zombies ploughed into him. And yet, as the seconds passed by there were no desperate screams. Confused, he chanced a look back. The zombies were fanning out to cut off his escape and Rob was standing at the side of the path eating pizza. His friend caught his gaze and waved.

Sliding over the bonnet of a parked car Geoff was faced with three zombies, one of which was the sprightly Miss Perkins, her greying hair scraped back.

"Hi Miss Perkins, is this about the bins?" blurted out Geoff.

Miss Perkins bared her teeth and lunged at him, "Uuurrrgghhh!"

In blind panic Geoff found himself running full pelt back to the flats. He could feel the full mass of the horde right behind him. Running past Rob, he slammed into the door. "Keys! Where are my fucking keys?" he cried. Looking back, he was surprised to see that he had built up a lead of around twenty feet and that the nearest zombie seemed to be just hanging around and making low groaning noises.

"I've got them," said Rob. "You gave them to me at O'Sheas and made me promise not to let you drive back."

"But I haven't got a fucking car anymore. You wrote it off. Hurry up, they're coming!" snapped Geoff, his eyes wide. While he was correct, they were now coming at a rate of inches and not the leaps and bounds of before. In fact, all of

---

[23] A recent scientific study in the well-respected Mexican Journal 'El Macho,' has found that saying, "We don't want any trouble," results in trouble occurring 94.72% of the time. Conversely saying, "Yes! We want loads of trouble you mother fucking cocksucking bastardo," reduces the instances of trouble occurring to a mere 4.2%. The caveat to that being that any subsequent instances of trouble show a vast increase in serious head splitting violence.

his pursuers had adopted a confusing, ambling approach to catching him. Some of them had lost all interest and turned to watch the road.

"Won't be a minute," said Rob.

"Hurry up!" The horde silently fanned out into a neat semicircle around Geoff. The entrance to his flat was now the only place he could go.

"Catch," said Rob.

Geoff spent the next thirty seconds fumbling the right key into the lock while the zombies watched him. Rushing up the stairs he breathlessly made it to the safety of the flat. By the time Rob joined him every light was on and every room had been checked. In the lounge, Mr Sox his black and white cat sidled over and purred his greetings.

"I'm calling the police," said Geoff, stroking Mr Sox. "Why did they chase me and not you?"

"Maybe they're like dogs and could sense your fear," replied Rob.

"Weren't you afraid?"

"Trust me, it takes more than a few bumps in the night to scare me."

Geoff put his mobile down. "How can the police be engaged? I was right – it is the zombie apocalypse."

"Why don't we wait until the morning?" Rob yawned. "They'll probably get bored and go somewhere else."

"They really don't seem to be the get bored and clear off sort of mob to me. They're more the chase and kill as many people as they can."

"But they didn't hurt you did they? Why don't we get some sleep?" Rob rubbed his eyes and yawned again. He began to sway and closed his eyes.

"Take it easy big guy I've got you," said Geoff as he manhandled Rob back down the corridor to his bedroom.

There was a padded *Thud!* as Rob crashed onto his bed.

Geoff retreated to the lounge. His heartbeat slowing but his mind still racing. Looking at the entrance door he shook his head. It was locked but would it stop any axe-wielding maniac worth his or her salt from breaking into the flat? He could already see Miss Perkins splintering the door with an axe bought at B&Q, forcing her contorted face through the gap, baring her teeth and screaming, "Here's Maggie!"

Geoff's eyes settled on the tired leather Barcalounger. Straining every muscle, he moved the oversized chair down the short corridor and wedged it against the front door and Rob's bedroom door. Making a cup of tea he searched for the last of the chocolate Hobnobs. They were all gone and the finger of suspicion was firmly pointing at his sleeping friend. Annoyed, he was reduced to suspiciously soft custard creams he found at the back of the cupboard. He picked up a block of knives and took his tea and weapons of minor destruction to his bedroom.

Moving his white chest of drawers behind the door Geoff wondered if the Swedes had ever considered their role in safeguarding people of the Western world against the crazed mobs of the apocalypse? He thought not. They were too nice and blonde and far too busy bringing cool things like Abba, H&M, government sponsored eugenics[23], Scandi anything, IKEA and boxy Volvos to the world's table.

After half an hour the novelty of watching a barricaded door in semidarkness began to wear off. Geoff phoned the police, but they were still engaged. Flicking on the television he channel surfed, his finger stopping at a documentary about the Battle for Stalingrad. By the time the Russians had secured the surrender of the Germans, he was fast asleep. Mr Sox curled up tightly beside him, idly flicking his tail.

β

Geoff stared down a pitch-black staircase. A small orange light grew and faded before he heard a deep Germanic male voice from the darkness below. "Geoffrey? Geoffrey Pike? Come with me if you want to live."

"What? Are you Arnie?" asked Geoff into the darkness.

"Come with me if you want to live," repeated the voice.

"Okay." Geoff hesitantly took the first few steps down.

"I'm only messing with you, don't be stupid you could fall," said a clipped Scandinavian voice. "Lights."

Immediately a row of paraffin lights burst into flame showing a long line of roughly carved stone steps leading down. Geoff couldn't see the end of the tunnel, which curved sharply to the right after around thirty steps. What he could see was an unbelievably cute, pure white, lop-eared rabbit sat up on its back legs

---

[23] Question: how much fun did the Swedes have in enforcing their state approved eugenics programme which sterilised 63,000 people (90% of them women) between 1934 and 1976? Answer: lots. Who would have thought that improving Swedish 'racial purity' as part of a policy of ethnic hygiene would be such wholesome family fun? For all of you who think that Swedes are tall, blonde but a bit boring – in your face.

smoking a cigarette. The rabbit had a small swastika armband and a pristine German SS officer's cap on.

"Hi, I'm Gus," the rabbit introduced himself.

"You're…"

"Yeah, I know I'm smoking. Filthy habit but what can you do? You better follow me kid. There is someone here who wants to meet you." The rabbit took a final drag and hopped down the tunnel. After a couple of turns the descent finished with a short level corridor. Stopping at a solid looking wooden door the rabbit rapped at its base three times with his back claws.

A thick German accent replied, "Enter."

Gus looked up at Geoff and pulled another cigarette from behind his ear. "You heard the man. Better not keep him waiting."

"Err, thank you Gus," said Geoff, twisting the handle and pushing the door open.

"Don't mention it," replied the rabbit as he hopped away. Turning he raised his right front leg. "Remember Heil Hitler. They still get a bit touchy about that around here."

The room was well lit by the same old-fashioned paraffin storm lamps. As Geoff entered, a tall German officer handed him a small glass of what smelt like brandy and offered him a seat. The officer took the matching seat opposite. There was a simple wooden chess set on the small table between them. A game had already started with two white pawns and a knight traded for two black pawns and a bishop.

"The clock is ticking," the officer said, "and it's your turn."

Chapter Eleven

"Bo wha biddy biddy bum biddy boo," – Hunter

Back Office, The Thirty Pieces of Silver Sports Bar and Grill

Jay sat back down, poured another drink and placed his cowboy boots on the coffee table. He gazed at the empty bottle; brow tightly knotted until his thoughts were interrupted by a soft knock at the door.

"Enter," he commanded.

The door did not move.

He looked up and repeated louder, "Enter."

The door remained closed. There was another knock from outside, firmer and more impatient.

"Sam?"

Jay put down his glass. Still no answer. "If that's you Pnakotic or Sister M I've already told you it's not cool for us to be seen together, especially here. We have rules for a reason."

Unfamiliar silence crowded the room. Jay frowned, he couldn't hear the bass thudding of the music, or the frequent high-pitched screams from the bar down the corridor. Stealthily he rose and crept to the filing cabinet, grabbing the baseball bat that leaned up against its side. He cleared his throat, "Seriously? Are you going to play that old daemon of mystery card with me?"

The whole door began to shake.

Jay moved swiftly to one side. "Whoever you are, we really need to talk about your passive aggressive approach. Is this some weird power thing where I have to open the door for you? If it is, I can recommend a great therapist." Flicking the handle, he kicked the door open and readied the bat. All he could see were slivers of light reaching into the darkness; all he could hear was silence.

He moved to the centre of the doorway and dropped his gaze a foot and a half. He stopped at the bald head of Lou.

"Oh…it's you? You had me scared for a while. What the heaven are you doing here?" asked Jay as he dropped the bat to his side and looked down the dark corridor.

Lou smiled.

Jay went on, "What's happened to the lights and music? We having a power cut? Where's my bitches?"

"Hello Judas," came from the shadows.

"Oh shit," muttered Jay.

Lou's smile turned into a golden glistening grin.

"Aren't you going to invite me in?" asked the voice.

"Nope," said Jay retreating into the light of his office. "What do you want? If it's about what I said to Sam I stand by it all."

Lou took two steps back and Emily appeared in the doorway dressed in dark green body armour the colour of her eyes. She pursed her lips and frowned.

"Well, most of it," said Jay.

Her frown deepened.

"Well, definitely the bit about me caring for Sam. He's like a brother to me, you know that."

"Is that a fact," said Emily striding into the room holding Jay's business card in front of her. "It seems to me that you set your brother up and I'm here to find out whether I'm right."

"I don't need to tell you anything," said Jay raising his bat. "This is my club and I've got rights."

Emily moved closer flicking the card at Jay's face, "You're not afraid of a little girl, are you?" she asked.

"No," replied Jay.

Emily punched him hard on his throat. "Wrong answer." Her right leg swept Jay's legs from under him and he crashed to the floor. "I suppose a tough man like you Judas needs a little bit of persuasion to cooperate."

"You can fuck right off, bitch," Jay snapped.

Emily smiled down on him. "Now, you are just being rude. I think we need to take this someplace else. Sorry, I meant to say take *you* someplace else."

Scrambling to his feet Jay backed away to the furthest corner of the room and held his bat shakily in front of him. "Bitches get stitches!" he warned.

"This is very disappointing behaviour," she sighed. "Would your mother like to hear you talk like that?"

"Really? You wanna dance?" asked Jay swinging the bat, "well I can fucking dance!"

"Remember I've already seen you dance," said Emily pulling a thick black stick the size of a truncheon from her back. With a twist of her wrist, it quadrupled in length. The seamless katana blade glistened. "It wasn't impressive then, and I can't see why it'll be any better now. You lack rhythm."

A minute later Jay lay wheezing on the floor, surrounded by splinters of his bat, still gripping its handle.

"Now are we going to play nice?" asked Emily. "Or do you want to continue this with Lou?"

"Hi Jay," said Lou eating a banana with one hand and holding a large, stained cloth sack with the other. "Do you want to do this the easy way?" he shrugged, "or the other way? I think you know which I prefer."

Twenty minutes later they arrived at Loading Bay C.

"When you said that you had a special sack of carrying, I thought it would be…you know, special," said Emily.

"What do you mean?" asked Lou holding up the sack up with one massive hand. "This is my special sack of carrying. I've had it since I arrived here. It's carried all sorts of things and people[24]."

"I just thought it would be magical and a bit smaller," said Emily.

"But if it was smaller you wouldn't be able to get a body into it, so it wouldn't really be special." explained Lou.

"Oh I see," she looked around. "So, if this bay is out of action with all the refurbishment why have we come here."

"Because I have a special…"

"Sack?" prompted Emily.

Lou clicked his fingers, "Way," he said as a pristine grey Panzer Tank trundled out of the tunnel.

"Well," said Emily. "I didn't expect that."

"Shall we?" asked Lou.

"Won't it be a bit slow?"

---

[24] Notable people that have seen the inside of Lou's special sack of carrying include: Salvador Dali; Jeffrey Epstein; Joseph Stalin; Michael Jackson; Jimmy Saville; Frederick Christ Trump; and Walt Disney. The more observant of you will have realised that there are a lot of moustaches and Js in this list. That is not a coincidence.

Lou frowned and clicked his fingers again. The tank disappeared, only to be replaced by a gleaming Austin Martin complete with side mounted machine guns.

"Bagsy driving!" cried Emily her eyes as wide as her smile.

Bowels of Freemasons Hall

"This is ridiculous," muttered Brian, "we've been here for over two hours and we can't even see the bloody door. What we are doing is really important, not like these bunch of amateurs."

"Would you like me to persuade the people in front of us to let us through sir?" asked Hunter.

"Tempting but no. We are English after all," smiled Brian. "But there really should be a better system. Did you book the Summoning Room Number Seven as I asked?"

"Of course, sir."

"Good. It's a bit roomier than the others and the central heating actually works," added Brian. "It's also out of the way, so we shouldn't be disturbed."

Under Freemasons Hall lies an ancient rabbit warren of tunnels, caves, secret passageways and rooms stretching out a quarter of a mile to five interconnected points like a gigantic pentacle. The queue shambled forwards allowing Brian and Hunter to turn another corner. Raising himself on his tip toes Brian looked down the corridor, "I can see, Lucinda and Boris near the front." He turned around and looked over the heads of the elemental students behind him. "But we seem to be surrounded by children. Well, at least we know they'll have what we need when we eventually get there. Oh, they're coming. They must have already been in. Look busy, Hunter."

"Of course, sir."

A tall thin woman with raven black hair in a tailored business suit approached them and gave a thin smile.

"Hello Lucinda."

"Hello Brian."

"Wonderful to see you. How's the witching business?"

"For the most part highly agreeable," she replied.

"You better not have taken all the virgin's blood?" chuckled Brian looking beside her. "Oh, I'm sorry I didn't realise you were here Boris. Still planning for the end of the world?"

"Hello Brian," said Boris, a short balding man. "It is going to happen this time."

"But of course it is. I don't suppose you want to share when the apocalypse will be taking place?"

"Maybe this Friday, but Sunday at the latest," answered Boris.

"So soon? That gives me a good two days to get my affairs in order. Well, it was really good to see you Lucinda, we should catch up soon, how are you fixed for next Monday?" Brian smiled. "Boris."

Thirty minutes later Brian gave an actual smile as he opened the double lead doors, clasped with a central silver pentacle surrounded by mystical symbols. Walking to the right of the brass counter that spanned the whole of the room he placed the *Book of Pnakotic* down and opened it at the single pink Post-it note.

"Hi," Brian looked up. "Now let me see, could I please have a two headed toad; a vial of manticore venom; and five, no make it six pints of virgins blood?"

The middle-aged man in a dark suit and a Freemasonry apron raised a bushy white eyebrow and cleared his throat. "You are particularly fortunate, sir, that we've recently completed a blood drive at the university."

"I fully understand the value of students for our work," smiled Brian.

The man did not smile back but took the top sheet from the stack to his left and carefully wrote a number of symbols in black ink on it. He placed the sheet in a small cannister and loaded it into a shiny copper tube running upwards and behind him. With a press of a button the cannister whooshed away.

"Could you please move to payment, sir," said the man handing Brian a yellow carbon copy of his order.

Brian moved along to the left and faced another man who was an almost identical copy of the first, with the addition of a pair of thin framed silver glasses. This man smiled, "Can I please have your order, sir?"

Brian handed his copy over.

"Is sir paying by card or coin?"

Hunter handed Brian a small velvet purse tied up with a golden drawstring.

"Coin," replied Brian passing over the purse.

"Do you have your Freemasonry Card?"

"Yes, but I think I've left it at home."

"No problem if you keep this receipt, you'll be able to redeem your points next time. Can you please take a seat while your order is being arranged?"

Once sat down on the second pulpit Brian whispered to Hunter, "I can see why the Freemasons are so wealthy."

Five minutes later another suited man standing at the far end of the counter shouted, "Two hundred and forty-two?"

"Here," said Brian standing up waving his order paper.

A large brown paper bag was pushed carefully across the counter to Brian.

"Your toad has been sedated. Judging by your order, I take it that sir is intending to perform a level five summoning?"

"That is correct," said Brian.

"Then I further assume that you have the required certificate and official stamps?"

"Of course," said Brian offering an A4 sized scroll.

The man carefully checked the scroll, picked up the Freemasonry seal and stamped it for the third time. "Have an efficacious day sir," he said.

Brian smiled, "Right Hunter let's go and do some proper summoning."

Summoning Room Number Seven

"This seems pretty straightforward," said Brian. "It's almost the same as this morning."

He looked at the pentacle carved an inch deep into the stone floor.

"Two headed toad in the box? Check. Virgins' blood filling the pentacle? Check. Summoning markings in virgins' blood? Check. Goblet of pure gold filled with virgins' blood mixed with the manticore venom in the centre? Check. I tell you Pnakotic really likes her virgins' blood. I wonder why? Right, we seem to be good to go."

"Would sir like some wine before performing this ritual?"

"No thank you. I need a clear head for this. I've heard that she can be a little difficult to deal with when you go off-piste."

"Indeed, sir," agreed Hunter.

"Dim the lights," said Brian, "I need to be in the right mood for this."

After five minutes of voice exercises Brian stood at the marble lectern at the head of the pentacle and flicked the microphone on.

"Oh seducer of all men," said Brian his voice slow and deep. "Do I sound okay? You know, do I sound the part?"

"Eloquent and masterful, sir," replied Hunter. "As always."

"That's good. You know the parts you need to sing?" asked Brian.

Hunter nodded putting on his black sunglasses.

"Right, let's do this. Oh, vile seducer of all men. Crusher of the most tormented souls in the fires of damnation I call upon you," boomed Brian before breaking into song. "A one, two, ah one, two three four. There she was just rocking down in Hell, screaming."

"Bo wha biddy biddy bum biddy boo," sang Hunter in his rich baritone voice.

"Crushing those souls and burning those feet, singing."

"Bo wha biddy biddy bum biddy boo," sang Hunter swaying and clicking his fingers.

"You looked mad, you smelled of brine and I'm sure you've lost your mind!"

Two minutes of enthusiastic singing later Brian smiled, "Those monks really knew how to put on a show didn't they? You can really hold a tune Hunter. Have you been practicing?"

"Thank you, sir, but no. My singing voice is from my mother's side."

The blood started to coalesce and move to the centre of the pentacle. A monstrously large two-headed snake slithered into existence. Rising up, it slowly morphed into a kind-looking, old woman in sensible shoes.

"Why do you look like that?" asked Brian.

"You mean like your mother?" the shape replied.

"Yes, precisely like my mother."

"Because I take the form you desire the most," Pnakotic explained, opening the box and pulling out the toad. Kicking and squirming it filled her mouth.

"Oh, I see," said Brian. "Wait a minute, you're not saying that you think I want my mother in that way?"

"You tell me?" she shrugged, picking up the goblet and downing its contents in one swift gulp.

"No more games," said Brian.

"Okay," said Pnakotic and grew into a multihorned, scaly mass. "Why have you summoned me again?" she shrieked from one of her many mouths. "You are not strong enough to hold me. Why shouldn't I just destroy you, worm."

Brian smiled, "You know the rules. The pentacle prevents you from leaving the circle in this plane, so destroying me would be a bit of stretch even for you. Secondly, while I realise you can return to Hell at any time, I have an offer that I wish to put to you oh great Pnakotic."

"What sort of offer?"

"You have great knowledge of all things and I have this," said Brian holding up the *Book of Pnakotic*. "It's an original as you can see. Slight markings in the corners of the hide but that's got to be expected given its age." He opened up the book and leafed through its pages. "Real artistry and all with one hundred percent virgins' blood. Yours for just a tad more information about this. Think about it? No pesky summoners pulling you away from whatever torturing spree you may be enjoying."

"Go on?" said the daemon. "What is it you wish to know?"

Brian picked up the cover of the *Book of Shenanigans*. "You've already confirmed that this is the Word of God."

"Correct."

"Then why was it in the hands of a daemon?"

The mass of flesh oozed, "That I do not know, but if I were you, I would be extremely suspicious of the motives of that daemon," she paused. "Would the daemon you speak of be known as Samuel Spade?"

Brian nodded with a smile, "Please tell me more oh great Pnakotic."

Chapter Twelve

"It is never too late to fight pure evil, dear." – Mrs Thornthwistle

The Mancunian Way, Manchester

Simon opened the window as the red Volvo swung onto the Mancunian Way. The night was awash with big city lights. It was the first proper night he'd seen for over ten years as Heaven was surprisingly like a Las Vegas casino, lit up twenty-four seven with cloudless blue skies, free food and absolutely no clocks. He looked at Sister Ruth's angular pixielike features, her small sharp nose and mouth. "So why did you answer Mrs Thornthwistle's card with you, err…"

"You mean with me being a nun?" Sister Ruth smiled. "I honestly didn't know whether I should contact her, but I prayed and here I am off to smite the Devil with a couple of angels. If that isn't proof of the power of prayer, I don't know what is."

"Do you really think that this could be the apocalypse?" asked Simon.

"I think you're better placed to answer that than me, but we are looking for the Devil in Manchester. I'm no Biblical scholar but doesn't that sound like end of days to you?"

"I suppose so. Do all the members of the Set believe that?" asked Simon.

"We're a bit of a mixed bag and some certainly don't share my Christian views," replied Sister Ruth.

"That's me," chirped Jacob from the driver's seat. "And I still don't believe that we are going to find the Devil per se, more likely just a lowly disgruntled ex-employee of your God."

"Isn't that precisely what the Devil is?" asked Sister Ruth.

Jacob sped up, took the second exit off the overpass and headed up Princess Parkway away from the city. As he turned onto Burton Road, the car slowed to an unexpected near crawl.

"I didn't realise the Set had so many members," said Simon.

"We don't," snorted Jacob. "Last time I checked there was only thirteen of us. Ruth, do you know any of these people?"

"Sister Agnes, my Mother Superior, is over there with a few nuns. She was keen to get in on the action when I phoned her but I have no idea who the rest are."

"Why are they all here?" asked Simon.

"Maybe they're here for you?" said Jacob.

"For us?" said Simon.

"Maybe they want you to do a miracle for them," explained Jacob.

"We don't do anything like that anymore," said Simon shaking his head. "Gabriel said such activities are strictly forbidden."

"I know that, but do they? You have been sent by their God after all," smiled Jacob.

"Please stop," said Sister Ruth. "I can see Mrs T over there. We should go and have a word with her. She'll know what's happening."

"I'll go," said Jacob pulling the Volvo up on the kerb. "Stay here and try not to draw too much attention to yourselves."

Simon watched Jacob weave swiftly across the road to Mrs Thornthwistle who was balancing precariously on a green wheelie bin while barking out orders to a group of around twenty people below.

"Now you all know what to do, dears?" said Mrs Thornthwistle. "Go and do God's work. Remember, your very souls depend upon it."

"Sorry we're late, Mrs T, I had to swing home. Who are all these people?" asked Jacob, watching the crowd disperse in a dozen different directions.

Mrs Thornthwistle's mouth pinched. "Tonight, is not the night for tardiness Mr Tucker. May I point out that this is your second unpunctual attendance in less than two hours."

Mogwai lying on top of the bin, lifted his head up and gave him a look of deep displeasure.

"Sorry, I had to pick something up," Jacob muttered.

"Very well, I will give you the benefit of the doubt but I strongly suggest that you do not make this a habit. Now could you please help me down and I'll explain what is happening."

Back on the pavement Mrs Thornthwistle brushed her tweed skirt and checked her brown shoes. "While you've been gallivanting, there have been a number of significant developments. In short, I now believe that we have hit the mother lode."

"What do you mean?" asked Jacob.

"All of these people have been drawn to this area. Specifically, they were all heading for Barry Court though the nuns picked them up before they could get any closer. None of them understood why they were doing this, but my guess is that they were driven by an unconscious fear of the Devil."

"I'm sorry, I still don't follow."

"Can you not see? Rachel is right. Her Satanist colleagues live in Barry Court which is acting as a magnet for all of these people. That cannot be a coincidence. I believe that these flats are the key to finding whatever evil currently resides in Manchester." She waited for her assessment to sink in. "Which means that the Devil could already be there and that Mr Smith and Simon can smite him all the way back to Hell. How wonderful is that, dear?"

"Yes, very wonderful," muttered Jacob, looking around. "There must be over a hundred people here and you think they are going to help us smite the Devil? That is, if he really exists."

"Don't worry, dear, he certainly does exist and yes these people will help us because they are scared witless by the alternative." In this light her face looked hard and sharp. "Are Mr Smith and Simon with you?"

"Yes, they're in my car."

"Well, go get them and I'll meet you at the car park over there."

Five minutes later, a group of nuns in full black habits marched out of the darkness. They were carrying a massive tubular beige sack, poles and shopping bags of pegs.

"Friends of yours?" asked Jacob.

"The one with the two silver stars on her shoulders is Sister Agnes, my Mother Superior. She's really nice once you get to know her," replied Sister Ruth.

"There's quite a lot of them," said Simon.

"I know and there's more to come," replied Sister Ruth, her eyes glistening. "We nuns are always up for a good scrap!"

Once the green camouflaged marquee was set up everyone stood back to admire it, or in Jacob's case, wonder why they needed something so massive. "Don't you reckon they'll be able to see it from the flats?" he asked.

"The wall and trees block their line of sight," replied Mrs Thornthwistle. "Please bring in the equipment, dears, and gather everyone together."

"Right, you worthless mongrels," barked Mr Smith. "You heard Mrs Thornthwistle, let's get everything in."

Obediently the nuns brought chairs, tables, piles of rocky road bars, trays of carrot and lemon drizzle cake, flasks of tea and coffee into the marquee. When everyone was crammed inside, Mr Smith lifted Mrs Thornthwistle onto a table in the middle.

"Please gather round, dears," she said through her megaphone. "There is something important I need to tell you."

"Silence scum," growled Mr Smith.

The marquee hushed as everyone stared at the old Scottish lady with gleaming grey eyes.

"Thank you Mr Smith. Now what I am about to tell you may sound strange but, in your soul, you'll know that it is true and once I've finished it will all make sense," she paused. "The Devil is in Manchester."

The crowd gasped.

"Silence!" bellowed Mr Smith.

"That is the reason why you've all been drawn here tonight. I believe that God himself has chosen each and every one of you to do his bidding. We have identified two Satanists who live at Flat 124 Barry Court. They are called Geoff and Rob. If you join the WhatsApp group #satanicscuminmanchester you will see photographs of them. They returned to Barry Court just over an hour ago and are likely to be very drunk and highly dangerous. We do not know if the Devil is already there, or whether he intends to make contact with them later. As some of you already know, Barry Court is being protected by a small number of known Satanists. When we strike, we will crush these scum and smite the Devil all the way back to Hell. Tonight, you must forgo the normal rules. You must forget the police as they may well be in league with the Devil. You must do what is absolutely necessary, for tonight you are battling for your very souls!"

The marquee erupted into wild applause.

As the cheering subsided, Jacob asked, "What are we going to do when we find the Devil?"

“Leave it to these two,” Mrs Thornthwistle pointed at Mr Smith and a blushing Simon. “They have been sent by God and are professionals at this sort of thing. If you find Geoff, Rob or the Devil, inform them at once. They know what they are doing and they will smite them straight back to Hell in two shakes of a lambs tail.”

The marquee erupted again, though this time into far more menacing cheers.

“Do we know what the Devil looks like?” shouted Jacob.

“No. At the moment we do not know what the Father of Lies looks like, but I believe that his evil manifestation will be clear to us all once we see it,” replied Mrs Thornthwistle. “If you go onto the WhatsApp group, you’ll see a few ideas of what we think he’ll appear as.”

“I see that Mrs T likes to be high up,” whispered Sister Ruth.

“Is it being high up, or do you think that she just likes the power it gives her?” replied Jacob.

As the raucous cries of the crowd died down, Simon left the marquee, closely followed by Jacob. Once outside, Simon pushed his glasses up his nose and noticed that it was raining again.

“Are you looking forward to leading your rabid mob of religious vigilantes?” laughed Jacob.

Simon shook his head. “All we’re missing are the torches and pitchforks. Here we are about to face the Devil and everyone seems to be laughing and joking about it.”

“This isn’t what I was expecting either,” said Jacob offering Simon a cigarette. “My people have got some experience with mobs. Are you certain that the Devil is here?”

“I don’t know. What I am sure about is that a lot of people are going to get hurt tonight,” said Simon. He took a cigarette and offered to return the pack.

“Keep them,” said Jacob. “I think you’ll need them more than me.”

“Thanks. I don’t know why but this feels wrong. Shouldn’t we be praying, or something more suitably religious?”

“I’m not really the praying type but let me know if you come up with something else.”

“I don’t even know how we’ll recognise the Devil,” said Simon, biting into a slice of carrot cake and taking a sip of coffee.

"Oh, I'm pretty sure you'll just know. That's one thing I think Mrs T did get right." Jacob gave a crooked smile and looked through the trees at Barry Court. "Of course, that's only if he actually exists."

A puzzled looking man in a brown uniform walked past Jacob and Simon. Clearing his throat, he shouted as respectfully as he could to no-one in particular, "Sorry to bother you but is there a Sister Agatha from the Order of Saint Gertrude of Nivelles and her Crazy Cats here?"

A formidably large nun wearing a red habit and holding a pick-axe stopped beside him. "What is your name young man?" she asked.

"Err Douglas."

"Well Douglas are you here to fight the Devil?"

"Err no, I've got a delivery for a Sister Agatha. Don't suppose you know her?"

"No. I'm afraid I don't know a Sister Agatha but you could help us fight those awful Satanists over there at the flats," replied the nun raising her pick-axe to show she meant business.

"Sorry I'm working, so I can't," replied the young man before adding, "Good luck."

The nun beamed, "Thank you, but we've got God on our side so good luck will not be necessary. Please let me know if you change your mind, I'll be over there and I'm Agnes."

"I will." Douglas looked back at the marquee and then at the mass of nuns milling around. *They really do not pay me enough for this,* he thought. He felt a soft tap on his shoulder and turned.

"I know a Sister Agatha," said Jacob.

"But you're not a nun," stated Douglas.

"True, but I do know her and she might be hard to find at the moment," explained Jacob.

"What with all these nuns?"

Jacob gave a shrug, "Yes, that and the fact she has a tendency to hide. She's surprisingly good at it. Best thing you can do is let me sign for whatever she's ordered. I'm certain I'll see her sometime tonight."

"You promise?" asked Douglas.

"You have my word."

"Can't say fairer than that," smiled Douglas handing over two identical square boxes. "Can I have your name?"

"Jacob Tucker."

"Great. There's another package in my van over there. It's a bit big."

Five minutes later Jacob turned to Simon. "How the devil are we going to find her? We can't wander around with this? What do you think it is?"

Simon looked at the package. It was a long, relatively thin cardboard box with four red, "Very Very Fragile," stickers at each side. "A really long feather duster?" he suggested.

"Too heavy for that and I can't imagine Sister Agatha as a domestic goddess," said Jacob. "What about a DIY pole vault? Bulgarians are known for their pole vaulting."

Simon gave this some thought before replying, "True, but don't pole vaulters need to be tall and thin? What about a periscope?"

"If we were near the sea I would say that would be a very good guess. What about a..."

A nun appeared at Jacob's shoulder and hissed, "Be still, your Sister Agatha has returned."

"Arrggghh..." cried Jacob. "We've got a few packages for you."

"Shush. Sister Agatha needs to be wary," She looked around, shook each package and listened to them. "Sister Agatha accepts your gifts."

"They're not really gifts, at least not from me," explained Jacob.

"Sister Agatha wonders why her servant is giving her such bounty?"

"What? Me? A servant? Listen here," said Jacob.

"Silence! Sister Agatha must ready herself for the dance."

"You're dancing? Are these props?" asked Simon.

"Tonight we dance the sedi donka," replied the nun her eyes triumphantly wide as she started to dance.

"The sedi what?" asked Jacob.

"Sedi donka, The dance of death. Sister Agatha will show you the moves. She is an expert in the national dance of her beloved country of Bulgaria."

"Thanks, but I think we'll pass on that," said Jacob.

When Sister Agatha had disappeared into the night Jacob whispered, "Remind me never to set foot in Bulgaria. Right, I'm going to find Mrs T and find out what the plan is."

∴

Mrs Thornthwistle sat down near the cake stall, absentmindedly stroking Mogwai and mulling over the night's events. She smiled as Jacob joined her.

"What are we going to do if the Devil doesn't appear?" he asked.

"There are Satanists protecting Barry Court and they must be doing that for a jolly good reason. But if the Devil doesn't come by two-thirty we'll secure Rob and Geoff for questioning."

"When you say secure, you mean storming into their flat and hauling them off in sacks, don't you?"

Mrs Thornthwistle's smile widened.

"But don't you think that's a bit vigilante of us?" Jacob frowned. "We don't know these people from Adam and then Rachel has some vision about one of them and suddenly we're going off to ambush them. It's all sounds a bit like Salem to me."

Mogwai arched his back and hissed.

"Or Nazi Germany," Jacob added. "I think that all this talk of smiting has got the crowd too worked up that's all. They may even end up killing people. What happened to due process?"

"You need to forget all your customary ways tonight, dear. This is a war against evil itself so any actions we take are not only going to be legal, but they are going to be moral and ethical as well."

Jacob considered whether waging war against evil gave you the right to do whatever the hell you wanted. He stroked his beard and checked his watch. "Do you not think that it will be a bit late?"

"It is never too late to fight pure evil, dear," stated Mrs Thornthwistle, her grey eyes bright and threatening.

"You don't think there's any chance of us fighting substandard or at least heavily degraded evil tonight? You know the sort that spends its time talking in cinemas and jumping queues?"

Mrs Thornthwistle shook her head and stroked Mogwai.

"Pure evil it is then," Jacob sighed. "You do know that there's going to be massive fireballs?"

Mrs Thornthwistle smiled.

Chapter Thirteen

"Heil Hitler!" – Geoff

Barry Court, Withington, Manchester

Geoff looked around the bunker and knew that he was deep underground. While seven flickering kerosene lamps provided adequate lighting for most of the room, a full-length scarlet curtain cut off the far corner. In the centre a large table was covered by a detailed map of what he assumed to be Stalingrad. Two swastika flags were hung on the side walls facing each other. One, frayed and discoloured, had a mahogany writing bureau underneath it; the other was pristine with vibrant colours of red, white and black.

The seated soldier waited patiently for Geoff to take in his new surroundings. He had lean aristocratic features, clean shaven with slicked back black hair and piercing brown eyes, giving him the presence of a wolf on the prowl, or a hawk on the kill. His brow was furrowed, his forehead deeply lined. The Iron Cross medal at the centre of his perfectly creased white collar glistened.

Geoff looked down. "Sorry, I'm new to this lucid dreaming."

"It's your turn Geoffrey."

"I'm not that good at chess but I'll give it a go." Geoff sat down and advanced a pawn two spaces forward and pressed the chess clock button down.

"Have you considered that this may not be a dream?" asked the soldier, waving his right hand around the bunker.

"Of course it's a dream. I was brought here by a talking rabbit and you're General Paulus if I'm not mistaken?" replied Geoff.

"Correct. I am Friedrich Wilhelm Ernst Paulus, General of the German Wehrmacht Sixth Army, awarded the Iron Cross with Oak Leaves."

"I was just watching an excellent documentary about you and your, err troubles in Stalingrad. This is…erm, don't tell me. 1942? '43?"

The general smiled.

The warmth of the brandy made Geoff aware of the intense cold. An ancient iron stove stood in one corner that had long since run out of heat.

Boom!

Boom!

A couple of shells landing nearby shook the bunker, causing dust to fall from the ceiling. They were followed by silence save for the ticking of the chess clock.

Geoff sniffed the brandy, but all he could smell was the overpowering chemical stench of the lamps. "Rob would love this," he said.

A look of bemusement crept over the face of General Paulus.

"My friend Rob's a big fan of the whole Third Reich thing. Hugo Boss uniforms and the elite SS. You had such great names for stuff: Barbarossa, Wolf's Lair, Stuka bombers, Gestapo and Panzer tanks. Obviously, he's not a big fan of concentration camps or anything like that. More about how cool you looked."

"We did look sharper than anyone else. They say the Devil has the best toys."

"You had those crazy MC Hammer pants with the polished black boots," continued Geoff. "Luger pistols, stick grenades and really cool medals."

"And still we lost," said the general.

"Yeah, sorry about that. I don't suppose that I can have a look at your pistol?"

"Of course," said General Paulus, unholstering his Luger and handing it over to Geoff. It was in immaculate condition.

"This is heavy. Can I shoot it?" asked Geoff.

The general nodded.

Geoff aimed and pulled the trigger. There was a bang and a hole appeared in the dishevelled flag. He handed the pistol back. "I've always wanted to do that," he said.

"No problem at all."

"This is the best ever dream. Everything feels so real," grinned Geoff, looking around.

"My question for you is why do you believe that this a dream? And if it is a dream, who is the one dreaming?" The general moved one of his bishops, taking an exposed pawn, and stopped the clock.

"But this has got to be my dream," said Geoff.

"You can call me Friedrich. You are amongst friends here, Geoffrey. As a counter argument, have you considered that this could be my dream and you are just a small part of it? Please follow me." General Paulus stood up and walked to the far corner, sweeping back the curtain to show a sleeping figure.

Covered in blankets it took Geoff a dozen seconds to work out that this dishevelled unshaven man was another General Paulus. This version did not look anything like the apex predator that stood beside him.

"As you can see, I am sleeping," said General Paulus.

"Is that really you?"

"To my shame I'm afraid it is. So who is the real dreamer? Could it be that we are both dreaming, or could it be that neither of us are dreaming?" The general closed the curtain and walked back to his chair.

"I don't understand why you would dream of me and how can we understand each other? I don't know any German so we must be speaking in English. You have a weird Essex-German accent, which must make this dream mine."

"An interesting observation and I agree that we understand each other perfectly, but from my perspective we are both speaking in German and you have a Bavarian twang like that blasted Bohemian corporal," said the general, his unblinking dark eyes boring right into Geoff.

"Bohemian corporal?"

"You know him as Adolf Hitler. We know him as our Fuhrer."

"I suppose he's the reason you're here?"

General Paulus nodded. "Or could this be a repressed memory unlocked in response to the change in your circumstances?"

"What do you mean by my change in circumstances?" Geoff could feel his brow knitting up.

The general smiled. "Surely that is for you to work out?"

Geoff took a pawn with his knight before standing up and walking towards the centre table. It was a map of Stalingrad, though confusingly it didn't appear to be monitoring troop positions. Instead, there were at least fifty black crosses with dates beside them. He looked up. "I honestly don't know whose dream this is. Does it really matter?"

"Honesty is truly the first casualty of war."

"What do you mean?" asked Geoff.

"Why do you think we came to Stalingrad?"

"By we I'm thinking you mean the Sixth Army, making it sort of a military we and not me and you? Wasn't the whole purpose of Operation Barbarossa to neutralise Russia and colonise parts of Ukraine to guarantee oil and gas supplies for the rest of the war? Stalingrad was a key part of that," Geoff reeled off the documentary's explanation.

"But is that the real reason why the Sixth Army was sent here? And if it isn't, what was the true purpose of us coming to this frozen hell?"

♥

A barely audible rustling swept through Geoff's bedroom. Mr Sox's ears twitched. The end of his tail gave a lazy snap and his whiskers stood erect. Eventually he opened his emerald eyes and watched a slight figure walk slowly over and turn the television off.

"Here, puss, puss. Who's been such a good kitty?"

Mr Sox uncurled himself and leapt down from the bed to pad over to the stranger's legs. She had a shock of white hair and lent over to stroke him.

"Have you been eating enough? You look thinner than I had imagined. Have you gone native on me?" The woman eased the baseball bat out of Geoff's sleepy grip and placed it under the bed. "If you have, I will be a more than a little disappointed."

Mr Sox shivered, though not from any coldness.

β

In the bunker General Paulus refilled the glasses with brandy. "I think you may have to leave to deal with a pressing situation."

Geoff sat back and cleared his throat. "But this is a dream? Either mine, yours or even ours?"

"It could be, but then again who really knows?" replied General Paulus.

"I'm not trying to change history or anything like that and I certainly don't want your lot to win the war. I mean, you had some really nasty people on your side, so you winning wouldn't be good. But you seem like a decent bloke and this is only a dream so what difference can it make?"

The general rolled the brandy around his glass.

"I just think you should know that your Romanian allies are going to be targeted by the Russians. They're your weakest link and once they collapse on your right flank you will end up being surrounded and forced to surrender. The end happens pretty quick. You may want to consider bulking up your Romanians with some crack German units. If you do that you may be able to hold on until reinforcements arrive."

"Thank you, Geoffrey, but I'm fully aware of the Russian plan."

"I don't understand. If you know this, why don't you do something about it?"

"Because this is the morning of 31st January 1943." General Paulus glanced at his gold watch. "At exactly two minutes to seven in the morning."

"Why does that ring a bell?" asked Geoff. "Of course. That's the day you surrender to the Russians."

"Earlier today the Fuhrer made me a Field Marshall. The papers confirming my promotion are about to arrive, along with the official seal, which I must remember to burn. I always seem to forget to do that. Well, that fool thinks that I won't surrender because no German Field Marshall has ever surrendered. He's mistaken. I can and I will."

"But your men don't surrender till later, do they?" asked Geoff.

"My men surrender on 3rd February."

"And almost all of them go on to die in the Siberian Gulags," said Geoff, immediately wishing he hadn't.

"I am afraid I know that too," said the general. "You certainly know your history."

"Not really. I was watching a documentary on Stalingrad when I fell asleep. Do you know that this was one of the key turning points in the Second World War?"

"I do."

"How can you know all of this?" Geoff felt the brandy warming his chest. The general's mouth opened but before he could reply another shell landed above them, this time closer, showering them with more dust.

♥

"Wake up Geoffrey." A soft female voice echoed like a ghost around the bunker.

"Can you hear that?" asked Geoff, noticing that none of the dust had stuck to the general's uniform.

"Your presence is needed elsewhere."

A sharp knock at the door was followed by a loud efficient German voice. "News from the front, Field Marshall."

"It would appear that I am needed here as well." They both turned to see the once sleeping version of the general brush the curtain to one side and get slowly out of the bed.

The chess playing general stood up and placed his cap on his head. "May I ask a favour of you, Geoffrey?"

"Of course."

"Can you give me permission to tell myself what you have told me?"

A whisper of a creak echoed around the bunker.

Geoff frowned. "Yes, I suppose so, but just so you know that's weird even for a dream."

"Even so, I thank you for that." General Paulus looked down at the board. "Your queen looks vulnerable."

"I did tell you that I was not very good at chess."

"May I offer you a word of advice before you go?"

Geoff nodded.

"You must protect your queen at all costs. Without her it is extremely difficult, if not impossible, to win this game."

"I'll remember that," said Geoff. "And thanks for the brandy and letting me fire your gun."

"Wakey, wakey, Geoffrey." The disembodied voice sounded much closer, female and Welsh.

"Well, I guess this is goodbye," said Geoff.

"Auf wiedersehen," replied General Paulus, firmly shaking Geoff's hand.

There was another set of sharp knocks, more urgent than before.

"Enter," yawned the general, looking straight through them.

The door opened and a baby-faced soldier with a rabbit smoking a cigar to his right stepped inside. The rabbit leaned up against the side of the door and raised his right eyebrow at Geoff.

"Heil Hitler! News from the front, Field Marshall," rattled the soldier.

The general in the corner started to pull his trousers on. He did not reply.

"Heil Hitler!" saluted General Paulus, the heels of his boots snapping together. "Sorry, force of habit," he said.

Geoff looked at the general; the board; the flags; and the map. "Rob would love this. Heil Hitler!" he saluted.

The general suppressed a smile. “Good luck to you, Mr Pike, and with all your future endeavours. I look forward to meeting you again.”

“I still don’t understand how you can know how the war ends. It’s only 1943,” said Geoff, remembering what he’d been thinking before the last shell landed.

“I know how the war ends, Geoffrey, because this is Hell,” replied the general.

“Well, I get that this must be really upsetting but that doesn’t explain why you know about the future.”

“I’m afraid that I haven’t developed some remarkable ability to move through time. I know that the real date is Friday, 18th March 20…”

BOOM!

A shell landed directly above them, shaking the whole bunker and causing everyone to lose their footing.

“But you said that you’re about to surrender,” said Geoff.

“It’s quite easy. When I said that this is Hell, I meant that just that,” said General Paulus, spreading his arms around him and moving his body in a slow circle. “This my own personal part of Hell.”

“Oh, I…”

Gus, the bunker, and General Paulus flickered and disappeared. They were replaced by total darkness.

“..see.”

β

It was still dark and Geoff’s eyes were firmly closed, but he knew he was back in his bed. He grunted and licked his cracked lips. In a heartbeat he also knew that something was wrong. A light scent of blossom and soft citrus wafted towards him. He tried to grip the baseball bat but it was gone.

“For fuck’s sake Geoffrey, wake up,” a Welsh whisper ripped into his consciousness like a honey-coated nail bomb.

Geoff froze as the voice continued, “If you’re going to pretend to be asleep, I’ll have to pretend to cut your balls off.”

He rolled away, opened his eyes and stared at the location of the voice. It was dark and grainy but no one was there.

“Morning gorgeous,” whispered into his right ear.

“Uuurgghhh!” Geoff sprawled out of bed with a *thud*, scrambling to his knees.

The woman with white hair and sparkling blue eyes stood with her hands on her hips in front of him. She was holding a paring knife in her left hand. “We need to talk.”

“Who the fuck are you?” he asked.

The woman stopped smiling and narrowed her eyes.

Part of Geoff demanded that he took control of this situation. “I said, who the fuck are you?” he asked again, though this time slower and deeper.

“Geoffrey,” she replied in a husky voice, her blue eyes sparkling. “I am the Devil.”

Chapter Fourteen

"Padre, you are even worse than the orangutans." – Alexis

Room 101, The Lowry Hotel, Salford

Crash!

The single knock was so heavy that it threatened to take the door clean off its hinges. Three further batterings and it began to creak inwards. Sam looked through the spy hole and opened the door as far as the security chain would allow.

Bernie the black suited Minotaur filled the whole of the doorway, his fists balled up. "The boss wants to see you."

"No problem, I'll just get my…"

"Now!" With a single blow Bernie ripped the door open and grabbed Sam by his ears, pulling him into the corridor.

"Owwhh!" Sam cried.

"Get the girl Saunders," ordered Bernie.

"She's not here," said Sam, "she's out shopping."

"Check the room Saunders and meet me at the car," ordered Bernie.

Saunders grunted and stepped through the doorway.

"Don't be late Saunders."

❽

The mobile rang for over a minute before it was answered.

"Spade."

"Hi Sam, what happened at the hotel?" asked Emily.

"I had a slight disagreement with room service. You get something nice?"

"Sort of. I ran into someone who really wants to see you."

"Really? I don't know anyone in Manchester. Who is it?" asked Sam.

"It's a surprise. Says he's one of your closest friends."

"I don't have any friends."

"Where are you?"

"I'm at the Freemasons with Brian."

"Can you get away?" asked Emily. "This is important."

"Not really. I'm a bit tied up. We're working through some things at the moment."

"Well, I guess it'll be okay for Daddy to meet your friend."

Brian glared at Sam.

"Look I've got to go. Brian wants to get things moving. I'll see you soon."

Freemasons Hall, Bridge Street, Manchester

Emily, Lou and his trusty special sack made their way down into the basement of Freemasons Hall.

"Don't you think that Sam sounded a bit weird when I called?" asked Emily. "That door was a mess."

"You worry too much, I think he sounded just like Sam," replied Lou. "Room service can be pretty annoying you know."

"Maybe." Emily doubted if Lou understood what room service actually was. "You stay here and I'll go and check that Daddy isn't up to no good." She turned and crept down the long corridor, deserted apart from stone busts of serious looking past Grand Masters of the Lodge. Slipping through a heavy wooden door she eased into another corridor, shorter and illuminated by a series of flickering torches bolted to the walls. She was about to turn left at a T-junction when she heard a series of mutterings that sounded like a deep growl.

"Go get that Saunders. Go get this Saunders. Hit him harder Saunders. You're stupid Saunders. Kill him Saunders. Get me a flat white with no sugar Saunders."

Emily stopped dead in her tracks.

The mutterings stopped long enough for a loud snort and then started again. "Just because he's my older brother and an inch taller than me doesn't give him the right to order me around. Next time, I'm going to show him."

Emily plucked a shuriken from her belt and extinguished the closest candles with her fingers.

"Who's there?" came from around the corner.

Flicking her wrist Emily launched the shuriken down the right corridor of the T-junction. Bouncing off the stone walls it made a satisfyingly loud clatter.

The voice started up again, though this time much less of a growl. "Just so you know, this is nothing personal but I'm having a very bad day. Like Machiavelli said, *'Men ought either to be well treated or crushed, because they can avenge themselves of lighter injuries, of more serious ones they cannot'.* I hope you understand that I'm in a crushing sort of mood, so I think I'm going to rip your arms and legs off and feed them to you." A massive figure marched past Emily. "Then again, maybe I shouldn't be so rash. It's not your fault that I'm having an existential crisis, so I should at least consider a counter argument put forward by Asimov, *'Violence is the last refuge of the incompetent'.* See what you've done now, I'm all conflicted. Why don't we see how the chips fall when I find you?" The figure stopped and snorted. "On reflection I think it's going to be simpler if I just do the arms and legs ripping thing. Okay what have we got here?"

Gripping her stiletto daggers Emily stealthily followed.

Saunders bent over to pick up the shuriken. When he righted himself, two very sharp points jutted into the sides of his neck.

"Uurrgghh," he grunted.

"Hi, I'm Emily and you must be Saunders, one of Daddy's Minotaurs?"

"Maybe."

"Pleased to meet you and for the record I'm always in Team Machiavelli. Now why don't you turn around very carefully and take me to Daddy. He's expecting me so don't do anything rash that will force me to slice open your jugular. I don't think he'll be very happy if you hurt me either."

Saunders turned slowly and walked back down the corridor. At the T-junction Emily told him to stop while she called for Lou.

"Saunders this is my friend Lou."

"Hi," said Saunders looking down. "I like your sack. It looks roomy."

"Thank you. It's nice to meet someone who appreciates that a sack can be special without being magical or small," said Lou looking at Emily.

"I've already apologised for that," she said rolling her eyes. "Why don't we go and find Sam?"

"You got a body in it?" asked Saunders.

"Yes," nodded Lou.

"Sweet," nodded the Minotaur.

At the end of the corridor there was a plain lead door with a brass plaque bolted above it that announced that this was, 'Summoning Room Number Seven'.

"Well?" whispered Emily.

"What?" asked Saunders.

"Get us in."

"Oh okay." Saunders knocked on the door and said, "Boss, Emily's here. Says she's your daughter."

"Bloody bollocks. We are in the middle of something," boomed Brian, adding, "come in if you must."

When Emily opened the door, two things struck her. One, her father was standing on a raised stone pedestal at the head of a very large pentacle with a marble lectern in front of him. He was speaking into a microphone. Two, a bare-chested Sam was hanging upside down in the centre of the pentacle with another Minotaur looming next to him.

Sam's hand shot out and grabbed Bernie by the balls and squeezed.

"Owwhh!" cried Bernie, a look of deep confusion spreading across his face. Sam and Saunders smiled.

Immediately Bernie raised his dagger to just above Sam's genitals.

Emily was the first to speak, "Now why don't you two boys be reasonable about this?" She stepped into the room with two stiletto daggers still pressed against Saunders' neck. "Mr Samuel Spade, please let go of this nice man's balls," she paused, "immediately!"

To Bernie's surprise and relief, the upside-down Sam let go of his balls.

"And now would this nice young man care to remove his very sharp dagger from Mr Spade's balls?" she asked.

Looking at Emily, her daggers and Saunders, Bernie sheathed his blade.

"You see, that wasn't so hard," said Emily, daggers dropping to her sides. "You boys will have to learn how to play nicely or someone is going to end up getting hurt and we don't want that, do we?"

"Why are you here?" asked Brian coldly.

"To see Sam," replied Emily. "I've got one of his friends."

"He doesn't have any friends," said Brian.

"Fair point, and I'm also here to make sure you're not doing anything nasty to him."

Brian looked at her, "Colour me suspicious, but I felt that certain people weren't being completely truthful about what is happening when we last met. Isn't that right Samuel? So I thought it best for all concerned if we had another friendly chat."

"We have different versions of friendly Daddy," remarked Emily looking straight at Sam.

"I'm sorry I just can't stand by and watch this," blurted out Lou, staring at the thin lines of blood carved across Sam's chest. "You're doing it all wrong."

"What?" asked Brian.

"The torturing. You're doing it all wrong," he repeated. "With a daemon like Sam what you need to do is…"

"Heh Lou, great to see you," cried Sam. "But what are you doing?"

"Okay strange short German I'll bite," said Brian. "In your opinion what exactly should I be doing if I really want to hurt Mr Spade?"

"Well, the first thing that he really can't handle is…"

"Lou!" shouted Sam. "They're torturing me! And I'm your friend remember?"

"I'm sorry, Sam's right. I shouldn't really be saying anything," replied Lou. "It's just a professional thing."

"I know I'm going to regret asking this, but what is in your sack?" asked Brian.

"My special sack?" Lou raised his arm as high as he could and turned the sack over. Jay fell to the floor, a mass of arms and legs. "This."

Jay stretched out and scrambled to his feet. "Heh Sammy, how's it hanging?"

"Jay?" asked Sam.

"Heh buddy it's great to see you," grinned Jay looking around the room. "You're obviously in the middle of something so how about we catch up later?"

"What the heaven are you doing here?" frowned Sam.

"You're bi… sorry I mean Emily, was very persuasive. She turned up at my place and had this ridiculous idea that I set you up with those Minotaurs. Crazy hey?"

"Did you?"

"Well, a bit, but not like she thinks," said Jay opening his arms. "I guess hugging it out is a bit of a problem. Tell you what, I'll get back in Lou's special sack and we can all nip back home and chat about this over some whisky."

"Daddy aren't you forgetting something?" asked Emily sharply.

"Damnit," said Brian shaking his head. "We're obviously not going to have any privacy now. Cut him down Hunter."

"Of course, sir."

"Can we have a minute?" asked Sam.

Brian nodded.

"What happened Jay?" whispered Sam as they got to a corner pillar.

"Well, when I said that Sister M was causing some problems, I was sort of helping her," he shrugged.

"What? Why would you be working against the boss?" asked Sam.

"You've probably not noticed, but the boss hasn't exactly put me on the career development fast-track. I want to do more and Sister M said she understood and if she took over, she'd make me into a real daemon. I'd even have my own minions. I've got real ideas on how to improve Hell and I know how people work."

"But you love that bar," said Sam.

"No Sammy, you and your bloody daemon mates love that bar, not me. I just manage it."

"But I've got an invite for a big party they're throwing for you in 2032."

"Yep. Two thousand years of running the same old bar. Guess what they're going to give me? Exactly the same that they gave me after a thousand years; thirty bloody pieces of silver. And the award for the most imaginative present goes to…"

"Sorry I didn't know," said Sam. "What did she have you do?"

"Keeping tabs on the Big Man and his top boys. Helping Pnakotic get hold of some secret work done by some scientists on time travel. That was where Darius came in."

"But what does this have to do with the *Book of Shenanigans*?" asked Sam.

"That I really don't know, but the person who gave Sister M copies was someone called the Greek."

"Never heard of him," said Sam.

"Same here. Definitely not a daemon so maybe an angel?"

Sam frowned, "I can't see why an angel would get mixed up in Hell politics."

"I am sorry for what happened to you Sammy. It was my bad to tell Sister M you were asking questions. People will have seen you at the bar, so I figured I needed to tell her something. Why do you think I gave you that card?" asked Jay.

"Because you're stupid?" suggested Emily appearing at his side. "And traitorous; Sam almost died."

"No. Think about it, it was a clue just for you. I was letting you know what was what. I was warning you buddy. I've always got your back."

"You could have just told me," said Sam.

"Walls have ears. It's Hell, and you know everyone is out for themselves. If I'd ever thought Sister M would send those killers after you, I would have never mentioned Darius," Jay smiled. "I knew you'd be able to handle whatever was sent your way."

"True," agreed Sam. "I was in complete control before Emily turned up and killed the one who was just about to spill everything."

"They were going to kill you Sam," Emily sighed. "Remember all the machine guns, body armour and grenades they had, and you didn't?"

Jay raised an eyebrow.

Sam shook his head, "That's just how I wanted it to look."

"No worries, everyone ended up okay," said Jay. "How was Darius? He still got those crazy cats?"

"They killed him," said Sam and Emily.

"Oh. So everyone is okay except Darius. That is a real shame. But we're all cool now?"

Brian's voice boomed out of the six speakers attached to the upper walls. "I'm sorry to break up this touching reunion, but the acoustics in this room are exceptional so I've heard everything you've said. Now that torturing Sam appears to be off the table, why don't we all have a little chat? Who are you Jay?"

"Judas Iscariot at your service," Jay replied with bow.

"My favourite apostate; big fan of your earlier work. So why were you in the bag?"

"I was kidnapped by your psycho offspring."

Brian shrugged and smiled, "I for one would like to hear what else you have to say."

"Like I was saying to Sammy, Sister Muerte is planning to make a few changes at the top in Hell. She's been working with a daemon called Pnakotic and they, amongst other things, have been collecting work on time travel. There is also someone called the Greek, who I don't know, who gave her copies of God's new work, the *Book of Shenanigans,* which I understand you've already seen?"

"This may be a bit off point but does anyone know who Santa Muerte actually is?" asked Brian looking around the room.

"Is this a trick question? Santa Muerte is Sister Muerte," ventured Jay.

"Yes and no. The truth is that Santa, or if you prefer Sister Muerte started off as Saint Gertrude of Nivelles."

"Who?" asked Jay. "I spoke to her today and she did that scary, husky, going to kill you slowly in your sleep voice. I can tell you that broad is definitely not a Gertrude."

"I am not questioning whether Santa Muerte is terrifying only that she began life as Gertrude. I've completed extensive research on this subject for an article I'm writing for the Demonologist Monthly and I can say with certainty that this Gertrude was born into a noble family in 626 AD in what is now Belgium. I think she may have had some daddy issues…"

"That is no longer acceptable," interrupted Emily.

"Well that is the only explanation I can come up with for her declaring aged ten that she would devote her life to God," shrugged Brian. "Any case, getting back to the story, she did just that and lived a life of humble devotion setting up a monastery which she became abbess of. Her reputation for kindness grew and on 16th March 659 she asked Ultan, an Irish pilgrim who was visiting her monastery, when she would die. Ultan replied "the very next day," which, as you can imagine, sucked the fun right out of the room. Gertrude thought deeply about this and decided that her best course of action was to avoid meeting death altogether. So she gave strict orders not to be disturbed and barricaded herself into her quarters. Shuttering the windows and using rags bathed in holy water to plug any gaps she got ready to ride it out until the 18th."

"It doesn't work like that," said Sam, "death isn't a real person."

“Thank you for that invaluable insight Samuel but as this was the Dark Ages Gertrude wasn’t as enlightened as yourself. There she was, completely isolated apart from her much-loved cats ‘Bubble’ and ‘Squeak’.”

“Really?” asked Sam.

“No of course not. I have no idea what her cats were called but they are rather important for this story. Months went by and Gertrude still did not appear. Finally the nuns couldn’t stand the putrefying stench any longer and on 14th July 659 they broke into her quarters. What they found was her dead body and two rather plump cats. Faced with starvation, Bubble and Squeak had chewed her face off, right to the bone. My guess is that they were responsible for her death.”

“You cannot trust cats,” stated Sam.

“But this is where it gets really interesting. In Heaven God is really pissed that Gertrude tried to avoid his divine plan for her. But God being God he’s also feeling bad about getting her cats to eat her face so he comes up with another plan. He makes Gertrude the Patron Saint of Cats.”

“But why do you think she’s Santa Muerte?” asked Sam. “They sort of play for different sides.”

“Because Gertrude did not appreciate the irony of becoming the ultimate crazy cat lady so she flipped.”

“She went mad?” asked Jay. “I’ve met her and I can easily believe that. That bitch is loco.”

“No. Gertrude flipped by going direct to Hell and asking for diplomatic asylum,” answered a smiling Brian. “As you can imagine, the Devil was ecstatic about this and agreed to take her in on the understanding that it’s all done in complete secrecy. She starts at the bottom but works really hard at all things evil while still acting as the dutiful saint. Over time she rebrands her Hell image as a very tall skeleton complete with scythe and orb to reflect her growing obsession with death. When God finally learns of her double life, he can’t denounce her because that would amount to admitting he was wrong, so Saint Gertrude and Santa Muerte remain one and the same. In fact, her feast day was yesterday, the same as St. Patrick.”

“That sounds pretty crazy to me,” said Jay. “What do you think Sammy?”

Sam frowned. “Brian could be right. I don’t remember Santa Muerte at all until after the First Crusade. I did some serious shit during The Dark Ages so they’re a bit of a blur for me but I can’t remember a daemon called Muerte.”

“That’s because she isn’t a daemon, merely a very hard-working human,” said Brian. “I assumed you would approve Judas, given your own daemonic aspirations.”

“I guess that explains why she offered me a promotion,” said Jay.

“But I must confess I did not realise that Pnakotic was working for her. What a small world we live in,” smiled Brian. “Do you know why they would be interested in time travel and who this Greek character is?”

“Nope and nope,” replied Jay. “No one can travel through time. My guess is the Greek is a codename for a very powerful daemon who likes to collect human oddities. They give him the complete set and he provides them with support when it matters. But that’s just my take on this.”

“Have you seen the rest of the *Book of Shenanigans*?”

“Again nope,” replied Jay. “But all of this has spooked the big man and he’s come down to Earth and judging by Shenanigan’s cover he’s here to get the Spear of Destiny. And that, is all I know.”

“And what about you,” Brian swivelled his gaze to Lou. “What is your part in all of this?”

“I’m a friend of Sam’s.”

“Sam doesn’t have any friends,” said Emily and Brian.

“Well then I’m a longstanding acquaintance who runs Loading Bay C in Hell,” Lou sniffed. “We get shipments of new souls and we introduce them to how it’s going to be for the rest of eternity.”

“But why were you in Hell?” asked Brian.

“I was a member of the SS.”

“Oh,” said Brian, “I guess that would get you there, but that’s part of my problem who decided that you went to Hell?”

“The boss,” replied Lou.

“That’s the Devil,” added Sam.

“Thank you Samuel, I would never have guessed. So why did the Devil decide you were his?”

“I did bad things,” smiled a nodding Lou.

"But that doesn't seem fair. You make some questionable decisions and then you're sent to Hell to be tortured," said Brian.

"But I did some really bad things and I liked it a lot."

"What, being tortured?" asked Brian.

"I'm more the torturer than the tortured," said Lou, his barrel chest jutting out. "Isn't that right Sam?"

Sam nodded, "Lou's the best. In fact, if you ever plan to torture anybody soon, apart from me that is, he'd be perfect."

"I'll keep that in mind. By some strange coincidence we all seem to share a common goal, which is to find the Devil and dispose of him." Brian pointed at Jay. "You want to facilitate a change in leadership to enable you to become a fully-fledged daemon." He pointed at Sam and Emily. "You both need to work for me to clear your debt." Finally, he pointed at Lou. "And you, if I'm guessing correctly, just want to torture people which works for whoever is in charge."

"But what happens when we do find him?" asked Sam.

"That's another question to be answered at another time," smiled Brian.

Lou loudly cleared his throat and everybody looked at the diminutive torturer.

"Sorry, was I supposed to speak?" He looked around settling his gaze on Brian, his eyes narrowing, "Do you have any bananas?"

"Can I just have word with Emily," asked Sam.

"If you must," smiled Brian.

"I'll do this in private if that's okay? Now we're all on the same team Lou and Jay can give you some professional advice. Won't be long."

Sam waited for the door to fully close before whispering, "We've got to go right now."

"I don't understand, what about Lou and Judas?"

"Forget them. I know where the Devil is…"

※

Internet searches on Geoffrey Pike delivered very little. He was obviously not a person destined for greatness. However, it did not matter why Santa Muerte wanted his balls, just that she did. At Mexico City airport the metal detector malfunctioned, an incident occurred nearby and Father Garcia calmly walked through security. Now on the plane the events of the last twenty-four hours caught up with him and by the time the plane left the runway he was soundly asleep. He woke to the smell of fresh paint, his coppery face breaking into a smile. Opening his eyes, he looked around the same deep red pit as before. Alexis was curled up in a corner.

"How?" Alexis whispered. "You are back padre."

"Come closer Alexis."

Alexis looked up at the lip of the pit and moved slowly to its centre. He was naked but untouched. "Padre please help me escape," he said squinting at his watch. "I've only two more minutes left before the orangutans come to help me."

Father Garcia smiled. "Of course I will help you, my son."

"How?"

"I have an idea. Give me your machete."

Alexis shook his head. "No. What can you do? I'm in Hell and you're just a hallucination. You cannot help me."

"But you are wrong Alexis. I am really here and you saw that Santa Muerte favours me. I am honoured by her unholiness and I believe that this is a test for you. If you give me your machete it will show her that you are truly repentant and she may spare you. If not, I can take care of these orangutans you speak of."

With shaking hands Alexis passed over the machete handle first.

Father Garcia gripped the weapon and grinned.

"Is that it?" asked Alexis, studying the priest's wide eyes. "Am I saved?"

As his words drifted away, Father Garcia's lips curved into a cruel smirk.

"No, padre."

The priest licked his lips. "Alexis you have much to fear my son. I now know that this was a test for me and not you. As an apostate you should be punished."

Beep. Beep. The alarm sounded.

"Please no, padre."

A breathless Father Garcia finally stopped, blood dripping down the blade hanging by his side. Alexis' head was attached to his body but that was all as various body parts twitched around the pit floor.

The priest looked up and shouted, "How did I do?"

From the floor a blind Alexis murmured "Padre, you are even worse than the orangutans."

Chapter Fifteen

"I present to thee essential smiting equipment." – Jacob

Just Outside Barry Court, Withington, Manchester

Emily looked around the marquee, "Don't you think that was impressive, turning a herd of scared little lambs into this pack of rabid wolves? Look around, that video is going viral."

"She's a witch and a strong one at that," replied Sam. Everyone was busy watching their phones. "That was a powerful glamour spell which beefed up her message to the masses."

Emily frowned. "Those nuns were pretty adamant that we weren't going to the flats. Whoever these people are, they seem pretty well organised. Are you absolutely certain the Devil is in those flats? They don't think he's there yet."

"He is. I don't know how he got in without them noticing but I can feel his presence. You've got to remember, we go way back."

"Do you think they could work out you're a daemon?" asked Emily in a serious tone.

"I don't think so. I've got my own magical protection and to them I'm just another one of these oddball disciples," said Sam, throwing his half-smoked cigarette away. "Mind yourself with her cat. He'll be her familiar, so that gives her an extra pair of eyes and ears."

"What about those angels?"

"I don't think they're proper angels, at least not like the ones I've met. Brian may be able to shed some light on them."

"Speaking of Daddy, don't you think we should have invited him to this little shindig? Meeting the Devil is definitely on his bucket list."

"You know we have some trust issues we're working through. The first being that I don't trust him and second that according to the *Book of Shenanigans* he's not supposed to be here anyway," said Sam.

"But I thought you didn't believe in predestination."

"I don't, but this one makes sense. It could get very messy if Brian and his thugs get involved."

"Mr Spade, I think it will get very messy tonight whoever is here," said Emily. "What's the plan now?"

"Split up and get speaking to people. Try and get a handle on what's going to happen and meet up at the car park in fifteen minutes?"

"Be careful Sam," smiled Emily as she walked away to a table laden with cake and coffee. "I don't want to have to come and save you from those nasty nuns."

"Hi, I'm Emily."

"I'm Rachel, pleased to meet you. I like your costume, very ninja chic. You fit in well with the nuns. Have you come from a party?"

"You could say that. I met with some of my partner's oldest friends this afternoon, so I thought I should make an effort," smiled Emily. "Though I didn't have time to change."

"I hope he appreciated it."

"Deep down I think Sam, that's my partner, is fully aware of what I do for him. He's somewhere around here. It's all a bit crazy but we both felt drawn to this place, like we needed to do some good."

Rachel laughed and looked at the two photos on her phone. The first was a drunken Geoff, the second a grinning Rob wearing a Guinness hat.

"Is that why you're here?" Emily asked.

"Not exactly. Did you see the scary Scottish lady giving the speech before? I'm sort of with her."

"So you're a professional at this sort of thing? If you don't mind me saying, but on first impressions you seem far too nice and normal for this."

"I used to be," Rachel sighed. "But I've been getting visions of what people really are for over a year now. I used to think they were nightmares, but now I know they're real. I can't explain why, but that's the reason I joined the Set."

"The Set?" asked Emily.

"Sorry, that's our group led by Mrs Thornthwistle."

"Right, the scary Scottish lady. But are you really certain about these two?" asked Emily. "They look too drunk and stupid, to be the poster boys of evil."

"I'm sure this one is," scowled Rachel, holding her mobile up. "That's Rob and he worships the Devil."

"How do you know?"

"I've worked with them for over two years and my visions all started with Rob. I can't prove it but he's done some horrible things. Then this morning they got fired and he ran over my partner just when the Devil comes to Manchester. That can't be a coincidence."

"That's terrible," said Emily. "Is he okay?"

"Thankfully just cuts and bruises. I befriended his mate Geoff so I could keep an eye on Rob."

"Speaking of Geoff, he just looks really confused as well as being very drunk."

"Mmm. You may be right about him being drunk and stupid but he's Rob's best friend so…"

"Evil by association?" Emily suggested.

Rachel smiled.

"Interesting logic," added Emily.

"Maybe, but I bet they're doing some evil Devil worshipping shenanigans right now and I swear I'm going to make Rob pay," said Rachel, her green eyes fierce and bright.

"Pay for what?"

"Being evil of course," answered Rachel. "I'm going to cut his balls off."

"What if he tells you everything before you get to torture him?"

"It doesn't matter, I'm still going to cut them right off," said Rachel, dipping into her bag and pulling out a kitchen knife. "And this is what I'm going to use to do it."

"It's been lovely talking to you but I think I should find out what Sam's doing, wherever he is," Emily smiled. "Good luck with the whole torturing thing. Remember the trick is to slice and dice and not to puncture. Think of them as a couple of juicy plums."

When Emily found Sam, he was standing alone near the trees looking at the Satanists gathered at Barry Court.

"If it isn't Mr Spade skulking around as usual. I thought you wanted us to blend in, talk to people and learn what's happening."

“I did my bit,” said Sam turning and smiling.

“Are you certain those angels aren’t a threat? You know, with you being a daemon and a once-valued ex-employee of the Devil?”

“I don’t think they’re proper angels and even if they are, they’re nothing I can’t handle.”

“Mr Spade, that is mighty big talk for someone who managed to get himself beaten half to death twice in the last seven hours, strung up, tortured and needed a weak, defenceless girl to fight his battles for him not once, but twice.” Emily winked and smiled, her teeth snow white.

“I had those Minotaurs exactly where I wanted them and Brian was just a bit upset. You know how he gets.”

“So you said. By the way, this carrot cake is to die for. I’m going to get the recipe from those nuns.”

“Em, you can’t cook.”

“How little you know me. I’ll surprise you with my cooking expertise if we ever end up owning a place with an actual kitchen. In any case, meeting your friends was most enlightening,” said Emily, a smile playing on her lips. “Once this settles down, we should host a dinner party and for that, I will learn to cook.”

“They are not my friends.”

“Sorry, I mean your associates. I keep forgetting that you don’t have any friends. Now who do I prefer? There is the one who sent a squad of Minotaurs to kill you. What was his name? Judas… Iscariot. I really like the way his name rolls off the tongue just like his lies. Doesn’t that give it away?” asked Emily, squeezing his hand.

“He had his reasons,” said Sam flatly.

“Do the people gathered here count as new associates? They seem to believe they can kill your ex-boss with a fearsome collection of garden tools, knitting needles and portable drills,” she said. “I particularly like Rachel, sweet and normal on the outside and a completely deranged wannabe torturing maniac on the inside.”

“What can I say?” shrugged Sam.

“And then, of course, there’s Louis your German SS friend, who is a real darling, though he did seem more than happy to beat the living shit out of you and then give Daddy pointers on how best to torture you. Oh to have associates, Mr Spade. Have you seen what they think the Devil will look like?” asked Emily, holding her phone up.

Sam looked at the three suggestions. Red, horned, with wings and a tail was common in all of them. "I think he'll be a bit subtler than these," he said. "But back in the day you should have seen him. If he decides to go all retro, I'd say they have it nailed."

"And what are we going to do when they attack?" asked Emily.

"As little as possible. I'm in no hurry to meet my old boss."

"Neither am I Mr Spade," shivered Emily.

"Remember we're here to observe that's all."

∴

At exactly one o'clock Mrs Thornthwistle led people out of the marquee in a surprisingly orderly manner and raised her right arm. A light rig burst into life, illuminating the surroundings.

"Wow! Where did that come from?" exclaimed Simon shielding his eyes.

"The nuns I expect," replied Jacob. "They seem very well equipped."

Mrs Thornthwistle's arm fell and the lights faded back into darkness.

Simon asked, "Talking about equipment I take it that we've got weapons? Guns and the like? Mr Smith will be a natural with anything that causes blood and death. I think he's a killing savant, but the rest of us will need some help."

"I don't think the nuns brought any of their guns tonight," replied Jacob. "Or tanks, or RPGs for that matter."

"Right. I just thought you might have some stockpiles," said Simon as he watched people form a queue in front of a large table in the car park manned by Mr Smith, Mrs Thornthwistle and Sister Agatha. "In case something like this ever happened?"

"You're right. We really should have predicted the Devil coming here and secretly armed ourselves with military grade weaponry. Why don't you go and ask Mrs T to call down an airstrike to obliterate Barry Court so we can all go home early?" asked Jacob.

"I get your point," said Simon, as he watched seven of the nuns place wheelbarrows full of weapons beside Mr Smith.

"You've got to remember that this is England and we are not Americans," added Jacob.

Mr Smith gave each person a carefully chosen weapon. Almost all of them had a kitchen, or garden maintenance feel. There were no guns, but there were still plenty of sharp, bludgeony items on offer. Each recipient shuffled to the right where Sister Agatha blessed their weapon with a flourish of holy water and the sign of the cross. Shuffling again, Mrs Thornthwistle shook their hand and said something short and meaningful. This production line proved to be highly effective and within ten minutes everyone was armed, blessed and scarily happy.

From nowhere Sister Agatha appeared between Jacob and Simon. "You will need these tonight. They have been blessed by God." She handed them two identical circular metal objects and vanished into the night.

"Do you think these were in the smaller packages?" asked Jacob.

"Probably," replied Simon.

"Strange woman that Agatha," whispered Jacob. He looked at the item. It was a Custom Axelerator and he already knew what was coming.

Simon looked at him. "I don't suppose you know why a couple of blessed yoyos are going to help us smite the Devil?"

Jacob did not answer, his breath condensing into small clouds in the cold as he studied the Devil's likely manifestations on his mobile. "You're saying that the Devil is real?" he finally asked.

"Definitely," replied Simon. "He's the boss of Hell. I think it's in the Bible and he's escaped."

"And you think that we're going to face him tonight?" Jacob rubbed his beard.

"Archangel Gabriel said that there was a ninety-eight percent chance that the Devil is in Manchester and Mrs Thornthwistle seems pretty confident that these two are a big part of anything evil happening here. Look at all these people, he could already be in those flats," said Simon.

"Mmm," muttered Jacob. "No offense, but if you're right I'm a bit surprised they didn't send someone with a proven track record. Not necessarily an archangel like Gabriel or Uriel, but someone like Michael, or maybe even Barachiel?"

"None taken. I know what you mean. I've had no training and smiting the Devil sounds pretty tricky to me," said Simon.

"I'll say. Have you heard of the Dead Sea Scrolls?"

Simon shook his head. All around them people were practicing their blood curdling cries, inspecting their blessed weapons and glaring through the trees at Barry Court.

Jacob continued, "It's an ancient Jewish text that's like an idiot's guide to angels. It gives different categories, hierarchy and the actual names of a bunch of individual angels and I don't remember you, or Mr Smith being mentioned anywhere."

"I'm afraid that was all a bit before my time," grinned Simon.

"Once again, please don't be offended, as we're all very grateful for your assistance but your colleague Mr Smith," Jacob paused, "well, he seems like someone who would play for either side as long as he gets to hurt people, and you just seem..."

"More like an accountant?" offered Simon. "Maybe a bit less of a force?"

"Exactly. I had you pegged as IT but you're right, accountancy seems perfect for you."

"That's probably because I was an accountant. That's when I was alive."

"I didn't realise that accountants could ever make it to Heaven," said Jacob.

"You may be right, there's not a lot of us up there," laughed Simon. He wondered if Isabel was a real qualified accountant.

"What happened to you?" asked Jacob.

"I was a tax specialist in London. It may not sound much but I really enjoyed it and then one Monday morning, I was going down St. James's Place on my bike and out of nowhere a bus swerved into the cycle lane to avoid someone crossing the road. Bam!"

"Ouch. That sounds painful. Were you wearing a helmet?"

"Yes, but it was no use. I was killed immediately so pain wasn't really an issue. One second I'm riding my bike to work, the next I'm stood outside the gates of Heaven."

"I know that this is a strange question but was being a tax accountant better than being some avenging angel sent to Earth to smite the Devil?" quizzed Jacob, his dark eyes shining.

"I honestly don't know," replied Simon, pushing his glasses up his nose. "This is a great honour but I don't think that smiting the Devil matches my skill set. I suppose I was handpicked by Gabriel, which must count for something?"

"I agree. The fact that an archangel sent you here shows they have faith in you," agreed Jacob.

"I hope you're right."

"I'll tell you what, once you've gotten rid of this Devil character, I'll write a story about your exploits. I'll call them the Manchester Scrolls. Before my father disappeared he used to draw pages and pages of religious stuff. He kept saying that God had told him secret important things about the future."

"You mean like prophecies?" asked Simon.

"I suppose they were, at least to him."

"Did he really know things?"

"No, of course not. He was into all these conspiracy theories and left us on my birthday. The last thing he said to me was that he had to devote his life to his work. Hard for an eleven-year-old boy to understand. He then disappeared, taking all his stuff. Maybe that's why I joined the Set. Oh, I almost forgot."

Five minutes later, Jacob returned from his car holding a long package, a pair of cricket pads, cricket gloves and a newish looking black cycle helmet. "It's for the battle." He solemnly handed the package to Simon and said, "I present to thee essential smiting equipment."

"Thanks. I played a bit in my time for the village team," said Simon, removing the bedsheet to examine a cricket bat. "This looks like it was used by Noah in his pre-Ark days. Where did you get it from?"

"It was my great-grandfather's."

"It's a bit old," said Simon, whooshing the bat through a couple of practice strokes.

"They don't make them like this anymore," said Jacob.

"They certainly don't."

"That's why it's perfect for smiting, they won't expect it," said Jacob, handing Simon the pads, the gloves and the cycle helmet. "I hope this one's more use than your last one."

"Thanks. I'll see what smiting I can do with this when the time comes." Simon laughed and made a couple more swings. "I think I can do some serious damage with this."

"And the rest of the stuff is to help when a fireball gets hurled your way."

Simon strapped on the pads and put the helmet and gloves on. He couldn't help thinking that the logical way to avoid fireballs was speed and this would only slow him down.

"You better take the yoyo as well," said Jacob, rubbing his beard. "Just to be on the safe side. In my experience, nuns know things."

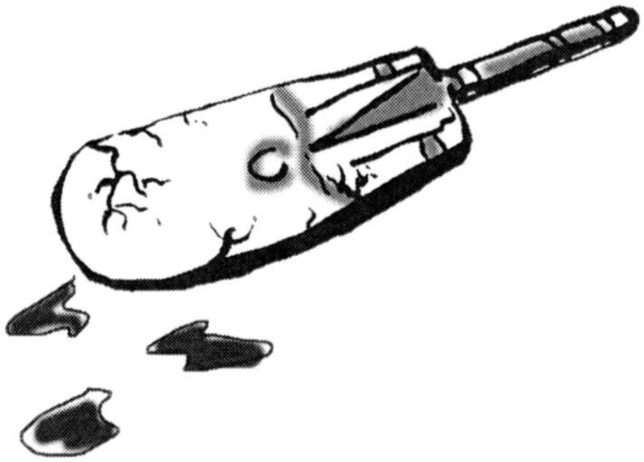

Chapter Sixteen

"Master, I am afraid that I have some bad news for you with regards to Geoffrey." – Mr Sox

Barry Court, Withington, Manchester

And just like that Geoff's composure wilted. He looked at the barricaded door. What had made perfect sense two hours ago was now looking decidedly shaky. Instead of keeping all the crazy people out, it was keeping him in with a person who believed she was the Devil. He made and then hurriedly broke eye contact with the white-haired woman.

"Use your words Geoffrey," she said.

He snapped. "Of course you're the Devil. Sorry, the lack of horns and cloven hooves threw me, can I ask where your pitchfork is?"

The woman smiled, slowly carving the air in front of her with delicate, precise strokes of the knife[25].

Mr Sox backed away slowly, his back arched.

---

[25] While there are many competing theories concerning the origin of the paring knife, it's actual genesis occurred in Ancient Egypt in 2001 B.C. It was the dawn of the summer equinox and Brexit Bistoph, the Chief Priest of Anubis (the jackal headed God of the Dead and no friend of cats or their own God Bast) decided he'd had enough of his neighbour's cat Mr Tiddles dirtying his floor. Picking up a misshapen knife he proceeded to ritually castrate Mr Tiddles. More recently, worshippers of Anubis have secretly infiltrated the makers of knife sets to add the paring knife in the hope that it will re-ignite widespread worship of Anubis through collective consciousness and the subsequent butchering of a great number of cats. This is why the paring knife seems completely useless unless you see a cat when holding one. Then, some strange instinct resonates through your consciousness and you suddenly know exactly what you need to do. "Here, kitty kitty. All praise Anubis!" More information on worshipping Anubis can be found at the C.C.C. website CatsConspiracyCabal.com.

Geoff shook his head. While he was asleep, all the knives and his baseball bat had been moved away from him. Naked and unarmed his madness ebbed away. "Did I bring you here?" he asked.

"No, I came alone."

"So how did you get into the flat?"

"I am the Devil Geoffrey, so I know a bit about breaking and entering," smiled the woman.

"How do you know my name?"

"I named you."

"You're crazy," he said, "and how did you get into my room?"

"I flew."

"Really?" Geoff frowned. "You're that girl from the pub."

"Yes," said the, woman making speech marks with her fingers. "I'm that girl from the pub. FYI, the right word for you to use is *woman*, though I'll let that go this time as you seem to be missing the bigger picture."

"What happened? Did you drug me?"

"Don't be stupid. You were very drunk," the woman replied, placing her hands back on her hips, "and The Wild Geese performed a Satanic ritual to help loosen things up."

"Rubbish. I met them before the concert and they were really nice."

"I'll have you know that many of my worshippers are decent, Devil fearing human beings. The ritual they performed is a groovy soul search, which affects people in different ways. For most, it gives the illusion of transforming them into the daemon they wished they were for a short time, but for a select few they have an out of body experience. Does that sound familiar?"

"How could you know that?"

"I was there," replied the woman.

"You said something to me. What was it?" asked Geoff.

"*Te es meus creatura. Ego Dominus Deus vester. Ego vere tui similis chorum*. I thought I was quite clear."

Those words came tumbling back. Geoff finally mumbled, "This is so fucked up. What do they mean?"

The woman sighed. "You are my creation. I am the Lord your God and I really like your dancing. Please tell me you know Latin?"

"No, and that's just bullshit."

"Please try to concentrate on the take-home message, Geoffrey." The woman waited a good ten seconds before continuing, "I am the Devil."

"What I'm concentrating on is that there is a mental woman who says she's the Devil who threatened to cut my balls off standing in my bedroom."

"I was only kidding about castrating you, it was just a bit of fun." The woman placed the knife on the floor. "See, the nasty mean knife has gone away. Now you can stop being a pathetic pussy and we can get down to business."

"Back off and let me put some clothes on. Then you can go on your nutty merry way or I'm phoning the police," said Geoff.

The woman handed over his mobile and said, "It won't work."

Geoff keyed 999 and, like before, it was engaged. "That proves nothing."

The woman frowned, "I don't understand."

Geoff hurriedly dressed, checking the intruder with wary eyes.

"I don't have the knife and you are sort of dressed so it's time for you to be more reasonable," she said.

"Reasonable!" snorted Geoff, pulling the chest of drawers from the door. "Once we get out of this room you're leaving."

"You didn't actually think that would stop me, did you?"

"This was not for you. It was to stop the other crazies that have been chasing me," said Geoff, poking his head through his faded blue T-shirt. Removing the final piece of furniture, he stomped off to the lounge and sat on the brown sofa. The woman followed him, holding the baseball bat, the chef's knife and once again the paring knife.

"You're Welsh," stated Geoff, rubbing his face and looking at Mr Sox.

"Well spotted. My present incarnation is female and Welsh and yes, you did see me at the pub and yes, we had a moment. Happy? I'm so pleased for you, but none of this is important."

"Okay, if you're the Devil make me fly."

"I can't. I'm not even supposed to be here and any use of my powers will piss God off."

"That's pretty convenient. I thought that pissing God off was your day job?"

"We have an agreement that prevents me from using my powers," replied the woman.

"What? You can't make me fly?"

The woman cleared her throat. "I could but I won't. Making you fly, making me fly, turning people to stone, old-style raising heaven – in fact, any show of supernatural strength is prohibited under the agreement. And the penalties for noncompliance are extreme and immediate. It works for both sides."

"Why did you say raising heaven?" asked Geoff.

"It's just a Hell thing," she replied.

"Right…but you said you flew here?"

"That was a lie."

"I knew it," exclaimed Geoff. "This is all bullshit. You're not the Devil."

"Heavens bells! What part of me being the Devil don't you get? Of course I'm going to lie. It's the first line of my contract of employment," said the woman, stroking a purring Mr Sox.

"Really?"

"No, you moron. That's another lie." The woman shook her head. "I stole your keys at the bar and hid under the bed. But none of this changes that I am still the fucking Devil!"

"But Rob gave me back my keys outside."

"No, I had them, see?" said the woman pulling a set of keys out of her jacket pocket and dangling them in front of her. "He must have given you his. If I do use my powers, it will alert God that I am here and that would not be a good thing for either of us. Take it from me, God's wrath can be pretty vicious if you're on the receiving end of it."

"I don't believe you. You're just a mad woman who's broken into my flat," Geoff said, picking up his phone.

"We haven't got time for this, let's take a break. Do you want a cup of tea?" the woman asked.

Geoff nodded, his eyes switching towards the baseball bat.

"Don't even think of using that."

Geoff's eyes swivelled to the knives.

"Or those. Think about this logically. Behind door A: If I am the Devil, do you think that you, with a baseball bat and a couple of knives would stand a chance against me? Or behind door B: I am lying, and you brought me home and threatened me with physical violence? What would the police make of that? Especially if I told them of your drinking and hallucinations. Which means your current end game is either: you lose and burn in Hell; or you lose and rot in prison." The woman raised her eyebrows and Mr Sox sauntered after her into the kitchen.

“Do you wish to say something?” asked the woman coldly as she closed the door.

“What a gloriously happy day, master. A truly joyous time indeed. This is such a great honour. Am I correct in assuming that the day of reckoning is near?” Mr Sox spoke in a delicate, feline manner.

“That is something I’m here to find out, Kerberos, my favourite Hell Hound.”

“I am so honoured to serve you, master, in any way I can.”

“You do look skinny,” said the woman, stroking Mr Sox. “I wish you’d chosen to be a dog, you know how much I dislike cats.”

“Well, master I can only agree with your infinite wisdom. I was terribly mistaken to believe that being a cat would allow me greater freedom to protect Geoffrey. Indeed, one of the dreadful drawbacks to being a cat is that, try as I may, I’ve not been able to develop the bulky lean muscle mass I was hoping for. I didn’t expect this but my puny bones just can’t take the weight of real muscle. Can you believe that on occasion I have had to run away from dogs? Small, pathetic dogs – and the cats are even worse,” cried Mr Sox. “I declare by all things unholy that when I return to my true form, Mister Bobbins, Jasper and of course that vixen Gracie will feel the full force of my vengeful wrath.”

"Poor you. But, more importantly, what has happened to Geoffrey?" asked the woman, stroking Mr Sox's splash of white chest fur. "He isn't exactly what I was expecting."

"I can assure you that nothing untoward has happened to my charge, master. I gave you my word that I would never allow anyone to harm him and as you well know, my word is my bond."

"Physically that may be true, but spiritually and concerning his personal growth, I feel that some opportunities must have been missed," she said.

"I can only wholeheartedly agree with you, master, but my understanding was that would be Azothoth's area of responsibility. My remit was physical protection, and one which I have dutifully fulfilled. May I point out that Geoffrey is thirty-three years old. Surely that shows my devotion and honour to you, master? Much as it pains me to say this, if you truly believe that anyone has failed you, I would sadly suggest that you ask Azothoth what he has brought to the cause," said Mr Sox, rubbing his body across the woman's legs. "As you are here master, which is so terribly wonderful and joyous as the end of days are undoubtedly close at hand, can I have your permission to speak openly?"

"Of course you can Kerberos. I have always valued your counsel."

"Master, I am afraid that I have some bad news for you with regard to Geoffrey." Mr Sox frowned, as he considered his position. "I'm terribly sorry and I don't know how to say this without offending you."

"Go on."

"The truth is that I am not entirely convinced that Geoffrey is a suitable candidate for what you have planned."

"Oh, that would be so disappointing, especially for you and for Azothoth," she said.

Mr Sox looked up, his eyes gleaming like little scimitars. He shivered, though not from the cold.

In the lounge Geoff scanned the room for other weapons, which made him feel like a ninja. A ninja biding his time, assessing the situation and getting ready to strike at exactly the right moment. He smirked, just like a ninja would.

"You are not a fucking ninja Geoffrey," said the woman, placing two steaming mugs on the table.

"Hey, my thoughts are private."

"Do you believe me now?" She looked Geoff up and down. "Thought not. I was hoping that this would be a good way of getting your attention and explaining what things need to happen but I was wrong. Everything was straightforward from the Garden of Eden to the Middle Ages when people really believed. And now how many people would happily get themselves burned, crucified, drawn and quartered, for their religious beliefs? People have lost their way."

"You mean Christians?" asked Geoff.

"No, I do not mean just Christians," snapped the woman, her mouth pinching up. "A great number of my followers suffered horrific deaths at the hands of the Catholic Church during the Inquisition. Did they complain? Did they say this is a bit hard? Or that it hurt a little? No. They took what was coming knowing that I would reward them in the afterlife."

"In Hell? How can that be a happy afterlife?"

"I agree it isn't that great for the souls God doesn't want and sends to me but for my true believers Hell is the Promised Land."

"Your delusion is really dark," said Geoff, sipping his tea.

Thud!

Crash!

"Geoff, the door's broken," shouted Rob. "Help!"

A further series of *thuds* and *bangs* echoed around the flat.

"Do you think I should move the lounger?" asked Geoff.

They both looked down the hallway at Rob's bedroom door. The handle twitched violently again.

"I can hear you! Who are you speaking to?" cried Rob.

The top of the chair crushed into the opposite wall and stuck firm.

The woman got up. "I'll make him a cup of tea. I think he's going to need it. By the way, it wouldn't hurt to get some decent biscuits in for guests."

There was a guttural roar and the upper half of the door exploded outwards in a storm of splinters, closely followed by Rob. "Why is my chair blocking the door? Let me out."

"Long story," replied Geoff, heaving Rob over the chair.

"Did I do it?" asked Rob.

"How could you barricade yourself in?"

"Did you do it?" accused Rob.

Geoff grinned.

"Oh right. Paranoia getting to you again? Scared I was a monster?" said Rob, making a monster face with jazz hands. "That was a crazy night. Where's the rest of my pizza?"

"In the kitchen."

Rob looked at the crumpled wall. "That's the last we'll see of our deposit."

"I know but I really need to tell you something," said Geoff.

"Let me get my pizza and then you can tell me all your freaky problems."

Geoff sat back down and smiled at the woman sitting opposite him.

"Really uncool dude. Really, fucking uncool. Who were you talking to? Sounded like a chick. Are Ruby and Sophia here?" asked Rob as he reappeared, pizza box in hand. His gaze settled on the pretty young woman balancing a knife on the tip of her forefinger. The Devil smiled.

"Aaarrgghhhh!" Rob's cry came straight from his bowels. He shifted his considerable weight between his feet and looked down the hallway. "Hi, boss. How's it going? Er…do you want the last piece of my pizza?"

"Don't you dare *boss* me!"

The woman flicked the knife up, grabbed the blade and threw it. Instinctively Rob pulled his pizza box up.

Thud. The blunt knife punctured a good two inches through the base of the pizza box.

"Wow," said Geoff.

Rob looked at the knife tip. "That was really dangerous, boss. You could have taken my eye out."

"Azothoth!" The woman jumped to her feet. "What the heaven have you been doing for the last thirty years? This," pointing at Geoff but glaring at Rob, "is completely unacceptable."

"I am here, you know?" said Geoff.

"In my defence I didn't have much to work with. I mean just look at him," said Rob. "I thought he'd be a pure thoroughbred, somebody I could carefully polish and be proud of. Maybe he should have gone through the programme to start off with. Kerberos agrees with me on this."

Mr Sox meowed loudly.

"But that was a key part of the plan, keep him a blank canvas to avoid God's attention. After all these years I expected to find a Monet or at least a Bosch, but what you've given me is this finger painting by a monkey."

"That hurts," said Geoff.

"Sorry, dude."

"Is this the opportunity that Ruby told me about?" asked Geoff.

Rob and the woman nodded.

"Geoffrey, what if I told you that the entities in this room represent the greatest concentration of pure evil this world has ever known?" asked the woman as she stood up.

Geoff scrunched his eyes and squinted at Rob who gave him an encouraging smile and then at Mr Sox curled up on a pair of grey sweatpants and finally to the woman. "Really? This is the best that pure evil can come up with?" he asked.

"Surely you must see the quiddity of evil before you," said the woman, spreading her arms.

"The what?" asked Geoff.

"Is it quiddity, or the concept of evil that's troubling you?" asked the woman.

"Both. It's far too early for made up words and talk of pure evil. Please just go and leave me be. Back me up on this Rob, she threw a knife at you."

Rob shrugged his shoulders. "She can do much worse."

"Geoffrey, quiddity is not a made-up word. It means the essential nature of something. I forget you're not educated to the standard I'd normally expect," said the woman, pinching her lips and flashing a look at Rob.

"Are you calling me stupid?" snapped Geoff. "Unbelievable."

"That's not what I meant. A person's vocabulary is a reflection of their education, rather than their intelligence. But we digress, do you really not see the raw power of wonderful evil that surrounds you?" She stretched her right palm towards Rob. "I present to you, Grand Duke Azothoth. The most powerful of all my Dukes of Hell. Captain of the Seventh Legion of the Damned and sometime wielder of the infamous Widow Maker. The Smiter of the Pure of Hearts and the Chief Nightmare Master for the under twelves of the Western world. Twice winner of the Hells Hammer Award for Unspeakable Evil for his pivotal role in the massacring of over four million defenceless souls in Eastern Siberia during Stalin's rule and his visionary establishment of the Cambodian killing fields during Pol Pot's rule with the Khmer Rouge. And for the last thirty-three years your mentor in all things evil."

Rob stood there in the corner, his flabby chest puffed out clutching the last slice of pizza. A broad grin spread across his face.

The woman then stretched out her left palm towards the newly awoken Mr Sox. "I give you Kerberos. The mightiest of all my Devilish Hounds of Hell. Scourge of the innocents. Torturer of the weak. Winner of the Best in Breed for the last two hundred and thirty-seven years. And for the last thirteen years your loyal protector."

Mr Sox raised his head and carefully licked his left paw before giving a deep yawn and stretching out on the slightly moist, fleecy material.

"And then there is me. Over the years mortals have given me many names: the Devil; Satan; Mephistopheles; Beelzebub; the Horned One; or, if you prefer my official job title, the Ravisher of Souls. Do you not see this?"

Geoff looked at her. She was very pretty. "Yes, if you say so," he replied.

"Finally some progress," she said.

"What should I call you? All of those names are cool but they'd draw attention to you."

"Mephistopheles is my favourite, but no one uses it now. I guess I miss tradition." The woman gave him a weak smile and added in a wistful way that made Geoff think of waves clawing at a rugged coastline, "Sooner or later everything changes."

A dozen seconds later, she spoke, "Call me Natasha."

"Why Natasha?" asked Geoff.

"Why not?" she countered.

"It's not really Welsh or evil. What about Cerys or Bronwyn?"

"Who wants to be a stereotype?" Natasha's lips curled into a warm smile. "And it suits me."

"I still don't understand," said Geoff. "If you're telling me the truth, and I don't believe for one minute you are, why are you all here?"

"Let's take this slowly," Natasha smiled. "Rob is Azothoth, a Duke of Hell. Have you got that?"

Geoff nodded. Playing along seemed to be his only sane option.

"Mr Sox is Kerberos, a mighty Hound of Hell. Are you certain that you have that?"

Geoff nodded again.

"Now this is the most important part. I am the Devil."

Geoff cleared his throat, but decided it was better not to speak and nodded.

"The people of the world are gathering like lambs for the slaughter. We are all here for you. Now is the time to grasp your destiny, which makes you?" asked Natasha.

Geoff thought long and hard before replying. "Really unlucky with his choice of flatmate, pet and girl he meets at a bar?"

"No," cried Natasha, cradling her head in her hands. "Given the urgency of the situation your humour is severely misplaced."

"I wasn't trying to be funny," protested Geoff.

"I realise this is all a bit new to you so I'll just say it straight. You are worth more than this. You can have a wondrous future ahead of you," said Natasha, interlocking her fingers in front of her chest.

"You sound like Ruby," said Geoff.

"But this will only happen if you fulfil your fate," she said.

Geoff looked around the flat. "Okay, if you say so."

"Geoffrey, you can be the ruler of the world."

"Steady on, let's not get too carried away."

Natasha paused and stared at him. "Geoffrey, you are my Anti-Christ."

Chapter Seventeen

"You're scaring me." – Geoff

Barry Court, Withington, Manchester

It took a couple more minutes before Geoff could find any words. Eventually he looked up at Natasha and spoke slowly, "You are fucking mad if you want me to play Anti-Christ in your made-up cosplay world. Get out of my flat now."

"We both know that I'm not going to leave your flat." Natasha's gaze was unflinching. "A great deal of time and effort has already been used to get us to this point and, as I'm sure you can understand, my time and effort are both incredibly valuable."

"No I don't understand any of this. You know you're not really the Devil and I'm certain that I'm not the Anti-Christ, so what do you want from me?" asked Geoff.

"Turn on the TV," Natasha ordered.

Geoff picked up the remote and started flicking through the channels.

"What about the prophecy boss?" whispered Rob.

"I don't know. Things have changed so much," replied Natasha, glancing at Geoff. "It's pretty fucking obvious that I didn't want you to watch cartoons!"

"Sorry," he said.

Natasha turned back to Rob. "We've both made mistakes." She shot another glance at Geoff. "Heavens bells, put the BBC News Channel on."

"Boss, can I ask you something?" asked Rob.

Natasha nodded.

"I was wondering if I could change my name." he paused, "to Rob."

"You want to be called Rob the Duke of Hell? Absolutely not. What is up with Azothoth, the name I gave you?" asked Natasha.

"It's not very modern, is it?" asked Rob.

"Modern!" she exploded. "We are all about traditional. Just so we're clear, that is a no, an unholy church no!"

They both turned to the TV. "Breaking news. We are getting reports of unplanned gatherings across the world. People are, for some as yet unexplained reason, being drawn to religious sites. In the UK, the emergency services have been overrun by calls and the COBRA committee is currently in session. Government sources have advised people to stay at home," said the newsreader.

"Do you see what's happening?" Natasha interrupted.

"It's the zombies, isn't it?" replied Geoff.

"No. I can assure you that this has nothing to do with zombies," said Natasha. "This is happening all over the world. People from all faiths are flocking to their religious sites seeking shelter."

The newsreader continued, "It appears that something quite extraordinary has shaken the world's shared consciousness. Cathedrals, synagogues, mosques, temples, and even football grounds have become sites for gatherings of hundreds of thousands of people."

Natasha looked at Geoff's confusion. "Turn it off, Geoffrey. The huddled masses are crowding together before the approaching storm. We are that storm. Sit down and be very fucking quiet," said Natasha, pacing around the lounge before turning her violent attention back to Rob. "Let me get this straight, Azothoth. You are telling me that this pathetic excuse is not your fault, and is not Kerberos' fault, but is actually my fault?"

"No boss. It's just that he has never shown any talent for the game," replied Rob, holding his palms up.

"Which is exactly why I wanted you to mentor him. What special skills have you imparted? What world class fighting abilities has he gained from years of your tutelage? Martial arts? Archery? Boxing? Fencing? Tell me what distinguishes him from the herd of dancing monkeys?" asked Natasha, somehow using her five feet and three inches to loom over Rob.

"We tried judo but he got thrown about a lot by women. It was undignified. And there was no one here that did fencing," replied Rob.

"I would have loved to learn fencing," blurted out Geoff.

Natasha flashed Geoff a look of burning contempt before growling back at Rob. "What about his mental growth? Surely he has an unprecedented understanding of history, philosophy, sciences, business, politics or even religion?"

"Like I said, he has no real talents," replied Rob, who was running out of space to retreat into. "That's why we ended up at the call centre. No one else would take him."

"Azothoth," said Natasha, in a measured reassuring tone that Rob found terrifying. "You must at least have given him a decent grounding in the Black Arts?"

Geoff looked at Rob whose face had gone a deep scarlet colour.

"When was your last specifically evil act with Geoffrey?" she asked.

"I tried to keep up to date with the local Satanic network and get him in as a member," replied Rob.

Geoff spluttered his tea over a surprised and angry Mr Sox, who had been watching this with feline fascination. Rob was not really an atheist.

"And how has that been going? You don't pray, you don't write and most importantly, you don't sacrifice? What am I to think?" asked Natasha.

"I did sacrifice once," said Rob, his arms outstretched.

"Really? And I suppose that makes up for all these years of silence?" Natasha asked.

"I was the Treasurer of the local coven. The guided tour of Boleskin, good old Ally Crowley's house was a real success but then they found that I was helping myself to coven funds and forced me to resign."

"And what did they think about him?" asked Natasha, casting her glare at Geoff.

"They didn't think he was their sort and I couldn't explain who he really was without blowing our cover," explained Rob.

"Are you talking about your amateur dramatics club?" asked Geoff. "Those weirdos dressing up in masks and robes?"

Rob nodded.

"Wasn't Miss Perkins a member?"

Rob nodded again.

"Azothoth, I feel it's important to get this right. You are telling me that you couldn't even get the fucking Anti-Christ into the bloody local Satanic coven? I asked you to make him into a lean, mean, evil machine and what do you give me after thirty-three years? Him!" Natasha turned on her heels and sat down on the corner of the sofa. "You could have at least home schooled him."

"Rob, let's kick her out and go back to bed," said Geoff.

Natasha's eyebrows arched sharply into a triangle.

"That would be a very bad idea," said Rob.

"Why?"

"Because she really is the Devil."

"Why does she keep calling you Azothoth?" asked Geoff.

"Because that's my real name. You saw a glimpse of me at the pub, but I didn't understand what was happening because I was too drunk. Remember this?" asked Rob, pulling the gold money clip from his sweatpants. "This was a gift from him, sorry, her. I'm Azothoth and she's Mephistopheles. I'm a Duke of Hell and that's what the DOH stands for on this clip."

"Rubbish. The stuff at the pub was just the booze and stress getting to me. I've known you since you were three-years-old and you're definitely not a Duke of Hell," said Geoff. "You're Rob and you bought that at a pawn shop at Saint Anne's."

"I lied."

Natasha stood up and raised her arms high as if she was being crucified. "The Dragon as prophesied in the *Book of Revelations* has arrived," she said.

"What do you mean, the Dragon?" asked Geoff. He turned to Rob. "See what I mean? She's as mad as a box of frogs."

Rob stepped in. "It's in the *Book of Revelations*. The Devil is the Dragon who brings about the end of the world and that is now Natasha."

"Like a zombie apocalypse?" asked Geoff.

Natasha answered sharply, "No fucking zombies. I can guarantee you that there will be no zombies in this apocalypse. Read your Bible."

"What about the people outside? Are you saying Miss Perkins is a Satanist?" asked Geoff.

"Amazing," said Natasha, shaking her head and smiling, "you've actually got something right."

Mr Sox stretched and purred. He felt conflicted by almost everything that had happened since waking up. He had spent thousands of years hunting damned souls that had the misfortune to cross his path, but now he was happy with more simple pleasures to be had from a generously filled saucer of milk and a warm place to sleep. In truth he hardly ever missed the look of desperation in his quarry's eyes, or the metallic taste of blood as he gnawed into their flesh. Mr Sox thoroughly preferred being a cat.

Of course, if Mr Sox was sent back to Hell, he would have to accept that a five-kilogram cat would fail to meet even the most basic job requirements of a

Hell Hound, that of striking unholy fear in humans and ravaging mortal souls. That was why he had a plan. Through television he had witnessed the fearsome brutality of lions and tigers and by adding more prominent fangs he felt sure that the 'Hounds of Hell' could be smoothly rebranded into the 'Sabre Tooth Tigers of Hell'. But for now, he couldn't see how loving strokes of his fur and access to food that didn't require him killing something was going to be high on the list of priorities of anyone in this impending apocalypse. Things were going to change and certainly not for his benefit. He looked down the hall and caught a glimpse of the cat flap behind the lounger. Mrs Hotchkiss, who lived next door, fed him mashed up cans of salmon and told him that he was, "the cutest thing in the world," was a clear relocation option.

"I intend to win my war with God this time," said Natasha, her features dark and sharp.

Mr Sox gave a soulful meow. He wondered whether the master knew that he had prayed to Gertrude of Nivelles, the patron saint of cats yesterday for aid against Gracie? It had been her feast day after all.

"Why should I believe any of what you are telling me?" replied Geoff.

"Because you're the Anti-Christ, dude," chirped in Rob.

"Then why don't I feel the slightest bit evil and why can't you prove any of this? Just telling me stuff doesn't make it real," said Geoff.

Natasha sighed. "We wiped your mind at birth and had you adopted by normal people. We cannot show our true selves because God will find us and bomb your flat back to the Old Testament before you can take another sip of tea."

"How come God doesn't already know you're here?" asked Geoff.

"Turns out that North Korean hackers are pretty evil and really good at their job. They overloaded Heaven's tracking system and tricked them into believing that I'm still in Hell."

"But going back to the bombing why can't you use your powers to stop that?" asked Geoff.

"Like I told you, we have an agreement with God that is literally carved in stone[26]," she replied.

---

[26] God has got pretty obsessive about the whole carved in stone thing. He now only uses elongated A4 size tablets which correspond with the Golden Ration (width x 1.618 = height). His tablet of choice is the light grey matt granite tablets from the Top Tartan Quarry in Scotland engraved in 'Times New Roman' font, size 22. It has proved itself to

"That's another lie, isn't it?" grinned Geoff.

"No, that's true. All agreements with God are carved in stone," explained Natasha. "But what's important is that with us contained in these mortal vessels the good people of Manchester will be waking up from restless sleep and be drawn to us. We have broken their pathetic status quo. Pure evil now walks amongst God's little lambs and like all lambs they will flock together waiting for their slaughter. Geoffrey, you can help me do all the butchering."

Geoff laughed. "I've always fancied a bit of butchering with my slaughtering."

"Now is not the time for humour," said Natasha.

"This all just seems like an elaborate hoax," said Geoff, looking at Rob. "This is the reason we stopped doing whisky chasers, Jaeger Monsters and voddybulls. Weird shit always happens when we do."

"But you really are the big AC," replied Rob.

"Don't be stupid."

Natasha sighed and placed her head in her hands.

"I've got an idea," ventured Rob. "Can we talk in private?" At this both Natasha and Geoff looked up expectantly.

"Sorry, I'm talking to the boss," said Rob, making guns out of his fingers and aiming them at Geoff's bedroom door.

"I'll make a brew while you talk about all things evil," announced Geoff. "Would my friendly neighbourhood Hell Hound like a saucer of milk?"

Mr Sox meowed. He reflected that his earlier misgivings could well be unfounded. Given Geoff's reluctance to accept any of this, there was a small chance that life would continue as before, albeit with some minor changes. Maybe the Devil would live with them, which would be really nice and very bad news for Gracie and her cronies.

Once in the bedroom Natasha closed the door. "Azothoth, I was in the middle of something, or didn't you notice? This needs to be very good."

"I think we should perform an intervention with Geoff," Rob said.

---

be far superior to the old sandstone stuff. To say that God was a bit miffed when the original Commandments disintegrated into dust is a bit of an understatement.

“A what?” Natasha asked, giving every indication that this idea did not come close to what she considered to be very good.

“An intervention. It’s when someone doesn’t realise the problems they’re causing and a group of people who love them gather in secret and confront them with a personal list of how they’ve let them down. This helps the person understand what they’ve done wrong and motivates them to change their ways and do much better in the future. What do you think?”

“Tell me more.” Natasha’s blue eyes narrowed.

Five minutes later, Rob and Natasha reappeared just as Geoff placed mugs of steaming hot tea on the table.

Natasha walked to the window and gazed out. Thick, seemingly immovable clouds of gun metal hung in the sky. In five hours, a new day would be stretching itself into place. All over the city people would be waking up; stumbling out of bed; showering; dressing; putting makeup on; leaving for work; and all the time being very, very scared. Sooner or later they would realise that this was not a fear they could understand. It was a gnawing, clawing primitive fear that people just could not put their finger on. In fact, they didn’t actually want to put their finger on it, or even their worst enemy’s finger. Something scary was walking amongst them and it needed to be pushed back into the darkness with a very long and pointy stick. Overnight the flimsy fabric of civilisation had been stretched over sharpened claws, hooves and horns. Her lips curled into a smile.

Geoff sipped his tea. He was confused and tired but felt that everything was going to turn out for the best. He idly stroked his index finger from the crown of Mr Sox’s head, along his back and all the way to the tip of his tail.

Mr Sox’s tail swished. He understood the importance of appreciating the smaller things in life, rather than worrying about the bigger picture, however worrying that might be.

Natasha turned from the window and gave a short nod at Rob who was facing Geoff.

“Dude we are going to perform an intervention,” said Rob.

“A what?” asked Geoff.

“An intervention. We are going to explain how much we love you and what you need to do to make things better. Do you want to start boss?”

Natasha stood there, hands on hips, gathering her thoughts. Finally, she smiled and spoke, “Geoffrey, I am the Devil and you are the Anti-Christ, so obviously I care about you. However, unless you get your shit together right now

I will torture your soul for eternity in the deepest layers of Hell." Her voice became deeper, her words dripping with malice as her blue eyes changed to an angry blood red colour.

Geoff's face went as pale as a white lily. He looked around the flat – everywhere was painted in fresh red paint.

Natasha continued, her voice rising ever so slightly with each passing word. "Hell Spiders the size of watermelons will suck your eyeballs out of their sockets. You will be castrated every hour with that blunt paring knife of yours by very mean, short-sighted orangutans. Daemons will feast on your burnt flesh, maggots will eat your insides and unpleasant and very bad things will happen to you each and every second of each and every day for the whole of eternity. I swear by all things unholy that I will make all of this come to pass if you continue to piss me off."

With two shaking hands Geoff took another sip of his tea. "You're scaring me."

"Oh good. The scary stuff is what I do." Natasha's voice was back to being syrupy sweet, her features all perky.

Geoff looked around and shook his head. The flat looked normal.

Mr Sox sighed. He felt certain that no one heard him, or frankly cared that he'd just sighed. He eyed the door and wondered how many cans of salmon Mrs Hotchkiss had waiting just for him.

Natasha looked at Rob with bright blue eyes and smiled hopefully. "So how did I do?"

Chapter Eighteen

"Oh yeah, that shit really hurts." – Rob

Barry Court, Withington, Manchester

Rob hesitated before breaking into a wide grin. "What can I say? That was amazing boss, you're a natural at intervening. Didn't she do well Geoff?"

"No, she bloody didn't," Geoff said. "She scared the shit out of me, did you see those eyes?"

Rob beamed. "Isn't she just the best?"

Natasha sat back down and gazed at Geoff. "Now that we all know where we stand, I'll give you some background information that will help you better understand our situation. In Hell we developed something called the Standard Anti-Christ Really Excellent Development Programme that's generally known by its acronym SACRED."

"What do you mean?" asked Geoff, his voice returning to something like normal.

"SACRED does exactly what you would expect," she replied. "The Anti-Christ is born into a wealthy Western family and all manner of luxuries are bestowed upon him. To focus the family's attention we simplify things by disposing of any siblings. He then receives the finest education in the world to sharpen his mind and personal trainers develop his body to Olympic standards. In short, SACRED produces Anti-Christs that are at the very pinnacle of mental and physical development."

Geoff nodded enthusiastically. Being the Anti-Christ may not be as bad as he first thought.

Natasha continued, "Strangely, it doesn't seem to matter whether the chosen family are Satanists or Christians. However, what is vital is that they have an astonishingly high level of wealth, which allows the Anti-Christs to go through life knowing that they can buy or sell anything on this planet. A small army of fanatical bodyguards protects them and everyone wants to be their ally, friend or lover."

Geoff grinned at Rob.

"However, for you, we decided not to fully implement the SACRED programme," she added.

Geoff's grin dropped. "What do you mean, not fully implement? Which parts will I go through?"

"Actually," paused Natasha, "none of it."

"This isn't an admission of me believing what you're saying but exactly who decided that?"

"We all did," she replied, looking at a nodding Rob.

"Define all?" asked Geoff.

"Well, when I say all, I sort of mean me. I am the Devil and the thing is that we've tried SACRED many times before and it never ends well for you."

"Well for me?" asked Geoff. "Have I done this before?"

Natasha smiled. "No, not you. There have been other Anti-Christs and ultimately it hasn't ended well for them. Of course, at the start everything is wonderful. They are successful, powerful and delightfully evil. They are everything that I could ever want."

"You're telling me that even though I am the Anti-Christ, I'm not going to do any of the incredibly fun stuff that goes with it?" asked Geoff.

Natasha nodded.

"And you think this is good for me? I work at a crappy call centre and live in this dump, so if you really are the Devil and I really am the Anti-Christ, why would you ever do this to me?"

"Simple," Natasha shrugged. "Like I was saying, it's always great to start off with and then it all goes terribly wrong. God learns about your existence and gives someone a vision, or a dream about you. Then, fuelled by this epiphany, they track you down and kill you."

"What about the army of fanatical bodyguards?"

"They get bought off or tricked. God's people get you alone and then." Natasha slowly scraped her forefinger across the middle of her neck, "no more Anti-Christ."

"Don't you need special daggers to kill the Anti-Christ?" asked Geoff.

"No, that's just movie talk. Once you're in a mortal vessel you're just as vulnerable to physical harm as everyone else. Being the Anti-Christ doesn't give you any type of invulnerability, just ask Jesus," said Natasha, folding her arms across her chest. "Recently God has been using anything that ends up with you dying in excruciating agony. So instead of guns there has been a fair share of knives, swords, an ice axe and even a couple of drills. I think God is sending me a message."

"Drills?" exclaimed Geoff. "Fucking hell. God has me killed by holy drills?"

"No. It's only a couple of your predecessors who've met their end with drills and like I said, they were not holy drills, just very painful," said Natasha.

"But being killed by a drill has got to be bad?" said Geoff looking at Rob.

"Oh yeah, that shit really hurts," Rob shook his head and grinned. "There is so much fucking blood when the drills come out to play."

"For the record, I do not want to get killed by a drill," stated Geoff.

"Geoffrey, please forget about the drills and focus on what this means. You've heard of the *Book of Revelations*? Well, according to *Revelations* you are supposed to rise up and rule this world. Diseases, famine, violence. Typical apocalypse playbook stuff. A small amount of good souls get whisked off to Heaven with the Rapture but the rest of humanity has a very unpleasant time under your rule. Happy so far?" asked Natasha.

"But I don't think God wants me to rule, given the stuff with the drills?" interrupted Geoff, who was some distance from being happy with this. "By killing me all those prophecies don't have to take place."

"Exactly," agreed Natasha. "God doesn't want you to rule, which is why we came up with this plan. We get you, the Anti-Christ, to your thirty-third birthday and see what happens."

"See what happens?" snorted Geoff. "What sort of a plan is that? It sounds like the sort of plan that gets me fucked up by drills."

"But that hasn't happened so far, has it? That's progress in my book. I'm sorry you didn't go through SACRED, but you're thirty-three years old and still alive," said Natasha, her eyes wide and blue, her finger pointing at him. "This was all top secret but we did set up a number of daemons to help you achieve your potential without alerting God."

"You mean Rob?"

Natasha nodded.

"And a cat?"

"Technically a Hell Hound," she corrected. "Kerberos is really scary."

Geoff looked at Mr Sox blankly. "But in the body of a cat."

"Yes."

Mr Sox meowed and did his very best to look scary.

"You do know I've had a terrible time all these years?" said Geoff, his arms folded tight across his chest.

"You've still got your health and you can't put a price on that," said Rob.

"But I have absolutely nothing," said Geoff, reaching for his tea. It was empty.

"Technically, that's not true," said Natasha. "You've got my eyes,"

"What?" asked Geoff.

"My eyes," she repeated. "See?"

"You've got blue eyes like me, so what?"

"Geoffrey, all celestial beings have blue eyes and yours are the exact shade as mine. It was one of the things I was adamant about you keeping. Cool eh?"

"Let me get this right. I got none of the crazy wealth and power but I got your blue eyes? What's so important about blue eyes?"

"Blue is God's favourite colour. The sky, the sea and celestial beings eyes. I wanted you to have something of mine. Look at Rob's," Natasha suggested.

Geoff fixed his gaze back on Natasha. "You do know that loads of people have blue eyes?"

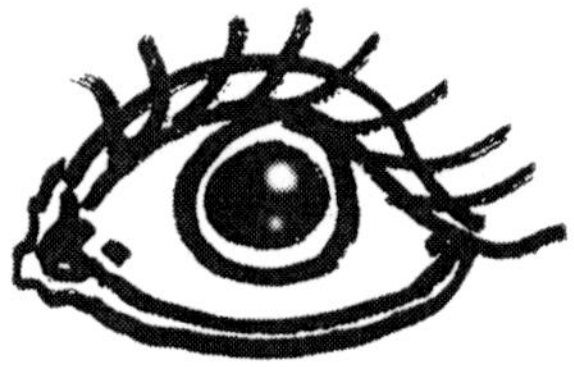

"Yes, but celestial beings *only* have blue eyes and only you in the whole wide world have exactly the same shade as mine. What other proof do you need?"

"It's true," nodded Rob.

"What about Mr Sox? Isn't he a celestial being?" asked Geoff.

"We got him fitted with contacts before he came down," said Natasha. "He's got the most wonderfully bright blue eyes. They sparkle like sapphires in sunlight."

Mr Sox purred his agreement and opened his eyes as wide as he could.

Geoff sighed and shook his head.

"So, to get back to my point, to keep you secret I couldn't have any contact with you," said Natasha, her voice softening. "But you have the soul of an Anti-Christ and how you've led your life so far is something that you need to take responsibility for. Look at it this way, your constant failures have kept you off God's radar which means you're the first Anti-Christ that has ever seen his thirty-third birthday. Isn't that something you can be proud of?"

"No," said Geoff flatly. "Why should I be happy living like this? It just makes me miserable."

Natasha smiled. "Well, it makes me proud."

"What happened to the others? Was it bad for them? You know, after they got killed?" asked Geoff.

"You mean once their souls were returned to me in Hell?"

Geoff nodded, his face breaking into a thin smile. The thought of all those smug Anti-Christs being punished for their failures comforted him. "I bet you gave them eternal damnation. The whole Hell Spiders the size of watermelons, maggots, freaky orangutans, daemons eating their flesh all the time because they failed you."

"They were all following the standard 444 Brimstone Protocol, a key part of SACRED," replied Natasha.

"Shouldn't that be 666?" asked Geoff.

"No," replied Natasha. "You shouldn't base everything you know on movies. It wouldn't hurt to read a book once in a while."

"Okay, so what happened to their souls?"

"As you can imagine we were all very disappointed. They had not been successful in making the apocalypse as foretold in the *Book of Revelations* a reality, but that wasn't their fault because God had tricked us. So once they came back to Hell I had them treated as heroes."

"You what?" spluttered Geoff. "Heroes?"

"Everyone already knew about them and how despicably evil their deeds had been. We'd have to celebrate their return, throw lavish banquets in their honour and give them a little slice of Hell to rule."

"But they failed you?"

"Geoffrey, we don't like to use the F word," replied Natasha.

"But you used it with me," said Geoff.

"That was different. The thing is, in Hell people need heroes and the previous Anti-Christs tick all the boxes. They're really good looking and extremely evil. You've got to understand that being the Devil is not an easy job. I've got lots of people I need to lead and keep happy," replied Natasha. "I only gave them a very small part of Hell."

“What’s going to happen to my soul when a crazed monk armed with a blessed chainsaw dismembers me?”

“I didn’t say anything about chainsaws,” snapped Natasha. “No one has ever used chainsaws. Why would you say that?”

“I don’t know, it just popped into my mind. But what happens if they kill me?” pressed Geoff.

Natasha bit her bottom lip. “Hmm.”

“What the hell does hmm mean?”

“Do you mean if you died right now?” she clarified.

“Yes, if I died right this second, no more Geoff.”

Natasha coughed and looked away. “That is one of the practical problems of you not following SACRED. My subjects don’t know about your existence so it’d be a bit tricky lavishing rewards on you when you return to Hell.”

“What does that mean?” asked Geoff, who carried on before Natasha could reply. “I guess I’ll have to enrol in the Hell part of this Anti-Christ Programme of yours. I’ll be like a mature student. Then you can pop me back on Earth with loads of money and the right backup so we can start again.”

“Sorry,” said Natasha, “I’m afraid that wouldn’t work. SACRED produces Anti-Christs who are refined, educated and charismatic. They have vast amounts of wealth and taste and that, I’m afraid, takes decades of work and effort.”

“Why can’t I do that? Rob, back me up on this.”

“Sorry dude, I’ve got to agree with the boss. That’s why she’s the boss.”

“Geoffrey, I’ve actually given your future a great deal of thought and this is what I’ve decided. I’m certain you’ll be very happy,” smiled Natasha. “If you die before doing anything noteworthy evil, I will arrange for you to join one of our Prayer Answer Teams, or PAT for short.”

“That doesn’t sound so bad, but hasn’t God got the monopoly on prayers?”

“Not at all. Prayers can be for good or evil. Granted, God has a higher volume but we do okay,” she replied.

“Great. But what is a Prayer Answer Team? Do I make prayers come true by doing evil stuff? Build up my reputation as an Anti-Christ?” said Geoff, sharing a grin with Rob.

“Not exactly.” Natasha scrunched up her nose. “When people of a certain disposition.”

“You mean bad people?”

"No, I mean truly evil people. Bad isn't enough to get your prayers answered by me. When evil people pray to me it is important that I show them that they're not alone, so I answer a percentage of their requests. Our response rate is around four percent, but I'm happy for it to double on special occasions like Christmas Day, Halloween and especially on Valentine's Day. Your role would be to monitor the prayer, log it and then grade it according to the severity of what they are asking for and the evilness of the person praying. The bulk of this is automated, but it sometimes needs a personal touch to make those borderline decisions. If it is worthy of answering, you will pass the prayer up to your Team Leader who will take it from there."

"That sounds just like a call centre," said Geoff, his voice as flat as a frisbee.

Natasha smiled.

"So I'd be working at a bloody call centre in Hell?"

Natasha broke into a grin. "I totally knew you would love it," she said.

"But..."

"You're right, it would be similar to the work you've been doing here for the past seven years. Given what Rob has said about your very limited skill set and total lack of ambition, I'd say it's a perfect match. It comes with a free uniform designed by Alexander McQueen[27] and a full two days' holiday each year. As a side point the uniforms are great, all red and gold, and if you work really hard you may even get your own team."

"How quickly would that be?" asked Geoff.

"Let me see," said Natasha, working things out. "A couple of centuries or so. All things considered it's a great opportunity for someone like you."

"Like me?"

"You know, someone who needs to prove himself."

"A couple of centuries?" repeated Geoff.

"Obviously I can't guarantee that at present and it would only happen if you worked really hard," smiled Natasha.

"So how long is the working day?"

"Twenty-three and a half hours," she replied.

"How many days?"

---

[27] The direction of Mr McQueen's soul was a great and unexpected coup for the Devil. Despite his homosexuality, he would not have been going to Hell until his untimely demise by his own hand. However, this silver lining allowed a complete overhaul of almost all of Hell's uniforms with a consistent military red and gold design. As it worked out, even in death Mr McQueen made a great many people very happy.

“Seven days a week,” replied Natasha. “We don’t like to respect the Sabbath.”

“I’d get thirty minutes off each day and no weekends?”

“As you’d be a soul, sleeping and eating are entirely optional,” answered Natasha. “And this is much better than being tortured.”

Geoff looked at Rob whose bulk filled the rest of the sofa next to Natasha. Throughout her explanation Rob had done a mixture of approving nods and supportive smiles. He was now nodding and smiling at the same time with great gusto.

“And what about him?” asked Geoff, eyes narrowing as he pointed at Rob. “Will my trusted companion be joining me in this great opportunity?”

Rob broke Geoff’s gaze and looked down at Mr Sox.

Natasha sat back and brushed a hand over her hair. “The person you know as Rob is actually Azothoth, a highly decorated Duke of Hell. He is part of Hell’s aristocracy and has a truly remarkable record of performing indescribably evil acts over the centuries. His noble face is even on one of our dollar bills.”

“Rob is on your money?” asked Geoff slowly.

“The three-and-a-half dollar bill. Taking everything into consideration I don’t think it would be very fair for Azothoth to join you at an entry level position, do you?”

“Fair!” exploded Geoff. “You want to talk about things being fair? Explain to me why all these other Anti-Christs have a wonderful life on Earth, get themselves killed by God and then go back to an even better life in Hell, while I have this shitty life on Earth, get dismembered by a mad monk with a fucking chainsaw and then go back to an even shittier life in Hell? Explain to me the fairness of that?"

Natasha answered swiftly. "The alternative is that you grasp your destiny and make this apocalypse a reality. That way everyone's a winner – or I could torture you for all eternity."

"You don't say." Geoff slunk back into the comfort of the leather sofa. For some time, the only sound in the flat was the air exploding out of his flared nostrils. "I've got to achieve something you haven't been able to do for over two thousand years? Or I'm going to have to work at a call centre for eternity."

Natasha shrugged her shoulders.

"And why does he get to go back to his old life, what use has he been?"

"Hey, I've tried to keep you on the evil path," protested Rob, standing up and walking to the window. "And I'd still come and hang out. It'd be like the good old days."

"Exactly what good old days are we talking about? Are we talking about those great days when we ran out of money and cooked beans in the kettle because the gas was turned off? Or those wonderful days when we had to catch the bus because my car wouldn't start? You want to talk about those fucking glory days? I bet I'll have so many new stories about the fun I'm having in Hell on my two days' holiday." Geoff rolled his hands up and down his face. "Or you could always come for a chat on the hour I get off each day."

"Just so we're clear, you only get half an hour off each day and you can't have your two days' holiday together," Natasha corrected. "Why don't you calm down Geoffrey, and try to see the bigger picture.?"

"I am calm, just very pissed off that's all. So why are you here? It's not like you've come to give me any good news. What do you think, Mr Sox?" asked Geoff. The cat meowed, slinked up and ran the full length of his shiny black head and body over his legs. "My life and even my afterlife could hardly get much worse."

"You're forgetting about what could happen with the drills," said Rob from the window. "And the chainsaws."

"But putting the likelihood of your excruciatingly painful death to one side," said Natasha, glaring at Rob, "you have your destiny to claim – which is why I'm here."

"From what you're saying, that doesn't seem very likely," said Geoff.

"I have some additional information, which is the other reason I'm here," said Natasha, pulling out a number of loose pages from her jacket pocket. "This."

"Boss, I really think you want to see this right now," interrupted Rob, peering out at the window. Natasha broke off midsentence, repocketed the pages and joined him at the window.

Geoff also got up but decided not to go and look earnestly into the night. Instead, he would make the most of this break and brew another nice cup of tea. Just as he opened the kitchen door a number of things happened all at once.

The first was Natasha saying in a slow and serious voice, "Oh dear. This is very bad."

Chapter Nineteen

"Blood bath! Blood bath! Blood bath!" – The Good People of Manchester

Just Outside Barry Court, Withington, Manchester

Simon stood there rooted to the spot in his cricket gear and cycle helmet thinking that only the bat made any real sense. "Thanks. I really don't know what to say. These are great." Before he could say any more an astonishingly raucous roar surged out of the marquee.

"Do you think they've started without us?" asked Jacob, checking his watch. "It's only one-thirty so there should be at least another hour before we attack. I suppose they could have seen the Devil but surely someone would have told you?"

"I don't know what's happening but Mrs Thornthwistle's pretty successful at riling these lot up," replied Simon.

"I agree. If this goes the way I think it could, #TheFirstLadyofSmiting could be going viral in the next couple of hours," said Jacob, shaking his head. "I think that everyone wants something to happen right now that involves lots of violence and bloody smiting."

Wide-eyed, contorted faces streamed out of the marquee behind Mrs Thornthwistle, cursing and brandishing their weapons.

"Do you think that being on the side of good with a couple of angels to help them has changed them?" asked Jacob.

"How do you mean?" asked Simon.

"Well, this lot look like they've found the God-given right to smash anyone who stands in their way into little pieces. Does being good mean that you can do absolutely anything you want to? Because I think what they really want to do now is to attack those poor people standing outside Barry Court."

"Remember they are Satanists," said Simon.

“How sure are you about that?” asked Jacob. “They look like normal people to me.”

“Fair point. I should try to do something,” said Simon, “or people are going to get hurt.” He cleared his throat and shouted as best he could, “Hey guys. Why don’t we just calm down? We don’t actually know what’s happening over there.”

To Simon and Jacob’s mutual astonishment a few people stopped shouting. Within seconds this spread and the angry mob was transformed into a quiet and reflective one. A sea of faces turned to Simon, eager to find out what the angel was going to say next. His face creased into a smile. “That’s it guys. We don’t know who those other people are, so why don’t we wait and see what happens? I don’t think anyone has gone in, and no one seems to be trying to get out, so Mr Smith and I will go over in the morning and have a quiet word with this Rob and Geoff and find out if they know anything. That way people don’t have to get hurt. I know you want to see some action, but deep down you don’t want a blo…”

“Blood bath!” Mr Smith roared.

Everyone, including Simon, stopped and looked at him in the middle of the crowd. His face was a mask of pure hatred etched in the half-light of the moon.

“Blood bath. Blood bath. Blood bath!” Mr Smith began to chant slowly, the vein at his right temple throbbing furiously.

A small group of nuns joined him, their voices high pitched cries.

“Blood bath. Blood bath. Blood bath!”

A low rumble rippled amongst the crowd as more people joined and the chant speeded up. Soon they were all glaring and shouting at the flats.

“Blood bath! Blood bath! Blood bath! Blood bath!”

“I can smell their Satanic blood,” cried Mr Smith over the wall of noise, his arms raised, his massive fists balled tightly shut.

Simon looked through the trees at the two hundred and fifty or so yards to Barry Court and decided that Mr Smith couldn’t actually smell Rob and Geoff’s blood. However, he was willing to accept that Mr Smith may think that he could smell their blood, which was almost the same thing and not really worth arguing about. He shrugged at Jacob who gave him a weak smile. The only certainty that remained now was that a lot of blood was about to be spilled.

Mrs Thornthwistle stood at the back of the crowd stroking Mogwai. She raised her small hand and the lighting rig burst back into life, flooding colour over the crowd.

Sister Agatha moved swiftly past them with an RPG strapped to her back. Stopping at the trees she aimed it at the flats.

"Oh that's what the package was," said Jacob cheerily.

A mechanical whoosh was followed by an explosion at the entrance to Barry Court.

"Who do you think gave Mr Smith the machete?" asked Simon.

"Probably the same person who gave him the chainsaw," replied Jacob. "It could be any of the nuns but my guess would be Sister Agatha. I think she likes giving people weapons, the way a cat brings in dead rodents." He watched her sprint forward with the vanguard. Even from this distance her battle face was truly terrifying.

Jacob and Simon walked back and took a good vantage point to the side of the now deserted marquee. Through a gap they watched a storm of righteous humanity erupt out of the trees and hurl itself towards the flats.

"Blood bath! Blood bath! Blood bath! Blood bath!" echoed in the night air.

"It's fair to say that didn't go particularly well," said Simon glumly. "I think I may have given them their chant. I hope that isn't going to be in your Manchester Scrolls?"

"Don't worry, I'll keep you out of it. At least it could be worse," said Jacob.

"You know I really can't see how."

"Well, for a start the bloodthirsty mob are on our side and the use of fireballs seems to have been very limited so far."

"That's true," said Simon.

"I say, those nuns are very keen to get in on the action," said Jacob as he spied a group of shrieking nuns leading the very tip of the charge. "Very keen indeed. I don't know how they're going to be in battle but just watching them scares the hell out of me."

"I know what you mean," agreed Simon.

"I'm sorry about bringing this up, but shouldn't you be joining in with this and give your friend a hand?" asked Jacob.

"My friend?" puzzled Simon.

Jacob's gaze drifted to the hulking figure moving at surprising speed towards Barry Court.

"Oh, you mean Mr Smith," said Simon. "He's not really my friend – more of a work colleague. I think he may be a bit too enthusiastic about the hurting aspect of our mission."

"You could say that about the nuns. They seem equally desperate on getting stuck in," pointed out Jacob.

"Fair point. I suppose that hurting the bad guys is okay? We are the forces of good after all and we have God on our side."

"What I'm saying is – shouldn't you be getting involved as well?"

"Gabriel told me that Mr Smith would do all the smiting," replied Simon.

"But even so, shouldn't you be joining this battle?" asked Jacob. "You're wearing the smiting gear and we're talking about the Devil and the forces of evil."

Simon shook his head. "Me? No. I think of myself as having a more administrative role. Blood and glory isn't really my thing. I don't think that violence ever really sorts anything out."

"That's a pretty interesting take for an angel sent here to smite the Devil. Don't know if God would share that view."

"Ah, but I wasn't actually sent here by God."

Jacob rubbed his beard. "I was given a noncombative role by Mrs Thornthwistle due to my fear of fireballs, pseudo-Judaism beliefs, and basic cowardice. But you need to consider what Archangel Gabriel will think when all of this is done. Didn't he say that you could make a real difference in the war against evil?"

Simon gulped heavily and thought about Gabriel's shiny black shoes. Looking Heavenwards he said in a loud but scratchy voice, "That is a very good point. I better go and do some smiting. Mr Smith probably needs a hand. Thanks for the gear. I'll see you later."

"Good luck," said Jacob as he watched Simon march away.

Simon, to his utter dismay, arrived at the fray far quicker than he had hoped, and found it to be much less appealing than it had looked from afar. Even from a short distance away there seemed to be a rhythmic flow to it all, a push and pull that gave the melee a polished, semi-choreographed look. However, up close it was just another bloody descent into humanity's dark heart.

Knitting needles pierced flesh, spades crunched bones and somewhere in the dark a couple of cordless drills whirred away. Apart from the nuns in their habits people didn't have uniforms to identify which side they were on, but that didn't seem to matter. Instinctively everyone knew who they were fighting and poked, scratched, smashed, bludgeoned and head butted with all their might. The "Blood bath!" chant faded as it was deconstructed into its component parts of blood, cries, cuts, bruises, groans, yelps, thuds, slashes, and broken bones.

About thirty feet from the entrance, a black suited middle-aged woman, known to Rob and Geoff as Miss Perkins, came out of the general melee and bared her teeth, gripping her hands like claws.

"Arrggghh!" she screamed at the top of her lungs as she threw herself at a bewildered Simon.

"Arrggghh," echoed Simon flinching and turning away. Just as it seemed his makeshift armour would be called upon, her heel stuck in the sodden turf, sending her sprawling in front of him. Completely prone she struggled to get up.

Simon readied his cricket bat, but before he swept Miss Perkins' head into deep fine leg she looked up at him, her eyes wide and full of hate. He gave her an apologetic smile.

Thud.

The metal yoyo hit Miss Perkins right between the eyes, spinning her backwards.

"Sorry about that," said Simon and he continued to the entrance. A dozen paces later a piercing scream caused him to look back. Three nuns and Douglas the courier, were happily giving his would-be attacker a serious kicking with their sensible shoes and rounders bats. As he continued, his gaze fell on a window on the third floor. It was one of the few flats with lights on, silhouetting two figures.

"Rob and Geoff, I presume?" said Simon as he entered the flats. The reinforced glass of the front door was punctured and starred in several places. To his right a bloodstained Mr Smith bellowed, "Smite the craven unbelievers!"

Simon stood silently as people charged all around him. After a few seconds he decided that the forces of good had the matter of smiting evil firmly in hand and that he should find somewhere else to do some searching for Rob and Geoff. *Somewhere less fraught and crowded would be ideal,* he thought. Spying a red door to his left that was well away from the action, he casually approached it and knocked several times. Hearing no answer, he nipped through the door and carefully closed it. He decided against turning the lights on as it would alert people to his presence. Instead, he made do with the grainy light that spilled through a small, high window. As his eyes grew accustomed to the dark, he could see that it was full of metal shelving and neat rows of cleaning products, mops and buckets. A blue door was nestled in the far corner and thankfully there was absolutely no indication of anything evil lurking in the shadows.

Simon put his bat down on an empty shelf and fished out the crumpled packet of cigarettes from his coat. The noise of battle was fading, which probably meant that the mob was closing in on Rob and Geoff's flat.

"This should be a good place to hide," muttered Simon. He looked up. "Maybe hide is not the right word. It's not like they really need my help – Mr Smith and those nuns seem have everything under control. Rather than hiding, let's call it making sure that nothing bad happens to me that sends me to Hell."

Suddenly the fire alarm crashed into life, adding to the general mayhem. Simon took another drag from his cigarette and waited to be whisked back to Heaven. Once back he promised himself that he would ask Isabel on that coffee date.

⁂

Father Garcia had been sleeping for hours before he was roused.

"Would anyone like any drinks? Snacks?" asked a high-pitched shrill voice.

He licked his dry lips. He needed strong coffee with lots of sugar. Opening his eyes, the inside of the plane lurched into view as did a very tall flight attendant. "Coffee, many sugars please," he muttered.

"Not for you," the flight attendant replied.

Father Garcia looked again. The harshness of the voice did not match how she looked.

"Come with me," she shrilled, passing over a large, milky orb.

His gaze settled on the orb and its swirling clouds. In seconds he'd seen all of his life flash by and then he was gone. The familiar smells greeted him but the view was very different. He was sat forty feet above the lip of the pit. He barely made out the figure curled up in a ball, but felt sure it was Alexis. Spread out as far as he could see from where he sat were identical pits in a radiating circular pattern. Dotted around the lips of the pits were orangutans slowly patrolling, checking their Casio watches every so often. He gripped the arms of his chair. It was made of smooth, bleached bone with a really useful drinks holder on the left-hand side. Looking down he saw a column of twisted bones culminating in a circular pedestal and his throne.

"Ahem," came from behind him. Turning, he saw Santa Muerte sat on a larger, higher throne.

"Your unholiness," Father Garcia said, bowing his head.

She smiled and leaned over, whispering in his ear. When she returned to her throne, Father Garcia was holding a glossy pamphlet.

All around faint alarms started beeping followed by screams and cries. Father Garcia breathed in deeply and smiled.

Chapter Twenty

"Mr Sox will introduce you to each of his fangs and each of his claws as he kills you with dextrous precision. Die! Die! And die again!" – Mr Sox

Barry Court, Withington, Manchester

Geoff heard the faintest knock from the front door. Stifling a mammoth yawn, he rolled his hand over his face and said loudly, "As zombies and maniacs don't knock, I'll go and see who it is. It's not like I've got anything better to do." He glanced back at Natasha and Rob. They seemed preoccupied by whatever they had seen outside. "Why don't you two have your secret meeting to talk about all things evil while I get the door?"

There was no reply from either Natasha or Rob.

"Fine, be like that." Geoff crawled over the lounger and looked through the door's peephole. He saw the frail figure of his neighbour Mrs Hotchkiss dressed in her fluffy pink dressing gown. As usual she looked like she was teetering on the very edge of mortality. He opened the door and smiled, checking his watch. "Is everything alright? I hope we haven't woken you up."

Mrs Hotchkiss smiled back through her wrinkles. "No, but I'm afraid that there is something wrong with Reginald. Can you please have a look at him?"

"Reginald?" asked Geoff.

"My cat," she replied.

Mr Sox's ears shot up.

"I didn't know you had a cat?"

"Yes I got him last week. I thought he could be a friend for Mr Sox."

Mr Sox rose. He certainly didn't want any feline friends.

"You know I'm not a vet but I'll have a look at him. Where is he at the moment?"

"On my sofa and he's not moving at all. Please help him," whispered Mrs Hotchkiss.

Mr Sox sauntered over and slinked around her bony legs, purring away. The arrival of a new male cat next door was unlikely to be good news for him. Three questions raced through his mind. *Is Reginald a bully? Does he like mashed up salmon? And is he cuter than me?*

"I'll just get my shoes," said Geoff turning back to the flat. Mrs Hotchkiss followed him and with surprising precision deftly kicked Mr Sox into Rob's bedroom, closing what remained of the door.

"What seems to be the problem?" asked Geoff, stooping to pick up his trainers.

"Die, spawn of Satan!" shrieked Mrs Hotchkiss, pulling two large kitchen knives from underneath her dressing gown.

As five-and-a-half-stone of Mrs Hotchkiss landed on Geoff's back the larger blade whooshed by in a swift, slicing motion. Craning his neck to see what was happening he narrowly missed the arc of the knife so that instead of carving his ear right off it merely lanced the skin off the lobe. Blood splattered to the floor.

"Oww!" cried Geoff.

They toppled over the chair and landed on the floor, a tangled heap of arms, legs, glistening steel and a fluffy pink dressing gown. Geoff squirmed around and gripped her bony wrists, forcing the knives away from his face. He wondered whether he would even make it to the Prayer Answer Team if he was killed by his doddery neighbour. The possibility of eternal torture loomed into view.

"Die, Baby of Beelzebub!" hissed Mrs Hotchkiss through gritted dentures. Her words were softer as the initial rush of adrenaline began to take its toll. Using his weight advantage Geoff bucked her off him and rolled on top, hitting his head hard on the facing wall.

"Oww. What are you going to do now, you crazy old bitch?" cried Geoff. "And you smell of piss[28]!"

Mrs Hotchkiss brought her left kneecap up with surprising force.

"Arrgghhh!" grunted Geoff, headbutting the wall again.

Mrs Hotchkiss, being a good Catholic, hadn't been that surprised when a vision from God had woken her earlier that evening. What she hadn't expected was the vision to tell her that Geoffrey, the nice young man from next door, was the Anti-Christ and that she should jolly well go and kill him. Once she was certain it wasn't one of the side effects of her medications, she decided to do just that. However, just as she was starting to enjoy herself, a sad wave of realisation passed over her face.

"Pop," a weakened valve ruptured in her heart and a second later Geoff was rolling on top of a corpse.

"Hah! I've got you now, you old bag!" shouted Geoff as he pinned her down. She was no longer struggling so he let go of her wrists and gave her a heavy slap. Her head rolled to one side, her eyes flat and lifeless.

The newly escaped Mr Sox sprang to Mrs Hotchkiss' head. His best relocation option was obviously no longer open to him. He turned to Geoff, hissed and stormed off.

"Oh shit, I didn't want to kill her," said Geoff, raising himself to his knees.

"But she wanted to kill you, didn't she?" pressed a smiling Natasha, standing by his side. "And what exactly was she saying?"

"She was calling me the Anti-Christ and that she wanted to kill me," mumbled Geoff. "But that was Mrs Hotchkiss. She was kind and made great cakes."

---

[28] Smelling of urine is Mother Nature's highly persuasive way of telling you that you are too old or too knackered and should be rounded up, culled and made into protein bars. This enlightened view of the circle of life is only likely to gain traction in the 2060's when climate change causes serious global food shortages. The Millennials think they've got problems getting on the property ladder and paying for the Covid pandemic. Just wait until they start getting hunted by Generation Z…

"But what does that tell you?"

"That I'm in a load of trouble and I'll have to explain why I killed my neighbour," replied Geoff.

Natasha caught his tone and placed her hand on his shoulder. "If it makes you feel any better, I don't think you killed her. She just died of excitement, the old dear."

"That doesn't sound evil," said Geoff.

"It's not," replied Natasha. "Oh, and you're bleeding."

"It's nothing," said Geoff, feeling his ear lobe. "Give me a hand putting Mrs Hotchkiss in my room, Rob." He picked up her ankles and began to drag her away.

"Why do I need to help?" asked Rob. "You're the one who killed her."

"Because you liked her." Geoff banged Mrs Hotchkiss' head first on the skirting board and then on the doorframe. Closing the door he turned to Natasha who was looking out of the lounge window. "What happens now?" he asked. "I know I'm not going on your stupid SACRED programme, but I guess I'll still need all sorts of training. I'm feeling a bit better about this."

"After killing Mrs Hotchkiss?" asked Rob.

"Yes, maybe I am the Anti-Christ."

"Killing people is so much fun," said Rob happily. "It's just the best."

"I don't want to spoil this moment but we need to run," said Natasha.

"I suppose that could be a part of my new regime. Bit of cardio to get me fit before I meet my subjects," said Geoff.

"We need to run away right now," barked Natasha.

Geoff scrambled to the window and found himself agreeing wholeheartedly with Natasha. The only amendments he would like to add were, as fast as he could and until his heart and lungs burst. "What about them being the fucking lambs huddling around waiting for the slaughter? Remember the we are the storm crap? Do some bloody storming," he pleaded.

"That was more of a best-case scenario to show you how good things could be if you really try," said Natasha.

"Oh God," Geoff thought he could hear a very faint whirr of a cordless drill somewhere down there. He was wrong. What he heard was a chainsaw drowning out the noise of the drills. The motley collection of Satanists fanned out and readied themselves for the attack. "It's like Braveheart," he said.

"I have that effect on mortals." Natasha's blue eyes were sparkling.

"A lot of people are going to get hurt," said Geoff.

"I have that effect on them as well. Don't worry, they'll get their rewards in Hell."

"Bet they can't wait for their two days holidays," said Geoff.

"And the Alexander McQueen uniforms," added Natasha.

"But shouldn't we help them?" asked Geoff. "There's a lot more of their lot attacking them."

"Help our people and save them from the murderous forces of God?" asked Natasha. "Interesting, but we really don't work like that. Let's stick to Plan A."

"Plan A?" asked Geoff.

"Run," shouted Rob, putting on his driving gloves and grabbing the baseball bat.

"That'd be Plan A I was talking about," said Natasha.

Opening the bedroom door Geoff stared at the serene face of Mrs Hotchkiss lying on the carpet. "You're not going to need this," he said. Prising her tiny fingers open he took the larger knife that still had droplets of his blood clinging to the blade.

At precisely one fifty-seven, the greatest concentration of evil to have ever set foot in Manchester, or anywhere else for that matter, strode out of Flat 124, Barry Court hoping to fulfil their collective destinies and bring about untold misery and suffering to all of mankind.

After taking six paces, Geoff went back to the door and checked the handle a couple of times just to make sure it was properly locked. Satisfied that it was, he re-joined the rest of the forces of evil.

"Let's catch the lift," said Rob.

"Really?" snorted Geoff. "It's just two floors."

"You know I don't like stairs," said Rob, pressing the call lift button. "They're such a waste of energy." He looked at Natasha. "Boss, we should get some of these installed at home. With all those circles they'd really help."

"Azothoth, I am aware of the advances in technology, but making life easier in Hell is not what we're all about," replied Natasha.

"What happened to running?" asked Geoff. "You made it sound pretty damn urgent thirty seconds ago."

"That's precisely my point," said Rob. "Why waste valuable energy reserves if we can preserve them for when we're really going to need them? Remember, the apocalypse is a marathon, not a sprint, which is perfect for someone of my stature."

"That makes no sense at all, but okay, you're the boss," said Geoff, catching a stern look from Natasha. "Sorry, you're the boss, not Rob. Rob is really not boss material. It's just a term."

"A term that doesn't get used to describe you very often, I'm guessing?" smiled Natasha.

"Now that is just mean and spiteful." Geoff looked down at Mr Sox.

Mr Sox yawned. For thirteen years his sole purpose had been keeping Geoff safe. At the start he had been his constant shadow, conducting risk assessments and stalking his every move. By the second year Mr Sox realised that Geoff led an unbelievably boring life and, Anti-Christ or no Anti-Christ, he had no enemies.

However, tonight Mr Sox had dropped the ball. How could he let an assassin of Mrs Hotchkiss' calibre get through to Geoff? Now it was time for him to gain redemption. All eighteen inches of him readied for a fight. Indeed, a bloody fight to the death against those pesky forces of good was exactly what this feline killing machine had been waiting for all these years.

Mr Sox looked back at the cat flap. No more fleecy warm spots; no saucers of warmed milk; no catnip; and definitely no more Dreamies. His tail floated upwards as he fought back tears. His emerald eyes narrowed – he fucking loved Dreamies, but the work of a Hell Hound was never finished. Six months ago, T.V. had introduced him to the wonders of visualisation. Harnessing the power of your thoughts was harnessing the power of your mind.

"Meow, meow, meow, meow, meow, meow! Meow! Meow! Meow, meow, meow."

This translated to, "Mr Sox is the ultimate weapon. Mr Sox's body and mind are pure in the arts of killing. Mr Sox will introduce you to each of his fangs and each of his claws as he kills you with dextrous precision. Die! Die! And die again! Mr Sox is the ultimate killing machine. Cower, puny forces of God. You are all about to die at Mr Sox's command!"

Mr Sox's heartbeat slowed as all of his five hundred and forty-nine muscles readied to erupt in a blaze of killing fury. *Mr Sox is waiting to kill you all*, he thought.

RING! RING! RING!

The relative calm was shattered as the building's fire alarm burst into life.

"We should take the back stairs," said Geoff. "Remember the Health and Safety course at work, Rob? Never use a lift when there's a fire."

"Don't be silly. Can you see any smoke? See, the lift's coming now," replied Rob.

"I still think we should take the stairs, just to be on the safe side," said Geoff.

"Are you okay?" asked Natasha, glancing at Geoff. "You're sweating and you're looking pale. You're not going to faint, are you? Please say you're not a fainter? I hate people who faint. It gets in the way of the torturing"

"No, I'm okay." Geoff breathed through his nose and gripped the knife harder. "Don't worry about me, I'm your new improved Anti-Christ. Not that I've had any training." He tried to smile but found he wasn't in the mood so he looked firmly at the lift instead.

"If that's your game face Geoffrey, we have some serious work to do," Natasha said.

As the lift arrived and the amber light faded out, Rob looked around and grinned. However, his smugness only lasted for a couple of seconds. The reason why this was so short lived was because two things occurred almost simultaneously.

The first was that the lift was already full and they'd have to take the stairs after all. More worryingly the lift was occupied by thirteen screaming, bloodthirsty nuns of all shapes, orders and sizes, plus Rachel. They bristled with spades, knives, rounders bats, a brass knuckleduster, two sawn-off shotguns, knitting needles, a cordless drill, and a razor sharp kirji.

Everyone went through three consequential phases. The first was that of complete surprise. Neither the waiting champions of evil, nor the homicidal servants of good had expected to be facing anyone as the lift doors opened.

For a rushed heart-beat everyone stared at each other before the second phase kicked in. Realisation. The nuns' orders had been clear. Capture Rob and Geoff for questioning, though they all believed that some blood would need to be spilled to do this. However, despite their violent intentions the nuns suddenly felt confused. Rob was grinning at them while Geoff was stroking a cute black and white cat. Their bewilderment was further compounded by the pretty young woman standing between the two Satanists. She had pure white hair, beautiful blue eyes and smelled of blossom and citrus. Was she an innocent in the wrong place with the wrong people at the wrong time?

For Natasha, Rob and Mr Sox this phase was easier to process. Their past experiences had shown that nuns were a highly trained, uniformed, crack force used by God to do some of his dirtiest work. They were the forces of evil and these nuns had come heavily armed. This helped fast track them to the third phase. Action.

However, it was a nun who was the first to make it to phase three, which was the second reason why Rob's happiness was so fleeting.

Sister Ruth plunged 'Fiddlesticks,' her sharpened knitting needle, firmly into Rob's upper thigh.

"Aaargghhh!" cried Rob. "Ouch. What the fuck!" He looked down at the needle lodged deep in his leg. He did not know the collective noun for nuns but if pushed he would guess it would be a 'hell'. Looking at their snarling faces, hearing the high-pitched shrieks and smelling the faint clammy odour of HRT, it seemed a most fitting term.

"Kill them all!" cried the nuns.

Geoff was already scampering down the stairs, closely followed by Mr Sox darting after him.

Mr Sox had decided that while visualisation was an exceptional tool, it needed some tweaking before it was put into live combative use against a squad of nuns. Instead of being the ultimate killing machine, Mr Sox was now a Mustang car being chased by a dozen police cars. He bounded past Geoff.

Natasha looked at the ferocious sea of black, white, grey and green clothed nuns armed with spiky, cutty, weighty and generally nasty objects of personal destruction. Beside her Rob hopped around, screaming in pain.

"Aaarrgghh!" Natasha screamed, baring her teeth. The nuns shrank back into the lift. Seeing her chance, she turned and fled down the stairs.

This left a bouncy Rob to face the imminent tidal wave of religiously fuelled female violence alone. He'd never been leader material. His work in Auschwitz, Stalingrad, Siberia and Cambodia had really been a case of the right Duke of Hell being in the right nightmarish place at the right nightmarish time. While he could take some credit for the millions murdered during these times, he was only riding the wave of atrocities that humankind seemed happy to overproduce[29]. However, what these experiences had given him was an invaluable insight into the levels of pain normal people would happily inflict on their fellow humans with a smile on their face and a spring in their step. Seeing the hatred on their faces he knew what his fate would be if he stayed. Pushing the first row of nuns back into the lift with the baseball bat he too turned and ran.

"Got you!" whooped Rachel, slicing open a strip of his belly.

"Ahhh fucking heaven!" Rob yelped.

The nuns now squandered their chance to press home their advantage by struggling to get out of the lift.

"He's getting away!" screamed Sister Agatha.

---

[29] On the 31st December 1999 at the 'Hell Crimes Against Humanity' awards ceremony Azothoth personally thanked a number of high-ranking Nazis, Stalinists and leaders of the Khmer Rouge for making all his dreams possible in his tearful acceptance speech. He went on to say how much he enjoyed their dedication and professionalism and how he sincerely hoped to work with them in the future. He added how much he missed the 'killing tree' at the Killing Fields just outside Phnom Penh and vowed to bring one to every town in England larger than Milton Keynes. As Natasha and Mr Sox can testify, when Azothoth had finished there wasn't a dry eye in the house.

All the nuns took a coordinated step back before rushing back towards the door.

"Excuse me, Sisters."

"Kill the fat one!"

"Kill them all!"

"Blood bath?"

"Sorry. I need the lavatory."

Only Sister Agatha escaped the lift by dropping to her haunches and combat rolling into the corridor.

Back down the stairs Geoff had seen enough movies to realise that if you are being chased it is a time consuming and potentially fatal mistake to look behind you. Invariably bad things happen to those people who give in to the need to glance back to get a better look at whatever is chasing them. An antelope being run down by a lion doesn't waste lifesaving milliseconds looking back. It knows exactly what a lion looks like at full pelt and has little need to know how many teeth and whiskers are chasing him.

A running Geoff glanced behind. He saw Natasha scampering down a flight of stairs. What he didn't see was Mr Sox who had stopped in front of a door up ahead.

"Arrrgghh!"

THUD!

Chapter Twenty-One

"Is it a tank?" – Rob

Barry Court, Withington, Manchester

Despite the fire alarm and general bloodshed he'd just witnessed, Simon felt surprisingly safe. As he lit his second cigarette in over ten years, two figures burst into the room. The first, a man, used his head as a battering ram to open the blue door.

"Arrgghhh!" he cried.

A large knife scattered noisily on the floor and came to rest at Simon's feet. The door swung back and hit the newcomer hard on the forehead.

"Oww!"

The second, a black and white cat, leapt gracefully into the room. Standing up quickly, the man peered through the small window at the top of the door. He also didn't see any need to put the light on.

Simon watched all of this in silence, the tip of his cigarette burning red in the darkness. The man was panting, bleeding and clearly upset.

"What the fuck! The world's gone crazy," muttered the man, touching the side of his head. It was sticky and wet.

Simon thought about saying something but before he could the man hastily reopened the door to let another figure in. The outside lighting briefly illuminated a young woman with chalk white hair. She slipped inside and closed the door. She was also visibly upset.

The curious cat padded over to Simon and brushed itself up and down the back of his right leg. He took a drag from his cigarette and reached down to stroke the friendly feline.

"Where's Rob?" whispered the man.

Simon froze. He looked at the cricket bat on the shelf and the knife on the floor.

As the man heard the cat's purring, he looked back into the shadows. "Shit!" he exclaimed. "Who the hell are you?"

"Hi, my name's Simon. Things are a bit, well, strange out there, so I'm sort of," he said, struggling for words. "You know, I'm sort of…"

"Hiding?" suggested the man, nodding sharply as he did.

The end of Simon's cigarette bobbed up and down as he returned the nod. He could now put a photograph to a grainy face that stood less than ten feet away.

"Hi, I'm Geoff."

"Hi, I'm Simon. Sorry, I think I've already told you that."

"Natasha," said the woman.

"Don't blame you for hiding," said Geoff. "Things are completely mental out there. Have you been playing cricket?"

Simon looked down at his gloves and pads. "No. They're for protection. It's like the start of the apocalypse out there."

"Absofuckingxactly," agreed Geoff.

"This is not the apocalypse," corrected Natasha in a flat voice. "I would know."

Simon gave Natasha a puzzled look. "Smoke?" he asked offering the pack.

They both shook their heads.

"Did you see any zombies?" asked Geoff.

"No. I'm pretty certain there aren't any zombies," replied Simon stubbing out his cigarette. "Just some pretty mad people."

"Can you believe that we're being chased by a group of psychotic nuns?" continued Geoff. "Nuns with guns."

"Really?" said Simon, pushing his glasses up his nose.

"Can you pass me that knife? I dropped it coming in."

Simon lent down and passed the knife over. "Is that blood?" he asked.

"Yes, it's mine," replied Geoff. "A crazy neighbour tried to slice my ear off. See?" He pressed his ear lobe forward. "World's gone mad."

“I think that you should stay here with us until it all calms down,” said Natasha. She was about to say more but was interrupted by a loud deep wailing from outside the room. Geoff quickly opened the door to let in another man. A scowling Rob tumbled in, holding a baseball bat. He was without his Guinness hat or happy grin and was panting, bare chested and bleeding from two cuts.

“Shouldn’t we make a run for it?” asked Geoff.

“Too many of them and they’re all really up for it.” Rob looked down at the blood oozing out of his belly before hissing at Geoff, “Rachel and a fucking nun stabbed me.”

“Rachel?” asked Geoff. “My Rachel?”

“Yes, your goody-two-shoes Rachel from work. That psycho bitch was in the lift,” said Rob, poking his finger inside the bloody gash.

“I didn’t see her,” said Geoff.

Simon gripped the packet of cigarettes tighter.

“That’s because you were too busy running away. That bitch stabbed me,” said Rob, pointing at his belly. “This, is a stab wound.”

“Oh,” said Geoff. “Was she alright?”

“Oh, she’s fucking peachy! Having a great time hanging out with some killer nuns.”

“Did she ask about me?”

“No, she fucking didn’t. She was too busy stabbing me. That woman has some serious mental problems.” Rob stopped and looked at Simon. “Who the heaven are you?”

“Hi, I’m Simon.”

“Hi, I’m Rob, pleased to meet you. Have you been playing cricket?”

“No, it’s for protection,” Geoff explained. “You know, from the crazies.”

“Cool, that’s a really good idea. We live at flat 124. You hiding here as well?” asked Rob.

“Yes, it seemed sensible with everything that’s happening,” replied Simon. “I’ve just moved in.”

Mr Sox meowed his own personal introduction.

“To be honest it’s usually pretty quiet around here. Nice really. Though the drains can sometimes smell a bit in summer,” said Rob.

“Don’t say that,” interrupted Geoff. “You’ll put him off and we need more younger people here, especially as the older ones have all gone psycho. You’ll have to come out for a beer with us.”

"That'd be great, thanks," said Simon.

"Really?" exploded Natasha, who'd been watching this from the other door. "Is everyone fucking happy now? Simon, this is Rob. Geoff, you've already met. The dog, sorry, cat is Mr Sox and I'm Natasha. Simon has just moved in and he's not playing cricket but he's hiding like us. Now that we know each other's names, can we please focus on not being slaughtered by those maniacs outside?"

They all nodded in silence.

"Thank you." Her voice was cold and hard.

"I blocked the door on the stairs but it won't hold them for long," said Rob. "What's the plan boss?"

Simon looked at Geoff waiting for a response but the answer came from behind him.

"If we're going to stay here we need to barricade the doors now. We've no idea what or who could be behind them," replied Natasha.

Simon had a very good idea of what was behind these doors. Mr Smith and a crazed bloodthirsty mob who would happily massacre everyone in this room with the hopeful exception of himself, the cat and the pretty girl. He wondered whether Sister Agatha was already priming a homemade pipe bomb.

Simon nodded his agreement at Natasha. He thought about running away but decided that they'd chase him and he was outnumbered two to one. Three if you counted the cat. Four if you counted the woman. Obviously it would be better to stay put and bide his time.

"Are you going to help?" snapped Natasha, her eyes flashing. "Now would be good."

Moving quickly, they turned over the metal shelving to create two solid barricades wedged against both doors.

"That should hold them for a bit," Geoff said.

Natasha stared up at the only window and shook her head. It was too high and too small to offer anything but an escape for Mr Sox. They were trapped. "Let me think. I need time to work this out," she muttered.

Silence filled the room as everyone watched each other in the semidarkness. This didn't last long as there was a muffled crash above them followed by a chorus of high-pitched screams.

"Keep your bloody voices down," hissed Natasha. "They're coming."

Seconds later the arrival of the cadre of nuns was announced by a garden spade smashing against the blue door.

"The nuns are here," bellowed Rob. "With that crazy bitch Rachel."

Crash!

♠

A smiling Mrs Thornthwistle picked Mogwai up and looked at Barry Court. "I think that is most of the Satanists dealt with, dear. Why don't we go and see what is left? Would you like to accompany us Jacob?"

"No. I'll stay here and guard the marquee if it's all the same to you. This seems like a pretty rough area and I'd hate for the nuns to lose their big tent," Jacob replied.

"As you wish, dear."

For a woman her age, Mrs Thornthwistle was surprisingly quick as she marched her way to the entrance of the flats. The groans and pitiful cries of the wounded littering her path did not slow her down at all, a fact that was not lost on a watching, Sam Spade.

"She is one stone cold witch," he grinned.

"What did you expect?" asked Emily. "You witnessed her pep talk and she doesn't strike me as the overly caring type."

"Let's follow her," said Sam. "I can still feel the Devil somewhere in those flats, so my guess is that there'll be lot more fireworks before this is over."

†

Douglas, the courier, had been wrong about the nuns. They were great fun to hang out with, especially Sister Agnes, who wielded her pick-axe with great strength and an infectious smile.

"Catch up Douglas," Sister Agnes cried as she stormed up the stairs. "Let's go and get more of them!"

Gripping his rounders bat tightly, Douglas bounded after her. It was only on the second floor he caught up with her. The reason for this was that Sister Agnes had stopped and was facing a rather dishevelled woman wearing a business suit and holding a fire axe.

♀

Miss Perkins was happy to be a lifelong Satanist. It had provided her with a fun hobby and a close circle of friends. She particularly enjoyed all the dressing up. However, she had been surprised when the Devil actually appeared to her and a little sceptical when she was told that Geoffrey, was the Anti-Christ. Years before, Rob had brought him to the covern as a prospective member, but everyone agreed that he wasn't really their type.

The Devil was also certain that because Geoffrey was the Anti-Christ, people would want to kill him. Armed with this information, she made a few calls and got the rest of the gang round. Though only eight hours ago, that seemed to be a lifetime away.

Miss Perkins had not expected the nuns to be so mean, or so violent. After being hit with a yoyo, she had been mercilessly kicked and pummelled with rounders bats. Limping back to her flat she picked up the fire-axe she had bought that afternoon. Shaking her head, she couldn't understand why she hadn't brought it down before. Closing the door she was about to nip down the stairs when her path was blocked by a large nun in a red habit. She was grinning and held a pick-axe.

"Oh bugger," sighed Miss Perkins.

†

The red door was hit by something large, fast and angry. It sounded like a medieval battering ram but a primal roar confirmed to Simon that it was Mr Smith.

"Support the doors," barked Natasha. "Hold them back."

Rob and Geoff threw themselves at the barricades at the red door, while Natasha, Simon and Mr Sox took the blue one. For a minute, the forces of evil, augmented by a heavily conflicted Technical Administrative Support Officer, appeared to have contained the threats from outside.

"They've stopped," said Geoff.

"What's that noise?" asked Natasha.

"What noise?" asked Simon. A power drill punched through the door inches from his head. "Aaaagggh!" he gurgled, bouncing away from the door, slipping to his knees in the centre of the room.

"That noise," said Natasha flatly, edging away as another hole appeared one inch lower than the first. It was followed by another and then another.

“They’re weakening the door,” said Simon.

A throaty, mechanical growl burst into life outside the red door. While Geoff had never attended any of the SACRED survival courses, he knew that it was in his best interests to get away as quickly as possible. Six inches of chainsaw blades ripped through the top of the door.

“They’ve got a fucking chainsaw,” exclaimed Geoff. “I knew it!”

“This is grim,” stated Rob.

“The doors won’t hold them!” cried Natasha.

“There’s too many of them!” shouted Simon, who instantly wished he hadn’t.

“Oh shit! Simon, go help Rob hold that door,” ordered Natasha.

Spinning Geoff to face her, Natasha placed her hands on his shoulders. “Geoffrey, it looks like they’re going to kill us so why don’t you do something that’s going to make me proud? This could be your only chance to prove yourself.”

“Easy for you to say,” replied Geoff. “They won’t be chainsaw-drill comboing you and you won’t be working at a bloody call centre for all eternity.”

♀

Douglas stepped forward, all the time eyeing the axe. He could feel his heart thumping like crazy, but felt he should show that he was a useful part of this partnership.

“Stop Douglas,” Sister Agnes smiled, placing her pick-axe in front of him. “This one’s mine!”

Miss Perkins returned her smile and raised her fire-axe, circling it slowly in front of her. Expanding and quickening the circles she moved towards the nun.

With the axe whirling around her head she cried, "Die!" With wild eyes and barred teeth she broke into a run.

The Satanist was less than eight feet away when Sister Agnes finally moved. She grabbed a pistol from a holster hidden in the folds of her habit, aimed, and shot Miss Perkins right between the eyes.

"Let's go and get some more!" cried Sister Agnes.

Douglas stared at the body laid out in front of him. *How do I become a nun?* He wondered.

As Miss Perkins soul began her descent to Hell her final thought was, *nuns really are rotten cheats.*

𝕽

"Right mate," said Rob, "we're going to hit whoever comes in first right in the face."

Simon gulped. When his friends broke in he'd have to turn on the people in this room. Weighing up his options, he decided that he wasn't going to hit the woman, the cute cat, or the scarily big guy, which just left Geoff. He wouldn't hit him that hard, though he'd definitely hit him from behind.

And so they all waited silently in the centre of the room, for the inevitability of what happens when a couple of doors meet a chainsaw and a power drill.

"What's that noise?" asked Natasha.

"Psycho harpy nuns trying to get in?" replied Rob.

"Or the power drill and chainsaw?" asked Geoff.

"No, it's something else," said Simon. "It sounds like a plane."

"So it's a plane. Get ready, they're about to break the doors down," cried Geoff, brandishing the knife in front of him.

"I don't think it's a plane. Can you hear it now? Whatever it is, it's getting closer," said Natasha.

For a second everyone in the room strained to hear whatever Natasha and Simon were talking about.

"Sounds like a bus," said Simon, who had personal experience of that form of transport.

Mr Sox's ears rotated before he spoke. "He could well be right, master. There are a great many buses in Manchester. Wilmslow Road is one of the most congested roads in all of Europe for that form of public transport."

Geoff and Simon looked down, searching for the source of the new voice. All they could see was Mr Sox.

The guttural engine sound outside grew louder and closer. The walls and the few standing shelves began to sway.

"But bigger," said Natasha.

By now the blue door was fully punctured in a neat inner door-shaped template. With the hard work completed a couple of nuns in sensible shoes began to kick it inwards.

"Is it a tank?" asked Rob.

The other door was being sliced through with a steady grinding motion. Simon knew that the person on the other side of the chainsaw was Mr Smith. He gripped the cricket bat and edged behind Geoff.

"Don't be silly," snapped Natasha.

"Please don't make me work at the call centre," pleaded Geoff.

Natasha stood back and spent a couple of precious seconds thinking about what she should say. The call centre was a necessary evil and as such, non-negotiable. The alternative was to torture Geoff though she doubted whether he would appreciate that. Those orangutans could be very mean. She smiled reassuringly and said absolutely nothing. A second later her face brightened. "Oh, I know what it is."

Everyone turned to catch her next words but Natasha only made it to, "It's a..." before the outside wall, ten feet away from their little room, noisily collapsed.

♠

Mrs Thornthwistle entered the flats and surveyed the carnage. To her left a wild-eyed Mr Smith was slicing open a door with a chainsaw, surrounded by a deafening mob. To her right metal stairs led upwards. She was about to join Mr Smith when there was a high-pitched cry and a nun landed at her feet. She had been thrown down the stairs, breaking her neck.

"That will not do, dear," she tutted, carefully placing Mogwai down. "I do believe that this warrants further investigation."

On reaching the first floor she asked a small group, "And who exactly are you, dears?" pulling a gnarled black stick out of her jacket pocket.

"Back away granny! Or you'll get what that nun got."

"Language like that will not be tolerated, dear."

❽

Sam and Emily had begun to creep up the stairs after Mrs Thornthwistle when they heard a muffled,

WHOOF!

Above them intense, but brief cries of agony exploded as a wave of extreme heat rushed down over them. Instinctively their eyes were drawn upwards to the freshly fire-damaged wall, heavily blackened with steam billowing out of bubbling sections of it. However, their gazes did not focus on that. Certain sections of the wall had remained completely untouched. Three figures were etched in white: a young girl; a pregnant woman; and a hunched over old lady.

"Mogwai," called Mrs Thornthwistle. "Where are you? You are such a scaredy cat. Let's go and find the Devil, I know he's here somewhere, dear."

"I think we should go," whispered Emily.

"I agree," replied Sam looking at the wall. "She may be a bit stronger than I thought."

"You reckon?" Emily suppressed a laugh as she backed away. "Only a bit stronger? She toasted those Satanists in the blink of an eye and what was that with the shadows?"

"I'll explain later, but I don't think Mrs Thornthwistle is what she appears to be. If those figures were the virgin, the mother and the crone I think she could be Hecate."

"Hecate?" asked Emily.

"The goddess of witchcraft," replied Sam.

β

Geoff blurted out, "Wha…" which, if finished, would have blossomed into, "…t the fuck is that?" as the back wall of the cleaner's room crashed inwards. Chunks of bricks and mortar showered the room. The impact catapulted everyone through the now weakened front wall.

Rob landed first with a belly flop, flattening a handful of nuns. He was followed by Mr Sox, who sadly found out that he had one life less than before, Natasha, Simon and then Geoff. For a second the forces of evil were at the mercy of the nuns that Rob had missed but then Seamus' foot slipped on the accelerator pedal and the tour bus of The Wild Geese jerked forwards through the load bearing wall, collapsing the ceiling and scattering the nuns.

Thick clouds of mortar dust clung in the brightly illuminated air, causing the filters of the power drills to clog up and splutter into silence. A thick chemical stench from the gallons of cleaning agents released from the burst containers assaulted everyone's nostrils.

Mr Smith picked up his chainsaw, which had been shaken out of his hands. Pulling sharply on the starter rope he fired it up and sliced through the final section of the door. The resulting sparks ignited the cleaning cocktail and towering flames erupted, licking at the ceiling. Kicking in what was left of the door, a raging Mr Smith stood silhouetted by the fiery blaze.

Cccrreeaaakkk!

This almighty groan from the ceiling commanded everyone's attention. Natasha, Rob, Simon, Geoff and Mr Sox crawled their way to the headlights of the tour bus. The flattened nuns screamed and prayed their way back down the corridor away from the collapsing room.

From his lofty viewpoint Seamus growled, "Buckle up!"

Sister Agatha cocked her crossbow and aimed.

Pow! The quarrel flew and hit the closest figure.

"Arrgghh!" cried Geoff, falling to the floor. Intense pain exploded in his shoulder. Struggling to his feet he was met by a wall of fire that had spread in front of him, cutting off his escape to the bus. He stood there like a statue in the centre of all the carnage. He looked at the top of his right arm. Something metal, pointed and very painful was sticking out of the back of it. His left kneecap was showing where his jeans had failed, grazed and bloody. A thick river of blood meandered from a deep cut gouged out of the right side of his head. With nowhere to go he raised his head and waited.

The surrounding shouts and cries of others became whispers and breaths. Eventually, even these were silenced and all that could be heard was the spasmodic buzzing of the electrical wire and the roar of the chemical fire. Geoff's silhouette looked like a shabby messiah.

"Geoff, come on!" shouted Rob and Natasha in unison.

Sister Agatha growled through gritted teeth at herself. She'd dropped the rest of her quarrels in the lift. Watching Geoff and the bulging ceiling her growl turned into a thin smile. At least one of the Satanists was going to die tonight.

Cccrreeaaakkk!

The final warning of the ceiling's intentions was a groan, swiftly followed by a deafening downward torrent of bricks, concrete and wood.

For a moment Geoff raised his arms and thought it looked exquisite and strangely wonderful. Then everything began to hurt and everything went black.

Chapter Twenty-Two

"Just so you know we will probably need therapy after this." – Geoff

Somewhere Different

Geoff woke up and realised that he was no longer at Barry Court. It was far too quiet. He wriggled his big toes and realised that he was naked, lying down and not in pain.

"Bugger."

He felt his shoulder. Where there should have been blood and metal there was now only soft skin. He felt his head and his knee. There was no sign of damage there either. He gripped beneath him. Silk sheets? He raised himself up by his elbows, opening his eyes as he did so. A suffocating blackness surrounded him. He blew out, "This is weird."

"It certainly is," replied a strangely familiar whisper from out of the nothingness. It seemed to come from a position directly facing him so Geoff reached out to touch whoever was speaking. He grasped a couple of times before giving up.

"Make that seriously weird. Hello," Geoff said.

A more confident, *"Hi,"* came back. *"You're awake. That's good, I was getting worried."*

"Who are you? And what are you doing in my dream? Are you using my voice? I think you are. And…"

The voice from the nothingness interrupted Geoff from behind. *"You really should know."* It was no longer whispering and it definitely sounded like him.

"Don't play games with me. Who are you?"

"Well." The voice paused and cleared its throat, *"I am you."*

"What?"

"Okay, I'll try to be more specific. I am part of you. I'm your subconscious and that's why I am using your, sorry, I mean our," he corrected, *"voice."*

"Oh, that's just great. I'm having a chat with my subconscious," Geoff sighed. "Is this another dream?"

"Well spotted. Yes, it could be a dream."

"But if you are my subconscious I guess you're in charge of all my dreams?"

"Correct. That is, apart from the daydreams, they're all down to you."

Geoff found the edge of what seemed to be a massive bed and sat up with his legs dangling off the side. There was no sense of a floor below him, a concern he dismissed as irrelevant as this was just a dream. "You've had your fun, but could you please put the lights on and explain what's happening? The last thing I remember was the ceiling falling on top of me."

"Sorry, but I can't."

"Why can't you?"

"I think I do a pretty damn good job under normal circumstances and..."

"What do you mean by normal circumstances?"

"I'm sorry, this is a bit embarrassing, but if this is a dream, it isn't one of ours. That's what I meant by normal circumstances."

Silence crowded around Geoff as he stared out into the nothingness. Finally he spoke, "It is a dream though?"

"Oh yes, this is probably a dream."

"But not one of mine?"

"No. This is definitely not one of your dreams."

"I'm stuck in someone else's dream? And in this dream there only appears to be you and me and technically you are me? No wonder I'm confused."

"Err maybe."

"What do you mean?" asked Geoff. "Maybe is not really working out for me. I may be the Anti-Christ and I may be travelling with the Devil and my best friend may be a daemon. Don't you think that I deserve something more concrete than a dodgy maybe from you?"

"Typical. It's not always all about you. For once try not to be so selfish. You're not the only one struggling with this. How do you think it makes me feel when I learn that we could be the Anti-Christ?"

"You mean you didn't know?"

"I had no idea. You think you know someone and then bam, you really don't. I mean, how can you be the Anti-Christ, you're not even that evil?"

"I know," agreed Geoff. "What about last night? Was that dream mine, or General Paulus'?"

"I think a bit of both."

"What sort of an answer is that?"

"I think the dream was partly ours and partly General Paulus'. I'm sorry but nothing like that has happened before. I'm just as confused as you."

"Okay, what can you tell me?"

"This feels like a dream but it's not like ours. We have really cool stuff in our dreams like flying, girls, penguins and this doesn't. This has nothing. We could even be dead and not know it."

"Dead!" exclaimed Geoff. "A second ago we were in someone else's dream and now we're dead."

"I didn't say that we are dead, it's just a possibility that's all. The last thing you did was stand under a collapsing ceiling and then bam, we're here. You could have killed us. Do you know why you did it?"

"I didn't really have any other choice, I was trapped."

"Doesn't matter."

"Wait a minute. If we're dead, shouldn't we be in Hell? Natasha was very clear on what would happen if I died without doing loads of evil acts."

"That would be true, but only if Natasha really is the Devil. She could just be crazy?"

"What about her eyes?"

"You could have been hypnotised like on TV?"

"I hadn't thought of that."

"You had actually," corrected his subconscious.

"So how strong a possibility is it that I'm dead?"

"I'd go for sixteen, maybe seventeen."

"What?"

"Oh, sorry. Seventeen out of fifty-seven."

Geoff did a rough calculation. "That's almost a third of a chance."

"To be honest I don't know. Why don't you just wake up? If you wake up we're not dead, right?"

"How do I do that?"

"Why don't you try slapping yourself awake?"

"I suppose it's worth a go," said Geoff. He slapped himself hard three times. "Nothing."

Geoff's subconscious smiled from somewhere in the nothingness. Subconscious' are, as a rule, duplicitous and devious.

"Then it doesn't matter if I'm the Anti-Christ or not because you think I'm dead and even if we're not we could be stuck here forever."

"I told you seventeen out of fifty-seven. That actually means I think we're alive."

"But you wanted to say higher, didn't you?"

Silence followed before his subconscious spoke again. *"Possibly, but I would have been completely wrong."*

"What?"

"The good news is that we are definitely not dead."

"That's great," said Geoff. "What's going to happen? Are we going to wake up?"

"I don't think so. It's good that we're not dead but I really wouldn't like to be in your shoes right now."

"You're my subconscious so you're always in my shoes."

"But not in a conscious way."

"So it doesn't count?"

"Well, I think this is going to be a touch worse for you."

"We're not dead, but you think it's going to be bad?"

"I haven't got anything specific because I don't work like that. What I get are vibes and right now I've got a seriously bad vibe."

"What sort of vibe?"

"Can't tell you."

"Are you telling me that you're a tree hugging hippy? Why don't you come a little closer?" asked Geoff, balling up his fists and thinking that his subconscious could well be a pacifist. If he was a pacifist he was going to beat the living shit out of him.

Geoff's subconscious backed away. *"Just so you know it's considered bad form for anyone to meet their subconscious. I deal with all the stuff you can't. The secrets, unrequited love, daemons, nightmares, fears, the bogeyman under the bed...some heavy-duty stuff. I sift through, rationalise, and repackage it all to make it safe for your conscious consumption."*

"Are you saying I'm a messed-up freak?" asked Geoff, unbaling his fists.

"Everyone is. Everyone has unresolved issues they can't face. I keep yours under wraps and I think I do a damn good job."

"I haven't got any unresolved issues. I'm totally fine. I might be the Anti-Christ but I think I'm doing pretty well all things considered."

"Told you I was good."

"That's not what I meant."

"You don't get many opportunities for recognition in my line of work, so what you've said means a great deal to me."

"I'm not praising you, I'm just saying that I'm perfectly normal," protested Geoff.

"You're making me blush. After everything that's happened, you still believe that you're normal. This is the pinnacle of my career. Thank you ever so much," said his subconscious triumphantly.

"What unresolved issues have I got?"

"Can't tell you. All the hard work I've put in concealing your problems would be wasted if I did. You'll have to trust me on this, but you have some Premier Division shit bouncing around in your head."

"Is it about being the Anti-Christ?"

"No. It's nothing to do with that, but you've got a whole world of new issues if you are. Just so you know we will probably need therapy after this."

"I'm not going to therapy with you."

"Just think about it. Sorry, but I really need to go. Remember to keep your chin up." Geoff's subconscious paused. *"I don't know whether that advice is applicable now."*

"What? Why? You're rushing off without me?" asked Geoff as he clenched his fists once more.

"I'm all for letting your anger out but would hitting yourself really help? Self-harm is usually a bad sign."

Geoff released his fists.

"Need to go. Take care." The voice faded into the distance. *"Good luck."*

For an indeterminable amount of time Geoff sat there looking out into the darkness waiting for some drastic change to happen. He waited and waited but none came. Eventually he began to trace the edges of the bed like an explorer mapping his known world for the first time. It was a very large square with no obvious headboard. He stretched his hands down the sides as far as he could. There was nothing.

Geoff was on the cusp of falling asleep when a tingling registered in the pit of his stomach. The hairs on his arms began to sway. He opened his eyes. He was still surrounded by nothingness but he was definitely moving. The speed quickly increased.

"Help!" cried Geoff, gripping the sides. Just as he felt like he was about to spin off and career into the nothingness, it began to slow. Seconds later it had stopped dead.

"What was that?" asked Geoff, hoping for a reply.

None came, but incredibly bright lights burst on and everything changed.

Chapter Twenty-Three

"You fucking killed that girl." – Simon

Barry Court, Withington, Manchester

"Go save them!" shouted Seamus from the driving seat.

The rest of The Wild Geese quickly disembarked. They had come prepared and sported thick hooded jackets, masks, head torches, goggles and fire extinguishers. Against this flow Mr Sox darted in and out of the fiery rubble into the bus. He was keen not to lose any more of his lives. What he saw when he stared out of the window was pure chaos.

Chemical fires blazed on three sides and shouts and screams came from every direction. It was beginning to feel a lot like home for Natasha, though despite this, she was not happy. She was propped up against what was left of Geoff's wardrobe, which had fallen through two collapsed ceilings. Her right hand was clamped to the middle of her forehead. She really didn't like the feel of her blood. Her head swam and her vision blurred in and out of focus. She began to understand the fragility of mortal existence and decided she didn't like that either.

"I've got her!" shouted Michael.

"Get her back to the bus," said Seamus Junior.

"Easy there," said Michael, placing Natasha's left arm over his shoulder and lifting her up. Seamus Junior appeared and did the same with her right arm.

"Geoff? You must find Geoff," whispered Natasha, her voice trailing away.

"We'll get you safe and then we'll get his body," said Seamus Junior.

"No!" cried Natasha just as her body fell limp.

"You bloody idiot," snapped Michael.

The cousins carefully carried her over the rubble, back towards the tour bus.

"Geoff! Geoff!" roared Rob. Thick clouds of masonry and fumes clung to the air. There was no sign of his friend. He started to feel his way through the wreckage, pulling away twisted metal, wood and bricks. To his left he saw Ruby putting out a small fire before dropping to her hands and knees. She was trying to get something or someone out of the debris.

"Get up! Get up right now!" she screamed, her fingernails scraping and breaking across a coffin-sized chunk of ceiling.

Rob eased her to one side and gripped the piece of masonry. With flaring nostrils and bulging eyes he slowly lifted it. Ruby, seeing her chance, dragged a lifeless body out by its two arms.

"Wake up," said Ruby.

The slab crashed down to the side.

"Who the bloody heaven is that?" asked Rob.

"It's Geoff," she said.

"That's not him," replied Rob. "Geoff doesn't wear dresses."

Ruby rolled the body over. It was a nun.

Pushing the nun to one side Rob resumed his search. "Is that an arm? I'll lift it up again." Straining as before he lifted the slab.

"It is Geoff!" cried Ruby.

"Is he alive?" asked Rob.

"I think so but his pulse is very slow," she replied.

"Help me get him back to the bus," said Rob, lifting the deadweight of Geoff onto his shoulders.

Ruby led the way screaming at no one in particular, "We've got Geoff."

In answer to her cries Seamus Junior and Michael appeared.

"We've got the master. She's back in the bus," said Seamus Junior. "There's also a cat that seems keen on escaping with us."

"Is that them all?" asked Michael.

Rob replied, "There's another bloke with us called Simon. He should be easy to spot, he's wearing cricket pads and a bike helmet. I think he may be one of us. Don't leave him to the nuns, they'll eat him alive."

Michael and Seamus Junior disappeared into the dust and smoke. As Rob made unsteady steps towards the sanctuary of the bus, one side of the chemical fire dimmed as something very large blocked it. It was Mr Smith. A machete rose and Rob turned, but it was far too late. The machete arched downwards and a petite figure in black dived in the way.

Sofia's head fell to the floor. With her eyelids still blinking, she saw Mr Smith tumble over the debris, her blood splattering on his machete. Her pupils dilated as she watched Rob carry Geoff onto the bus. Her eyes stopped blinking and her soul fell down into Hell.

"No!" shouted Michael.

Blood splayed out of the stub of Sofia's neck from the ragged endings of her arteries. Mr Smith slowly regained his feet and smiled.

"You bastard!" shouted Michael as he ran towards him.

Mr Smith stood to one side and with a single blow with the flat of the blade he sent Michael sprawling. Turning, he licked the dust off his lips. The machete sliced downwards but a bucket-sized piece of brickwork hit him hard. Losing his balance, he tumbled to one side.

"Get back to the bus," shouted Rob.

Rob and Michael scrambled to the entrance of the bus to find Seamus Junior arguing with a man wearing cricket pads.

"I'm okay," spluttered Simon.

"Is this your bloke? Says he wants to stay," said Seamus Junior.

"I'm okay," repeated Simon, this time to Rob. "I'll be alright."

"Whatever you do keep away from the nuns," said Rob. He shook his head and looked like he was going to continue the discussion but thought better of it as more shadowy figures loomed around them. "Right, let's go. Are you certain about staying? You'll be safer with us."

Simon sincerely doubted that and shook his head. "No, I'll stay."

Surrounded by the swarming mob, Seamus began to reverse and the doors began to close. However, before they had snapped tight shut, two massive hands appeared and began to force them open.

"Arrghhh!" Mr Smith groaned as the doors opened to the width of his face.

Rob stumbled along the bus gangway and kicked him square in the face. "You bastard!" Once, twice, three times.

On the final kick, Mr Smith crumpled backwards and the door closed with a satisfying hiss. As the red tail light disappeared, he stood up and grinned. Walking back into Barry Court through the gaping bus-shaped hole he stopped and kicked Sofia's head into the heart of the fire.

"You fucking killed that girl," snapped a tight-jawed Simon. "She wasn't even armed."

"We are good, they are evil. We smite evil." Mr Smith pointed at the fiery head. "This is what smiting looks like."

Before Simon could continue there was a noisy commotion around a large disjointed pile of rubble.

"Hurry up!" cried Mrs Thornthwistle. "We need help."

Mr Smith brushed Simon to one side and took hold of the largest slab at the bottom of the heap. With a single ginormous heave, he lifted it to one side where it crashed loudly.

Everyone gathered around the hole that Mr Smith had just created. In its centre lay a motionless Sister Ruth, her hands crossed over her chest like a corpse. Her blue eyes twinkled in the dust.

"She's alive!"

"It's a miracle!"

"Are you okay, dear?" asked Mrs Thornthwistle.

Sister Ruth checked herself before nodding. "Yes, I am."

"And can you tell me why you did that, dear?" asked Mrs Thornthwistle.

Sister Ruth shrunk into the hole. "I tripped. I'm very sorry. It just happened."

"You do realise that it was your duty to destroy them?" smiled Mrs Thornthwistle.

Sister Ruth nodded.

"And yet you saved Geoffrey, one of those vile Satanists from certain death." Mrs Thornthwistle paused and drew breath. "May I ask if you feel possessed, dear?"

Sister Ruth checked herself again. She had no idea what possession felt like. "I don't think I'm possessed," she said.

Mrs Thornthwistle did not seem convinced. "Some Devilish force has been at work here. What else could explain why you saved a known minion of the Devil with potentially fatal consequences to yourself?"

"It was dark and there were lots of things to fall over," explained Sister Ruth.

"She has a point," Simon said. "It was really dangerous out there. I also think it takes a very special person to kill someone in cold blood." Simon shot a scathing look at Mr Smith.

"But Simon, that was the plan," said Mrs Thornthwistle coldly. "You do remember all that talk about smiting? And now they've escaped."

"Have you thought that this could be God's way of letting us know that this wasn't his plan?" asked Simon.

"Are you speaking for God now, dear?" asked Mrs Thornthwistle.

"No, but look at Sister Ruth. She doesn't look in the slightest bit possessed. Shouldn't she have oozing sores and be speaking in Latin with a scary voice?"

"That's how things worked in my day," admitted Mr Smith, nodding his head.

"And the fact is that by tripping Sister Ruth saved a soul from eternal damnation. That soul now has the opportunity for redemption. Why wasn't she crushed by the ceiling? Against all odds Sister Ruth survived and suffered no harm. No cuts or bruises. That's what I call a real miracle and I should know because I'm from Heaven," said Simon.

"Actually I did twist my ankle," said Sister Ruth. "And I've got some bruises on my arms. And my…"

"I don't want to break this up but judging by the sirens the police are going to be here soon," said Jacob, his beard peppered white with dust. "I think that we should fall back to Thrifty Flowers. We may need some Divine Inspiration to find them again."

"Do not worry thyself," said Mr Smith. "We will find these craven cowards wherever they flee."

"How?" asked Simon.

"Trust in the lord thy God," said Mr Smith, high fiving Sister Agatha.

"I press this," said Sister Agatha, "and the hunt for the serpent continues."

"You've got a GPS locator?" asked Jacob. "Is that with someone on the bus?"

"I placed it under their mechanical carriage," replied Sister Agatha. "The serpent is truly weak if he cannot throw his fireballs."

Jacob nodded.

"So where are they going?" asked Simon.

"North," replied Sister Agatha, looking at a black box. "They are on one of your large roads."

"I know exactly where they are heading, dear," said Mrs Thornthwistle with a thin smile as she stroked Mogwai.

β

Rob placed Geoff's body on a bottom bunk at the back of the bus.

"Is he dead?" whispered Natasha.

"No," replied Ruby. "We've got that arrow out but his breathing is really shallow. I think he could have internal bleeding. We need to get him to a hospital."

"We can't," said Natasha. "Doctors would kill him out of instinct. Can you please look after him?"

Ruby placed her hand over Geoff's and squeezed. "Of course master."

"Don't worry about your sister. Sofia is a true Heroine of Hell," said Natasha solemnly.

"I know," replied Ruby, fighting back hot tears. She looked up at Natasha and said in a voice that could launch a thousand air strikes, "Just make sure the bastard who killed her dies horribly and we win this war."

"I will. Sofia saved a Duke of Hell and the Anti-Christ from certain death. She has gone to a far better place than this shithole and I swear that a horrible death awaits the person who killed her."

"Thank you, master," said Ruby.

"Geoff must survive and be our Beast of the apocalypse," said a stony-faced Natasha looking straight at Ruby. "He must, or else all this is for nothing."

†

"Jacob?" called Simon from what was left of the flattened marquee.

"Just packing up," replied Jacob, holding the remains of a crushed chair in one hand and a slice of lemon drizzle cake in the other. "The nuns aren't too happy with the bus driving through their big tent."

"I just wanted to say thanks for the gear. It's all here, though some of it's a bit dented."

"I'm glad it was useful. At least the Devil didn't throw any fireballs. Do you think he was actually here?"

"I don't know," said Simon. "If he was, he certainly didn't look like we thought he would."

"Shame they got away."

"Jacob, I need to tell you something. I was in the room with them and they were really scared. Really scared of us."

"Scared of us? That makes sense, we were trying to kill them after all."

"They were particularly scared of the nuns," added Simon.

"Well, so am I," said Jacob.

"They," Simon pushed his glasses up, "seemed nice and normal. We may be getting a bit carried away with all of this talk of smiting. Did you see what Mr Smith did to that poor girl? He sliced her head right off."

"But isn't that what this is all about? If the Devil is here, he must be stopped and that means cutting him and his mates into little pieces and sending them recorded delivery back to Hell. What if everyone had been fried to ashes by one of his fireballs? Where would your extra crispy conscious be now?" asked Jacob.

"You may be right but Mr Smith enjoyed decapitating that woman," said Simon.

"War is hell? If that's true those bastards should be pretty used to this by now," said Jacob.

β

With an unexpected jerk Geoff's whole body began to crumple and convulse.

"Help!" screamed Ruby, her eyes shiny and wet. "He's dying."

Chapter Twenty-Four

"Don't ever call me a girl again!" – Natasha

Somewhere Different

A shock of brilliant white light crashed through Geoff's eyelids. He spun his head one hundred and eighty degrees and opened his eyes. For less than a second he struggled to gain focus before another bolt of searing white light hit him.

"Bloody hell!" he gurgled. Scrambling to his knees, he stumbled sideways and ran into what felt like two thick taut ropes, one across the top of his chest, the other across the top of his thighs. He risked a hooded glimpse at what had changed and then closed his eyes even more tightly than before.

"Why am I in a boxing ring?"

Geoff was still hoping for a reply when it became obvious that something else had changed. He opened his eyes fully and found he was wearing white satin shorts, a dressing gown, boots and boxing gloves. While the ring was now brightly illuminated the same thick black nothingness still surrounded it.

"Mustwakeup! Mustwakeup! Mustwakeup! Must…"

A booming voice that seemed to come from everywhere and nowhere thundered,

"LET'S GET READY TO RUMBLE!"

"ARE YOU READY TO RUMBLE?"

Geoff felt his heart pounding against his rib cage.

"ARE YOU READY TO RUMBLE?" the voice repeated with a sprinkling of irritation. A couple more seconds passed before the voice added, **"GEOFFREY! ARE YOU READY TO RUMBLE?"**

"Err, not really, I'm not much of a fighter so can we talk ab..."

"EXCELLENT!"

Geoff took a proper look at his surroundings. There was a large advertisement for *The Thirty Pieces of Silver Sports Bar and Grill* splashed across the centre of the ring. Beneath his feet the canvas floor felt bouncy.

"HAILING FROM THE FIGHTING CITY OF MANCHESTER, ENGLAND."

"I'm actually from Milton Keynes."

"THE SPAWN OF SATAN! SOON TO BE THE NEW RULER OF THE WORLD!"

Geoff couldn't help but grin.

"YOUR NEW ANTI-CHRIST! GEOFFREY. PIKE!!!"

Geoff raised his arms in the air and then just as quickly put them down. A lone pair of hands began clapping wildly somewhere out there in the nothingness.

"Go get 'em champ. You can do it!"

"Why don't you come here, you bastard?" asked Geoff. To this there was a couple of whoops and a single piercing whistle.

"How come you can whistle? I can't whistle," said Geoff.

There was another whistle, this time louder and more piercing.

"HIS OPPONENT."

I bet it's going to be that rabbit, thought Geoff.

"HAILING FROM THE FIGHTING REALMS OF HELL."

Or it could be Rob. If it is, I'll just run around until he has a heart attack.

"THE MASTER OF DISASTER!"

Geoff frowned. The noise surrounding the ring began to grow.

"THE PROPHET OF DOOM!"

Geoff wanted to wake up from this nightmare.

"THE UNDEFEATED!"

Before anything really bad happened.

"THE REAL DEAL!"

To him.

"AH... SATAN!"

"Oh shit," gulped Geoff.

The crowd surrounding the ring exploded into berserk approval. A slight hooded figure flipped into the ring. "The Real Deal – AHSATAN!" was stitched in gold on the back of the black robe. The figure turned to face him.

"Natasha?"

"Ah, Satan to you," she corrected, her eyes flashing like a couple of razor-sharp daggers.

"But you're not really the Devil?" Geoff looked at her. "I know you did the redeyes thing but that was just a trick. I think you hypnotised me. If you were the Devil you'd really look the part. Is this your dream?"

Natasha smiled and the robes disappeared.

"Ding!" A bell rang and Natasha advanced.

"You know that I would never hit a girl. Even if it is just a dre..." Geoff's nose crumpled and the crowd went wild.

"Oww! That bloody hurt."

Geoff spun away, briefly glimpsing General Paulus, Gus the rabbit and a tall Emperor penguin with a large silver Mardi Gras headdress sitting together. The penguin was eating popcorn.

"Now, listen here Natasha," said Geoff as a black leather glove hit him just below his right eyeball. Raising his fists he bobbed away. At a safe distance he felt his nose. It didn't feel broken.

Natasha closed, hitting his solar plexus. Air fought to emerge from his lungs and his guard dropped just as she launched an uppercut.

"Smack!"

Geoff didn't need to check. His nose was broken and bloody.

"Stop it!" Geoff demanded in a high-pitched nasally voice. "I'm not going to fight you. You're only a girl."

Natasha stalked him with silent menace.

"Shouldn't we have a referee?" said Geoff, looking around. "This doesn't seem fair."

Natasha spoke softly, "Don't be stupid Geoffrey. We don't need a referee." She faked a right jab and connected with a left cross.

"Oww. Stop this right now!" Geoff shouted. Above the wall of noise of the crowd he could hear a familiar voice. *"Bob and weave! Bob and weave!"*

"Smack!"

Another roar from the crowd.

"Bob and weave, champ! Remember, she's only a girl!"

"Show your true self, Geoffrey. Face your destiny. Fight me and live."

"I am myself. Please stop."

"You really have no idea?" Natasha's fists dropped to her sides. "Maybe this will help you understand?"

The crowd fell silent.

"What are you talking about?" he asked.

Without breaking her gaze Natasha unleashed a vicious kick to Geoff's groin.

"Aaaarrrggghhhuuuurrrrr," Geoff buckled to one knee, his eyes watering.

"Low blow! Low blow!"

"Does that clarify the situation for you?"

Geoff's head dropped as he fought back tears.

"Let go. Fight me and live," Natasha's black gloves rested on the elasticated gold waist band that hugged her hips.

Geoff's reply was pure instinct. Springing up he hurled a sweeping right hook, glancing the side of her head.

Natasha's smile was replaced by a look of sheer horror. "You hit me in the face!" she accused.

"I'm so sorry. I don't know what happened. Please forgive me," he cried.

"That's it, champ. Let her have it. Go in for the kill." Geoff's subconscious could be clearly heard over the hushed crowd.

Fighting back tears welling up in her eyes Natasha spoke in a quiet broken voice. "How could you hit me? How could you hit a girl?"

"I'm really, really sorry. I don't hit girls – ever."

Natasha's teary eyes looked back at Geoff.

"Hit her again, champ!"

Geoffrey spun to face his subconscious, "Shut up!"

"But you did hit me and you did kill Mrs Hotchkiss, Geoffrey," snarled Natasha. "And you are the fucking Anti-Christ."

"Uhhh? You said Mrs Hotchkiss had a heart attack and I don't hit girls."

"Don't ever call me a girl again!"

Natasha's uppercut lifted Geoff off the floor and for a split second his body was horizontal, sailing four feet above the centre of the red and blue advertisement lettering.

With a *thud* Geoff's unconscious body crashed down. The crowd went wild as Natasha raised her arms in victory and marched around the ring.

"Good fight. Good fight."

Chapter Twenty-Five

"This could be the actual end of the world." – Simon

The Sweet Surrender Coffee House, Deansgate, Manchester

Despite the early hour the Sweet Surrender Coffee House was buzzing. People whispered away on distressed leather sofas under low level lighting next to open brick walls. Hits of caffeine, overpriced pastries and hipster company was proving to be a partial antidote for the unnamed fear that gripped them all.

Standing in a corner Simon scanned the room, "He's late." He undid and retied his tie. It looked exactly the same as it had done before.

A seated Mr Smith looked over his dark glasses, "The most holy archangel is not late. You must keep thy faith."

"Why is he coming? Won't it break the agreement?"

"We are here to tell and inform him of our progress, or lack of it. I believe that the archangel will know exactly what should be done."

"Do you think he'll be annoyed?"

"No," Mr Smith paused, "at least not with me."

Simon's face scrunched up. He looked at the three empty cups on the table. "Do you think I could have another coffee? It was the best coffee that I have ever had. Why does no one eat or drink in Heaven?" Before he could go on a firm hand clamped itself onto his shoulder.

"I think that a coffee would be excellent," boomed a voice behind him.

"Gabriel!" Simon exclaimed. "Thank you for the new clothes and the rest of the stuff."

"Well, I think it's important for you as Technical Administrative Support Officers to look the part." Gabriel maintained his smile. "You are my A-team, after all. Mr Broomhead, would you be so nice as to order a double espresso and a croissant for me? And for you, Mr Smith?"

Mr Smith shook his head.

"And whatever you fancy Mr Broomhead. I've heard that the breakfast pastries here are amazing," said Gabriel, dropping a black leather messenger bag at his feet.

"Most holiness, he is irritating," said Mr Smith once Simon had left.

"Come now, you must remember your first time. Simon just has a bad case of reintroduction overload. In his eyes every sensation is magnified. It's the most beautiful sunset, the most gorgeous sunrise and for everyone it's the most wonderful coffee they have ever tasted. Strange thing, caffeine, gets everyone first time. Give it a day and he'll be over the worst of it."

"He is also a craven coward," said Mr Smith.

"Perhaps, but I seem to remember that I sent you here to do all the smiting, not him?" said Gabriel. "And please try and keep your language modern. We don't want to draw attention to us."

Simon arrived tray in hand.

"Ah, excellent Mr Broomhead, that was quick. And with my espresso and croissant, I see." Gabriel smiled and gave his coffee a single stir. "I understand from Mrs Thornthwistle that things didn't go according to plan last night. She has kindly provided me with the bare bones, but would you please add the meat by explaining exactly what happened?"

Fifteen minutes later a red-faced Simon apologised, "I'm really sorry about failing to smite them."

"Why are you sorry, my boy?" Looking around the café Gabriel smiled reassuringly. "Evil walks amongst them and they bloody well don't like it. Billions of people have been given a short sharp shock. Once you start crunching the numbers this is truly excellent. Praying has gone up by over two thousand percent. Atheism has dropped to a record low and true belief has skyrocketed. We really should have considered the possibilities of letting him loose before. And to cap it all off, because the Devil is our personal manifestation of evil we are storming way ahead of all the other faiths. It's a good job we had him patented from day one."

"Really?" asked Simon.

"Of course not, Mr Broomhead," said Gabriel, breaking his croissant in half and dipping it into his espresso. "That was a joke. So back to your story, you've got them surrounded with no means of escape and yet we end up with nothing to show for our efforts?"

"We were about to complete our mission by securing and massacring the inhabitants of the room," replied Mr Smith.

Simon coughed weakly.

"Apart from Mr Broomhead, but then an armoured tour bus appeared and ploughed into the base of the building. This collapsed loadbearing walls and some of the ceilings. Members of a Satanic folk band called The Wild Geese who were on the bus, extracted the targets before we could successfully slaughter them," said Mr Smith, "or capture them for questioning."

Gabriel nodded while slowly chewing his soggy croissant. "I understand you were actually with them, Mr Broomhead? That must have been awful for you, my boy. Caught in there with all that evil."

"To be honest they all seemed really scared," said Simon. "Scared of us."

"I did warn you that they are very sneaky," said Gabriel. "What about these four? Was one of them our man?"

"I think that the Devil may have taken on a somewhat unconventional manifestation," replied Simon, handing over a grainy photograph.

Gabriel looked up. "Please explain why I am looking at a cat?"

"That's Mr Sox," replied Simon.

"I don't care what it's called Mr Broomhead, the fact remains that it is just a cat. Why would you ever think this could be the Devil?"

"He was one of the four that escaped and it seemed sensible to include him," explained Simon.

"I applaud your assiduous approach but I refuse to believe that the Devil would ever walk the Earth as a cat. They are truly monstrously vile creatures and I know for a fact that he personally despises them." Gabriel finished off his croissant. "I suppose for thoroughness' sake I should ask if this Mr Sox appeared overtly evil?"

"No, he seemed very friendly and purred a lot. I suppose that could be a trick and the Devil is using Mr Sox as a vessel before he possesses a human," said Simon.

"I seriously doubt that," said Gabriel.

"And," Simon paused, pushing his glasses up his nose, "I also think he spoke."

"You're saying that this cat actually spoke to you?" asked Gabriel.

"I think so. He was talking about the number of buses in Manchester. He seemed very knowledgeable on the subject."

"But did you actually see him talk?"

"No…but…"

"Why don't we put that down to the great stress you must have been under? Who else was in the room with you?"

Simon handed a photograph of Natasha to Gabriel.

"It's a woman," stated Gabriel, "and she appears to be bleeding."

"Part of the ceiling had just collapsed on her," said Simon. "She's called Natasha."

"Nice name. She's rather fetching, don't you think?" laughed Gabriel. "Though I'm afraid that I can't see the Devil coming back as a pretty young girl. He's got succubi for that, you know?"

"But she was very bossy," added Simon.

"Women generally are Mr Broomhead, the Almighty made them like that. Did you see what shoes she was wearing?"

"No."

"Well, that settles it," Gabriel snorted. "She'll just be another Satanist, or possibly an innocent caught up in all of this. I for one would lose a great deal of respect for the Devil if he stooped to possessing a pretty young girl."

"Mr Smith says you already know about the next one," said Simon, passing over a photograph of Rob.

"Well, well. Where have you been hiding all these years, Azothoth?" Gabriel looked at Mr Smith and chuckled. "Didn't he work with you on the First Crusade?"

"Indeed, he did sire," said Mr Smith, looking at Simon. "You never forget your brothers in arms."

"He's been living in Manchester for ten years and calls himself Rob," said Simon.

"Now that makes more sense. I've not heard of Azothoth for a great number of years. He's put on some weight and doesn't usually wear a hat – something about his horns getting in the way – but that is definitely him. Do you think he's gone native and the Devil was taking him back home?"

"I don't think so your holiness. He seemed relieved to escape on the bus," answered Mr Smith.

"What about this one?" asked Gabriel. "He looks suitably sneaky."

Mr Smith replied. "That sire, is Geoffrey Pike. He's in his early thirties. From what we can gather he has no distinguishing talents or events that tie him to anything evil apart from his friendship with Azothoth who he's known since childhood. They have lived together for ten years and, up until yesterday, worked together. However, I think he must have known something of Azothoth's real nature. You can't spend that much time in the company of such evil and not know his true nature unless you are ridiculously stupid."

"Interestingly, a number of strange events happened to him last night. The first being that he watched The Wild Geese with Rob at a pub called O'Sheas near here. The second being this," added Simon, passing over a series of seven smaller photographs to Gabriel who laid them down in a landscape row in front of him.

"I take it that Geoffrey is the fellow being chased," asked Gabriel.

Simon nodded.

"Do we know who the people doing the chasing are?"

"Minions of Satan and others with craven black hearts who were drawn to the evil that resided in Barry Court," said Mr Smith.

"Did they catch him?" asked Gabriel.

"Not exactly, but they did cut off his escape and forced him back to Azothoth and their flat," said Simon.

"So this Geoffrey character tries to escape but is brought back by a collection of Satanists to a Duke of Hell. An unfortunate result for him under any circumstances," snorted Gabriel. "I think we can rule him out as being the Devil, don't you agree?"

Mr Smith nodded.

Gabriel finished his espresso and placed it carefully on the table. "It would appear that the Devil may not have contacted them at all last night, or I suppose he could have been with The Wild Geese. With all that happened do you think we could have missed him?"

"I don't think so – why would all those people guard the flats?" said Simon. "There was another thing that happened later on to Geoff. He stood under the ceiling when it collapsed."

"Do you think he was trying to kill himself?" asked Gabriel.

"He was cut off from the rest of them after a nun with a crossbow shot him," Simon replied. "Then, just as the ceiling collapsed, another nun tripped over and pushed him out of the way. I guess we'll never know whether he was trying to kill himself. Do you think he was the anointed vessel for the Devil? If he was, he didn't seem particularly pleased by the prospect. That would explain why he was trying to get away earlier on and why he stood under the ceiling when it collapsed."

"Did he die?" asked Gabriel.

"We don't know. Rob, I mean Azothoth, pulled him from the wreckage and took him back to the bus. By all accounts he was unconscious and bleeding heavily," said Simon.

"This is more than a little puzzling," agreed Gabriel. "Your anointed vessel theory does seem to make more sense than the cat or the girl. Right. From what you've told me there are three distinct possibilities. The first is that the Devil was in the room with you Mr Broomhead and escaped. The second is that the Devil was on this bus and coordinated the extraction. And the final one is that the Devil was elsewhere but still coordinated the extraction and met with them later. Whichever is correct, finding that bus and smiting everyone on board appears to be our best option."

"Agreed sire," growled Mr Smith.

"While this has given us an extraordinary boost in our approval ratings, we are playing with fire by having the Devil on the loose. Especially as we still have no idea of what he is planning." Gabriel tossed Geoff's photograph back onto the table. "There is one thing that may help us. The golden rule that applies to everything that the Devil has ever done is that he loves an audience so we should find out what he's planning pretty quickly."

"We know that they headed north and our last confirmed location before the signal was broken just before Junction 36 of the M6," said Mr Smith, pulling out the black GPS locator and placing it on the table.

Gabriel picked up his black messenger bag and a clear plastic folder fell out onto the table. The title page read, *Making and Fulfilling Your Own Prophecies – A Working Guide.*

"Sorry about that," said Gabriel, as he quickly placed the folder back in the bag. "It's just a working title at the moment. If it all goes well I'll be seeing my agent later on today." He then pulled out a number of luminous pages and placed them on the table. "I'm afraid I'm being a touch disingenuous. This came to my attention before our meeting, Mr Broomhead. This is a new Word of God."

"I don't understand. It's a comic book," said Simon as he looked at the glossy front cover of the *Book of Shenanigans*. "And this is the Word of God like the Bible?"

"As you can see it has the official seal," said Gabriel, pointing to the top righthand corner which stated in shimmering gold, "Word of God."

"And that makes it like the stone tablets?" asked Simon.

"No, it doesn't make it like the Ten Commandments. They were carved in stone while this is, as you so rightly said, a comic book."

"But still God's Word?" asked Simon.

Gabriel nodded.

"What does, "Deciding the fate of the World and the Universe" mean?" asked Simon while staring at the cover. The shimmering colours had a strange hypnotic effect.

"It means that we live in very interesting times Mr Broomhead," replied Gabriel.

"Can I look at it sir?" asked Simon.

"Seeing as you are one of our Technical Administrative Support Officers and this is the Word of God, it would seem appropriate for you to examine it," replied Gabriel.

Carefully, Simon picked up the pages and began reading. It took another five minutes before he looked up wide-eyed and disbelieving. "This is very bad." He looked at Gabriel. "This could be…" He paused for a long time, gulped and finally said, "The actual end of the world."

"I think that is highly unlikely, Mr Broomhead. Where is your faith in the Almighty?" said Gabriel.

"But this meeting is in here. Our meeting. Even the cool suits and me checking the time; it's all in here. How can that be?"

"I do not know," replied Gabriel. "It is a prophetic work after all, and thus a manifestation of God's will."

"Why does it stop at page thirteen?" said Simon, placing the *Book of Shenanigans* pages down on the table and picking up his coffee cup.

"I simply do not know that either, my boy," said Gabriel. "This appeared anonymously on my desk through the internal post. I only received the first four pages to start off with, but then I got the rest this morning, once again through the internal post."

"And you've never seen it before?" asked Simon.

"No, and to my knowledge nobody else has either," explained Gabriel.

Simon looked at Mr Smith. "Don't you want to look at this?" he asked.

Mr Smith shook his head.

"Your colleague has already seen parts of it back at the office," said Gabriel.

"Okay. I see that there are no zombies in this," said Simon flatly as he held the cover up to Gabriel and pointed at the, "Special Bumper 64 Page No Zombie Edition," flash at the bottom right hand corner. "So why don't you just go and see God and ask him to explain what this is?"

"I would." Gabriel paused, steepling his hands in front of him. "Though I'm afraid that God is currently on a lengthy sabbatical and is therefore noncontactable."

Simon just stared at the archangel as his tenuous grip on his cup failed. It dropped, spilling the dregs of coffee over the wooden floor. "Err…what do you mean, sir?"

"It's very simple Mr Broomhead. God is currently unavailable," replied Gabriel in a thoughtful tone.

"We've lost God and the Devil at the same time?" asked Simon.

"We haven't lost God. He's been under a great deal of pressure for centuries and it was decided to give him time to recharge his batteries so to speak. This is a planned break with a clear management structure put in place for the duration of his absence. I think it's time for us to put things back in order. I have a strong suspicion of where the Devil is now heading, and if I'm right, it should be quite simple for us to locate him and smite him all the way back to Hell," beamed Gabriel.

"Agreed holiness," said Mr Smith, tapping the black GPS locator on the table.

"Us?" asked Simon.

"Yes, us, Mr Broomhead. You obviously require some assistance to clean up this mess, wouldn't you agree?"

Simon nodded weakly. "But doesn't that break the agreement?"

"This is one of those situations where the end justifies the means. Right my boy, we should hurry up. Mrs Thornthwistle is already going north with the nuns and many of those who turned up last night. I've also got some people waiting for us in The Lake District and to top it all off I've left Uriel's sword in the car. Let's get a move on and go and do some serious smiting," declared Gabriel as he stood up.

Simon looked down. His own shoes were sparkling.

Terminal 1, Manchester Airport

England was far greyer, far colder, far wetter, and most definitely far madder than Father Garcia had ever imagined. He had expected to find a reserved and refined group of gringos. Instead, as he stepped off his plane in Manchester, he was greeted by a population that was on the verge of mass hysteria. *And they say that Mexico has problems*, he mused, as he walked out of Terminal 1 with his suspiciously long, thin carryon bag.

To his left, a burly shaven-headed taxi driver was mercilessly kicking a red shirted football tourist who was curled up tight in a ball. The taxi driver looked up and leered at Father Garcia, his eyes bulging and a prominent vein throbbing in his temple.

Father Garcia smiled and kicked the prone man in the face. Stepping to one side he scanned the concourse for his ride.

A thick cheery Mancunian, "Hola mate," came from a lean, track-suited figure directly in front of him. "How you doing? You Garcia from Sinola?"

Father Garcia nodded.

"Welcome to sunny Manchester. You had a good flight?"

Father Garcia paused and narrowed his dark eyes before replying, "I am very impressed that you can speak Spanish."

"Okay, easy man. I can't speak Spanish, I only know "hola." I speak English so we could have a communication problem if that's all the English you can say."

"But you are speaking in Spanish? Have you spent some time living in Mexico City?" asked Father Garcia, who desperately needed a coffee. His face suddenly brightened as he worked it out. "Ah, I understand what is happening. Santa Muerte works in very mysterious ways."

"Santa what? Let me take your bag. No other luggage?"

"No other luggage. I do not intend to be here for long," said Father Garcia as he passed over his bag.

The man looked down at the bag and decided that he understood exactly what was happening. He looked up at Father Garcia and gave a brief nod of his head.

"Let's go and slice off Geoffrey Pike's balls with my incredibly sharp sword!" Father Garcia's coppery features eased into a smile.

"I like a man who knows what they want. So why does the cartel want this Pike bloke dead?"

"Not the cartel. Santa Muerte wants Geoffrey Pike's balls and you are going to take me to him," said Father Garcia.

"That sounds like a plan. Name's Benny," he said, offering his hand.

"Like Senor Hill?"

"Exactly, and I'll be your driver and guide to our fair city of Manchester."

From a side pocket Father Garcia pulled out a glossy colour A5 pamphlet and gave it to Benny. "She wants you to read this."

"Thank you. *Santa Muerte and the Successful Criminal – 10 Easy Steps To Ultimate Power*. Looks like an interesting read. I'll have a look at this later," said Benny as he turned it over. On the back cover an extremely tall skeleton wrapped in a robe and holding an orb and a scythe was standing next to a man in a suit. The skeleton was definitely trying to smile.

"So where can we find this Geoffrey Pike?" asked Benny.

"Take me to Wastwater in your Lake District," said Father Garcia from the back seat of the car.

"Lake District? That's not in Manchester," said a confused Benny.

"I know." Father Garcia smiled, the skin around his eyes creasing.

"That's a bloody long way," replied Benny.

"Then you better drive fucking fast, Benny," stated Father Garcia, patting his bag with his right hand. He wasn't smiling anymore.

Chapter Twenty-Six

"I think Daddy tried to kill you." – Emily

Restricted Library, Freemasons Hall

"Why didn't you answer any of my calls?" asked a seated Brian. "I knew something big was happening."

Sam stepped in from the doorway, took his hat off and placed it on the table. "I had things to do. Don't you ever sleep? You were phoning all night."

"On occasion, but I've trained my body and mind to be less reliant than most people."

"And why have you decided to set up shop in all these creepy locations? You really need to get out and see the sun once in a while, smell the roses, maybe meet normal people."

Brian stood up and looked around the small Restricted Library, the cloth books and manuscripts stretched up two stories. "The Victorian Daemonologists who built Freemasons Hall and the rooms beneath it ensured that it gave excellent magical protection, which is why I spend a great deal of my time here. It all boils down to self-preservation, which considering you went to meet the Devil on your own last night without informing me, I suspect is a trait that you no longer possess."

"I did take Emily with me."

"Bravo, your point being?"

"Well, I'm just saying that I wasn't alone and I didn't actually meet him. I've given you the extra pages of *Shenanigans* and as you can see, you're not in any of them. What could you have done if you'd been there? There was no God and more importantly for you, no Spear of Destiny. Would it be worth blowing your cover without two of the major players? You may have got a meet and greet session with the Devil but without the Spear you couldn't take him on. So would you have challenged him to a heated debate about the terrible injustices waiting for human souls in Hell?"

"It would have been nice to be asked that's all. Tell me exactly what happened?"

Minutes later, Sam said, "It looked like a scene out of Braveheart."

"Which scene?" asked Brian.

"The battle scene of course. The famous one where they line up and Mel Gibson gives that speech," Sam paused, "I think we're getting a bit off message. Are you certain you're getting enough sleep?"

Brian shrugged, "I still believe that my presence would have been advantageous for us both."

"But surely having all the information without any of the risk is exactly what you want? Remember I know the Devil. He is meticulous in his complete and total attention to detail. He wouldn't risk everything that he has planned for some last-minute escape. It's just not his style."

Jay coughed from his seat in the corner, "Sammy, I really think you should be nicer to Brian. He's a pretty cool dude. Hunter knows his wine and gave us great food. Do you know how long it's been since I've had a rare organic fillet steak partnered with vintage Spanish wine? Fucking never is the answer."

Sam turned, "You do remember Brian was torturing me?"

"Hah, but did he really?" Jay grinned. "Lou seemed to think he was playing around. Ain't that right?"

Lou nodded his head and said, "He gave us loads of weird fruit, not just bananas," pointing at the large basket on the table. It was almost empty.

"What do we do now?" asked Brian.

"That's simple," replied Sam, "we pick Emily up, she's watching them."

"And then what?"

"We follow the angels."

Two black limousines slipped slowly out of the underground car park and made their way from Freemasons Hall to the Sweet Surrender Coffee House.

In the leading car Brian ordered, "Pull over Saunders. There's Emily."

Saunders grunted and slowed to a halt. Five minutes later he started following a convoy of three coaches, numerous cars and two red double-decker buses full of nuns. They headed North and the city shadowing the sides of the motorway turned into town, which slowly turned into rural villages surrounded by green fields. It was only then that the silence was broken.

“Do we know where they’re going?” asked Emily.

“No but Sam was right to follow the angels, I’m certain God is guiding them as we speak,” replied Brian.

“Hell was truly awful Daddy,” said Emily looking out of the car window, her jaw tight. She breathed in, “The orangutans were really cruel.”

“I’m certain they were, but you did break their rules which is why you ended up in Hell. It’s very simple, the Bible tells you that if you commit suicide you will be tortured for eternity.”

Saunders turned his massive neck back from the driving seat, “Miss Emily, like they said when SpongeBob and Patrick stole a balloon, ‘If you can’t do the time, don’t do the crime’.”

Emily looked at Brian. “I thought Sam had died on one of your stupid missions. I was so upset and not thinking straight. Why haven’t you asked me about it? Do you even care?”

“Of course, I care! But you broke their antiquated rules and by doing so you played right into their hands. And then Samuel took it upon himself to save you by stealing a book of great power from me and taking it to the Devil to trade for your return.”

“Sam upset a lot of the major daemons by giving the Necronomicon to the Devil. They’d all told him that it had been destroyed at Damascus. He made them look silly,” said Emily.

“That sounds like a Samuel problem to me,” said Brian. “That book wasn’t his to trade.”

“You were going to leave me to suffer for eternity because I broke a rule of a system that you’ve devoted your life trying to destroy?”

Brian sighed, “Not that it matters now, but I did have my own plans to save you, plans that didn’t involve people stealing from me. And then when you did return you chose to avoid me. Have you any idea how much that hurt?”

“I wanted to see you, but Sam thought you would still be angry so it seemed better to let you cool down.”

“It’s been over five years, Emily.”

“What is your plan now?” she asked.

“The plan is what it’s always been; destroy the Devil and God and finally free humanity from this pointless charade,” replied Brian. “The two questions that need answering today are whether the Spear of Destiny is here and if I can take it.”

“They’re pulling into the services boss,” said Saunders. “Should I follow them?”

“Saunders, what part of follow the angels do you not understand?” said Brian. “Of course you follow them!”

Lancaster motorway services had never been so full. In the car park the meaty smell of hot dogs and sweet candyfloss filled the air.

“Ten quid for Devil on Tour T-shirts,” barked a middle-aged man doing a roaring trade with the nuns, “Twenty-quid your hoodies.”

Rising above it all was the plump observation tower in complete darkness. Emily watched as more nuns piled off their bright red buses.

“Hi, how are you?” asked Rachel appearing by her side.

“Good I think,” laughed Emily.

“This is my friend Sister Ruth, she’s one of the Set and as you’ve probably guessed a nun. Ruth this is Emily, we met last night.”

“Hi, pleased to meet you,” said Emily shaking Ruth’s hand. She looked back at Rachel. “Did you have any luck with your torturing plan?”

“Not really. We didn’t capture Rob, or anyone else for that matter, but I did get a decent stab in. I was aiming for his groin, but I think it was a just a flesh wound on his disgusting belly. Hard to tell with him being so fat.”

“I take it you’re chasing them?” asked Emily.

Ruth answered with a smile, “Yes one of the other nuns put a GPS tracker on that bus, but Mrs Thornthwistle seems to know where they are going anyway. She thinks we’ll be able to corner them. It’s all very exciting.”

“Can we follow you?” asked Emily. “We’re not professionals like you lot but we’d still like to help.”

“Looking around here I’d say the more the merrier,” laughed Rachel. “Who is that with Mrs Thornthwistle near the minibus?”

Emily followed Rachel’s gaze to two black suited figures flanking Brian. “Oh, that’s my dad. He wanted to come along as well.”

“He looks very familiar,” said Rachel.

“He’s been on TV,” admitted Emily. “A couple of years ago.”

“I’ve never met anyone whose been on TV,” said Sister Ruth.

“That’s it,” exclaimed Rachel, “he’s Brian, the archaeological bloke. He’s pretty handsome. Didn’t he?” Her question fell silent.

“Yes, he was involved in some controversy and the BBC terminated his employment.”

“I’m sorry.”

“Don’t be, worse things happen all the time,” Emily smiled. “Would you like to meet him? And you could introduce me to the scary Scottish lady.”

“Come with me,” said Rachel. “Before we see her, do you like the monarchy, cats and being on time?”

When they sat back down in the limousine, Emily was the first to speak, “I think Mrs Thornthwistle took a shine to you Daddy.”

“Sam was right, she’s a powerful witch,” replied Brian. “The good thing is that she’s happy for us to tag along. Hopefully, the Spear will make an appearance and we can take matters into our own hands. Follow them Saunders and please keep up.”

“What will happen to Sam if you’re successful?” asked Emily.

Brian paused and looked into Emily’s green eyes before replying, he smiled, “That I do not know. According to Samuel he’s a free agent, so if that’s true my guess would be nothing. But it doesn’t change the fact that he’s a daemon.”

“Meaning what?”

“Just that I had such high hopes for you. I trained you to be a warrior to protect all mankind. I expected you to understand the importance of my work and eventually take it on. It wasn’t just the stealing, it was more the feeling of betrayal I was left with when I realised you were in love with a daemon. Not even a major daemon, just a pawn, that I knew I would have to sacrifice at some point.” Brian’s voice trailed away.

“No!” Emily’s voice rose, “You tried to have him killed didn’t you? That’s why I sliced my wrists open and that’s why I ended up in Hell.”

Brian did not reply and the rest of the journey was completed in silence. They came off the motorway at Junction 36 and followed the convoy winding through the National Park. At Wastwater Head they parked up at a grassy verge next to a car driven by a track-suited man and a copper faced gentleman holding a suspiciously long thin black bag.

It was obvious that this was the end of the journey and everyone got out to stretch their legs. Seeing Emily alone staring into Wastwater Sam came to stand beside her.

"Did you have a good journey? Brian talkative?" he asked.

Emily replied without changing her gaze, "It was interesting. I think Daddy tried to kill you."

"I figured as much. That's why I gave him time to cool down. It doesn't matter now," said Sam gripping her waist.

Emily turned and smiled, but before she could say anything else she was interrupted by an amplified Scottish voice, "Listen up, dears. This is the plan."

Chapter Twenty-Seven

"This is practically fucking Romeo and Juliet." – Natasha

The Wild Geese Tour Bus, The Lake District

Natasha went to the rear shower cubicle and ten minutes later she reappeared wearing Sofia's black jeans and Motorhead T-shirt. "He'll be okay now," she said quietly.

Geoff's back arched rigid, eyes shot wide open and his lungs clawed for oxygen.

"He's awake!" cried Ruby.

"Finally. Do you feel okay?" asked Natasha.

"Bruised and groggy. I think you broke my nose," replied Geoff.

"Let that be a valuable lesson to you. From now on you'll need to fight just to stay alive and you'll need to fight even harder if you're going to get what is rightfully yours," Natasha smiled.

"Where am I?"

"We're with The Wild Geese. They saved us last night. The sound we heard in that room was their tour bus crashing into the flats," said Natasha.

Ruby kissed him on the cheek. "Morning, handsome."

"What's the last thing you remember?" asked Natasha.

"I got hit by something which knocked me over," said Geoff, feeling his shoulder. It was freshly bandaged. "When I got up I was trapped, then the ceiling collapsed but a nun pushed me out of the way. Why would she do that?"

"I don't care and neither should you. For every sweet nun who doesn't want you dead, there'll be a thousand more with chainsaws and drills who do," explained Natasha. "Nuns are vicious little creatures. You need to start thinking like an Anti-Christ, Geoffrey."

"Could she have been possessed?" asked Geoff.

"That had nothing to do with me," said Natasha, holding her hands up. "My guess would be that the nun was acting on autopilot. We are talking about someone who has dedicated her whole life to being good and it was probably just a kneejerk reaction. She saved you because it's in her nature to do the right thing, which fortunately for us, has kept you alive."

Geoff tried to get up off the bed, but only got as far as sitting. "Where's Sofia?" he said.

"Some psycho bastard killed her at the flats," a stony-faced Rob said. "Weirdly he looked just like someone I worked with during the Crusades."

Geoff looked at Ruby, "I am so sorry."

"On a happier note I could make things much better for you if you like?" smiled Natasha.

"What do you mean?" asked Geoff, his eyes narrowing.

"Between you and Rachel. Rob explained your situation."

"How would you do that?"

"For a start, Rachel is mortal so I can easily destroy her life," explained Natasha.

"That doesn't sound particularly romantic."

"What do you expect? She stabbed Rob and was probably going to kill you and you still expect the whole hearts and flowers show?"

"Even so, ruining her life won't help me," Geoff said.

"Ah, you'd think that but hear me out. What if I take a personal interest in making her life a complete and utter misery? Eventually she'll crack and commit suicide, sending her direct to me," Natasha smiled and fluttered her eyelashes. "Cool, eh?"

"Err, really cool," muttered Geoff.

"Okay, top of the head again but what if everyone she loves in the world is killed in truly horrible ways? That should do the trick. Once she arrives in Hell all broken and upset you two lovebirds can have a little chat on how you can save her from an eternity of torture. And this is the kicker, you can only do this if she loves you with all her heart. This plan is amazing."

Geoff paused. "You make Rachel believe that suicide is the only option left to her?"

Natasha and Rob grinned and nodded.

"Then I threaten her with eternal damnation in the afterlife unless she loves me?" asked Geoff.

"That is so brilliant boss," said Rob.

Natasha beamed. "I'm beginning to think that I get some of my best ideas when I'm limited to a human-sized brain."

"Wouldn't Rachel hate me?" asked Geoff.

"Not if she knows what's good for her," stated Natasha.

"But she'll only love me because she doesn't want to spend the rest of eternity being tortured?" Geoff felt his forehead and found a thick bandage.

"Bingo!" cried Natasha.

"That sounds pretty terrible to me," said Geoff looking at a scowling but silent Ruby.

"What do you mean? How old-fashioned do you want this romance of yours to be? It's as old as the Garden of Eden. Boy meets girl. Boy loves girl. Girl breaks boy's heart. Boy takes action. Girl forced to reconsider her position faced with either a) superior firepower, or b) exceptional circumstances. Geoffrey, this is practically fucking Romeo and Juliet," said Natasha, unfurling her arms.

"I'm guessing blackmailing her with the business end of Hell falls under exceptional circumstances?" he asked.

"Bingo again, you are on fire."

"I don't know. It sounds like it's all based on cheating, a serious power imbalance and some heavy-duty coercion."

"Which is why it is all so perfect," said Natasha.

"Mmm."

"You've got to remember I'm the Devil and you're the Anti-Christ, so hearts, poetry and flowers aren't really our way. Fluffy little kittens get used for target practice and unicorns, well, you really don't want to hear what unicorns are forced to do in Hell."

"You haven't had that much experience of romance, have you?" asked Geoff.

"Not as such, but as you can see I'm a very fast learner. I know Rob would really like to help with the murdering. Will you at least consider it?"

Geoff nodded.

"That's the spirit. Just try to keep an open mind to our ways. Hell really isn't that bad if you're high enough up the food chain," said Natasha.

"Why don't you do some of that old style Biblical magic stuff and make sure we really win this time rather than threatening Rachel?" asked Geoff.

"I've already told you why. I signed an agreement with God in 1979 to cut right back on manifestations of power in a series of gradual phases," said Natasha.

"But that's my point, didn't God do all the miracles before then?"

"Technically, yes."

"So what exactly did you do?" asked Geoff.

"So many to choose from," Natasha said. "What about the untamed butchery of the Crusades? The raft of genocides that have occurred throughout the ages?"

"That's sort of what I'm saying. Your stuff happens because humans are, if left to their own devices, pretty evil. What did you have to do with Rwanda? Kosovo? Syria? Weren't they after 1979?" replied Geoff.

"There are many times in history where I've guided people to do the wrong thing," said Natasha. "I feed peoples' worst desires and that works pretty well for me. Rob was at Rwanda and at Kosovo, though more as a tourist I think."

Rob grinned at Geoff and gave him a fleshy thumbs up.

"All you've really done is watch normal people kill other normal people while giving them a few words of encouragement from the sidelines. I'm just saying it's not that impressive," said Geoff.

Natasha flinched. "What exactly are you driving at Geoffrey?"

"Don't you think that God could be a couple of steps ahead of us? Have you thought that he could be the cat to our little mouse?"

Mr Sox turned his head and purred as he thought about the many good times he had enjoyed with Mrs Hotchkiss. While he wasn't totally sure that Reginald existed, he hoped that if he did, that he was going to die of starvation stuck in her flat.

"You may have a small point about the past but the *Book of Revelations* is our time. It's when being evil will be the coolest thing on the planet. It's our destiny to rule the world and make all humans fear and worship us. We'll be the ones with all the drills and chainsaws then," said Natasha.

"You really believe that?" asked Geoff.

"Of course I do. You know nothing, Geoffrey Pike," Natasha smiled. "And you look terrible so try to get some sleep."

Geoff rubbed his face with the palm of his hand and yawned. By the time Natasha turned away he was fast asleep.

As the bus rumbled through The Lake District, the first shafts of dawn broke through the thin cloud cover. Natasha looked out and thought that if she ever got

the chance she would make more of the Earth as beautiful as this. A healthy number of genocides, famines and cranking up global warming should do the trick. At the righthand fork they headed towards Wasdale Lower.

When Geoff woke up Ruby was sat next to him. He looked around and saw Natasha and Rob in conversation at the front of the bus.

"Feel better?" asked Ruby.

"A bit. What do you think those two are discussing?" he asked.

"It's the Devil and a Duke of Hell, so I guess that they'll be talking fluffy stuff like kittens, rainbows and unicorns. You know, standard evil topics," explained Ruby.

"I'm really sorry about Sofia," said Geoff. "I feel terrible that she died saving me."

"It was her choice," said Ruby, looking away. "And she was really saving Rob."

"Even so."

"She's in a better place now, and we all knew it could happen," Ruby sighed. "Remember I've got the Gift and so had she."

"Speaking of your Gift, I take it that this is my great opportunity to make something of myself?"

Ruby nodded. "People have died for you now. Not only Sofia but some of those who guarded you at the flat. You'd better make the most of this, or their deaths will have been for nothing."

"I suppose you're right. I have a responsibility to make this work even if it means starting the apocalypse," said Geoff as he stood up.

Ruby's dark eyes widened. "I knew you had a good old-fashioned apocalypse in you, Mr Pike."

Geoff smiled. At least one person believed in him. "Don't you find all this daemonic Hell stuff a bit strange? Most people don't even know this exists and you seem okay with the whole thing at twenty-one?"

"Twenty-three," Ruby corrected.

"So where did you grow up? A nice leafy suburb of Hell? You're not a daemon, are you?"

Ruby forced a thin smile. "No, I was born and raised in Cobh, a small port east of Cork. You may have heard of it because it was the last stop for the Titanic – before she sank, that is. The head of the local coven was my great-grandmother and she had a wager with the Bishop of Cloyne. She said she could sink the Titanic as a test of faith, a good versus evil thing. His congregation prayed for its safe crossing and her coven did their thing and the rest is history. Once it sank to the bottom of the Atlantic we became the most famous coven in all of Europe for a while."

"You're kidding?"

"No, that's all true," replied Ruby.

"Do you know what happened at the pub? Natasha said it was something to do with your music?"

Ruby smiled. "It was – we performed a little Satanic ritual. You see, on special nights we can use our music to harness the audience's energy and make things a little more interesting for everyone."

"What about your soulstone? It was huge and hovering in mid-air."

"It acts as a focus for the spells we cast. I'll show you a few other rituals once we have more time. Did you like it?" asked Ruby.

Geoff shook his head. "Not really. Everything was frozen and I was chased by monsters."

"Ah, what you experienced was a crude form of True Sight and that's very rare. You saw what people wanted to be, rather than what they are. Rob was the only true daemon there."

"What do you mean, crude?"

"You couldn't distinguish between what was real and what was a person's projection. They chased you because of the great power you have within you. It's very impressive for a first go," said Ruby. The bus turned and slowed. To the right a dark lake stretched out at the foot of a mountain. "I think we're almost there."

Five minutes later the bus slowed to a halt at the side of an abandoned barn, which had a thick coating of dark green moss growing on its roof. Further down the road was a large stone pub.

"Time to grab hold of your destiny, Mr Pike," said Ruby. "Are you ready?"

Geoff nodded and Ruby leant over and kissed him softly on the cheek. "For good luck," she whispered.

Outside Natasha was speaking to Seamus. She was looking back down the valley and frowning. "There's only one way in and out of this place," she said.

Seamus shrugged and took a couple of mouthfuls from his hip flask. "You said you wanted to speak to the Greek and this is how you do it. On the plus side we've got three-inch steel ramplates, bulletproof glass and a double gearbox that'll take us off road if necessary."

Standing outside the barn door Geoff was despondently looking at his mobile. "I can't get a signal here," he muttered.

"Laddie, you haven't been able to get a signal for the past hour," said Seamus. "The Lake District has something called mountains that don't get on with your fancy mobiles. It wouldn't work anyway as the phone masts will have been destroyed by our people by now. Much better to have one of these." He handed Geoff a black walkie-talkie. "They're military issue and have a range of about five miles."

"Thanks," said Geoff.

Seamus placed seven more walkie-talkies on an overturned rusting bucket and raised his voice. "Pay attention. This is important. Everybody take one of these and use channel thirteen if you see anything out of the ordinary."

"So why are we here?" asked Geoff as he followed Natasha to where a thin path snaked upwards.

"We're going to meet the Greek," she replied.

"And he lives at the top of this hill?"

"No. This is a mountain but there's a cave complex about halfway up and she lives there. There's a good chance that she'll already be waiting for us," said Natasha. "The Greek is very good at that sort of stuff, she's special."

"You mean like you and Rob special?"

"No. She's a very different type of special and has a unique hobby, which means she likes to be alone." Natasha had dark circles forming under her eyes. She looked back at the pub and the barn. Michael and Seamus Junior were taking high points on the other side of the valley.

"How come Rob isn't coming?" asked Geoff. "Or Mr Sox? Shouldn't they be shadowing my every move now that people are trying to kill me?"

"Rob and the rest of them are going to make sure we don't get ambushed like before and." Natasha gave a pause. "And the Greek scares him a little."

"Scares Rob? Isn't he this famous Duke of Hell?"

“I’ll explain it all later,” said Natasha, looking at the lake. It was peaceful with shafts of sunlight dappling on its still water. “But now we have to move.”

Trudging up the path that disappeared into the early morning mist Geoff had a strong feeling that he may well dislike the whole outdoors thing. It seemed far too cold and wet. After an hour of strenuous exertion, he decided that nature was not for him. If he was going to rule this apocalypse one of his first actions would be to get the whole of The Lake District flattened and tarmacked.

Suddenly Natasha stopped and looked up. There was a man standing on a ridge twenty feet above them. He was facing away and was very still.

“Is that her? She looks human,” whispered Geoff.

“She is, sort of, but looks can be deceiving. Come on.”

“And she looks like a bloke.”

As they approached, the figure turned. Somewhere in his fifties, he had shortish red hair and a salt and paprika beard. He looked at them through heavily bloodshot eyes. His face looked mottled, grey in some areas and angry red in others. A strange putrid smell hung around him.

The Greek smiled and offered her hand to Natasha.

“I was expecting you earlier.” Her voice sounded like the spidery writing of a stroke victim, all disjointed and weak. It was also the voice of a man. The Greek was wearing a bright red walking jacket, which had seen much better days. “It’s good to see you, Mephistopheles. It’s been a while,” she said.

“It’s good to see you too. You know how it is with these desk jobs,” smiled Natasha. “We were delayed, but I’m guessing that you already know about that and all about Geoffrey?”

“Indeed I do. Pleased to meet you Geoffrey, you can call me the Greek,” she said, giving Geoff a firm handshake. “Now if you would like to follow me.”

The Greek turned and walked diagonally upwards away from the path for ten minutes. She then stooped and disappeared through a hidden and extremely tight gap in the wet Cumbrian stone saying, “Please follow me. You are perfectly safe.”

Geoff shook his head as the Greek vanished into the mountain. He didn’t feel safe. For the last nine minutes he had been watching her right ear. It was covered in shiny dark green pus and seemed to be on the verge of falling off her head.

“You said no zombies,” breathed Geoff. “What about that ear? And the smell?”

“Not a zombie Geoffrey. Now keep close to me and keep your wits about you,” whispered Natasha as she glanced back at him. “If this goes wrong, neither of us will be getting out of this alive.”

Chapter Twenty-Eight

"She is not a God." – Natasha

Scafell Pike, The Lake District

"Isn't that the sort of information you share with someone beforehand?" hissed Geoff through clenched teeth. "You know, before they disappear into a mountain with some hillwalking zombie?"

"She is not a zombie. And if we'd discussed this before you wouldn't have agreed to come with me," replied Natasha, manhandling Geoff into the gap and pushing him forward. "It's better this way."

A further five minutes of claustrophobic ducking, edging and crawling later they emerged into a large roughly circular cavern. An industrial-sized generator hummed in one corner with a series of floor mounted electric lights rigged up to it. There was no bed and nothing that resembled a kitchen or a bathroom, though there was a gleaming metal door on one side. In the centre there was a large white marble table with six matching chairs.

"Please forgive the webs, you know how it is when guests are seldom," said the Greek as she ushered Natasha and Geoff to a seat.

"Before we begin, can I ask your views on spiders Geoffrey?" asked the Greek, her eyes dark and shiny.

Geoff looked at the edges of the cave and saw there were even more spiders and webs than he had noticed when he first came in. "They kill flies so that's good. My flatmate Rob's scared of them so I have to deal with them."

"You don't suffer from arachnophobia?"

"Not really," replied Geoff. "I always help the spiders in our flat. I never kill them but I do think Mr Sox eats them when I'm not there."

The Greek's lips pursed, her brow furrowed.

"He's our cat."

"Of course he is," replied the Greek, her features softening to a smile under the straggled beard.

"Is that why Rob's scared of you? Because you collect spiders?" asked Geoff.

The Greek threw her head back. As her throaty laughter echoed around the cavern, she showed two sets of perfectly white teeth. Geoff shivered. Some teeth looked like they'd been filed to a point.

"I like you Geoffrey. You've got a good heart," said the Greek finally.

"Shouldn't I have a black evil heart?" laughed Geoff.

"Possibly? Were you surprised that I asked you about spiders?"

"Not really. You live in a cave, there're lots of spiders here and you're probably a bit attached to them. It must get lonely up here in the middle of nowhere."

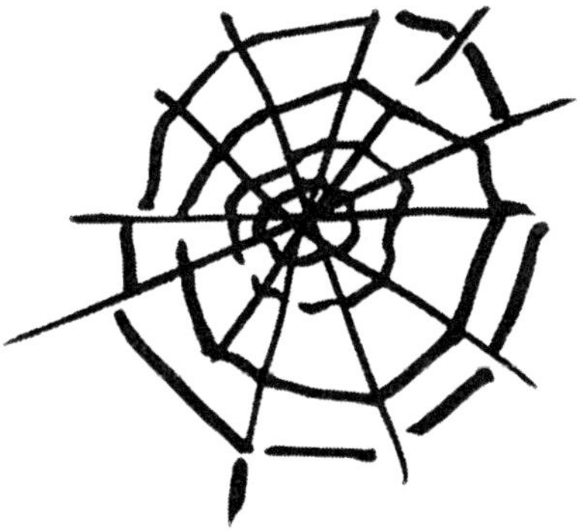

"A bit attached to them?" The Greek savoured each word, looking down as a large hairy spider the size of a small espresso saucer crawled up the table leg and onto her left arm. Carefully she scooped it up with her hand, allowing it to crawl up and over, up and over. "Attached?" She lowered her hand and allowed the spider to creep down to the marble table. Once there the spider stopped moving and stared at Geoff with all of its eight eyes. "My interest in spiders is for the most part scientific. Pound for pound spider silk is as strong as the Aramid filaments used in Kevlar vests, and a single silk fibre could go around the world and weigh only sixteen ounces. They are truly amazing creatures."

"I can see that," agreed Geoff, who felt he needed to be polite.

"They are also born predators who live for the kill. Out of the forty thousand species known to man only one is not a hunter. Native Americans believe that the spider is the 'Thinking Woman' who has the power to create or destroy the world as she sees fit."

"All very impressive," nodded Geoff.

"However, despite all of these advantages, spiders have failed to develop any type of brain that could match that of you monkeys, so you win the evolutionary race. Such a shame."

With one fluid movement the Greek grabbed the spider off the table and shoved it unceremoniously into her mouth. Two hairy back legs spasmed over her lower lip. All the colour drained from Geoff's face. "You…"

The Greek's tongue expertly licked the legs up before there was a dull crunch followed by a heavy gulp.

"Eat spiders? Yes, I do. They are delicious and an excellent source of protein. Would you care to have a little nibble? There's plenty to go round."

"That is dark," replied Geoff, shaking his head and looking at Natasha.

"Well, as you already know they call me the Greek." Her voice was getting stronger with each word as if she was remembering how to talk. "However I am not from Greece, but I do possess a unique talent that allows me to work out the most likely turn of events in complex situations when given mere scraps of information."

Geoff watched the floor at the outer reaches of the cave ripple slowly towards the table. The air in the cave felt cold and stale with a stench of rotting flesh. He shot Natasha a look, but she was gazing at the Greek with a smile playing on her lips. *That must be why we are here,* he thought. "So you're like Sherlock Holmes?" he said.

"I suppose there are similarities though he is a fictional character while I am very real. Would you like a demonstration?"

"Yes, that would be great," answered Geoff.

"Can you please stand up and face me? Good. Can you stand on your right leg and touch your nose with your left index finger? Excellent. Hold that position."

A couple of minutes passed with Geoff swaying and touching the floor with his right leg three times before the Greek told him to sit back down.

"You are Geoffrey Archibald Pike. A thirty-three-year-old male. I'll round up the probabilities to make it easier for you to understand."

"Okay," he said.

"You are five foot nine inches, though there is a ninety-seven percent probability that you tell people that you are five foot ten. There is an eighty-nine percent probability that you have failed to have any truly significant romantic relationships during your life and there is a ninety-nine percent probability that you harbour feelings of unrequited love for a woman you have worked with. There is a seventy-four percent probability that she is a Rachel, Ruby or Rebecca. There is also a sixty-three percent probability that she has attempted to kill you in the last twenty-four hours." The Greek paused. "How am I doing?"

Geoff managed a gulp followed by a nod.

"There is a ninety-one percent probability that you have been involved in a life and death struggle with people who believe that you are either a Satanist, or the Anti-Christ. There is a one hundred percent probability that you prefer tea to coffee and that your favourite food is spaghetti carbonara. Other one hundred percent probabilities are that you have a cat, your favourite colour is red, you're a terribly bad dancer and of course that you are the Anti-Christ."

"So I *am* the Anti-Christ," said Geoff, smiling at Natasha.

"Indeed you are," smiled the Greek. Some of her teeth had definitely been filed.

"That's amazing. What was the use of me standing on one leg and touching my nose?"

"I wanted to see how gullible you are," the Greek replied. "I originally thought ninety-one percent, though I've subsequently raised that to ninety-nine percent."

"That's just mean," said Geoff.

"Of course it is and I am sorry," said the Greek as she held out both her hands. There were small movements under her skin. She turned to Natasha. "Have we got time for truthful introductions?"

Natasha nodded, though she narrowed her eyes. "If you must. I am guessing that you haven't had too many opportunities to speak over the past few years, but please make it quick?"

The Greek turned back to face Geoff. "Seeing as you're so desperate to know, I'll tell you my story. I am a native of Phalangia, a planet in a parallel dimension. At least, that is roughly the sound of what it translates to into English."

"That means you're a…" whispered Geoff his eyes wide.

"Yes," interrupted the Greek. "I am what you would classify as an alien life form and I am also female."

"But you don't look alien?"

"I'm part of a highly intelligent and supremely advanced race of cyborg solifugae."

"A soli…what?" asked Geoff.

"A primitive version of our distant ancestors lives on your planet. Think of a ten-legged spider if that makes it easier for you. Obviously, we are far more evolved and have developed twelve legs and fourteen eyes. Like you, we are a carbon-based life form, though we are significantly augmented by robotic enhancements."

"But you look human."

"Yes, you are correct," said the Greek, placing her hands on her chest. The number of spiders teeming around her seemed to have doubled since they sat down. "As a race we have an ability to couple with inferior beings in a semi-symbiotic manner. I came to this miserable rock over three thousand years ago. When I arrived you monkeys had no idea about how the universe works. The basic science and wonder of it all completely eluded you. Do you have a working knowledge of string theory?"

Geoff shook his head.

The Greek gave a fleeting smile. "Your ignorance does not surprise me in the slightest so I'll give you a simplistic summary. String theory unifies everything: matter, force, space and time. Everything is composed of tiny vibrating strings."

Geoff listened in silence.

"If you are capable of faster than light propulsion you are able to move from one string universe to another. We were the masters of our universe and our mission was to explore new dimensions and enslave them. However, while we made it through to your universe, we miscalculated and our fleet crashed into your Earth. Almost all of us perished and the majority of survivors found that being deprived of our technology and being dwarfed by ignorant monkeys was just too much. Those few of us who had the will to survive chose to adapt."

"Are you saying that humans aren't really human?" asked Geoff.

"No. Not at all. We simply took over certain individuals and managed their subsequent thoughts and actions."

"That's pretty creepy," said Geoff. "So how do you control a person?"

"Adaptation on a cellular level occurs over a short period of time. Silk thread encases the subject's head and an acidic secretion weakens the back of the skull to allow us to physically split it open and join with the inferior monkey brain after around twenty-four hours. We provide psionic suggestion which gives the host an intense feeling of euphoria to compensate for any discomfort. We then reseal the skull, reposition the host brain and take over operational control of the body and the mind. Snazzy, eh?"

"Yes, real snazzy," agreed Geoff.

"Alternatively we force our way into the brain through the eyes, ears, or nasal passages. Though that can cause extreme pain and disfigurement. Either way works for me, though I do accept that this way is a little bit less snazzy?"

"So why would people volunteer for this?"

"Because I offer them a free ride of millennia of experiences and a true understanding of the universe that's way beyond their dreary mortal expectations and abilities," explained the Greek. "They get to learn about everything from my Godlike intellect."

"You are not a God," said Natasha flatly. "Gods do not live in caves and eat spiders."

"I can sort of see why some people would like that, but isn't it a bit cramped?" asked Geoff, looking at the ear.

The Greek laughed, "True. My exquisite body needs wriggle room which means that we dispense with certain sections of the host brain."

"You eat bits of the brain?"

"Quite a bit over time. You do not use large parts of it so you don't really miss it. The longevity of the host varies. Many live for decades, others die in a matter of months. Those who volunteer willingly generally fare much better."

"You're like a hermit crab?" asked Geoff.

"I suppose it is similar, but we have a living shell. My current manifestation is one of the more disappointing examples. We all do what we must to survive. Wouldn't you agree Mephistopheles?"

"But why do they call you the Greek?"

"As even you must know, the Greeks brought the concept of civilisation into this world through their work on philosophy, science, art and literature. That was down to me. Archimedes, Pythagoras, Aristotle, Plato were all vessels guided by me and thus the nickname stuck. As the years went by the other survivors also did their part. Controlling your understanding of the universe was surprisingly fun."

"The dancing monkeys would have eventually found out about science with or without you," said Natasha.

"Possibly, but how long did it take them to discover fire? I think I speeded things up by at least a millennium. As centuries passed we found that even your best minds were far too slow. I was all for setting up a rival race of super solifugaes starting with our pure bloodline but mating with the savages on this planet was considered heretical and I was outvoted by what remained of my crew."

"So how can you live for so long if you're not a God?" asked Geoff.

"She is not a God," repeated Natasha.

"Compared with your limitations we are practically immortal. When the host body dies, we move on to another and rejuvenate. However, most of my crew eventually went mad or simply gave up. They starved themselves to death and died, hoping that their souls would make it back to the Golden Web."

"Enough of the introductions, we need to talk now," said Natasha.

"Fine, but let me explain to Geoffrey why you are here," replied the Greek. "When we sliced through the barriers that separated our dimensions something else happened. My already impressive psionic abilities were vastly increased and I developed an uncanny precognition ability, which allows me to see things that have not yet happened. I believe that this was caused by a time gap between our realities. Think of it as different time zones on Earth. Your reality is at midnight but if I'm in Beijing my reality is eight o'clock. I move to your reality at midnight and suddenly I can see what happens from now until eight o'clock in the morning."

"This isn't a religious thing then?" asked Geoff.

"Not at all, but I see Natasha grows impatient," said the Greek. "I will need to speak to her privately if that's okay with you Geoffrey? You don't have to leave, we'll use telepathy."

"Why in private?" he asked.

"It'll be better for you that way," replied the Greek.

"Oh great," said Geoff, watching Natasha and the Greek close their eyes. A minute later he muttered, "Bugger this," closed his eyes, placed his forefingers on his temples and began to think really hard. His brow furrowed, eyes bulged and his face reddened to the colour of a ripe radish.

Pop.

Geoff realised he could hear exactly what they were saying.

Chapter Twenty-Nine

"My advice to you is to think of Geoffrey as a big lump of cheese." – the Greek

The Greek's Lair, Scafell Pike, The Lake District

"You are, once again, trying to bring about your apocalypse through the ascension of your offspring," stated the Greek. "I must confess that I am impressed by your commitment to this dream of yours."

"Pot, kettle, black?" replied Natasha. "But yes, I am guilty as charged. What can you tell me?"

The Greek glanced at Geoff's deep concentration before shaking her head, "And why do you think that this one is going to be any different?"

"He's thirty-three years old and still alive."

"Even so I'm afraid it's not going to happen," said the Greek.

"Are you certain?" asked Natasha.

"Putting his numerous deficiencies to one side I still can't see how this," the Greek sighed, "individual of yours can become the world devourer. He simply doesn't have it in him. The truth is the truth and sometimes it hurts. I am sorry."

Geoff could feel his face reddening but kept his eyes firmly shut. He didn't want to miss a word.

"You must be mistaken." There was a soft quiver in Natasha's voice.

"Mephistopheles, why do you think that Geoffrey is going to succeed where all others have failed? Your SACRED programme has produced some excellent candidates. As for Geoffrey, he has nothing that sets him apart from the average dancing monkey. I'm not trying to tell you how to run your business but I would try to be more selective in future."

Natasha's face hardened as she bit the inside of her cheek.

"Do you believe in him?" questioned the Greek in a slow whispery voice that sounded like snakes, not spiders.

"Yes," she replied. "Even though he's not much to look at, he has my royal blood. He is the Anti-Christ and has lasted for thirty-three years, which is more than Jesus managed."

"But don't you see that Geoffrey's longevity can be attributed to the fact that he poses no credible threat to God? Put yourself in his sandals – would you lose any sleep knowing that the new Anti-Christ works at a call centre? I can provide a probability if you wish?"

Natasha shook her head.

The Greek went on, "You know full well that pure blood does not guarantee success. Geoffrey will remain an excessively dull person of no real worth with or without your actions. I suppose your PR team could repackage him and try to sell him to the masses as a dumbed down people's Anti-Christ?" she chuckled.

Geoff spoke. "I know that you're talking telepathically but I can hear you and I think you should know that before someone says something that's going to hurt my feelings."

"How do I know that you are telling the truth?" asked Natasha, ignoring Geoff.

"You already know that I'm telling you the truth," said the Greek. "What could I possibly gain from lying?"

"I can hear you both," stammered Geoff, his eyes firmly shut. "And I'm not even trying to concentrate anymore."

"Maybe you could use him as bait?" suggested the Greek.

"I heard that as well."

The Greek turned to face Geoff. "Of course you did, darling, because we are speaking."

"Are you?" Geoff opened his eyes and levelled his gaze at Natasha.

"Yes," she replied. "We stopped using telepathy when you went bright red. I thought that if you were willing to cause yourself a stroke you had a right to hear what the Greek said."

"I feel a bit stupid now."

"See what I mean?" said the Greek. "There is a ninety-nine percent probability that Geoffrey is getting used to feeling really stupid."

"I'm not the one?"

"Precisely, you're the Anti-Christ in name only, darling," explained the Greek, turning to Natasha. "See, he's taken it very well, don't you think? He knows deep down that he isn't the one who's going to ascend to the throne of the Anti-Christ."

"But they'll still try to kill me, won't they?" said Geoff.

"Yes," replied Natasha and the Greek in unison.

"I'm afraid that Natasha coming down to see you has set those wheels in motion. My advice is to try to go back to your dull and boring life," said the Greek in a happy tone. "Maybe get your job back at the call centre? And then God may realise that you're not a serious threat and let you live a long, uneventful life."

"So this has all been pointless?" asked Geoff.

"You mean for you?" The Greek's dark eyes sparkled like polished stones. "One hundred percent yes."

"Oh," said Geoff glumly.

"Cheer up, would you like to see my work?" asked the Greek, pointing at the metal door. "I'm sure you'll find it fascinating."

"Make it quick," said Natasha. "And don't do anything rash. Rob and my followers are close by."

"I know that Mephistopheles. Now please follow me." The Greek rose and shambled slowly through a steel doorway into a small metal room. Once Geoff and Natasha entered, the door behind them locked with a heavy clunk and the room was bathed in an ultraviolet light. Hundreds of small spiders fell off the Greek to be swept up by a circular robot.

"This is a harmless scan to make sure none of my spiders follow us," said the Greek, turning to a grey box at head height. A retinal scan gave a faint whir as she looked down and tapped in a thirteen-figure code. There was a buzz and the second door swung open.

"How did you get all of this here?" asked Geoff.

"Amazon makes deliveries at the pub. I pay people to bring it up the mountain, then I lobotomise them so they don't feel the need to discuss this location, or me."

"Snazzy," said Geoff.

The room ahead was brightly illuminated and scrupulously clean. Thirteen separate walls gave it a circular shape and feel. Twice as large as the previous cave, gleaming white tiles covered the floor and a vast array of scientific equipment stood at almost every wall. In the centre was an operating table while banks of computers whirred away on one side. Monitors showed a view of space from the James Webb Space Telescope; security footage played from an underground facility; a call centre; and the interior of a small florist shop. Elsewhere on circular tables stood cellular equipment; microscopes; small refrigerators; and four online casino sites. A silent black generator easily the height of Natasha, completely filled one corner with thick black cabling spilling out of it.

"Wow," said Geoff. "So why does Rob hate you?"

"I fucked him during World War Two," stated the Greek.

"That explains it," said Geoff. "He's a really bad loser."

"I don't think that you understand, darling. My host then was a sweet young actress working with the Gestapo and Azothoth, or Rob as you know him, was a dashing SS-Sturmbannf with an Iron Cross around his neck. Back then neither of us knew what the other was and there was even some talk of marriage until I came clean and explained my somewhat unique situation. The stupid oaf did not like that at all."

"Oh, that does makes sense," said Geoff, standing in front of a wall that was covered by hundreds of dead spiders and solifugae in special pods, labelled and framed. "What are all these?" he asked.

"Welcome to my extended family," said the Greek. "Five and a half years of genome sequencing and splicing and I still haven't stopped them eating each other. It's as if your God himself is out to thwart me."

"He does that," shrugged Natasha. "I take it your work here supersedes anything taking place out there?"

"Of course it does, darling, and yet…" the Greek touched the glass cabinet of the largest spider. "I have failed to use my perfect DNA to spawn a new breed of intelligent solifugaes. What limited success I've had has been with arachnids. All my work is contained in this," said the Greek, holding up a sleek black portable hard drive.

"I thought you said you were prevented by your crew from mating with the locals?" asked Geoff.

"That only counted when they were alive," replied the Greek.

"Did your current host go for the snazzy option?" asked Geoff.

"Regrettably not, which has resulted in a few problems down the line with his ears, one of which I believe you've already noticed."

In front of the computers stood a number of metal tables covered with books, devices and strange artefacts. The Greek lumbered up to one of the computers and started typing. The resulting words on the monitor screen looked like gobbledygook, or as they actually were, Phalagian script.

Geoff hovered over a small porcelain Victorian doll on a wooden stand. He was just about to pick it up when a shrill call from the Greek stopped him. "Please don't touch anything in this room without my permission. It has taken me literally hundreds of years to acquire this collection."

"A collection of what?" asked Geoff.

"What you're looking at are primarily artefacts of the occult. With the progress of science so slow I dabbled in supernatural phenomena looking for alternative solutions to my dilemma. It was then that I ran into Mephistopheles," said the Greek. "Of course back then, she was a he."

"But why?" Geoff asked.

"I was hoping to escape back to my dimension, or at least find some way of contacting Chairman Z. All hail Her Fangs!"

"Chairman Z?" asked Geoff.

"All hail Her Fangs! Yes, the most powerful being in any dimension. Like your God but with a more fangs on approach. She is the ruler of the Golden Web," said the Greek wistfully.

"Is that something like Heaven?" asked Geoff.

Natasha shot Geoff a glance.

"Similar, but with more slaughtering of our enemies," answered the Greek. "I believe that Mephistopheles should help me go back home so I can spend eternity with Chairman Z. All hail Her Fangs!"

"We've already discussed this. I can't do that because gods and demigods from different strings appear to be unaware of each other's existence," replied Natasha. "And I wouldn't have the slightest idea how to pass over to a new dimension, nor would I ever want to."

"Can you at least help me collect certain items from this room?" asked the Greek.

"What do you want?" asked Natasha.

"See the purple rucksacks over there? Please fill them with stickered items. Natasha, if you could pick up all the items with red stickers, leaving the blue ones to you, Geoffrey. You should both collect thirteen items. I would do this myself but as you can see my body is failing me," said the Greek while tapping away. "You'll need the head torches as well."

"Why do you want these now?" asked Natasha. "Planning on going somewhere?"

"I'll explain everything once we get out of here," replied the Greek, painfully shuffling towards the door.

Two minutes later the rucksacks were filled with the stickered items: five musty books; two daggers; four small thermos flasks; two amulets; a ring; a crystal skull; a silver mirror; a kaleidoscope; a paperweight; two mummified spiders; a pair of goggles; two leather messenger bags; a jewellery box; a flash drive; and a large revolver.

Geoff began to follow the Greek and Natasha out of the room when a small plastic gun caught his eye. It had a white body, purple nozzle and a bright red trigger. Whilst not stickered it quickly found its way into the bottom of his rucksack.

Once they were back in the cave, the Greek stumbled and whispered, "I'm afraid that I need to sit down."

"Err...you've lost an ear," said Geoff. The other ear was beginning to melt away.

The Greek raised her hand and found only green pus. "Damn. Please give me a moment."

Geoff looked around. Thousands upon thousands of arachnid eyes peered back at him. The floor, the walls, the ceiling were an organic mass of legs, plump bodies and glistening black eyes. "What's happening with the spiders?" he asked.

"They sense that my body is decaying and my arrival is imminent. In short, they all wish to see and worship me," explained the Greek.

Two thick hairy legs of an overly large spider appeared over the Greek's shoulder. This was followed by a bloated body the size of a pasta dish with one large blue eye in the centre of its face surrounded by nine smaller black ones. The mutated spider looked at Geoff.

"I think we need to be…" he whispered to Natasha.

"Proud? Is that the word you're looking for? For indeed I am." The Greek scooped the spider up with a cupped left hand and began to stroke it. The abomination purred. "Jasmine likes you Geoffrey. Would you like to hold her? She won't bite, unless she senses your fear."

"You did say you liked spiders," smiled Natasha with raised eyebrows.

Taking two heavy gulps Geoff slowly stretched out his palm across the table. Jasmine's four front legs slowly crept onto his hand followed by her body and the rest of her legs. She was easily twice the size of his hand.

"Hi, Jasmine," croaked Geoff. "Aren't you a beautiful spider? Yes, you are."

"I like. I Jasmine, please meet you."

"She spoke to me." Geoff shivered. "In my mind."

"Well done Jasmine. I have had some success in passing on a small fragment of my intelligence and telepathic ability."

"You cute," Jasmine said. The voice in Geoff's mind was deep and plummy.

"Thank you very much, Jasmine. This is amazing," replied Geoff.

"You have a big…" Jasmine paused and showed her pure white fangs. She seemed to be smiling and smelt of Chanel Coco Mademoiselle.

Geoff breathed in and slowly reached out and touched her. His hand immediately shot back from the thick carpet of throbbing hair.

"Juicy brain!" cried Jasmine, rearing up and sinking her fangs into Geoff's palm.

"Oww!"

She ran quickly up Geoff's arm, her front legs wrapping around his chin.

"Arrrgggghhhh!" he cried.

Thud!

Natasha punched Jasmine square in the face, spilling her over the far side of the table. "Enough of your games, Greek," she said.

"She bit me!" cried Geoff.

"You showed fear," snorted the Greek.

"I feel woozy," said Geoff, studying the two puncture marks on his hand. They were deep and bloody.

"I assure you that Jasmine is not poisonous and that was just a playful peck," said the Greek, picking Jasmine up and placing her back on the table.

To Geoff's horror three similarly mutated spiders, all slightly larger than Jasmine, joined her. They all had an additional large blue eye and twelve thick legs.

"The black one is Bert; the red and black is Nancy; and the purplish one is Terrence. These are my most recent children."

Geoff managed a subdued, "Hi."

Each of the spiders fixed their beady eyes on Geoff. Finally, the black one moved forward and spoke in his mind in an Australian accent, *"I am Bert."*

He was followed by a soft delicate Japanese voice, *"I am Nancy and very pleased to meet you,"* followed by a heavy South American voice with a slight lisp, *"My name is Senor Terrence. Pleased to make your acquaintance."*

Geoff stared at them. He gripped the walkie-talkie in his pocket but thought it would be no use this far underground. The spiders returned his stare while Jasmine cleaned his blood from her fangs.

The Greek's breathing became erratic and her head began to roll from side to side. "My body is failing, darlings. Please do not be alarmed Geoffrey, but I am about to meet you in person," she grunted.

A thin red dot appeared at the bottom of her forehead which quickly spread to the left, right and up. Blood oozed out of these lines creating a gruesome red mask below them. Her eyes bulged before they popped out of their sockets. Her head crashed forwards hitting the marble table with a sickening *thud*. Her head rose again before crashing back. On the third attempt the top of the skull cracked, spilling a mixture of hair, skin, and bone across the marble. A cocooned brain rolled slowly onto the bloody mess still attached to the spinal column.

A small twelve-legged spiderlike being with a golden metallic body, bulbous torso and a large blue eye surrounded by thirteen smaller black ones was sat atop the brain. Each eye was protected by a brass goggle and each leg poked out of a small circular metal colander with dainty hairs emerging at regular intervals. The Greek gave a shake of her body, loosening the bloody bits of brain that still clung to her.

"Ta dah!" Her physical voice had a scratchy, throaty purr.

"Never, ever let her do that to me," said a white-faced Geoff to Natasha. "Rob is so fucking right to be scared of her."

"Pleased to meet you, Geoffrey," cooed the Greek.

From every part of the cave a faint rustle started, like the crushing of dead leaves underfoot. Gradually this living tide grew. It was as if someone had fired a starting gun as every single spider began to march towards the table.

The human host reached down and clumsily tried to return his brain, skull and eyes to their original locations. Bits of eye kept slipping through his shaking fingers, smearing the marble with a thick translucent sheen. Geoff couldn't be certain but the host seemed to be smiling while gurgling bubbles of blood at him.

"What the fuck is happening?" asked Geoff.

"That, my darling, is a particularly good question. My subjects are making their pilgrimage to the sacred site of my residence."

"You mean his skull, don't you? What will they do once they get there?"

"Like all devout pilgrims they will feast."

"But look at him. He's hardly got any brain left," cried Geoff.

"I admit that I have had a few nibbles of the frontal lobes. He was such a monstrous bore with a brain function to match, but it's not just the brain that is considered holy. The whole of his body will be consumed."

"We're done with this arachnid freak show. Geoffrey, we're leaving," said Natasha, as a moving carpet of spiders covered the host's face.

"Mephistopheles, it has been a great pleasure, but you need me if you want this to end with your apocalypse," said the Greek with a smile.

"But you've already said that Geoff isn't the one," Natasha said.

"Indeed I did, but I know of a certain game changer that can get you your apocalypse with or without a functioning Anti-Christ."

"This will not end well for you if you're playing games with me," snarled Natasha, her eyes blazing red. "What do you want from me? My patience ends right now."

"I want a safe journey back to my dimension," said the Greek, scuttling towards Geoff.

"I've already told you I can't send you back."

"True, but I think I can show you how it can be done," replied the Greek.

The host spasmed, his hands slipping off the top of his skull while Bert, Terrence and Nancy prised their way in. Only Jasmine remained on the table staring at Geoff.

"I need details now," said Natasha.

"I'd love to explain but we really need to go," said the Greek, watching her three children split open the broken skull and sink their fangs into what was left of the brain.

"Uuurrgggh," grunted the host. There was a sickening *thud* as he fell to his right and started crawling to the exit. He was covered head to toe with spiders of every conceivable size and shape. He let out another blood splattered groan.

"Details now," repeated Natasha. "Or we leave."

"I believe that there is a seventy-seven percent probability that the apocalypse can occur and usher in a new age of darkness," said the Greek quickly.

"But how is that possible?" asked Natasha.

"Darling, explaining how makes my role somewhat redundant. Something I can tell you is that your God has disappeared, which gives you a far better chance of success." The Greek scuttled to the edge of the table.

"He is not my God," said Natasha.

"Nor mine," said the Greek.

"God's gone?" asked Geoff. "Just so you both know, he's not mine either."

"I also believe that there is a forty-two percent probability that I can make it home and finally join Chairman Z. All hail Her Fangs! if you help me."

"That sounds low?" said Natasha.

"Only because I require your apocalypse to occur before I can attempt to make my journey," stated the Greek.

"What about Geoffrey? What role does he play in this?" asked Natasha.

The Greek sighed. "I wouldn't get overly attached to Geoffrey, Mephistopheles."

"Why not?" cried Geoff.

"Well, if he remains with you and becomes a threat to God, we both know how that ends. But if he goes it alone they will catch him and undoubtedly kill him. Your interest in him has sadly sealed his fate."

"But you said God was missing," said Natasha.

The Greek shrugged, "Missing yes, stupid no. You know how God feels about your Anti-Christs."

"That's really unfair," said Geoff.

"And yet that is how it will be. My advice to you is to think of Geoffrey as a big lump of cheese. If God's people are busy chasing him, you can pursue your apocalypse with my assistance. That changes him from a liability to an asset."

"I'm not a lump of cheese!" exclaimed Geoff. "I'm the Anti-Christ."

"Shhh. Be quiet Geoffrey," soothed Natasha, placing her hand on his shoulder. "Cut to the chase."

"I have stipulations. The first is that you provide me with a new host. My preference would be a young, sexually active female."

Natasha nodded, her features frozen in the half light.

"The second is a personal guarantee of my safety. I want your word that neither you nor your subjects will cause me any harm. This applies most stringently to that monster of yours, Azothoth."

Natasha nodded once more.

"My final stipulation is that should an apocalypse come to pass, you promise to assist me in my attempt to return home. This is the most crucial one. Do you agree with my terms?"

"I agree with your terms," said Natasha in a cold voice, "but I also have a stipulation. You must promise not to aid God."

"I've already told you that my returning home is dependent on the apocalypse coming to pass," said the Greek. "Your God is of no use to me."

"Then I have your word?" pressed Natasha.

"Yes," replied the Greek.

"What just happened?" asked Geoff.

"I just made you into an asset, Geoffrey." The Greek looked at him, her blue eye sparkling, and said to Natasha, "In our world we close a deal by gorging on the brain of a weaker member of our species. I don't suppose that I could interest you in doing it our way, darling?"

Chapter Thirty

"Bad Brad!" – Jasmine

The Greek's Lair, Scafell Pike, The Lake District

"I will travel with you, Geoffrey. We can have a nice get to know you session." The Greek scuttled onto the back of Geoff's overturned chair.

"What?" growled Geoff. "No fucking way!"

"Look, darling, I promise not to mind meld you. I give you my word. If you don't want me attached to your head I can ride on your rucksack."

Geoff clamped his mouth shut and shook his head.

"I feel so rusty, I've been cooped up for far too long," purred the Greek, stretching her legs and wiggling her bulbous body. "Mephistopheles, the clock is literally ticking."

"What do you care?" asked Geoff. "You're immortal so you can catch us up."

Natasha pulled Geoff to one side. "She cannot keep up with us and time is our scarcest resource. We don't know how close our enemies are and there is only one way out of this valley. I'm afraid you will have to carry her."

"No way," he replied, eyeing the Greek and her four children on the marble table. They were all watching him with small bits of brain hanging from their fangs. Their conversations crowded his thoughts.

"Surprisingly chewy," said Nancy.

"I love warm brains in the morning," lisped Terrence.

"Geoffrey is stupid name," stated Jasmine. *"I will call you Brad."*

"I am Bert."

Natasha put her arm around Geoff's shoulders. "Just think, a seventy-seven percent chance of the apocalypse. Do you understand how wonderful that is?" Her eyes sparkled.

“Maybe for you, but I’m just a great big lump of cheese in all of this,” snapped back Geoff.

“No you’re not. You may even get to rule here, we just don’t know the practicalities yet, but if you help make the apocalypse a reality I will be able to honour you at home after all.”

“In Manchester?” he asked.

“No, Geoffrey, in my home, your real home,” sighed Natasha. “I like to call it Hell.”

“I have to die?”

“Everyone dies but when you do you’ll be a real antihero.” Natasha gave Geoff’s bicep a squeeze.

“No call centre?” asked Geoff.

“That’s right,” confirmed Natasha, “no call centre.”

“I suppose I could do this, for the cause and for you, that is. Just promise me that I won’t end up like him,” said Geoff, pointing at the Greek’s host. He wasn’t smiling now, which wasn’t surprising as a group of spiders were busy dragging off his lower lip.

“I promise.”

From the chair the Greek interrupted, “Darling Mephistopheles, this is all very touching but we need to move. I feel my subjects are becoming a touch agitated.”

“Do not bite me, or do anything weird, okay?” said Geoff.

The Greek whispered, "Yes, whatever you say, but we really do need to go now. I fear my subjects are seeing this as a kidnapping."

"Say what?" said Geoff.

The four large spiders reared up, their long fangs flashing.

"They're realising that I'm about to leave them and they are becoming unhappy," stated the Greek. "Very unhappy."

"And that's bad?" asked Geoff, placing his head torch in the centre of his forehead and flicking it on.

"Depends on whether you are comfortable with upsetting over a hundred thousand spiders," replied the Greek.

"To be fair, most of them are pretty small," said Geoff, looking around. "Even the ones on the table don't look that tough."

"Bad juicy brain! Eat bad juicy brain!" The four spiders screamed in unison in Geoff's mind as they crawled slowly across the table.

"I think you've upset them Geoffrey," said Natasha.

"There is also an additional matter that you are unaware of. I would prefer not being in this cave in exactly one hundred and ninety-six seconds," said the Greek.

"That's pretty precise. Is that one of your probability predictions?" said Geoff as he picked up the rucksack.

"There are hundreds of years of work in my laboratory which I do not wish to share. We Phalagians are biters and do not play well with others," said the Greek. "Like I said, the clock is ticking and we need to go this instant."

"What do you mean?" asked Geoff.

"The computer screen," stated the Greek, looking over the metal door. With fourteen flat eyes it proved to be more difficult to guide Geoff's gaze than she had anticipated. She sighed. "The screen above the door."

"I would never have guessed that," said Geoff, as he stepped away and looked up. A series of letters flashed.

MGBURFYHTVDS

In a second they changed:

MGBURFYJWQR

In another second they changed again:

MGBURYHYKG

Another second passed by:

PVWRTQNGT

"Oh shit! We need to go!" shouted Geoff.

Natasha was already at the exit. She dropped to her hands and knees and without looking back she disappeared down the tunnel. The Greek jumped off the chair and onto Geoff's rucksack as he scrambled out of the cave. The walls were a writhing mass of hairy bulbous movement.

Geoff glanced behind him. A thick carpet of spiders over six inches deep was flowing out of the cave towards him. At its head the four large mutated spiders were being carried on the bodies of others. His heart thumped harder, they were clearly gaining on him. He flailed along the tunnel, which narrowed right in front of him. Stopping to see whether he was able to get through with the rucksack on his back, the Greek dived over his head and scurried away.

"Sorry, darling, I should have called you a big fat fly. Say hello to Jasmine next time you see her."

Geoff hurled himself through the gap and promptly found himself wedged tight to the walls. "Help!" he cried.

There was no reply ahead of him, only a seething mass of movement behind him. Unbuckling his rucksack, he grasped at a low hanging rock and pulled his body forward. Intense pain surged through his shoulder.

"Crack!"

The light of the head torch disappeared.

"Oh fuck."

Geoff pulled the rucksack through and scrambled away on his hands and knees. He could feel his palms bleeding, his knees bruising.

"Hurry up!" shouted Natasha from up ahead as Geoff scraped his body through another crevice.

Halfway through the next section of tunnel Natasha found herself well and truly stuck, unable to move forwards, backwards, or either side. Struggling to breathe she felt the tunnel closing in on her. "Help me." she hissed.

Geoff hurtled around the corner and went face first into something living and small. Instinctively, he bit into a hairy, part-metallic cushion that had at least two heartbeats.

"Aaarrggghhh." Geoff spat out a mixture of thick matted hair and black skin moistened by alien blood. It tasted like over chewed blueberry bubble gum.

"Oww!" screamed the Greek, spinning round with her front legs raised, her fangs poised. "What the hell do you think you're doing? You bit me, you filthy monkey."

"I'm stuck!" Natasha shouted.

Geoff spoke quickly, "Sorry, I didn't mean to bite you. I lost my torch and couldn't see. Please help Natasha?"

"Grrhhh!" menaced the Greek.

"Remember we're all going to die if you don't."

The Greek turned and climbed onto the lower part of Natasha's back. Gripping the rucksack with her four back legs she used the others to scratch at the sides of the tunnel. Within seconds Natasha felt the tightness ease and wriggled through the gap.

"Go now Mephistopheles," ordered the Greek, climbing up Natasha's leg and diving onto her back. "Immediately!"

Natasha was off down the tunnel.

Geoff felt a soft wave of matter flow over his ankles. In no time his legs became a mass of spiders climbing over and under his jeans. "Help," he mumbled as the light from Natasha's head torch disappeared around a corner.

"Peekaboo juicy brain, Brad," sang Jasmine. *"Come play with me."*

Thrashing around, Geoff punched, kicked and crushed everything behind, around and on top of him as best he could. Even in this state his main concern was where the four mutated children of the Greek had gone. As he scrambled around a corner his brain was relieved of this task so it could concentrate on another, more pressing matter. What to do when four large spiders land on your head? "Aaarrgghh!" he cried.

"Hello good looking. You leave me without a kiss," Jasmine purred. In the darkness he could smell her sweet perfume.

"Face me like a man, senor! Why you run? What are you afraid of? Are you a coward?" said Terrence.

"We good friends with you," cried Nancy. *"Same, same but different."*

"I am Bert."

With the spiders gripping firmly onto different parts of his face and head Geoff threw himself down the tunnel. Clawing, kicking, elbowing, kneeing, he scrambled away.

Terrence sank his fangs into Geoff's ear lobe, trying to rip open the ear canal with his forelegs. *"I am coming for you, senor."*

With her body at the centre of Geoff's forehead Nancy, the red and black spider began to prise open his eyes. However, while her hairy legs prodded and poked, getting a decent grip on the squishy blobs proved to be more difficult than she had anticipated. *"Stop moving!"* she demanded.

Despite his constant thrashing, Jasmine carefully crept down Geoff's face until she was positioned just above his nose. Carefully she eased two thick back legs up his nostrils.

Bert simply stayed where he was, wrapped around Geoff's Adam's apple. He was enjoying the ride and was happy to find out what would happen next. *"I am Bert."*

In all of this chaos Geoff heard a gentle voice, *"Calm down kid. You'll be alright if you just keep moving."*

Jasmine's hairy legs tickled the outermost cover of his brain and Geoff's world, which had descended into a horrific nightmare in such a short period of time, suddenly became terribly worse. "Aaarrrhhhhh!" he cried, opening his mouth.

Jasmine seized her chance and forced five legs into the soft fleshy cavity.

"Juicy brain mine."

"Calm down. This will be over soon," Geoff's subconscious said in a soothing flat tone, before adding in a fluster, *"But obviously I mean in a good way. Not in a way that involves your horrible death in this spider-infected tunnel or being blown apart as that would be very bad."*

Terrence, who had bitten through Geoff's ear lobe, was finding the ear canal frustratingly small. *"Senor, could you please open up your ear and we can discuss this like men?"*

Geoff threw his head to one side, catching a jutting rock.

"Crunch!"

"Oh bugger senor!"

Seven of Terrence's eyes, a chunk of his brain and half his abdomen was ripped from his body. What was left fell to one side, leaving a single fang still embedded in Geoff's ear lobe.

Nancy unhooked her grip on Geoff's forehead and reared up, all fearsome fangs and bristling legs readying to bite into a single eye. Before she could, Geoff bucked and hit a pointed rock, landing face down.

"Ouch!" cried Geoff.

Nancy screamed, *"Nooooo!"* as she was flattened into a bloody hairy pancake.

Bert, seeing and feeling the demise of his two siblings, decided that certain things were simply not worth it. He would go back to the cave and ascend to his rightful role of heir to God.

"I am Bert."

Skipping down Geoff's back Bert scuttled towards the cave. Obviously, he would have to do something with the decor. Lose the lights; go with more webs; drastically thin out male challengers; build his harem; and get into that bloody special room. There was so much to do.

Caught in the moment Jasmine squeezed her fangs into Geoff's mouth and latched onto his upper gum behind his two front teeth. From here she could see his tonsils. They looked delicious.

"Oww," spluttered Geoff, opening his mouth wider. Jasmine took her chance and dived fully into his mouth. Her forelegs gripped his fleshy cheeks, allowing her fangs to bite deep into the back of his soft palate.

"Jasmine and Brad sitting in a tree," she sang.

While Jasmine had received some training for this, she had never really grasped the dangers of gaining entry through the mouth.

"Aaarrrggghhh!"

Twenty-eight teeth clamped down hard, severing four of Jasmine's legs and a good third of her ripened body like a bloody organic guillotine. Realising her mistake, she tried to escape.

"You hurt me!"

Bits of Jasmine exploded in Geoff's mouth, oozing over his taste buds. She tasted like flowery chicken. He opened his mouth as wide as he could allowing the bleeding Jasmine to messily squirm away. A single hairy leg tickled the back of his throat triggering his gag reflex. Teeth clamped back shut, messily decapitating what was left of her brain.

"Bad Brad!" she screamed.

No longer feeling any of the mutated spiders on him, Geoff opened his eyes and saw a sliver of daylight at the end of the tunnel less than twenty feet away. Taking hurried lungfuls of air he crawled forwards. The rest of the spiders began to stream back to the cave where Bert had arrived.

"I will call this Bert's," he said. *"So this is what real power feels like."* Scuttling to the centre he made himself at home in the skull of the Greek's former host. It was still warm and he gripped the remaining grey matter close to his body like a cloak. With so many arachnid eyes fixed upon him he felt the need to say something.

"Good day, I am Bert, first of my name and your new king. I will be a hard but fair ruler; bend the knee and worship me and you'll be saved," cried Bert, snapping his fangs together. Dutifully all of the watching spiders kneeled before him.

Bert looked around at his subjects. *"This feels rather nice. I understand now why everyone strives for this. Absolute power gives you a warm glow. It is very, very warm. Now how am I going to get into that special room?"*

The countdown dropped silently from a big green **RASWX** to a big red **KNODW.**

BOOM!

An almighty mountain-shaking explosion rocked Scafell and resonated around the valley below. Natasha screamed as Geoff flew out of the tunnel.

"Geoffrey!" she cried as she slapped his face hard. He was covered in mud, burnt spiders, bits of Jasmine, Terrence and Nancy. Two hairy legs poked out of his nose and a solitary fang clung to his ear lobe.

"They tried to kill me," Geoff opened his eyes. "So many spiders."

Natasha smiled, cupping his head in her hands. "But you're okay now," she smiled.

Geoff snorted bits of Jasmine's legs down his nose and spat parts of her body out of his mouth. "No. I am fucking far from okay," he hissed.

The Greek moved slowly towards Geoff from the rock she had been standing on. "I feel that I should apologise for the behaviour of my children. I did not think that they would attempt to impregnate your brain – for that I am truly sorry."

"We should kill her," said Geoff, his jaw tight, his eyes fierce. "Rob was right. We should kill her right now."

The Greek backed away. "Well, that would be one of your options, but I'm afraid your master has already granted me safe passage for my unique and invaluable assistance, darling. Are you able to see into the future, Geoffrey, because I can?"

Geoff pulled Terrence's bloody fang from his ear lobe and rolled it between his thumb and his forefinger. He looked at the Greek and crushed it.

Natasha raised her head. "Geoff's right. You almost killed us. Unless you have some amazing last words I feel that it's time for no more Greek. Why don't we find out whether you can make it back to this Chairman Z?"

"All hail Her Fangs!" said the Greek. "Okay, let's all calm down and not do anything rash. I still have valuable information for you."

"Speak now or die," said Natasha, standing up.

"Okay, the game changer I speak of is the Spear of Destiny."

"What?" asked Natasha.

"My brother Sebastian may have been the last holder of the Spear of Destiny. He believed that it would grant him great power and even allow us to go back home. For you there is an eighty-six percent probability that ownership of the Spear will make your apocalypse a reality."

"I thought it was seventy-seven percent?" said Natasha.

"It increases to eighty-six if you wield the Spear; seventy-seven percent if the Spear is in play."

"Why have I never heard of this Sebastian before?" asked Natasha.

"He was always more reclusive than I," replied the Greek.

"Where is he now?" asked Natasha.

"I have no idea. I haven't spoken to him for over seventy years. The last time we met was during the Second World War in Stalingrad."

"Stalingrad?" asked Geoff, lifting himself up on his elbows.

"It's a city in Russia, Geoffrey," explained the Greek slowly. "The Germans and the Russians had a very big battle there."

"I know that," he snarled.

"Sebastian believed that the Spear of Destiny was in a vault somewhere in the city. The speed of the German advance had prevented the Russians from pulling it back to Moscow. Under Hitler's orders the Germans systematically searched every Church basement, bunker and vault in Stalingrad looking for it. I know because I was there, as was Azothoth."

Geoff thought about General Paulus' map.

"Did they find it?" asked Natasha.

"That I do not know. Winter has never agreed with me and that winter in Stalingrad was the bitterest of them all. I left for Paris on 6th of June, 1942 and that was the last time I saw him. Whether he found it is unclear, though I can say that there is a ninety-eight percent probability that the Spear of Destiny was in Stalingrad in 1942."

"Tell me more and you might live," said Natasha.

Thirty minutes later the Greek scuttled away at the sound of people below.

"Remember our deal, darling," she said, disappearing up a weather-beaten tree trunk.

Natasha nodded and looked down the path at the figures in the mist. "Hi Rob," she shouted with a broad smile.

Chapter Thirty-One

"… this is no throbber." – Rob

Scafell Pike, The Lake District

Halfway down the path Rob rushed up to meet them. He rattled off his words between short, laboured wheezes, "What was that? You okay? We were coming to meet you. I was worried. Told you. Cannot trust the fucking Greek."

"We are fine, Azothoth," assured Natasha.

"Really?" Rob looked her up and down twice. "Boss, you look like you've been dragged through a sewer by your ankles and he," pointing at Geoff, "he looks like absolute shit. What the heaven happened?"

Geoff cleared his throat. "There was an explosion and lots of spiders." He sat down and dropped the purple rucksack by his side. "They wanted to eat my brain."

Ruby and Mr Sox arrived, gathering around Geoff in a rough semicircle, their eyes wide and questioning.

"Geoffrey, I think you're being a bit overdramatic and I don't think that Rob needs to hear about that right now," said Natasha, smiling weakly.

"Did that abomination do this? I told you she's tricky boss. Why does no one ever listen to me?" Rob turned to Geoff, sensing that he was more likely to get answers from him. "Was she trying to breed that bloody master race again? Did she try getting into your head? Is she still alive?"

Geoff nodded.

"We should have killed her centuries ago," accused a red-faced Rob. "Where is she?"

"Killing her is not an option Azothoth," said Natasha.

"But she…" began Geoff.

"Has a very unique skill set," interrupted Natasha.

"Why have you got rucksacks? Did you steal her stuff? She would really hate that," said Rob.

"Not exactly," said Natasha as she spun him around. They walked another dozen or so steps away from the group before she looked at him. "You know, I've been thinking about what you said about changing your name and Rob is beginning to grow on me."

"Really? That's great. You didn't seem too keen when I mentioned it before."

Natasha cooed softly. "Well, I've given the matter a great deal of thought and decided that if my favourite Duke of Hell wants to change his name to a more modern one, so be it."

Rob's mouth broke into a wide grin.

"Of course you'll always be Azothoth to me, but if you really want to be called Rob I am open to discussing it. It's your name, after all. I honestly think it would make me a bad boss if I didn't see that certain concessions are necessary to keep my people happy."

"Hey, wait a minute." Rob stopped dead, his blue eyes narrowing. "You never say honestly and you never ever give concessions. You hate being truthful and you really hate giving stuff away. Why would you say this to me?"

"I have no idea what you mean, Rob?" Natasha looked innocent and a good deal scarier.

"Oh heaven," Rob shook his head. "Is it that bad?"

"You may disagree with some of my decisions but I'm still your boss and you will do as I say."

"You're not talking about changing my name to Rob anymore, are you?"

"No, we have a new ally in our quest," said Natasha, her face a study in cold power.

The blood drained from Rob's podgy face. "You mean the Greek, don't you? I know you reckon that you've got this under control, but that hairy fucking cockroach can't be trusted. She has her own agenda boss, and I'm certain it doesn't match ours."

"Maybe so, but she is going to help us and that is all that matters."

"But she's never helped us before," said Rob. "Why would she help us now?"

"Things have changed," replied Natasha, brushing the front of her jacket. "It has become mutually beneficial for both of us. The truth is we need her. She knows how we can make the apocalypse happen, maybe even get Geoffrey to ascend to the Anti-Christ's Throne of Thorns."

"But she has no honour. Not like you and me boss."

Natasha sighed and said, "I'm afraid that on this occasion needs must."

Geoff appeared at Natasha's side, his face scrunched up like he was sucking an overripe grapefruit. "I agree with Rob. She tried to kill us and she doesn't even believe I'm the real Anti-Christ. This is a terrible idea."

"Geoff's right," said Rob. "Come on boss, we should never agree to do anything with that monstrosity. Let's just kill, or better still torture her."

"I've already made my decision. Do either of you want to challenge me on this?" glared Natasha, her jaw high and tight.

"No," replied Rob and Geoff in unison.

"Remember Geoffrey, this could be the key to making you the first proper Anti-Christ," said Natasha, in her sweetest, honey-dripped voice.

Something shiny and metallic caught Geoff's eye, hovering about ten feet above them. Before he could say anything, it fell on Rob's head.

"Arrrghhhhhhh!"

Blinding him with her thicker front legs, the Greek gripped Rob's temples and the thick nape of his neck. "Have you missed me fatty?" she cried.

Spinning wildly Rob crashed into a tree before hurtling backwards over a drystone wall. By the time he stood up the Greek had bounded back onto a high tree branch.

"I'm going to kill it!" roared Rob. "Kill it!"

"Urrgghhh! You're even more disgusting than I remember," said the Greek.

Rob picked up a large stone and threw it with all his force. The Greek neatly sidestepped it. "Saw that coming. I've got a forty-eight percent probability of being able to work you up into a heart attack."

"Stop this at once!" demanded Natasha. "Geoffrey, take Azothoth away and calm him down. Greek, follow me now or face immediate extinction. We need to agree some ground rules."

"Calm down mate," said Geoff, placing his body between Rob and the path upwards. "She's not worth it."

"We should squash her right now," said Rob, through tightly clenched teeth.

"I know how you feel. She said that I wasn't apocalypse material and all I was useful for was bait."

"So let's kill her."

“I’m all for that, but Natasha has given her word which means we can’t touch her,” explained Geoff as he unslung the rucksack, squatted down and began rooting through it.

“What’s in there?” asked Rob.

“Just some crap that the Greek wanted us to bring. I know we can’t steal it unless Natasha says so, but what I’ve got is this.” Geoff pulled out the white gun.

“What’s that?”

“It was in this laboratory that the Greek had set up. I wasn’t supposed to bring it but I thought it might be useful.”

“Why? Does it squirt water?”

“No idea,” answered Geoff. “It’s heavier than it looks and it also throbs when you hold it.”

“A throbber you say?” Rob’s interest perked up. “Gimme.”

“Don’t let anyone see it,” said Geoff.

Shielding the gun with his body Rob aimed at the pub below. He pulled the trigger but nothing happened. His right eyebrow arched up like a well-fed caterpillar. “You’re right, it’s too heavy for plastic, but you’re wrong my friend, this is no throbber.”

“Really? Give it back then,” said Geoff. “See, it throbs for me.”

“What else you got?”

“Just more junk,” replied Geoff emptying the rucksack.

“What’s this?” asked Rob picking up the jewellery box.

“A crappy box.”

Rob turned it over and saw the carved initials at its base. Looking up the path he said slowly, "you're right. I bet there's millions of them."

Away from the others Natasha and the Greek were speaking quietly.

"Who's going to be the lucky lady?" asked the Greek, hungrily eyeing Ruby.

"That's not going to happen. I have plans for her," smiled Natasha.

"But we had a deal," accused the Greek. "And you gave me your word."

"You do realise who I am, don't you? I am the Devil. Breaking my word can hardly come as a surprise to you. I would think you'd say a one hundred percent probability? But for the record I am not breaking my word. I said that I would get you a host body, which I will."

"But will you help me go back to my dimension? You gave me your word on that."

"If I get my apocalypse, I promise that I will personally kick your disgusting body all the way back home."

When they got back to the bus Rob pointed out that every army that had ever tasted success did so on a full and happy stomach. They didn't seem to have been followed so it was decided that they would eat breakfast at the pub while Natasha planned their next move. Thirty minutes later Geoff was absentmindedly moving a couple of untouched sausages around his plate.

"Come on, it's not your fault," said Rob, putting a comforting arm around his shoulder. "People take time to adjust to being pure evil. Just look at Hitler, he was a sweet boy when I first met him."

"You're just saying that. I'm supposed to be this unbelievably evil Anti-Christ, but the only unbelievable thing is me," said Geoff, wriggling free. "The Greek knows I can't bring about the apocalypse. Have you any idea how that makes me feel? I've failed everyone, or at least I will do when I get the chance."

Rob found conviction in his voice. "That hairy cockroach knows nothing. I don't care how much of a badass you are, the first time you pick up a pair of pliers and torture someone to death, you'll have nightmares. Everyone does when they get to the pliers end of their first gig."

Geoff smiled.

"Stop being so hard on yourself. You don't have to complete SACRED to be the Anti-Christ. You just need to believe in yourself," said Rob, clenching his fist and slamming it on the table.

"But I'm too bloody nice."

"Rubbish. Look at me. You wouldn't think that I'm a fearsome Duke of Hell, would you?"

"I guess not," agreed Geoff.

"But I fucking well am," grinned Rob, his blue eyes blazing in their sockets. "A whiff of torture, rape or genocide and I'm on it like a car bonnet. You can still decide who you really want to be and that means you can choose to be the most motherfucking evil son of a bitch Anti-Christ ever."

"What nice things have you done over the years before you became real evil?" asked Geoff.

"Well," Rob moved his weight, causing his chair to creak. "That's a bit tricky. You've got to understand that I've been strictly evil for millenniums."

"What about Sue, your last girlfriend? She seemed really sweet. I bet you did nice things for her."

"Umm," Rob ran the palm of his hand slowly over his face, over his balding head and began massaging his thick neck.

"You bloody well killed her, didn't you?" accused Geoff.

"Mmm," Rob replied.

"I bet parts of her body are vacuum packed under your bed? That smell had nothing to do with the drains, did it? Have you been feeding Mr Sox her heart and liver? Is that why he's looking all glossy?"

Mr Sox bristled. He racked his brain on whether he had recently eaten human heart and liver. He didn't think he had but Geoff was right, his coat was looking much shinier.

"I wouldn't do that," defended Rob, with the conviction of a thief who had just been caught red-handed.

"Are you telling me the big bad Duke of Hell didn't kill her?"

"Okay, I did sacrifice her, but I swear it didn't mean anything" said Rob slowly. "It was just the once."

"Oh brilliant!" exclaimed Geoff. "I'm supposed to be the Anti-Christ, but do you let me get involved with any of your sacrifices? No, of course you don't. You didn't even get me into the coven. How can I become evil if you don't show me things?"

"I'm sorry, I didn't think you'd like it."

Geoff held out his hands. "Rob, these are the hands of a killer. Mrs Hotchkiss knows that and I tell you I enjoyed every damn second of it."

"To be fair I think she died from a heart attack," said Rob.

"So? It was a heart attack brought on by fighting me. You won't even give me that. I'm just a bloody disgrace to you," said Geoff, storming outside.

The long wooden table fell silent. Natasha looked at Rob and shook her head. "Go find him Ruby," she said.

Outside Geoff was propped up by the painted white stone wall. During breakfast a stiff wind had come in from the Irish Sea, bringing with it a downpour of heavy rain.

"What's up?" asked Ruby.

"I got blown up and thousands of spiders tried to kill me."

"I mean what's up now?" asked Ruby taking his hand.

"The Greek said I wasn't the Anti-Christ who'd get the apocalypse and that Natasha should use me as bait."

"So?" smiled Ruby.

"That isn't funny."

"That all depends on where you're standing," she said.

"But isn't it a big deal? Natasha believes in the Greek," said Geoff, looking into her eyes. "So how can she believe in me?"

"Rob said that Natasha has been failing to deliver the apocalypse for centuries. It should have happened years ago and the locals in Hell aren't happy. Think of the pressure she's under and the Greek is offering a different type of hope."

"Don't you think it matters what the Greek says?"

"Heaven no. Rob says she's a sneaky alien spider who'll do anything to get back home," said Ruby, "and I believe him."

"But what if she's right about me?"

"If this apocalypse happens it will be down to you, Geoffrey Pike, and not because some alien predicted it. You have the Devil's royal blood flowing through your veins. I know what I saw when I read your palm and I believe in you. Remember, you have a responsibility to everyone including Sofia and me," said Ruby as she stood up on her tiptoes and kissed Geoff on the lips. "Let's go back in. You need to keep your strength up."

In the corner booth Natasha sat opposite Donald whose eyes no longer darted around. They were deathly still, with pitch-black pupils covering the whole of his irises.

"I have kept my part of the bargain," said Natasha.

"This isn't what I wanted but I suppose he will do for now," replied the Greek, sitting on top of Donald's head which was encased in tight strands of silk.

"I wasn't asking for your approval."

"I appreciate his willingness to open his mind to new experiences," said the Greek. "Though I would have preferred someone more fit for purpose and less likely to die of old age."

"He's a leprechaun."

"But he's a very old leprechaun," stated the Greek.

"Well, we don't always get what we want, do we?" said Natasha. "Let's get down to business. You do realise that no one has seen the Spear for years?"

The Greek's eyes sparkled like small, polished stones. "Which is why it will surface now. Would you like me to guess on the probability of the Spear turning up when God is absent from Heaven and the Devil walks the Earth?"

"High?" she asked.

"Ninety-four percent probability."

"But why do you believe that the Spear can be the key to delivering my apocalypse?"

"You haven't been paying too much attention to the Spear of Destiny, have you darling?" smiled the Greek, cleaning her fangs.

Natasha blushed. "I've had a great deal of work to do, piles of administration, it's just not that easy to have time for any hobbies. Any case, when the Spear was here, all it did was scratch Jesus and a make a Roman soldier feel bad. Hardly impressive."

"Luckily for you I have devoted a great deal of time studying the Spear since Stalingrad and I believe that Sebastian was right, it is truly unique. A sentient being of unimaginable power that can cause all manner of things to happen when used correctly. Things like your precious apocalypse or my equally precious journey back home to the Golden Web."

"The Spear of Destiny has a soul?" asked Natasha, sucking in a quick breath.

"That I do not know, but it is certainly alive and truly immortal. I think it craves power, absorbs souls and travels across parallel dimensions."

"How?" asked Natasha, moving closer, her lips pulled tight.

"I haven't been able to identify the source of its power, but once we find it I'll show you what happens when an irresistible force meets an immovable object," answered the Greek.

"Whatever plans you have, you'll need to factor this into your calculations," said Natasha, pulling out an envelope and pushing it across the table.

"There are a great many documents of interest in this world and I dare say that I have seen almost all of them at one time or another."

"I seriously doubt that you will have seen this one," said Natasha.

"I suppose I can humour you," said the Greek. She crawled down the old man's face onto the table. Donald continued to stare unblinkingly ahead.

"A comic?" snorted the Greek. "You believe this is worthy of my intellect? I may have seriously overestimated you, Mephistopheles."

"Yes, it's a comic, but look at the seal, it is also the Word of God. I think it may be the prequel to the *Book of Revelations*," said Natasha. "It also mentions the Spear."

The Greek was already animatedly scanning the cover. "Fascinating. Absolutely fascinating. I've never cared for any sort of religious predestination myself. My talent is a logical result of the tearing through the spacetime continuum. This document appears to be a prophecy made by your God. A prophecy which you yourself strangely seem to be following."

"I wouldn't say that," said Natasha.

"Have you seen how the artist catches my good side? It's simply exquisite. I also seem to have a few more words than the rest of the characters. Do you think that makes me the chief protagonist?"

"No, and you are not a God," replied Natasha. "But does this change any of your calculations?"

"I haven't had time to fully assimilate this new information so I cannot authoritatively say either way. Though I do think it proves my theory on the Spear of Destiny being a key part of whatever is about to unfold?" said the Greek, looking up with her large blue eye.

Natasha nodded and pulled the pages of the *Book of Shenanigans* back towards her.

"Have you got the rest?" asked the Greek.

Natasha shook her head and pocketed the pages.

"I have a great many questions about this. To begin with…"

Before the Greek could utter another word, Seamus appeared beside them. "We have company. It's time to leave," he said.

"How did they find us? Let's see what that contraption of yours can really do," said Natasha, standing up.

"Don't you worry," grinned Seamus. "I'll handle whatever nunmobile is chasing us."

Five minutes later a wide-eyed Seamus cried out the most obviously pressing observation. "They've got a fucking tank!"

Chapter Thirty-Two

"Have you heard of the fighting Irish?" – Seamus

Wasdale Head, The Lake District

"And a bloody helicopter," added Geoff in frightened amazement. The helicopter banked to face the bus.

Ratatat! Ratatat! Ratatat! Ratatat!

Ratatat! Ratatat! Ratatat! Ratatat!

Geoff hurled himself to the floor. When he opened his eyes, he found he wasn't alone on the gangway. The windows were marked and starred with white cracks like large spider webs but held, at least for now.

"That's a gunship," corrected Natasha.

"And nuns," barked Rob. "I bet there's lots of nuns." While he hadn't seen a single nun, a shiver raced down his spine. He just knew that the same hell of nuns he'd faced before would be sharpening their knives and knitting needles further up the valley. He traced the hole in his stomach with his forefinger and winced. "And bloody Rachel."

“Geoffrey, given the forces looking to kill you right now, I would estimate that there is a probability of ninety-three percent,” said the Greek, perched on Donald’s head.

“That’s not so bad.” Geoff looked up at the bullet marks. “I’d take those odds on surviving.”

“Darling, I’m afraid you misunderstand me. The ninety-three percent probability is of you dying in the next ten minutes.”

“Everybody off the bus,” ordered Seamus. “Now!”

†

Simon heaved another shell into the breach loading mechanism and bolted it shut. There wasn’t much to see in the cramped interior of the tank but he was strangely enjoying it. He was sweating, the grey flame-retardant suit, hood and gloves saw to that, but at least he felt safe. The outside of the tank was camouflaged for a desert conflict in beige and sand colours, which was of no use in the lush green of the Wasdale valley. Inside it was completely different, decked out in interlocking configurations of sharp grey steel.

BOOM!

The shell landed twenty or so feet from the hastily retreating bus, showering it with clumps of earth.

Sister Agatha, in her full Nazi grey habit, slipped up a gear and steered round a small bend in the one-track road.

“Damn you infidels,” said Mr Smith as he scanned the range finder and recalibrated the gun. The turret moved ever so slightly to the left.

Simon heaved another shell into the breach mechanism.

BOOM!

This shell landed right on Seamus’ seat, flipping the whole bus skywards. As it crashed to the ground it burst into a raging fireball. It was a firework of Biblical proportions.

“Everything is going according to God’s Word,” shouted Gabriel, who had made a point of doing this old school. No fancy communications. No computer aided targeting. This smiting was going to be done simply by an archangel with a sword, a couple of Technical Administrative Support Officers, a borderline psychotic nun, and a tank.

"Turn on the music!" Gabriel ordered, his eyes flashing cobalt. "How on earth could I forget my trumpet?"

Sister Agatha pressed her phone and ominous chords joined by an electric guitar filled the valley from the raft of speakers strapped to the front of the tank.

"I can see it coming in the…"

An electric guitar howled.

"I love the smell of Satanists burning in the morning," smiled Gabriel.

Walking behind the tank, Mrs Thornthwistle stroked Mogwai who was safe in her arms. It had been a truly excellent morning. She turned and spoke to the man walking beside her. "I really enjoyed your programmes on the BBC, dear. They were always very entertaining and incredibly informative."

Brian watched another shell land before replying, "That is so very kind of you to say so. This is all very exciting, Mrs Thornthwistle. Is that really Archangel Gabriel?" With the tour bus in flames the rest of the forces of good began to charge noisily down the valley.

"Please call me Alice and yes it is," Mrs Thornthwistle winked. "Your friends are," she paused, looking the black-suited hulks up and down, "strapping and formidable gentlemen."

"I just wanted to do my bit," said Brian. "We are talking about the Devil, after all."

"I agree. Smiting him was never going to be easy, though this time I believe we have him by the short and curlies so to speak," she replied.

"Have you any idea why he's come to Manchester, Alice?"

"None at all, I'm afraid," Mrs Thornthwistle replied.

"I don't suppose you've seen a spear?" asked Brian. "Something like Gabriel's sword?"

"What a peculiar question," she replied with a frown. "No I haven't seen a spear like that, dear."

8

Sam looked down at Emily and wanted to question her choice of footwear. Instead he caught her eye and gave her a short smile. She smiled back. *At least they would have Wastwater*, he thought, *whatever the Heaven that may turn out to be.*

Catching Sam's mood Emily leaned over and whispered, "What are we going to do Mr Spade?"

For once Sam did not have a plan. "As little as possible," he replied looking at Mrs Thornthwistle, as another shell landed in the distance.

Emily raised her eyebrows. "Don't you worry, Mr Spade I'm certain you'll come up with something. Remember that famous knack you have?"

"I love you one hundred percent Em."

BOOM!

The shell exploded thirty feet to the side of the barn, which was now the only thing that stood between the forces of good and evil.

Gabriel put down his binoculars and snapped a command to the bowels of the tank, "Onwards! Fire at will!"

★

"So no hard feelings?" asked Jay.

"Why would there be any hard feelings?" shrugged Lou as he marched behind the tank. "You went into my sack without complaint."

"True but I didn't feel I had a choice."

"You've always got a choice, yours would have been painful that's all."

BOOM!

"I've stayed here because I'm tired of running that bar and I'm scared of running into Pnakotic or Sister M back in Hell, but I don't understand you why you've stayed?" asked Jay.

"I like Brian and I think he'll give me more responsibility."

"What do you mean?"

"He seems pretty confident that if he gets the Spear of Destiny he'll be able to whack God and the boss. That could make me redundant so we had a chat. It could even be like the good old days."

"What good old days?"

Lou gave a throaty smile, "The Third Reich of course."

∴

"Does anyone know who he is?" asked Jacob, giving a sideways glance at the swarthy man carrying a katana sword. It looked razor sharp.

"No idea," replied Sister Ruth. "He was probably drawn to this like everyone else."

"He looks very foreign. My guess is he's here with Sister Agatha," said Jacob.

Sister Ruth looked at the stranger and frowned. Jacob was right, he did look awfully foreign.

"Don't you think the Devil will use his fireballs now we've got a tank?" Jacob asked.

She shook her head and bit her top lip. *Sister Agatha had known about fireballs* she thought.

β

Geoff poked his head around the corner and tried to see through the noxious smoke, which swirled and bellowed upwards from the burning wreckage of the tour bus. For the most part he saw exactly what he expected to see. Hundreds of complete strangers shouting and rushing towards him brandishing makeshift weapons. However, there was one thing that he hadn't expected to see. With feverish eyes he looked back at Natasha. "The bloke on top of the tank. He's got a big burning sword." He didn't need SACRED to tell him that any sword that blazed with the light of a thousand suns was not going to be good news for him.

Natasha and Rob edged around the corner. A second later they were back.

"Therefore the Lord God sent him forth from the garden of Eden, to till the ground from whence he was taken," said Natasha solemnly. "So he drove out the man; and he placed at the east of the garden of Eden Cherubim, and a flaming sword which turned every way, to keep the way of the tree of life. Genesis Chapter 3 Verses 23 and 24."

"What the fuck?" exclaimed Geoff. "Why are you quoting the Bible?"

"It could be Uriel?" said Rob. "Or possibly Gabriel? He's always stealing Uriel's sword, but if it is Uriel, he's a real nasty bastard. They call him, 'God is my light'."

"We're all going to die, aren't we?" asked Geoff, his face pleading with Natasha who looked away.

The Greek scuttled onto the wall beside Geoff. "Darling, that probability for you is now at ninety-nine point seven percent." She shrugged. "They've brought a heavenly sword."

Geoff closed his eyes and heard many things. The helicopter blades circling above them; the clamour of the crowd; Phil Collins; the chugging roar of a tank; and of course, above it all, he could hear the mechanical clatter of at least one chainsaw and a large number of drills.

"Well?" Natasha interrogated the Greek. "What should we do?"

"My advice would be to give them Geoffrey and tell them he's the Anti-Christ," replied the Greek.

"What!" shouted Geoff. "Give me to the people with the big sword?"

The Greek went on, "Utilising him in this way will give an eighty-four percent probability that everyone else will be able to escape and work towards your apocalypse."

Natasha looked at Geoff before turning. "No," she replied. "Come up with something else."

"I don't understand Mephistopheles, this is his cheese moment," said the Greek, shaking her head. "There is no other option. Why would you jeopardise your apocalypse for him? Like I told you, he is not a workable Anti-Christ."

"I will not betray him, so think harder," said Natasha.

"I'm sorry but I did not see this eventuality coming to pass. I think it would be better for all concerned if I make my exit. I think you should too," said the Greek, her blue eye darting around. "You can keep Donald though, I don't think he's up to doing much escaping."

"You're going nowhere Greek," snarled Natasha. "Except possibly extinction?"

"But I'm no use to you now, am I?" said the Greek. "There is no other way out of this valley and you refuse to give up Geoffrey."

"None of that matters," said Natasha, her features dark and sharp. "You wanted a spot on Team Evil, well, this is what it's like."

Geoff spun Natasha round. "Do something Devilish! Throw fireballs. Bring down a meteor storm, just get us out of here."

"I'm sorry, I can't. It breaks the agreement," she said.

"What? How does an angel with a big flaming sword on a tank with a helicopter not break it?"

Natasha paused. "I think the sword is more of a statement and it doesn't actually break the agreement unless he uses it. Just keep away from it because it will annihilate your soul, you will literally cease to be. On the plus side I think the tank, gunship and raging mob are going to be enough to kill us without them needing to use the sword."

"This is grim," agreed Rob.

"We've got to run," said Geoff as he felt for the plastic gun in the rucksack. No one replied so he crawled to the other corner of the barn and pulled out the pistol. It gave a heavy throb that resonated through his hand. It felt alive.

≅

"Have you heard of the fighting Irish?" said Seamus to Natasha. He raised his eyebrows and repositioned his hat. "Don't you worry. Attack is the best form of defence[30]."

Seamus, Michael, Patrick and Seamus Junior ran quickly behind what was left of the tour bus crying, "Faugh a Ballagh[31]!"

BOOM!

The valley shook once more as this shell landed on the crown of Seamus Junior's head, dismantling him into his component atoms.

"Arrgghh!" gurgled Michael as shrapnel ripped him into five largeish parts. Two more souls were catapulted straight to Hell.

"Bloody heaven!" shouted Seamus. He turned on his heels and ran back to the barn with Patrick in tow.

ℜ

"What are you doing?" hissed Rob.

"What does it look like I'm fucking doing?" replied Geoff.

"Losing your mind would be my guess. Bringing a water pistol to a tank fight?"

"Natasha is quoting the Bible," said Geoff, shaking his head, his jaw tight. "We are all going to die. I fucking hate Phil Collins. The Greek had this for a

---

[30] Seamus' views on fighting tanks are remarkably similar to that of Colonel Kazimierz Mastalerz who thought that ordering a squadron of Polish Lancers to charge the Germans at Krojanty on 1st September 1939 armed with a selection of pointy sticks was a bloody good idea. What's the worst that could happen? Sadly, Colonel Mastalerz died before he could answer that.

[31] 'Faugh a ballagh' is a battle-cry of Irish origin meaning 'Clear the way'.

reason and even if it's just a water pistol, what have I got to lose? They are going to cut me up into little pieces with either a bloody chainsaw or a burning sword."

Rob's fleshy lips broke into a crooked smile. "Cool your jets on the personal attacks on Phil. He was undervalued by Genesis and still made it as one of the greatest singers of his generation. As for the rest, fair point."

Twenty-five feet away the Greek froze and asked Natasha, "What is he doing?"

"Who?" she replied.

"Geoffrey, that is who," said the Greek, pointing her two larger forelegs at the Anti-Christ huddled in the corner.

"Does it matter? We're all going to die," said Natasha.

The Greek fell silent until she caught a glimpse of the brilliant white barrel and cried a throaty, "Stop! Stop at once! Stop! It's not ready!"

Geoff edged around the corner and aimed the gun. He squeezed the red trigger and the purple nozzle glowed. A sharp thin burst of colour exploded from the barrel and raced down the valley. A series of pulsating rectangular holes the size of LP covers surrounded the tank. Their edges bled into a shimmering kaleidoscope of everchanging colours.

POP!

The tank disappeared. The music stopped.

Where the tank had previously been, a small but very powerful wind rushed from all four corners to the centre, ripping up the road.

Geoff sprawled backwards. In a second Rob loomed over him, his face pink and triumphant. "That's insane dude!" pointing at the space where the tank had been a second before. "Let me have a go."

"But it doesn't throb for you," said Geoff.

"Then bloody fire it again!"

The remaining members of the Set looked at the vacant space. They could see where the tank's tracks had stopped. They looked again, but there was definitely no tank standing there now.

"What the fucking hell was that?" asked Brian.

"Language, dear," rebuked Mrs Thornthwistle with one of her most withering looks. There were limits to the charms of any individual unable to handle himself under the pressure of battle, however handsome they may be.

"What happened to the tank?" asked Rachel disbelievingly.

"We should find some cover," said Jacob. "There could be fireballs coming, or more of the disappearing thing."

"That's an excellent idea," said Emily as she grabbed Sam's arm and steered him behind a wall. Everyone in the rear guard followed their lead. That is, everyone apart from Father Garcia who walked into the centre of the space where the tank had been, closed his eyes and fell to his knees. "Santa Muerte, I beseech you. Guide me to do your will."

β

Geoff sat up, gripping the gun. It felt warm like freshly baked bread. The throbbing had now reduced to a shadowy hum.

"You don't know what you're doing!" screamed the Greek as she scurried towards him at full pelt. "Stop immediately, you stupid monkey!"

The helicopter banked to the left.

Ratatat! Ratatat! Ratatat! Ratatat!

Ratatat! Ratatat! Ratatat! Ratatat!

Bullets raked the far end of the barn scattering the remaining forces of evil. Scrambling away on his hands and knees Geoff weighed up his options. All he had was a toy gun, but it was cool and made a tank disappear. With trembling fingers he aimed and squeezed the trigger.

The pulsating lights streamed towards the helicopter. The pilot desperately manoeuvred to the right but the colours seemed to know this and veered to meet him. Ten feet from impact the colours slowed and then stopped dead. For a couple of seconds they hung shimmering in the air.

"Oh shit," Geoff said. At least that is what he would've said if he was given more time. As it was he muttered, "Oh," as the stunningly bright kaleidoscope of colours plunged back towards him.

POP!

With a shimmer everything pixelated and Geoff bled out of reality.

⁂

Father Garcia slowly traced the burnt edges of the tank's footprint with the tip of his blade. It felt hot. He was joined by the others.

"I guess that's that, Brian," said Sam. "Even the mortals can feel that the Devil's no longer here. My guess is that he's gone back to Hell."

"Yes sorry, Daddy," said Emily. One of her shoes was frustratingly missing a heel.

Brian looked down the valley and breathed out.

"Maybe there'll be a next time?" said Sam.

"I doubt that," frowned Brian. "This seems to be the end of the story and as I am a man of my word this clears your debt to me and, more importantly for you, that of Emily."

"Thank you Daddy," Emily smiled.

"That's mighty white of you," said Sam. "You know, maybe your war with God was never meant to be won?"

"*La tristesse durera toujours*, is that what you're saying Samuel?" muttered Brian. "We'll fucking see about that."

Ž

High up on the side of Scafell Pike wisps of smoke were billowing out of a small crack in the rockface. Deep within the mountain nothing living remained and hardly anything else was recognisable. The exception to this was several thin metallic sheets that were untouched. In the pitch black no one would ever read them but they all said, *Book of Shenanigans.*

∴

Jacob smiled. "I suppose we should all go home now. People are saying that there is no sign of any of them, so I'm guessing that it's over. Did we win?"

"Yes dear," replied Mrs Thornthwistle. "It would appear that we have vanquished the Devil but I must confess that it doesn't feel quite right. He may have gone, but this all quite unsatisfactory if you ask me."

"I know what you mean," said Sister Ruth. "It feels like an anti-climax."

"We should have their heads on pikes," stated Rachel, brandishing her knife. "Especially that fat pig Rob."

"The Devil may not have thrown any fireballs, but he did make a tank and an archangel disappear, and then vanished himself before anyone could catch him," said Jacob. "Pretty impressive if you ask me."

"What do you think happened to the tank?" asked Sister Ruth. "I really liked Simon. He was very nice. Don't you think that we should say a few words about them?"

"I suppose so, dear," said Mrs Thornthwistle.

They all stood in silence around the last place of the tank. Finally Mrs Thornthwistle spoke, "Sister Agatha was one of the most resourceful women I have ever known. She told me only this morning how excited she was to have the opportunity to try out her tank skills against the forces of the Devil. That proactive, can-do attitude will be sorely missed by all the members of the Set."

"Quite," muttered Jacob as he examined his yoyo.

Mrs Thornthwistle continued, "While I remember, I've got Sister Agatha's infrared goggles and Kevlar body armour, both in small nun size, back at the shop. If anyone would like to make a small donation they can have them. Would anyone else like to say a few words?"

"I think Simon was very sweet," said Sister Ruth. "He wasn't your typical angel but he had a good heart and was willing to help with all the smiting even though he hadn't been trained for it."

Father Garcia, who knew a solemn ceremony, stuck his katana in the wet ground and pulled a vial from out of his jacket pocket. Unscrewing it he tipped out some cocaine onto the back of his hand. He snorted the powder and looked around.

For once, Mrs Thornthwistle was unable to find the right words.

Sister Ruth came to her aid, speaking slowly and loudly. "Did you know Sister Agatha? Was she your friend? Would you like to say something about her? Can you speak English?"

Father Garcia nodded and fell to his knees.

"Is he crying?" asked Jacob.

Sister Ruth's understanding of foreign people and their customs did not add up to much. However, she had heard that they could be inappropriately overemotional in public gatherings. "Maybe he knew Sister Agatha very well?" she said.

"He is crying," whispered Jacob.

Father Garcia wiped the tears from his eyes. Throwing his head back he shouted, “I have failed you, Santa Muerte. I gave you my word that I would cut off the balls of Geoffrey Pike and bring them back to Mexico. Now I beseech you, Santa Muerte, please kill me like the worthless dog I am and take my soul.”

“Steady on, that’s a bit much, don’t you think?” said Jacob. “Is Santa Muerte one of yours, Ruth?”

Ruth shook her head, “I don’t think so.”

Sam shot a worried look at Emily. Before he could speak his question died in his throat.

BURP!

A vivid discoloration sparkled and everyone standing there disappeared.

Chapter Thirty-Three

"…and it's all my fault." – Geoff

Somewhere Else

"What the heaven just happened?" hissed Natasha.

"Got her boss!" shouted Rob, his boot pressed down hard on the Greek's bloated body. "Want me to crush her?"

"Noooooo!" cried the Greek. "Stop hurting me you stupid oaf."

Broken glassed cracked as Natasha walked beside them. She breathed in sharply. "This is your doing," she said.

"Er… possibly," replied the Greek with a shrug.

"Azothoth."

Rob pressed down harder through his heel. The Greek yelped in pain.

"Where are we?" asked Natasha.

"I think there is a ninety-nine percent probability that we are…" the Greek paused.

"Well?"

"Somewhere else," the Greek finished.

Natasha took in her ruined surroundings. She was standing in a collapsed building with a smattering of snow on the ground and angry dark clouds whirling high above her. The lush green valley had vanished, replaced by ravaged urban greyness. She stooped down and looked into the Greek's blue eye. "You do not say. Would you like a final opportunity to clarify your response before I lose my patience, or Azothoth's enthusiasm gets the better of him?"

The Greek cleared her throat and whispered, "er… another timeline."

"What?" snapped Natasha. "How did this happen?"

"It wasn't me. I think the Spear of Destiny summoned your ridiculous monkey."

"You're blaming Geoff for this?" growled Rob.

"No, that's not what I meant," cried the Greek. "Though he did steal my gun."

"That white toy gun?" asked Rob.

"Yes. That was my first prototype allowing time travel by ripping through the space time continuum with a focussed bolt of energy oscillating around an exact frequency. When I first melded with Archimedes I gave mankind a long-term project which I buried deep within his subconscious. How to travel through time. I did it as a joke and quickly forgot about it. I mean how could these apes help me to go back home by travelling back through time?"

"I assume the probability was low?" asked Natasha.

"Infinitesimal. Literally too low for even me to calculate it."

"What changed?"

"Everything. About six months ago I began to pick up chatter deep within the international scientific community. Strangely they were using a code hidden in the Codex Sinaiticus which you know is in Greek. Even stranger was what they were saying." The Greek stopped.

"Go on," demanded Natasha.

"I would be far more comfortable explaining this without Azothoth's boot crushing me. Trust me, I have literally nowhere to run."

"Azothoth."

Rob slowly lifted his boot and the Greek righted herself.

"Well?"

"Your stupid monkeys somehow worked out the science underpinning time travel. The small acorn I planted in Archimedes' brain had flourished into a massive tree of secret work. Your best scientists had established a covert organisation called 'The Seekers' which they used to pass down their work to the next generation. Never tainted by national, political or religious identity all of this was kept away from the powers that be, even God I believe. It was as if the whole of human civilisation had been trying to answer my question."

"What did you do?" asked Natasha.

"I contacted some mutual associates of ours and arranged for them to track down the major pieces and then began the design of my prototype."

"But that gun wasn't one of the stickered items; why would you leave it behind?" asked Natasha.

"It was my first prototype. I stole plutonium from Sellafield, the nearby power plant and distilled it into the handle."

"That's why Geoff said it was a throbber," said Rob.

"Indeed. However, on running my final calculations I discovered a fatal flaw. There was a ninety-two percent probability that you could travel through time but a hundred percent probability that you couldn't control where you ended up in both time or geographical position. Looking back, it was all my fault. I should have stated that precise control of time travel would make-up fifty percent of the final mark. Maybe that would have given me something workable at the end. As it is I cannot risk going back to your Dark Ages."

"What happened when Geoffrey fired it?" asked Natasha.

"I do not have the data to provide probabilities on that but I do believe the gun wanted to be used and fused with Geoffrey. For the record, I calculated a ninety-seven percent probability that you would sacrifice him to get out of that valley."

Natasha smiled.

"I also believe that the Spear of Destiny called your off-spring to this place. Our following him is likely to have occurred because we were so close to him. The more pressing matter is the ninety-four percent probability that we are now in a parallel universe." The Greek gave a weak smile. "Sorry."

"Where is Geoff now?" asked Natasha.

"Somewhere here, but where I have no idea," replied the Greek.

"And what has the *Book of Shenanigans* got to do with this? It cannot be a coincidence that it appeared now, unless you are working for God?" Natasha's features hardened.

"No. I told you God isn't here, at least he wasn't in our timeline."

"Grab her Azothoth!"

Rob seized the Greek from behind and dangled her down.

"Stop this at once," demanded the Greek. "What are you doing?"

"It is obvious that you require additional motivation to tell me the truth behind this," said Natasha as she pulled the pages of *Shenanigans* out of her pocket. "You have so many eyes and legs, far more than you actually need. Azothoth feel free to find out how many legs our friend can dispense with."

Rob took a firm grip on the Greek's body and selected a single hind leg. He began to pull.

"Noooooo," cried the Greek.

"Last chance," said Natasha. "What have these pages got to do with you?"

The Greek looked at Natasha. "Okay. I wrote those pages after calculating your reactions to various situations I designed, or at least could partially control. I stole God's seal which allowed me to forge them into a passable Word of God."

"But why did you use a comic?" asked Natasha.

"I thought a graphic novel would be an interesting modern take on God's Word and I have an excellent artist friend who was able to help. In fact, he already had many of the sketches. I sent significantly different pages to other beings including Archangel Gabriel in his capacity as the acting CEO of Heaven and an ex-employee of yours Sam Spade."

"Why send pages to Sam?" asked Natasha. "He's a civilian."

"Interesting things happen ninety-seven percent of the time whenever he's involved. As my plan was to get everyone together to coerce the Spear of Destiny back to your universe he seemed to be a logical choice."

"You dared to use me as bait," barked Natasha.

"But only to help you gain your apocalypse," hurriedly said the Greek.

Natasha frown deepened.

"And eventually help me," added the Greek. "I was being truthful, all my calculations point to the Spear being sentient and immensely powerful. Used in the right way I believe that your apocalypse has an eighty-six percent probability of happening. I could then use the monkeys discovery and the power of the Spear to travel back to before I came to your universe. My calculations then give me eighty percent probability that I'd be taken back to Chairman Z. All hail Her Fangs!"

"You're saying that we have travelled through time as well?" asked Rob.

"Yes, you buffoon, both time and geographical position. I cannot understand why I ever fell for you."

"I see you kept the jewellery box I gave you," said Rob.

"Only because it has important things in it. Look around you stupid. Surely even you recognise where you are?"

Rob's brow knitted as he surveyed the destruction.

A sharp burst of machine gun fire erupted nearby followed by shouting.

Rob grinned. "Oh we're at…"

∞

The watching entity looked over the final clue for the five-dimensional crossword puzzle. *"I get the Texan miner to dispose of unwanted pests."* Thirteen letters across: *E__E___N_T__N.* It smiled and took a sip of the Yorkshire Gold tea. *E-X-T-E-R-M-I-N-A-T-I-O-N* for the seventh time. The rest of the puzzle was littered with many instances of DOOM; DESTRUCTION; APOCALYPSE; DEATH; STEWED TEA; DOWN THE PLUGHOLE: and NUNS WITH GUNS.

β

Geoff landed face down in what smelt and tasted like dirt. He felt like all the air had been forced out of his body. He coughed and spat on the floor and then, without thinking, rolled onto his back and breathed in. It was very dark and the air was cold and smelt of rotten cabbages hidden in wet socks. He was getting used to strange arrivals but this felt different. He opened his eyes and began to pick out rough shapes on the ceiling and upper walls. He was wondering where everyone else was when someone appeared out of thin air six feet above him and fell.

Thud, the landing was cushioned by Geoff.

"Aaarrrggghhh!" they both shrieked.

"Devil worshipper!" shouted a nun, who threw a small fist that glanced Geoff's ear. It caught him where Mrs Hotchkiss had bloodied him earlier that day.

"Oww!" Geoff rolled to one of the rough stone corners. "Calm down," he said.

"I've got a knife," said the nun, holding out Fiddlesticks. Her eyes hadn't adapted to the darkness though she thought she was aiming it at Geoff. "Come any closer and I will cut you up."

"Wow. Listen, crazy lady, I don't mean you any harm. My name's Geoff."

"I know who you are and I also know that's just what a Devil worshipper would say," she said.

"I'm not a Devil worshipper."

"So you admit that you're the Devil himself?"

"No, I'm Geoff."

"That's just what the Devil would say."

"I can't be both the Devil and a Devil worshipper, can I? I think my best friend Rob got me mixed up in all of this and I honestly don't know what I'm doing here."

"Your job can sometimes help define you. I'm a nun of the Order of Saint Gertrude of Nivelles and her Crazy Cats. What do you do?" asked Sister Ruth.

"I used to work in a call centre."

"That sounds suitably evil. That's just what..."

"No more of what the Devil would say. My job was really boring and the pay was terrible. Some people are saying I'm the Anti-Christ but I don't think that's really true either."

"Are you saying you're not really evil?" asked Sister Ruth.

"I don't think so, I'm just normal."

"How can the Anti-Christ not be evil?" she asked.

"Exactly," replied Geoff. "Which is why you shouldn't try to stab me."

"I promise you, evil one, that I will smite you back to Hell if you're lying about this," proclaimed Sister Ruth with as much viciousness as she could muster.

"That's okay. But for now, is there any chance we can have a bit less of the smiting, eh? Can I just check that you haven't got a drill with you?" asked Geoff, standing up.

"No, just my knitting needle Fiddlesticks," she said. "But it's very, very sharp."

They were in a rectangular room with a large single door at one end. A thin sliver of light could be seen under the door. "Was it you who saved me last night?"

"I may have," replied Sister Ruth. "But I didn't mean to, I just tripped."

"Even so, thank you for saving my life. Are you okay? I hope you didn't get hurt?"

"No, I'm okay though I did twist my ankle. I did promise Mrs Thornthwistle that next time I met you I would smite you back to Hell," said Sister Ruth defiantly. "And now I know that you could be the Anti-Christ – well, you can see my position."

"Why? You saved me and now you want to kill me? You don't even know me."

Sister Ruth frowned, annoyingly he had a point.

Geoff moved slowly towards the door. It was locked and didn't have a handle on this side. "I think we're in some type of cell."

"Like in prison. What happened?" she asked.

"It's a bit hard to explain," said Geoff as he inched towards her. "But my guess is."

"Stay back! I've still got Fiddlesticks you Devil something or other," exclaimed Sister Ruth. Things may not be too clear at the moment but getting close to someone who could well have Satanic leanings could never be a wise move for a nun such as herself.

"I was just going to show you this," said Geoff, holding out a white pistol. "It's like a toy gun but it caused all of this."

"You mean you made the tank disappear?"

"I think so. When I pulled the trigger there were lots of colour and the tank vanished into thin air."

"That really is what the Anti-Christ would do," stated Sister Ruth.

"I just didn't want to die and you were shooting at us with a tank. I didn't know it would do that."

"What happened to the people in it?" Sister Ruth asked.

"I'm sorry, I don't know. Were they friends of yours?" replied Geoff.

Sister Ruth nodded.

"I think there's a good chance that they're okay," he said.

"Okay, if you're not evil, do you know who the Devil is?"

"Well, I think I do. She's actually a really nice woman."

"What do you mean, she?" asked Sister Ruth, her voice rising. "How can the Devil be a woman? How can she be nice? Is she the one with the white hair?"

"Yes, she's called Natasha, but it's a long story."

"Okay, do you know what's happened to us?" asked Sister Ruth.

"I fired the gun at the helicopter because it was shooting at us, but it didn't properly work. I think it was out of juice so it gave up and went back into the gun. There was a weird shimmer of colour and I landed here about a minute before you arrived."

"That happened to us when we stood on the spot where the tank disappeared."

Geoff put the gun back in the rucksack. It was stone cold to the touch and didn't throb anymore. "Sorry about your friends," he said.

"Is your gun still working?" asked Sister Ruth.

"No," Geoff thought for a second. "I think it needs recharging, though I don't know how to do that."

"Where are we?" asked Sister Ruth, looking around.

"I've no idea, but please promise not to do any stabbing until we get out of here. Truce?" he said.

"I promise, nun's honour."

"Is that really something?" asked Geoff.

"Of course."

"Oh, pretty cool. Well, I'm pretty certain that we aren't in The Lake District, so that's one good thing," he smiled.

"Do you think that we could be in Hell?" asked Sister Ruth, her voice wavering with every word.

"Why would you be in Hell, you're a nun?" asked a puzzled Geoff.

"I saved you last night and some people think you're the Anti-Christ, so if I'm dead this could be my punishment, spending the rest of eternity with you," said Ruth, her voice as crisp as autumn leaves.

"I'll try not to be too offended by that," said Geoff. "But I don't think we're in Hell, it would be much hotter with lots of screams and smell of fresh paint."

"Fresh paint?" she asked.

"Doesn't matter," he replied. "It's also really cold down here."

"You're right. Hell is very hot, or so I've been led to believe," said Sister Ruth.

"We could be underground in some type of a bunker," said Geoff, as a worrying thought flickered through his mind. "No one else seems to be here."

"Have you actually called out for them?" she asked.

Geoff and Sister Ruth began shouting into the rock, the silence and the darkness.

"Natasha?"

"Mrs T?"

"Rob?"

"Jacob?"

"Ruby?"

"Simon?"

"Mr Sox?"

After two minutes, they stopped and sat down in their respective corners. Seconds later two strips of golden light crept under and over the cell door. This was followed by booted footsteps and a small metal window being opened in the door at eye level. More golden light and the thick smell of kerosene burners flooded into the cell. They sprang to their feet though only Geoff approached the door.

"Hello, Geoffrey Pike." The voice was slick, polished and German.

"Oh shit," whispered Geoff.

"What?" asked Sister Ruth.

"I think I know where we are," hissed Geoff.

"Where?"

"Stalingrad."

"What?" asked Sister Ruth.

"I think we're in Stalingrad and it's 1942," explained Geoff.

From outside there were more footsteps, a muffled voice and the rattling of keys. The door opened slowly.

"I'm so sorry about this. I think the Nazis are winning World War II and it's all my fault."

"Hello, Mr Pike."

Geoff turned slowly to face the figure silhouetted in the doorway. "Hello, General Paulus."

"Hello Mr Pike. Follow me. The Spear of Destiny has been expecting you."

To be continued…